THE ANCIENT LANGUAGE AND THE DIALECT OF CORNWALL

THE ANCIENT LANGUAGE

AND THE

DIALECT OF CORNWALL

WITH AN ENLARGED

GLOSSARY

OF

CORNISH PROVINCIAL WORDS.

ALSO AN

APPENDIX,

CONTAINING A LIST OF WRITERS ON CORNISH DIAECT, AND ADDITIONAL INFORMATION ABOUT

DOLLY PENTREATH,

THE LAST KNOWN PERSON WHO SPOKE THE ANCIENT CORNISH AS HER MOTHER TONGUE

BY

FRED. W. P. JAGO

KALPAZ

ISBN: 978-93-5128-610-3

First Published in 1882
Indian Reprint in 2017

Published by

Kalpaz Publications
C-30, Satyawati Nagar,
Delhi – 110052
E-mail: kalpaz@hotmail.com
Website: kalpazpublications.com
Ph.: +91-9212142040

Cataloging in Publication Data—DK
Courtesy: D.K. Agencies (P) Ltd. <docinfo@dkagencies.com>

Jago, Fred. W. P. (Frederick William Pearce), 1817- **author.**
The ancient language and the dialect of Cornwall : with an enlarged glossary of Cornish provincial words, also an appendix, containing a list of writers on Cornish dialect, and additional information about Dolly Pentreath, the last known person who spoke the ancient Cornish as her mother tongue / by Fred. W.P. Jago.
pages cm
Cornish and English.
"First published in 1882"—Title page verso.
ISBN 9789351286103 (PB)

1. English language—Dialects—England—Cornwall (County)—Glossaries, vocabularies, etc. 2. Cornish language. 3. Cornwall (England : County)—Languages. 4. Pentreath, Dolly. I. Title.

PE1851.J34 2017 DDC 427.94237 23

CONTENTS.

Page.

PREFACE.

Long-descended from Cornishmen, the writer, like others of his countrymen, has a clannish fondness for Cornish words and phrases.

From May 1879 to October 1880, the compiler of this book wrote lists of Cornish Provincial Words, which, through the courtesy of the Editor of the "Cornishman," (published at Penzance), were then allowed to appear in that paper.

These letters appeared to interest a good many persons, and lists of provincial words were often asked for, but compliance was impossible without printing, and so, a glossary in the form here given was then decided on.

But there were questions which required to be answered.

How should a glossary of Cornish provincial words be arranged? Since there is so much difference between the eastern and the western dialect, should there be a glossary for East, and another for West Cornwall?

This seemed a plausible method, but another difficulty arose. What was to be done with that very large class of words common to the *whole* of Cornwall? Such words could not be included in an eastern *and* a western glossary without a very useless repetition. To do this would be calling the same words, eastern dialect in one glossary, and western dialect in the other.

Then again, words, if one may use the expression, are constantly travelling about, and dropping here and there as the people move, and so, to keep an eastern and a western glossary *correct according to their titles*, would be an impossible, or endless task.

Again, it may be asked, where is the boundary between the east and the west dialect? In reality there is no actual limit, although, as stated in the following pages, there is a shadowy boundary, a sort of neutral ground.

In fact, the Cornish dialect changes by interrupted, or irregular degrees, all the way from one end of the county to the other.

Reflecting on these difficulties, the writer concluded that *one* glossary for the whole county would be simpler, and practically the better.

The other plan to be correct would require, 1st—A glossary for West Cornwall, 2nd—A glossary for East Cornwall, and 3rd—A separate glossary of words common to *all* Cornwall. In reality three glossaries for one county!

Nevertheless, the English Dialect Society, in 1880, issued a glossary for East, and another for West Cornwall, but none for those words common to the whole county.

That for West Cornwall is by Miss M. A. Courtney, who has evidently worked hard in compiling a valuable glossary to which the present writer is much indebted.

The glossary for East Cornwall is not so extensive as the former, but very good. It was compiled by Mr. Thos. Q. Couch, to whom the writer owes many thanks.

Good as these glossaries are, their division into Eastern and Western, is, the writer thinks, confusing, and the cause of a needless, but under such a plan, an unavoidable repetition of words in each division.

In writing on the provincial words, so many of which are ancient Cornish, a notice of the decline, and of the remains of that language is required, and as standard Cornish Histories are rather scarce and expensive, a sketch, as nearly as possible in the authentic words of Cornish historians, is given.

The writer has collected a number of words as spoken in Cornwall at this very time, and he has compared them with similar ones used by Chaucer 500 years ago. The resemblance is an interesting peculiarity of the Cornish dialect; and for illustration, quotations from Chaucer are given for each word used provincially.

A great many apparently barbarous, unmeaning, and uncouth words are evidently derived from the ancient Cornish language. By making *comparisons* between such words, and those formerly used by the old Cornish people, the writer has tried to make such obscure terms more clearly understood.

No doubt there are many faults in spite of every care in compiling this glossary of about 3700 words.

Many words have been purposely omitted because they seemed too common in other districts outside Cornwall, and probably, many which should have been excluded, are left in the glossary.

However this may be, and to whatever extent this book may be considered by the critic as meagre, and imperfect; yet it is hoped that such a volume as this may be of some use, or interest to those who desire to possess a memento of the Cornish dialect as spoken about, or a little before the beginning of this century, and still in use to a very great extent, but becoming more and more disused as time goes on.

Some words quoted from Carew, &c., are of course of an older date, but the writer could not very well omit them, as many are still in use.

In conclusion it may by said, that even now the Cornish people are speaking a large number of Celtic, or Ancient Cornish words, without being very much aware of it.

The Cornish dialect may be called the shadow, or penumbra of the ancient language; the link between the old and the new tongue; between Celtic and English.

FRED. W. P. JAGO.

21, Lockyer Street,
Plymouth,
A.D. 1882.

The Ancient Language and the Provincial Dialect of Cornwall.

THE DECLINE OF THE ANCIENT CORNISH LANGUAGE.

BEFORE saying anything about the provincial dialect of the Cornish people, it may be of use to give a sketch of the decline of the old Cornish language, and also notice what has been attempted in the preservation of its remains.

It appears necessary to do this, because, as the old language decayed the English took its place, and a long time was occupied in the process. Indeed, this transitional period may be called an *interregnum*, during which the provincial dialect of Cornwall became gradually formed.

In thus reviewing the decline of the old Cornish language, we are passing on to the dialect which took its place. Like its predecessor the Ancient Cornish, it is in its turn doomed, and rapidly changing into ordinary English.

Many reliable authorities have given a great deal of information about the old Celtic language of Cornwall, among whom are such writers as Carew, Lhuyd, Pryce, Borlase, Polwhele, Hals, Tonkin, &c., and scattered accounts may be found in various publications.

The particulars, as given in the History of Cornwall compiled by Hitchins, and edited by Samuel Drew, in 1824, are very simple and clear, and Drew's account may be quoted with advantage. He says:—

"The language which was once spoken in this county by our British ancestors, awakens our solicitude from motives of local attachment, and becomes particularly interesting from the singular circumstance of its being now no more. At present we behold its mighty shadow in the pages of our history, and even this is gradually disappearing. The only scattered remnants which have survived its oral existence, may be found in those provincial phrases, and local names, for which Cornwall is so peculiarly remarkable.

"The Cornish tongue is generally admitted to be a dialect of that language, which, till the Saxons came in, was common to all the western parts of Britain, and more anciently to Ireland and Gaul.

"When the Romans came and subdued this country, the changes which they introduced, affected the language as well as the manners of the inhabitants. It does not however appear, that the Romans had any fixed design to extirpate the British language; yet its gradual decline followed as a necessary consequence of their solicitude to diffuse and establish their own. Hence in those parts where they had more fully established their power, the language of the people suffered most from the general innovation; so that its purity seemed to retire from the Roman presence, and to seek an asylum in those mountainous or retired regions to which the invaders could not without much difficulty have access.

"In these western territories, the original language of the natives had less to fear than that of most others, if we make an exception in favour of Wales; and perhaps from this Roman invasion it suffered least.

"Hence, throughout the Cornu-British language we have, comparatively speaking, very few Latin idioms, and very few Latin words.

"But it was not from the influence of the Roman language, that the Cornish tongue was doomed to perish. It survived the shock which it had sustained, and secured its independence by retiring to the Cambrian mountains; to the retreats which Danmonium afforded it; and by emigrating to the continent, and there starting up as a new dialect on the shores of Armorica. (Brittany).

"When the Romans abandoned their conquests in this island, and the Saxons succeeded them, the inhabitants of Britain retiring before their victorious arms, sought a refuge in Wales, Cornwall, and Brittany, carrying with them once more that language which was originally common to them all. This language, in process of time for want of a more frequent intercourse between the inhabitants, became differently pronounced and written, and in various degrees mixed with different languages.

"It does not appear that anything was ever *printed* in the Cornish language till the year 1707, when the learned Mr. Lhuyd published his Cornish grammar.

"A few years before this, Mr. Lhuyd visited this County, in order to make himself acquainted with its natural history and monuments, but more particularly so with the language of Cornwall which was rapidly on the decline.

"But although nothing in the Cornish language was ever printed till the days of Mr. Lhuyd, several Cornish manuscripts have been preserved; but excepting one, none of any considerable age. This one according to Bishop Gibson, was written in 1036 in an old court hand on vellum. (This was 'The History of the Passion of our Saviour.')

"The Cornish language, it appears, was current in a part of the South Hams in the time of Edward 1st (1272 to 1307). Long after this it was common on the banks of the Tamar, and in Cornwall it was universally spoken.

"But it was not till towards the conclusion of the reign of Henry 8th (1509 to 1547) that the English language had found its way into any of the Cornish churches. Before this time the Cornish language was the established vehicle of communication.

"Dr. Moreman, a native of Southill, but vicar of Menheniot, was the first who taught the inhabitants of his parish the Lord's prayer, the Creed, and the Ten commandments in the English tongue; and this was not done till just about the time that Henry 8th closed his reign. From this fact one inference is obvious; which is, that if the inhabitants of Menheniot knew nothing more of the English than what was thus learnt from the vicar of the parish, the Cornish must have prevailed among them at that time'.... 'and as the English language in its progress travelled from East to West; we may reasonably conclude, that about this time it had not penetrated far into the County, as Menheniot lies towards its eastern quarter.

"From the time the liturgy was established in the Cornish churches in the English language, the Cornish tongue rapidly declined.

"Hence Mr. Carew, who published his 'Survey of Cornwall' in 1602, notices the almost total extirpation of the language in his days. He says, 'the principal love and knowledge of this language, liveth in Dr. Kennall the civilian, and with him lyeth buried; for the English speech doth still encroach upon it and hath driven the same into the uttermost skirts of the shire. Most of the inhabitants can speak no word of Cornish; but few are ignorant of the English; and yet some so affect their own, as to a stranger they will not speak it; for if meeting them by chance, you inquire the way, or any such matter, your answer shall be, '*Meea nauidua cowzasawzneck;*' I can speak no Saxonage.'

"Carew's 'Survey' was soon followed by that of Norden, by whom we are informed that the Cornish language was chiefly confined to the western hundreds of the county, particularly to Penwith, and Kirrier, and yet; "(which is to be marveyled) though the husband and wife, parents and children, master and servants, do naturally communicate in their native language; yet there is none of them in a manner, but is able to converse with a stranger in the English tongue, unless it be some obscure people who seldom confer with the better sort. But it seemeth however, that in a few years the Cornish will be by little and little abandoned."

Such was the state of the Cornish language, according to Norden, about 1610, the year in which it is probable his history was written.

The parish of Menheniot was the *first* in which the inhabitants were taught the Creed, the Lord's prayer, and the Ten Commandments, in English; (about A.D. 1540). The parish of Feock was nearly the *last* in which Ancient Cornish was used in the church service.

The Cornish was so well spoken in the parish of Feock by the old inhabitants till about the year 1640, "that Mr. William Jackman, the then vicar, and chaplain also of Pendennis Castle at the siege thereof by the parliament army, was forced for divers years to administer the sacrament to the Communicants in the Cornish tongue, because the aged people did not well understand the English, as he himself often told me." (Hals).

"Although, says Drew, the Cornish language appears to have been excluded from all our Cornish churches except those of Feock, and Landewednack, as early as the year 1640, yet it was not driven from common conversation until a much later period.

"So late as 1650, the Cornish language was currently spoken in the parishes of Paul, and St. Just; the fish-women, and market-women in the former, and the tinners in the latter, for the most part conversing in their old vernacular tongue."

Mr. Scawen, in his manuscript, says, that in 1678, the Rev. F. Robinson, rector of Landewednack, "preached a sermon to his parishioners, in the Cornish language only."

"From this period, continues Drew, the Cornish language appears to have been driven from the Cornish churches entirely; or if not wholly banished, we have no further record of its being retained or used on any occasion in the service of public worship.

"And so rapid was its declension throughout the County from this period (1678) in all the ordinary concerns of life, that Mr. Lhuyd, in a letter to Mr. Rowland, dated March 10, 1701, observes, that the Cornish language was then only retained in five or six villages towards the Land's End.

"In every stage through which we pursue the Cornish language, we thus perceive that its limits become more and more circumscribed. From five or six villages towards the Land's End, in which the Cornish tongue was spoken in 1701, we must now descend to individuals, and from them trace it to its grave."

Drew relates how that in 1746, Captain Barrington took a seaman from Mount's Bay who understood Cornish so well as to be able to converse with some sailors of Brittany, and it is very natural to suppose that many others knew the Cornish language at the above date, but Dr. Borlase thought, in 1758, that it had "altogether ceased so as not to be spoken anywhere in conversation." But, says Drew, "this opinion appears to be rather premature. It might be true, that the language was no longer spoken in common conversation from choice, but that several persons were then alive who could hold a conversation in Cornish on common topics, is plain from accounts of a subsequent date, to which we shall refer."

In the year 1768, the Hon. Daines Barrington, brother of Captain, afterwards Admiral Barrington, went into Cornwall to ascertain whether the Cornish language had entirely ceased or not, and in a letter written to John Lloyd, Esq., F.S.A., a few years after, viz. on March 31, 1773, he gives the following as the result of his journey, and as it refers to old Dolly Pentreath, a name so well known not only in, but out of Cornwall, it is well worth quoting.

Says Mr. Barrington, "I set out from Penzance however with the landlord of the principal inn for my guide, towards Sennen, or the most western point; and when I approached the village, I said that there must probably be some remains of the language in those parts, if anywhere, as the village was in the road to no place whatever; and the only alehouse announced itself to be the last in England.

My guide however told me that I should be disappointed; but that if I would ride about ten miles about in my return to Penzance he would conduct me to a village called Mousehole, on the western side of Mount's Bay, where there was an old woman called Dolly Pentreath, who could speak Cornish fluently. While we were travelling together towards Mousehole, I enquired how he knew that this woman spoke Cornish; when he informed me, that he frequently went from Penzance to Mousehole to buy fish, which were sold by her; and that when he did not offer her a price that was satisfactory, she grumbled to some other old women in an unknown tongue, which he concluded therefore to be Cornish.

When we reached Mousehole, I desired to be introduced as a person who had laid a wager that there was not one who could converse in Cornish; upon which Dolly Pentreath spoke in an angry tone for two or three minutes, and in a language which sounded very like Welsh. The hut in which she lived was in a very narrow lane, opposite to two rather better houses, at the doors of which two other women stood, who were advanced in years, and who I observed were laughing at what Dolly said to me.

Upon this I asked them whether she had not been abusing me; to which they answered, 'Very heartily' and because I had supposed she could not speak Cornish.

I then said, that they must be able to talk the language; to which they answered that they could not speak it readily, but that they understood it, being only ten or twelve years younger than Dolly Pentreath.

I continued nine or ten days in Cornwall after this, but found that my friends whom I had left to the eastward continued as incredulous almost as they were before, about these last remains of the Cornish language; because, among other reasons, Dr. Borlase had supposed in his Natural History of the County, that it had entirely ceased to be spoken. It was also urged, that as he lived within four or five miles of the old woman at Mousehole, he consequently must have heard of so singular a thing as her continuing to use the vernacular tongue.

I had scarcely said or thought anything more about this matter, till last summer, (1772) having mentioned it to some Cornish people, I found that they could not credit that any person had existed within these few years, who could speak their native language; and therefore, though I imagined there was but a small chance of Dolly Pentreath continuing to live, yet I wrote to the president then in Devonshire, to desire that he would make some inquiry with regard to her; and he was so obliging as to procure me information from a gentleman whose house was within three miles of Mousehole, a considerable part of whose letter I shall subjoin.

'Dolly Pentreath is short of stature, and bends very much with old age, being in her eighty-seventh year; so lusty however as to walk hither, to Castle Horneck, about three miles, in bad weather, in the morning and back again. She is somewhat deaf, but her intellects seemingly not impaired; has a memory so good, that she remembers perfectly well, that about four or five years ago, at Mousehole, where she lives, she was sent for by a gentleman, who being a stranger, had a curiosity to hear the Cornish language, which she was famed for retaining and speaking fluently; and that the inkeeper where the gentleman came from, attended him.

(This gentleman, says Daines Barrington, "was myself; however I did not presume to send for her, but waited upon her.")

She does indeed talk Cornish as readily as others do English, being bred up from a child to know no other language; nor could she (if we may believe her) talk a word of English before she was past twenty years of age; as, her father being a fisherman, she was sent with fish to Penzance at twelve years old, and sold them in the Cornish language, which the inhabitants in general, even the gentry, did then well understand. She is positive however, that there is neither in Mousehole, nor in any other part of the county, any other person who knows anything of it, or at least can converse in it. She is poor, and maintained partly by the parish, and partly by fortune-telling and gabbling Cornish.'

I have thus, continued Mr. Barrington, "thought it right to lay before the Society (the Society of Antiquaries) this account of the last sparks of the Cornish tongue; and cannot but think that a linguist who understands Welsh, might still pick up a more complete vocabulary of the Cornish than we are yet possessed of; especially as the two neighbours of this old woman (Dolly Pentreath) whom I have had occasion to mention, are not now above seventy-seven or seventy-eight years of age, and were healthy when I saw them; so that the whole does not depend on the life of this Cornish sybil, as she is willing to insinuate." *Daines Barrington.*

It appears, says Drew, from this letter of Daines Barrington "that in the year 1773, Dolly Pentreath was in her eighty-seventh year; and it appears from an epitaph on her grave, that she died at the advanced age of 102; so that she must have lived fifteen years after Mr. Barrington's letter was dated and consequently must have died in 1788.

"She was buried in the churchyard of the parish of

Paul, in which parish, Mousehole, the place of her residence is situated. Her epitaph is both in Cornish and English, in both of which languages as it is a literary curiosity, it is here inserted."

CORNISH.

* Coth Doll Pentreath cans ha Dean ;
Marow ha kledyz ed Paul plêa :—
Na ed an Egloz, gan pobel brâs,
Bes ed Egloz-hay coth Dolly es.

ENGLISH.

* Old Doll Pentreath, one hundred ag'd and two ;
Deceas'd, and buried in Paul parish too :—
Not in the church, with people great and high,
But in the church-yard doth old Dolly lie !

It is evident from there being an epitaph on Dolly Pentreath, that the Cornish language in A.D. 1788 was known, and could still be written.

Polwhele says, "the author of these verses, of which I have given a literal translation, is a Mr. Tomson a native of Truro, and by profession an engineer." The epitaph was translated by a Mr. Collins, who gave it to Mr. Polwhele.

In July, 1776, "Mr. Barrington upon more minute enquiry," presented a letter to the Society of Antiquaries written both in Cornish, and English, by William Bodener, a fisherman of Mousehole. This fisherman asserted that there were still four or five persons in Mousehole who could talk Cornish.

---

* Although this epitaph was written as described there is no present proof that any inscribed stone was ever placed on Dolly's grave. The present monument is modern. For Jeffery, Dorothy, *see* Appendix.

In 1777 Mr. Barrington found another Cornishman called John Nancarrow, of Marazion, aged 45 years, and able to speak Cornish. John Nancarrow said, that "in his youth he had learnt the language from the country people, and could then hold a conversation in it; and that another, a native of Truro, was at that time also acquainted with the Cornish language, and like himself was able to converse in it."

This last, is supposed to be the Mr. Tomson to whom, says Drew, "the world is indebted for Dolly Pentreath's epitaph."

It appears from additional testimony, that even up to the preceding dates the Cornish language had not entirely died out, and Dr. Pryce intimated that the language was known in Mousehole "so late as 1790."

From the foregoing narrative it is clear that the Cornish language did not die with Dolly Pentreath, but lingered on, gradually becoming more and more forgotten.

A language dies hard, and the gradual decay of the venerable language of the old people of Cornwall, resisted for centuries the ever advancing English tongue, the old Cornish receding from it towards the west, until, even in the extreme western end of Cornwall, it ceased to be a spoken language.

It has been supposed that the bible was once written in Cornish, but this is very doubtful, if we may form an opinion from the following remarks by the learned author of the "Ancient Cathedral of Cornwall." In this work Mr. Whitaker, with his usual and emphatic manner, says (Vol. 2. p. 37. in a note) "the English too was not *desirea* by the Cornish, as vulgar history says, and as Dr. Borlase avers; but, as the case shows itself plainly to be, *forced* upon the Cornish by the tyranny of England, at a time when the English language was yet unknown in Cornwall. This act of tyranny was at once gross barbarity to the Cornish people, and a death-blow to the Cornish language."

Mr. Whitaker alludes to the first use of the English liturgy in Menheniot church, and says, "that had the liturgy been translated into Cornish as it was in Welsh, the Cornish language would have been preserved to the present moment." Had there ever been any translation of the scriptures into Cornish, it would surely have been noticed by so learned an antiquarian.

If what Borlase asserts be true, then the Cornish people themselves are to be blamed for having used very potent means for the destruction of their own original language.

Although Whitaker asserts that the English language was "forced" upon the Cornish by the tyranny of England, yet, Borlase is just as positive to the contrary.

In Borlase's Natural History of Cornwall, at page 315, it is said that "when the liturgy at the reformation was appointed by authority to take place of the mass, the Cornish desired (Seawen p. 49) that it should be in the English language, being apprehensive that it might be injoined them in their mother tongue, as it was with regard to the Welsh. By this means and the gentry mixing gradually with the English, the Cornish language lost ground in proportion as it lay nearer to Devon."

When two such writers differ in this manner, it may

be fairly presumed that the truth lies in the middle. The English language had become familiar to, and perhaps fashionable with the *gentry*, while the lower orders of the people pertinaciously clung to, and retained the use of their mother tongue. The latter appeared to view with suspicion, and dislike those who spoke to them in English, which to them, in those days, was a foreign language. When spoken to in English, although understanding it to a great extent, the reply was in Cornish—"Meea nauidua cawzas sawzneck," I can speak no Saxonage as has been already mentioned.

But now, even a tradition of a Cornish instead of an English language having been formerly spoken seems to have died out, except among educated people, in the eastern part of Cornwall.

In 1878, the writer being at Menheniot and conversing with a native there, enquired whether the people in that district had any tradition of the use of a former and different language, and also of the first introduction of English in their church service. No, at least he had never heard of it. He thought they had always spoken English there!

In the "Cornishman" (a newspaper published at Penzance) there were in 1879, glossaries of old Cornish words, one by Mr. B. Victor, and another by Mr. Pentreath. Each list contained about 140, or, 150 words. These last remains are very interesting as affording evidence that even now, there are many words of the old tongue still known by men now living, and which they have learnt apart from any books.

ON THE REMAINS OF THE ANCIENT CORNISH LANGUAGE.

Pryce, referring to Lhuyd's unfinished Archæologia Britannica, considered that Lhuyd's death rendered the recovery of the ancient Cornish tongue very hopeless, for had he lived to finish his work, "not only the recovery of the dialect would have been effected, but, it would have been adorned with every elegancy and improvement from the unceasing labours of such a consummate philologist."

The ancient Cornish has for ever ceased to be spoken, yet that such an old language may be preserved and even understood, just like Latin and Greek, there seems good reason for believing.

The materials have largely accumulated, and are becoming more available for students.

The labours of many writers, viz., from Lhuyd to Williams, and of others since, have been hastening on the time when the ancient Cornish tongue will be fixed and rendered permanent as a *dead* language. This would be attained by a perfected Cornish grammar, an *English*-Cornish in addition to the *Cornish*-English Dictionary of Williams, and the collecting together of all other remains, whether in the form of histories, phrases, or even single words.

We are indeed much indebted to the eminent author of the Archæologia Britannica, Lhuyd, whose work printed in 1707, will always remain a memorial of learning and industry. Some idea may be formed of this author's labours, by reading the following list of the contents of his book.

1.—A comparative etymology, or remarks on the alteration of languages.

2.—A Latin-Celtic dictionary, or, a vocabulary of the original languages of Britain and Ireland.

3.—An Armoric grammar.

4.—An Armoric-English vocabulary.

5.—Some Welsh words omitted in Dr. Davies's dictionary.

6.—A Cornish grammar.

7.—A catalogue of British manuscripts.

8.—An essay towards a British etymologicon.

9.—A brief introduction to the Irish or ancient Scottish language.

10.—An Irish-English dictionary.

Borlase, also, in his "Antiquities," has given much labour to, and rendered good help for, the restoration of the old Cornish language, by collecting such remains as were existing in manuscript and in print. His Cornish-English vocabulary contains about four thousand words, perhaps more, and formed "chiefly" as he says, from the Archæologia of Lhuyd.

In 1790, Dr. William Pryce of Redruth, Cornwall, published the "Archæologia Cornu-Britannica, or an Essay to preserve the ancient Cornish language—containing the rudiments of that dialect in a Cornish grammar and Cornish-English vocabulary compiled from a variety of materials which have been inaccessible to all other authors, wherein the British original of some thousand English words in common use is demonstrated, together with that of the proper names of most towns, parishes, villages, mines, and gentlemen's seats and families, in Wales, Cornwall, Devonshire, and other parts of England."

In his dedication of the above book, he says, that it is "a work intended to rescue from oblivion the original language of a County."

It may be useful to give a brief account of what Pryce says respecting the ancient Cornish language.

Speaking of the high antiquity of the British language, "of which the Cornish is most indisputably a very pure dialect" he remarks in the Preface, that "it must be acknowledged, that a local inquiry and disquisition into the antiquity of our Cornish-British language has not been so particularly attended to as it deserves."

Polwhele, in his History of Cornwall, &c., has also helped the work of restoration, and his writings contain many of the old Cornish words with observations thereon.

In Polwhele's "Historical Views of Devonshire" (p. 187) are remarks on the language of the ancient Britons, and in comparing it with the Phenician the author says, "that its affinity with the Irish is proved beyond all controversy by Vallancey."

It will be interesting to compare the Phenician with a language allied to old Cornish, viz: the Irish.

In the Pnulus of Plautus, there are certain sentences known to be Punic, and on comparing them with Irish, there is found a remarkable likeness, as may be seen in the following extract.

Punic.—Chim lach chunyth mum ys tyal mycthi barii im schi.
Irish.—Chimi lach chuinigh muini is toil miocht beiridh iar mo scith.
English.—A support of weak captives; be thy will to instruct me to obtain my children.

Punic.—Lypho can ethyth by mithii ad œdan binuthii.
Irish.—Liomhtha can ati bi mitche ad eadan beannaithe.
English.—Let it come to pass that my earnest prayers be blessed before thee.

Punic.—Byr nar ob syllo homal o nim! ubymis isyrthoho.
Irish.—Bior nar ob siladh umhal; o nimh! ibhim a frotha.
English.—A fountain denied not to drop to the humble; O Deity that I may drink of its streams."

(From *Polwhele's Historical Views of Devonshire* p. 187.)

Pryce says, that "the dialect of Cornwall must certainly have obtained that purity, for which it is celebrated, from its immediate introduction by the Phenician navigators, especially as the character and orthography are so greatly softened, and the language is divested of that rough guttoral pronunciation, which is retained to this time by the Cambro-Britons. In fact, the Cornish, and the Armoric dialects are the most nearly allied in character, orthography, and sound, of any two of the British dialects. The Welsh, Irish, and Erse differ from each other greatly; and the two latter differ from the Cornish and Gaulish (Armoric) very much. Indeed the Welsh is closely related to us.

"Hence we may easily account for the similarity existing between the Cornish and Armoric; for the coasts of Bretagne (Brittany) are opposite to the shores of Cornwall.

"This is evidenced by the colloquial resemblance to this day (1790) subsisting betwixt the Cornish on the south-western margin of the County, and their opposite neighbours at Morlaix, and other parts of Bas Bretagne, where the low French and the Cornish seem almost one and the same dialect."

Pryce remarks, that if he had not been otherwise well apprised of this fact, his opinion would have been confirmed by what he had heard from a very old man now (1790) living at Mousehole near Penzance, who as Pryce believed, was at that time, the only person capable of holding half an hour's conversation on common subjects in the Cornish tongue. The old man told Pryce "that about three score years ago (in 1730) being at Morlaix on board a smuggling cutter, and the only time he was ever there, he was ordered on shore with another young man to buy some greens, and not knowing a word of French as he thought, he was much surprised to find that he understood a great part of the conversation of some boys at play in the street; and upon further inquiry, he found that he could make known all his wants in Cornish, and be better understood than he could be at home, when he used that dialect"

Pryce, referring to a correspondence between Lhuyd and Tonkin, says that "Mr. Lhuyd had gone great lengths towards the formation of a Cornish-British vocabulary, and he stated at the end of his Cornish grammar (Archæologia p. 253) that looking over the sheets of his grammar he must recall the promise made in his preface (p. 222) of a Cornish-English vocabulary, there being no room for it in that volume of glossography, and therefore must defer it till the next."

Lhuyd died about the year 1709, two years after his great work was printed, which death, says Pryce, "must have been the greatest loss to this pursuit that it ever had, or ever will meet with, on account of his profound learning and singular attachment to the recovery of our primitive language."

Hals, about 1715, took uncommon pains to heap together a mass of words which he entitled "Lhadymer ay Kernow, or the Cornish Interpreter." Mr. Tremayne lent this manuscript of Hals to Dr. Pryce, who says of it that "it is a most strange hodge-podge of Hebrew, Greek, Latin, and British words," but as it contained some words worth notice he selected them for his vocabulary.

About the year 1709, Messrs. Tonkin, Keigwin, and Gwavas, with other associates, kept up a correspondence in their native tongue, as well as they could, by collecting all the mottoes, proverbs and idioms, on which they could lay their hands, and Dr. Pryce availed himself of their manuscripts.

The grammar of the ancient Cornish by Pryce contains in the first part, "the marrow of Mr. Lhuyd's grammar, with some additions." The second part contains a Cornish vocabulary of about four thousand words, collected and arranged from the materials already mentioned. The third and last part consists of many Cornish names of places, "with their distinctions of the old and the modern Cornish."

As ancient English differs from modern, so does old

Cornish differ from modern, and this may be illustrated by a very short example, thus:—the phrase "Many thanks to God" expressed in old Cornish was, "Maur gras tha Deu," in modern Cornish it was "Meor 'ras tha Dew," which is contracted into one word "Merastadu" and meaning the same.

Although Dr. Pryce has been praised for the Cornish grammar and vocabulary bearing his name, yet it should be noticed that the greater credit is due to Tonkin and Gwavas.

Besides the writers of Cornish History, &c. already named, Davies Gilbert, Whitley Stokes, and Williams, have done a great deal in preserving the remains of the old Cornish language.

To Whitley Stokes we are much indebted, as may be seen stated in the Preface to Williams's Cornish Dictionary, of which further notice will be taken.

From what precedes, and follows, it will be seen that the remains of the ancient Cornish language are much more extensive than is generally supposed.

In the "Western Morning News" of August 2, 1871, there was published a list of the Gwavas manuscripts, which is very suitable for insertion in this place, and so useful, that it cannot fail to be of interest to any one who feels any liking for the subject.

At the end of the list are a few remarks about Gwavas, &c.

THE GWAVAS MANUSCRIPTS.

The Gwavas manuscripts were formerly in the possession of the Rev. William Veale, of Trevaylor. After his decease they passed to the Rev. William Wriothesley

Wingfield, the vicar of Gulval, by whom they were presented to the British Museum. They are in a bound volume, lettered Gwavas MSS. and are known as "British Museum Additional MSS., 28,554."

Letter from Davies Gilbert, dated East Bourne, 22nd July, 1836, to Rev. W. Veale; p. 1.

Three letters from John Boson, dated Newlyn, 1709, 1711, 1720, to W. Gwavas, Brick Court, Middle Temple, London; pp. 2, 10, 12.

Letter from W. Gwavas, dated 1711, to Oliver Pendar, merchant, Newlyn; p. 3.

Letter from O. Pendar, dated Newlyn, 1711, to W. Gwavas, London; p. 4.

Letter from W. Gwavas, dated Middle Temple, 1711, to J. Boson, Newlyn; pp. 8-9.

Letter from W Gwavas to ——, dated March, 1731, etate 55; p. 11.

Three letters from Thomas Tonkin, dated Polgorran, 1735, to W. Gwavas, Penzance; pp. 14, 18, 22.

Three letters from W. Gwavas, dated Penzance, 1735-36, to T. Tonkin; pp. 16, 20, 23.

Copy of "The Creation, finished by J. Keygwin, gent., in ye year 1693,"; pp. 24-49.

Copy of "Mount Calvary," amended and corrected by W. H., 1679-80; pp. 51-58.

The Lord's Prayer in Cornish; p. 50.

Cornish glossary—A to Cl.; pp. 59-78.

Cornish vocabulary— A to W; pp. 80-89.

Cornish verses, &c.; pp. 91-97.

The ten commandments in Cornish; pp. 97-99; By T. Boson, 1710; pp. 107-108; pp. 110-114.

The third chapter of Genesis in Cornish; pp. 100-101.

The fourth and seventh chapters of St. Matthew in Cornish; pp. 102-106.

The creed in Cornish, by T. Boson, 1710; p. 106; by W. Gwavas; p. 143.

Sundry Cornish writings, pp. 115-25.

Story of a Man and Woman in St. Levan, "in a place called the house of a Ramm" (unfinished); pp. 128-29.

Letter from Jane Manly to W. Gwavas; pp. 130-32.

The First Chapter of Genesis in Cornish; pp. 126-27.

Cornish song to the tune of "The modest maid of Kent; p. 131.

Copy of "Carmen Britannicum Dialecto Cornubiensi" (6th cent.), by Edwd. Lhuyd, from the original, with Mr. Jenkin, of Alverton; pp. 132, 34.

Song, "Fair Maid," Cornish and English, for Edwd. Chirgwin; p. 135.

Song by Mr. Jenkins, of Alverton; p. 136.

Inscription in Cornish for "My Ball," by Thos. Boson; p. 137.

On death of Mr. J. Keigwin, 20th April, 1716, by J. Boson; p. 142.

Song; p. 138.

Letter from J. Keigwin, dated 1693, to W. Gwavas; pp. 139-40.

Cornish Derivations, by W. Gwavas, dated Penzance, 1735; pp. 144-46.

Tenants' names versified in Cornish, by Mr. Collins, parson of Breage, dated 1723; p. 147.

Pilot's motto on a ring, dated 1734; p. 148.

On fishing, &c.; pp. 154-55.

Sundry Cornish writings, by W. Gwavas, dated 1731; pp. 156-65, 167-68.

Monumental inscription to be put on my tomb, dated 16th September, 1719; Wm. Gwavas, parish of Sithney, son and heir of Will Gwavas; p. 166.

Mr. William Gwavas was the son of William Gwavas, and was born in 1676. He became a barrister of the Middle Temple, where he for some time resided in Brick-court. He was impropriator or lay vicar of Paul, and in that capacity had various disputes with the fishermen of that parish respecting the tything of fish. A printed document referring to this matter, a copy of which is now in the possession of Mr. Henry Williams, of the Mount's Bay Bank, Penzance, bears the following title, "Private case between William Gwavas and William Kelynack, and 116 parishioners and fishermen, relating to the right of tything fish. An appeal before the House of Lords, 1730, fol. Privately printed." Some time ago there was published "Some observations on the Rev. R. Williams's preface to his Lexicon, by Prince L. L. Bonaparte [London, May, 1865,] s.sh., 4to." This work contains "A copy of a letter from the Rev. (*sic*) W. Gwavas to T. Tonkin," dated Penzance, 25th Jan., 1732, and is, as far as we know, the only other document referring to Mr. Gwavas besides those already mentioned. Some of Mr. Gwavas's Cornish writings have been printed by Borlase, Pryce, and Polwhele. Mr. Gwavas died in 1741, and was buried at Paul, on the 9th Jan. in that year."

In 1865, was published the Lexicon Cornu-Britannicum by the Rev. Robt. Williams, M.A. This dictionary of the

Cornish language is a work of great labour and learning, and has supplied to a very great extent the want so much lamented by Pryce; viz., in Lhuyd having died before a second volume of his great work the "Archæologia Britannica was printed.

Whether any manuscript of Lhuyd's intended second volume still remain, it seems hopeless to inquire, perhaps a copy may be lying hid somewhere even now. However this may be, the Cornish Dictionary by Williams is indeed a great advance towards the preservation of the ancient tongue.

So instructive is the preface to Williams's Lexicon Cornu-Britannicum that it seems very necessary to include it in this little book, for after the list of the Gwavas Manuscripts, just given, Williams's remarks appear to be all that are required to complete this division of the subject.

The object of the Editor of the Lexicon Cornu-Britannicum "was to collect and explain all the remains of the ancient British language of Cornwall." The book contains about 9000 Cornish words, with an immense number of quotations to render the meanings clearer, also the first chapter of Genesis, the Ten Commandments, the Creed, the Lord's prayer, &c. in the orthography of the Cornish dramas. It is published in quarto, and contains 400 pages.

Perhaps an enthusiastic student by the help of Williams's Dictionary, a Cornish grammar, and the translations of old Cornish into English now in print, might actually learn the language, and even get at the pronunciation, by observing how Cornish words are still spoken.

Is not the ancient tongue worth preserving just as, but not perhaps to the same extent as Greek and Latin?

We have only to consider the labours of those who have contributed to the accumulation of the remains, and we shall be led to answer this question in the affirmative. The language, as we have seen, was once spoken by a numerous people, over a large extent of land, and remained a vernacular speech for many centuries, indeed from a time lost in the obscurity of ancient history.

The history of the Cornish branch of the Celtic tongue extends so far back into the dim past, that even on such grounds the Archæologist and the Philologist may easily be induced to befriend its preservation.

The language, which was spoken when the Phenicians voyaged to the coasts of Cornwall, must, from its antiquity alone, demand affection and respect, especially from Cornishmen.

THE PREFACE TO THE CORNISH DICTIONARY BY WILLIAMS.

The following is the Preface already referred to as written for the Lexicon Cornu-Britannicum, by the Revd. Robert Williams, M.A., and dated 1865.

"The object of the Editor in the compilation of this work was to collect and explain all the remains of the ancient British language of Cornwall, and by comparing the words with the synonyms in the cognate dialects to supply an acknowledged want in Celtic literature. The sources for the supply of material are very few, and may be briefly enumerated.

The learned philologist Edward Lhuyd, in his Archæologia Britannica, (fol. Oxford, 1707;) first published a grammar of the Cornish language, as spoken in his time, being then in a state of corruption and decay. He also gave a promise of a Cornish vocabulary, which he did not live to accomplish.

In 1769, (the present writer's copy is dated 1754, with a vocabulary) Dr. Borlase published a Cornish-English vocabulary, in his Antiquities of Cornwall, which is chiefly derived from Lhuyd. The next work published was the vocabulary of Dr. Pryce, in 1790, 4to. This is so full of errors that the Editor soon felt satisfied that Pryce was entirely ignorant of the Cornish language, and had no acquaintance whatever with the Welsh. The discovery of the original manuscript, now in the possession of Prince Louis Lucien Bonaparte, shews the work to have been compiled in 1730, by Tonkin or Gwavas, and disingenously published by Pryce as his own. These printed works relate to late Cornish, but more important documents existed, which would furnish examples of the language, when spoken in a state of purity, and which it was desirable should be properly elucidated.

The earliest is a vocabulary of Latin words with Cornish explanations, preserved in the Cottonian Library, in the British Museum, and there entitled 'Vocabularium Wallicum,' (Bibl. Cot. Vespas. A. 14). This was first noticed by Lhuyd in the Cornish Preface to the Archæologia, (p. 222,) and proved by him to be not Welsh but Cornish.

It has been printed in the same order as it is written, and elucidated by Zeuss, in his Grammatica Celtica (2 vols. 8vo., Leipsic, 1853.) It has since been printed alphabetically by Mr. Norris in his 'Cornish Drama,' with additional illustrations from the cognate dialects. This vocabulary is of great philological importance. The manuscript was written in the thirteenth century, and may have been a copy of an older original, even of the ninth century, as it closely agrees with the Welsh of that age, and it contains important proofs that the Welsh then more closely approximated to the Cornish than in later ages. The next important document is a poem, entitled Mount Calvary; a manuscript of the fifteenth century; it contains

259 stanzas of 8 lines each in heptasyllabic metre with alternate rhymes. The subject of this Poem is the Trial and Crucifixion of Christ. There are four copies of this manuscript, the oldest being in the British Museum, and the other three appear to be copies taken from it. Two of them are in the Bodleian Library, and in these a translation by John Keigwin is written on the opposite page. This poem was published by Mr. Davies Gilbert, in 1826. The typographical errors are so numerous, that Zeuss observes that it does not seem to have been corrected after leaving the hands of the compositor, and eight errors in every stanza are below the average. The Editor had carefully collated the manuscript in the British Museum, with the intention of adding a corrected copy as an appendix to the Dictionary, but the necessity no longer remains, as an excellent edition has lately been printed for the Philological Society under the care of a most able Celtic scholar, Mr. Whitley Stokes, of Lincoln's Inn, (8vo., 1862).

The text now given is very accurate, and the numerous errors in the translation have been rectified. The only other work accessible was a Drama, called 'The Creation of the World with Noah's Flood,' which was written, as stated upon the manuscript containing it, on the 12th of August, 1611, by William Jordan. Of this Drama the oldest manuscript is in the Bodleian Library, and there is another in the British Museum, with a translation by John Keigwin, in 1693. This was also printed by Mr. Davies Gilbert, in 1827, and is equally remarkable for its typographical errors. A new and corrected edition, by Mr. Whitley Stokes, was printed for the Philological Society in 1864.

This Drama, being of much later date, shews the Cornish language to have become greatly corrupted, and it is full of English words. The above mentioned works comprised all the accessible material for the Dictionary when the Editor drew out the plan some thirty years ago.

Lhuyd had mentioned that there were three Dramas preserved in the Bodleian Library, of which he gave the first lines, and the Editor, finding that his Dictionary would be a meagre performance without obtaining a copy of them, in vain endeavoured to meet with a transcriber to supply him. Several commenced, but after a short attempt they gave up the task in despair. This circumstance has delayed the Dictionary for many years, and it would never have been completed but for the publication of these Dramas in 1859. They turn out to be of much greater importance than could have been supposed; they are of greater amount than all the other remains of the Cornish language taken together, and are most invaluable specimens of it when spoken in great purity.

The three are of the same antiquity as the Poem of Mount Calvary. The series represents scriptural subjects from the Creation to the Death of Pilate, the first being entitled Ordinale de Origine Mundi. 2, Passio Domini Nostri Ihesu Christi. 3, Ordinale de Resurrectione Domini; and they are of the same kind as the old Mysteries, or Miracle-plays, so common in the middle ages.

They were published by the University of Oxford, in 2 vols. 8vo., being most ably edited by Mr. Edwin Norris, who has added a literal translation on the opposite page.

He has also added a Sketch of Cornish Grammar, and the early Cornish Vocabulary, with a valuable appendix.

By the appearance of these volumes the editor's difficulties were overcome, and he hastened to complete his cherished work. The whole of the Dramas, and other documents are now incorporated in the Dictionary, and copious examples are given for the illustration of the words.

To complete the subject the editor intends publishing in due form a copious Grammar of the Cornish, compared with the cognate dialects, and an essay on the characteristics of the six Celtic languages, together with alphabetical tables of words, common to two or more of them. A list of words will also be given of words borrowed from Latin by the Welsh during the stay of the Romans in Britain, which will be found much more extensive than is generally imagined. The whole, it is presumed, will be found of service in arriving at the history of the population of the British Isles."

A FEW SPECIMENS OF THE ANCIENT CORNISH LANGUAGE.

Norden, writing of the Cornish people and language, about the year 1580, says: "The Cornishe people for the most part are descended of the Britishe stocke, though muche entermixed since with the Saxon and Norman bloude; but untill of late yeares retayned the Britishe speache corrupted as theirs is of Wales; for the South Wales man understandeth not perfectlye the North Wales man, and the North Wales man little of the Cornishe, the South muche.

"The pronunciation of the tounge differs in all, but the Cornish tounge is farr the easieste to be pronounced; for they strayne not ther wordes so tediouslye throwgh the throate, and so harshlye throwgh and from the roofe of the mouth; as in pronouncing Rhin, they fetch it with Rh. Rhin, and LL with a kinde of reflecting the tounge.

"But of late the Cornishe men have muche conformed themselves to the use of the Englishe tounge, and ther Englishe is equall to the beste, espetially in the easterne partes; even from Truro eastwarde it is in a manner wholy Englishe. In the Weste parte of the Countrye, as in the hundreds of Penwith and Kerrier the Cornishe tounge is most in use amongste the inhabitants."

Carew, writing about the same time, and whose "Survey of Cornwall" was published in 1602, gives us more information about the ancient Cornish language.

Norden is said to have been a native of Wiltshire, and naturally would not take the same interest in the old language as Carew, a Cornishman, and a member of an ancient and honoured Cornish family. We shall not be disappointed on enquiring what Carew has told us.

Of Cornish names he says, most of them begin with Tre, Pol, or Pen, which signify a town, a top, and a head.

> "By Tre, Pol, and Pen
> You shall know the Cornishmen."

but Camden im his "Remains" (p. 114) has a much more expressive rhyme, viz:

> "By Tre, Ros, Pol, Lan, Caer, and Pen
> You may know the most Cornishmen."

Carew, like others, says the "Cornish is more easy to be pronounced" and softer in its sound than the Welsh.

To the Englishman, the following examples must appear very uncouth and uninviting, yet doubtless his opinion would be changed, could he hear the old Cornish *spoken* in its original purity, but this is now impossible of course.

Carew names a friend of his, "one Master Thomas Williams," who judged that the Cornish was derived from, or resembled the Greek, and Polwhele, in his Cornish History, compared a number of Greek and Cornish words; but this is a question for the experienced philologist, and is only alluded to here to explain the introduction of a list of words given by Carew.

Greek.	*Cornish.*	*English.*
Teino	Tedna	Draw
Mamma	Mamm	Mother
Episcopus	Escoppe	Bishop
Klyo	Klowo	Here
Didaskein	Dathisky	To teach
Kyon	Kye	Dog
Kentron	Kentron	Spur
Methyo	Methow	Drink
Scaphe	Schapth	Boat
Ronchos	Ronchie	Snorting

Carew's Survey published by Lord de Dunstanville in 1811, (at p. 150) contains a note respecting the above words, as follows:

"Whoever will read Mr. Lhuyds' Archæol. Brit. p. 267, will not wonder that several of the Cornish words should agree with the Greek, since he there says, that both the Greek and Latin are but of one common origin, viz., the old Gaulish or Celtic; and that several of the greatest philologists of England and France have maintained that the tongues spoken in Cornwall, Wales, and Bas-Bretagne, are the chief remains (if not the whole) of the Celtic language."

Latham, in his "Elements of comparative philology," (and as other writers inform us,) says that the Celtic languages are divided into two branches: 1st the British; as known by the Welsh, the Cornish, and the ancient language of Brittany: and "that it is almost certain that the old British, and the ancient language of Gaul, belonged to this branch."

2nd; The Gaelic or Erse; as represented by the present Irish Gaelic, the Gaelic of the Highlands of Scotland, and the Manks of the Isle of Man.

The following table of numbers will give the reader some idea of the resemblances between English, Welsh, Cornish, and Breton, as given by Latham.

English.	*Welsh.*	*Cornish.*	*Breton.*
One	un	onan	unan
Two	dau	deu	daou
Three	tri	try	tri
Four	pedwar	peswar	pevar
Five	pump	pymp	pemp
Six	chwech	whe	chuech
Seven	saith	seyth	seiz
Eight	wyth	eath	eiz
Nine	naw	naw	nao
Ten	deg	dek	dec
Twenty	ugain	ugens	ugent
Hundred	cant	cant	cant

That quaint old writer Andrew Borde, who died in 1539, gives the numerals in Cornish thus:—1, Onyn; 2, dow; 3, tray; 4, peswar; 5, pimp; 6, whe; 7, syth; 8, eth; 9, naw; 10, dec; 11, unec; 12, dower; 13, tredeec; 14, peswardeec; 15, pympdeec; 16, whedeec; 17, sythdeec; 18, ethdeec; 19, nawdeec; 20, igons; 21, onyn war igons; 22, dow war igons; 23, tray war igons; 24, peswarygons; and so on up to thirty.

Borde says "no Cornyshe man dothe number above XXX, and this is named, Deec warnegons. And whan they have told thyrty, they do begyn agayn."

For a hundred they said "kans," and for a thousand "myle."

Carew gives for 40, Deaw Eigganz; for 100, cant; 1000, mille; 10,000, molla.

He also quotes the following simple phrases, viz:—

Durdatha why.—Good morrow to you.
Ternestatha.—Good night.
Fatlaghan a why?—How do you do?
Da durdalatha why.—Well I thank you.
Betha why lawanneck.—Be you merry.
Benetugana.—Farewell.

The following are examples of old Cornish from the Lexicon Cornu-Britannicum by Williams.

1.—Ru'm fay, lemmyn a'n caffen, er an ascal y'n toulsen yn creys an tân.

By my faith, now if I could catch him, I would cast him in the midst of the fire.

2.—My ny won pyw e cammen.

I know not who he is at all.

3.—My a'd câr mûr.

I love thee much.

4.—Y welas ef ny gara na bôs yn y gowethas.

He loved not to see him, nor be in his company.

5.—Cariah an stuff stena an stumpes.

Carry the tin stuff to the stamping mill.

6.—Mi rig gwelas an carnow idzha an idhen môr kil y ge neitho.

I saw the rocks where the sea-birds make their nests.

7.—Ni allaf cavos powes.

I cannot find rest.

8.—Mar menta gwelas an ost an chy kî da'n gegen, ha enna ti a'n câv.

If thou wishest to see the host of the house, go into the kitchen, and there thou shalt find him.

9.—Stean San Agnes an gwella stean en Kernow.

The tin of St. Agnes (is) the best tin in Cornwall.

10.—Ysedheuch yn kesoleth, râk scon why a fŷdh servys.

Sit down in quietness, for you shall soon be served.

11.—Sens dhe clap, na fydh bysy, râk ny fynnaf dhys crygy.

Hold thy prating, be not busy, for I will not believe thee.

12.—Out warnas harlot, pen cok, scon yn mes a'm golok.

Out upon the rogue, blockhead, immediately out of my sight.

13.—Rag cola worth un venen, gulan ef re gollas an plâs.

For listening to a woman, he has quite lost his place.

14.—Kyn pen vîs.

Before the end of a month.

15.—Eva, kyns del vy serrys, my a wra oll del vynny.

Eva, rather than thou shalt be angry, I will do all that thou wishest.

THE FIRST CHAPTER OF GENESIS IN OLD CORNISH.

(As given by Williams in his Lexicon Cornu-Britannicum, in the orthography of the Cornish dramas).

AN CENSA CABYDUL A'N LYVYR AN GENESIS.

1.—Yn dalleth Dew a wrûg nêf ha'n nôr.

2.—Hag ydh esé an nôr heb composter ha gwâg; ha tewolgow esé war enep an downder, ha Spyrys Dew rûg gwaya war enep an dowrow.

3.—Ha Dew a leverys, bydhens golow, hag ydh esé golow.

4.—Ha Dew a welas an golow may fe da: ha Dew a dhyberthas an golow dheworth an tewolgow.

5.—Ha Dew a henwys an golow dŷdh, ha'n tewolgow ef a henwys nôs: ha'n gorthuer ha'n myttyn o an censa dŷdh.

6.—Ha Dew a leverys, bydhens ebren yn creys an dowrow, ha gwrêns e dhybarthy an dowrow dheworth an dowrow.

7.—Ha Dew a wrûg an ebren, ha dhyberthas an dowrow esé yn dan an ebren dheworth an dowrow esé a uch an ebren: hag yn delna ydh o.

8.—Ha Dew a henwys an ebren nêf: ha'n gorthuer ha'n myttyn o an nessa dŷdh.

9.—Ha Dew a leverys, bydhens an dowrow yn dan an nêf cuntullys warbarth dhe un tyller, ha bydhens an tŷr sŷch dyscudhys: hag yn delna ydh o.

10.—Ha Dew a henwys an tŷr sŷch an nôr, ha cuntellyans warbarth an dowrow ef a henwys môr: ha Dew a welas may fe da.

11.—Ha Dew a leverys, gwrêns an nôr dry râg gwels, ha losow ow tôn hâs, ha'n gwŷdh ow tôn avalow warlerch aga echen, nêb usy aga hâs ynné aga honan, war an nôr: hag yn delna ydh o.

12.—Ha'n nôr a dhrôs râg gwels, an losow ow tôn hâs warlerch aga echen, ha'n gwŷdh ow tôn avalow, nêb usy aga hâs ynné aga honan warlerch aga echen: ha Dew a welas may fe da.

13.—Ha'n gorthuer ha'n myttyn o an tressa dŷdh.

14.—Ha Dew a leverys, bydhens golowys yn ebren nêf dhe dhybarthy an dŷdh dheworth an nôs, ha bydhens y râg tavasow, ha râg termynyow, ha râg dydhyow, ha râg bledhynnow.

15.—Ha bydhens y râg golowys yn ebren nêf dhe rey golow war an nôr: hag yn delna ydh o.

16.—Ha Dew a wrûg dew golow brâs: an brassa golow dhe rewlyé an dŷdh, ha'n behanna golow dhe rewlyé an nôs: ha'n stêr ef a's gwrûg yn wêdh.

17.—Ha Dew a's goras yn ebren nêf, dhe rey golow war an nôr.

18.—Ha dhe rewlyé an dŷdh ha'n nôs, ha dhe dhybarthy an golow dheworth an tewolgow, ha Dew a welas may fe da.

19.—Ha'n gorthuer ha'n myttyn o an peswerê dŷdh.

20.—Ha Dew a leverys, gwrêns an dowrow dry râg pûr vêr an taclow ûs ow gwaya gans bewnans, hag edhyn dhe nygé dres an nôr a lês yn ebren nêf.

21.—Ha Dew a wrûg an morvilow brâs, ha ceniver tra bew ûs ow gwaya, nêb a rûg an dowrow dry râg pûr vêr, warlerch aga echen, ha ceniver edhen gans ascal warlerch hy echen; ha Dew a welas may fe da.

22.—Ha Dew a wrûg aga benygé y, ha leverys, bydhouch luen a hâs, ha drouch râg pûr vêr, ha lenouch an dowrow yn môr, ha gwrêns an edhyn dry râg pûr vêr yn nôr.

23.—Ha'n gorthuer ha'n myttyn o an pempes dŷdh.

24.—Ha Dew a leverys, gwrêns an nôr dry râg an taclow bew warlerch aga echen, an lodnow, ha'n taclow cramyas, ha bestes an nôr warlerch aga echen; hag yn delna ydh o.

25.—Ha Dew a wrûg bestes an nôr warlerch aga echen, ha'n lodnow warlerch aga echen, ha ceniver tra ûs ow cramyas war an nôr, warlerch aga echen: ha Dew a welas may fe da.

26.—Ha Dew a leverys, gwrên dên yn agan del ny, warlerch agan havalder; ha gwrêns y cemeres gallos dres an pusces an môr, ha dres an edhen an ebren, ha dres an milyow, ha dres ol an nôr, ha dres ceniver tra cramyas ûs ow cramyas war an nôr.

27.—Yn delna Dew a wrûg dên yn havalder y honan, yn havalder Dew ef a'n gwrûg; gorrow ha benow ef a's gwrûg.

28.—Ha Dew a wrûg aga benygé, ha Dew a leverys dhedhé, bydhouch luen a hâs, ha drouch râg pûr vêr, ha lenouch an nôr, ha bydhouch dresto; ha cemerouch gallos dres pusces an môr, ha dres an edhyn yn ebren, ha dres ceniver tra vew ûs ow gwaya war an nôr.

29.—Ha Dew a leverys, mirouch, yma reys genef vy dheuch ceniver losow ow tôn hâs, nêb ûs war ol an nôr, ha ceniver gwedhen, ûs an avalow an gwedhen ynny ow tôn hâs, dheuch y fŷdh râg boys.

30.—Ha dhe oll an bestes an nôr, ha dhe geniver edhen an ebren, ha dhe geniver tra ûs ow cramyas war an nôr, ûs bewnans ynné, yma reys genef ceniver lusuan glâs râg boys, hag yn delna ydh o.

31.—Ha Dew a welas ceniver tra esé gwreys ganso, ha mirouch, ydh o ve pûr dha; ha'n gorthuer ha'n myttyn o an wheffes dŷdh.

THE PROVINCIAL DIALECT OF CORNWALL.

In the preceding account we have seen how the old Cornish language had been driven from the East to the extreme West of the County by the onward and unceasing progress of the English tongue.

A little more than three hundred years ago, the ancient Cornish was understood, and spoken, from one end of Cornwall to the other. About the year 1700, we find its use confined to the Land's End district, about St. Paul, and St. Just, and there used only by fishermen, market people, and tinners. By the end of the last century it had become all but utterly extinct, and now, (1881) as an oral language, scattered words are all that are left; and so ends the use of a fine old language which dates back to almost unknown time.

We must, however, except the names of persons, towns, farms, villages, hills, valleys, &c., and also the technical names used by miners, farmers, fishermen, &c., a great proportion of such words being actual remains of the old Cornish language.

During the long period that the old tongue was being superseded by the encroaching English language, the people of Cornwall had gradually become accustomed to the use of the new language, and the remote, almost island-like position of Cornwall, is no doubt the cause of the retention in the Cornish dialect of so many old English words in use to this very day.

We have in the provincial dialect a singular mixture of old Cornish and old English words, which gives so strong an individuality to the Cornish speech.

As, in speaking English, a Frenchman, or a German uses more or less of the accent peculiar to each, so it is very probable that the accent with which the Cornish speak, is one transferred from their ancient Cornish language.

The "sing-song," as "strangers" call it, in the Cornish speech is not so evident to Cornishmen, when they listen to their own Dialect.

It has been observed, that when Tregellas, in any place out of the County, gave one of his inimitable lectures on the Cornish *patois*, it was not appreciated as it deserved, yet Cornish audiences richly enjoyed it; but then the latter were more Celtic, and those in distant places more Saxon.

The cerebral, and subtle difference, between the Celt and the Saxon, may be the reason why the former perceived the wit and fun, and the latter little, if at all. Truly of this may it be said that appreciation is one of the talents.

As the old Cornish gave place to English, a provincial dialect composed of both being the result, so the last in its turn, as we are witnessing in our day, is rapidly passing away, and there threatens to be at no distant time a similarity of speech everywhere. As this general levelling proceeds, a large number of forcible and quaint words, and phrases, will be lost unless they be recorded.

It may be thought that to preserve such dialectic words will be neither useful nor ornamental to English speech, on the contrary, that it would be better for such barbarous, vulgar, and uncouth modes of speech, to be thrust aside.

But are they barbarous, vulgar, and uncouth? What if the charges were reversed? Suppose modern English condemned as vulgar, and an order given that the Cornish dialect should be used instead. In a short time the dialect which had become *fashionable*, would be found to be of high polish, elegant, and expressive.

Somebody said that "grammar was made for language and not language for grammar," and as to words being vulgar, it depends on the manner in which they are used, and from whose mouths they fall. The *words* are not so much in fault, for we have often heard sentences full of grossness and vulgarity, expressed in very elegant language.

It would be startling and amusing, if, in an English drawing-room, an elegant lady were to turn to a friend and make a request, thus, "Woll'ee ax en plais"? instead of saying "Will you ask him if you please"? yet all that could be said of it would be, that the former expression was spoken in a dialectic form, and the latter simply in current English.

Now as to the word 'Ax' (for ask), we are told by Toone in his "Dictionary of obsolete and uncommon words," that *Ax*, though now considered as vulgar and ungrammatical, was in use centuries before the modern word '*ask*,' to signify the same thing; in truth the latter word is corrupted from the Saxon.

> " *Axe* not why, for tho' thou *axe* me
> I *wol* not tellen God's privitie.
>
> *Chaucer*, " *Miller's Tale*."

In this quotation two of the words in the lady's request, *ax* for *ask* and *wol* for *will*, have very good authority for their use, and we find them still retained in the Cornish dialect.

Words like them, therefore, are not vulgar, they are simply disused by the educated of modern days. As to a dialect being vulgar and ungrammatical, there may be found in Latham's Elements of Comparative Philology some instructive remarks on this very subject. He says "of that particular form of his mother tongue which any individual uses, the speaker is thoroughly, and in every sense, the master. He uses it as an instrument of his own. He uses it as he uses his arms and legs: to a great extent unconsciously, but almost always instinctively. He cannot err in this, so long as he is at one and the same time, unconscious, spontaneous, and intelligible. If he thinks about grammar, and, by so doing, modify its spontaneity, it is *pro tanto*, a language influenced *aliunde*.

"As long as he speaks it simply from his instincts it is in good grammar; being simply what he makes it. What is called bad grammar is a detail in which he differs from some one else who calls *his* form of speech good grammar.

"It does not follow however, from this that there is no such thing as bad grammar. The term has two meanings, if signifies the actual *representation* of a language and the *formal scheme* of a language.

"*Language as a fact, must be taken as it is, and represented as it best may be.*

"If language at all times and in all places, stands in the same relation to its ideas as an exponent *it is equally good as a language.*"

But, whatever difference of opinion may exist as to the elegance or the rudeness of a language or dialect, one thing seems very certain, that at no distant time, that arch-enemy of all dialects, the modern school-board, will rapidly bring about a great change in Cornish speech.

Already, to a large proportion of Cornish people, especially the young, the Cornish dialect is become almost a dead language, and many of the words are to them as unintelligible as Sanscrit.

The greater intercommunication during the past fifty years has made a great change, and this has been much accelerated since the opening of the Cornwall railway in 1859.

Formerly, instead of one Cornish dialect there were many, which differed more or less from each other, indeed, even in adjoining parishes there were different modes of speaking. Still, taken as a whole, there was, and is, a marked distinction between the dialect of Cornwall and the other parts of the kingdom.

Rude as the *patois* of Cornwall may appear to strangers, yet no Cornishman familiar with it, listens to it other than with fondness. Whether at home, or in the distant colonies, the sound of the homely Cornish dialect falls pleasantly on the ear, and revives a host of kindly thoughts and feelings.

As a dialect, it may be asserted, that it is one of the most quaint, expressive, and friendly-sounding of any in the kingdom, and its characteristics seem to be the reflex of the civil, manly, and independent character of the inhabitants themselves; terms of eulogy given to them so long ago by Diodorus Siculus.

The shadow of the dead Cornish language still hangs over the dialect, and gives it a character not easily described; due probably to the intermixture of words, and the constant use of names of places, persons, &c., such names being of ancient Cornish origin.

The dialect is very capable of expressing odd ideas with fun and wit, and the "sayings" whether imported or native, are frequently very amusing, and characteristic of the Cornish people, thus:

"Laughing like a piskey,"

is curious as referring to the traditionary merriment of the fairies. Again:—

"Like Collins's cow," (*i.e.* worried in mind).

Then again, the fun and superstition combined in the following proverb, which however is spoken out of Cornwall also:

"A whistling woman, and a crowing hen,
Are two of the unluckiest things under the sun,"

also, the quaint adaptation of the name of a place of bad repute, to anything expressive of dirt and disorder, as

"The place is like Lanson jail,"

meaning, what *old* Lanson jail was formerly, viz., dirty and disorderly.

Then the fun and the fear in the following rhyme:

"Jack o'the lantern! Joan the wad
Who tickled the maid and made her bad
Light me home the weather is bad."

Couch's "Polperro."

The terse proverb used of a good catch of pilchards is very Cornish like,

"Meat, money, and light,
All in one night."

Ibid.

and satirical sayings like the following, have the peculiar vein of Cornish fun and wit, and when uttered in the Cornish dialect sound droll enough.

"He is like the Mayor of Calenick who walked two miles, to ride one."

"Like Nanny Painter's hens, very high upon the legs" (said of a tall thin person).

"He is like the Mayor of Falmouth, who thanked God when the town jail was enlarged."

R. Hunt's "Romances of the West of England."

But such "sayings" fall flat on paper, they have only to be heard spoken by a Cornishman in his native dialect, to be appreciated. If the reader desire more real and characteristic examples of the *dialect*, he should read the

"Tales" by Tregellas, Forfar, Daniel &c. (See the Appendix.) Tregellas was "thorough," and it may well be asked, where shall we find his like again? Who again will so amuse with droll Cornish stories as they were told by William Hicks, of Bodmin. What tales! and with such a hearty relish too in relating them!

The stories of Tregellas, really amusing and faithfully illustrative as they are, fall far below what they seemed when told by the living man himself. His perfect assumption of character and Cornish accent, his expression, action and fun, were irresistible provokers of mirth, and his listeners were sure to have aching sides after hearing him.

The writer has heard him lecture again and again, more than forty years ago. It was something to listen to Tregellas, the very master of the Cornish dialect, and the King of Cornish fun.

The dialect of Cornwall is a compound one, as already stated, and its name should be "motley" for it is found to be composed of, 1st, The remains of the old Cornish language; 2nd, Many old English words; 3rd, English words used in a provincial manner; 4th, Many words which apparently are mere slang. The origin of the last there seems no method of accounting for, probably, like "Topsy" in "Uncle Tom's Cabin," they "growed"; and 5th, Purely English words spoken in the usual manner.

About forty or fifty years ago, there were just as many shades of the dialect as there are towns in the County, and as at that time there was comparatively but little inter-communication, the people of different districts were easily known by certain peculiarities of speech.

Tregellas used to notice this in his lectures, and give illustrations, so that his listeners could at once perceive the difference even between two mining districts.

Although there were, and still are, many minor shades of Cornish speech, yet speaking generally it may be said for the sake of making a convenient distinction, that there are two dialects in the County, one which may be called that of the husbandman, the other that of the miner.

Where they border on each other they intermingle, where districts are more widely separated, in each the dialect is more distinct and characteristic.

This is observed in the towns also, although as may be supposed the difference is not so marked.

During the past half century the peculiarities of speech in the towns, and indeed in the rural districts also, have very much altered, and have been tending to greater uniformity.

Formerly it was very easy to distinguish between a man of Bodmin, and one from either Launceston, Liskeard, Withiel, St. Columb, and more especially from St. Agnes, Redruth, or St. Just.

In the west of the County we find a considerable number of old Cornish words still in use, but they become much fewer as we go eastwards. In distant parts of the County, the words are often the same, although spoken with different accents. Indeed, the provincial words are so inextricably mixed up, that it is hard to say as regards a large proportion of them, which are of the eastern and which of the western dialect. The accent of the husbandman is intensified towards the east, that of the miner towards the west, but with various interminglings of each.

It is hard to point out a line of demarcation, so insensibly do the branches of the dialect overlap each other, and become gradually shaded away.

The writer considers that somewhere between Bodmin and St. Austell, a line drawn north and south from sea to sea across the County, would indicate the locality where the dialect of the miner and that of the husbandman merge into each other. Mr. T. Q. Couch, in the introductory remarks to his glossary of East Cornwall, considers that such a line should be further west, viz: "from Crantock Bay, on the St. George's Channel, to Veryan Bay, on the English Channel." This question is not very easy to decide.

The story (given further on) of Richard and Betty at St. Austell is intended by the writer as a specimen of the dialect of that part of the County. It will be found to be, not exactly a miners' dialect, or very much that of the husbandman, and yet there is in the tale a mixture of both.

The miner holds to his peculiar form of speech, apparently with more tenacity than the husbandman.

It requires close attention to discover any provincial accent among the educated classes. It is however noticeable more or less among them as we travel westwards, and especially near the mining districts.

This is perceptible in travelling the short journey from Bodmin to St. Austell.

There is a difference between Launceston and Liskeard, but in both the English accent among the educated is very good, so also in Bodmin; in St. Austell there is more of the miners' accent, but it is not very perceptible without close attention.

In Truro the English accent has been noticed even by the old writers to be remarkably pure, and so it continues to this day.

This is rather surprising when we remember how short a distance separates Truro from the mining population.

The Cornish *idiom* can be understood by a stranger to the County by reading such tales as those by Tregellas, Forfar, &c., &c., but of course to understand the *accent* it must be heard; perhaps it is only a genuine Cornishman who, in in what looks like simple fun, can discover, or appreciate the very spirit and humour of the tale.

The Cornish sometimes attend their funerals in great crowds, and it is a custom to sing hymns as the coffin is being borne along. When all are silent, and walking slowly along, the aspect of the crowd is, of course, sad, or, as we say in Cornwall, "wisht."

As some, in deepest grief, break out into laughter as if defying sorrow, so this trait in human nature is seized upon, for some other occasion, * by Tregellas, who, in two simple but humorous lines gives the signal for cheering up with singular felicity,

"To shaw our sperrits lev us petch
The laast new *berrin-tune*."

---

* See "The St. Agnes Bear Hunt," by Tregellas.

The following speech said to have been made at a farmer's dinner not far from Wadebridge will serve as an illustration. Whether it referred to landlords, or to tenants, is not certain, perhaps to both.

> "Eff yiew wur te dew, as yiew oft te dew, yiew wud dew a guddel bettur then yiew dew dew."

Compare this with the miners' dialect as in this sentence:

> "That's awnly paart uv et, 'tes my belief thee doan't knaw whan thee'rt wale awf."

In the Cornish dialect we find ordinary English words, a large number of old English words, many of which seem spoken as in the time of Chaucer, and as before noticed a great number of names of places, persons, &c., derived from the old Celtic language of Cornwall.

The following is a specimen of the dialect in a form which is fast becoming disused:—

> "A es pinnikin, palchy, an totelin, a es clicky, an cloppy, an a kiddles, an quaddles oal daa,—
> Tes wisht."

which, turned into the ordinary English, means, "He is little, weakly, and imbecile, he is left-handed and lame, and he fidgets idly about all the day long. Tis sad." It is not the object of the writer to explain to any great extent, the origin of such words, such a task is very willingly left to the practical philologist, who certainly has a wide field for his exertions in dealing with the dialect of Cornwall. That there are many common words, and even

Cornish forms of expression, and thought, to be found in the writings of Chaucer, seems evident from the comparisons and quotations from that poet, as given further on.

It is difficult to say what was the exact pronunciation of English 500 years ago when Chaucer wrote, but it is startling to find so many words common to him, and to the Cornish dialect of the present day, and judging by the rhyme, after making due allowance for the poet's license, prononnced in the same manner.

In the Cornish pronunciation we commonly find that *i* is pronounced like *e*, as *selver* for silver; the *e* like *ai*, as *raide* for read; the *a* like *aa*, as *traade* for trade; the *o* like *aw*, as *awnly* for only; the *s* like *z*, as *zaid* for said; the *u* like *oo*, as *oogly* for ugly; the *f* like *v*, as *vaather* for father, and the *g* is almost always dropped at the end of a word, as *writin* for writing, *settin* for sitting. There are other differences also; the miner may be said to speak more broadly than the husbandman, and to more frequently use *aw* for *o*, and *v* for *f*.

There is a frequent use of the word *do*; instead of saying, *I know*, it is, *I do know*, or, as in the western dialect, *I de knaw*; the Cornishman in saying, "I do know," does not use the word *do* with emphasis, as in ordinary English; and also for *I think* the western man will say, *I de theenk*, which in the eastern dialect is expressed by "semmee to me."

In such words as thick, thing, and thin, the *th* is pronounced not like *d*, or like *th*, but in a manner halfway between the two. The vowel is doubled, or prolonged, and the words become theek, theeng, and theen. This is apparently a transmitted peculiarity from the old Cornish language.

Williams in his Cornish Dictionary (Celtic) has no word beginning with *th* in the ancient language, and he says of the letter *d*, that in the Cornish, "when radical it changes its construction into *dh* which has the sound of *th* in the English words *this*, *than*." In some parts of Brittany, they pronounce *dh* as *z* to this very day.

It is well known how hard it is for foreigners, to pronounce *th* and the writer well remembers how great were the attempts of a Frenchman to say

"They think that they are thoroughiy thrashed" after many efforts his despairing cry was "mais c'est impossible" and so it was to him; but we know that it is not so with all foreigners. Four or five hundred years ago when the Cornish began to lose their ancient language, they may have had the same difficulty with *th*, and there is a trace of this in their manner of saying *theeng* for *thing*. *Now*, as a race the Cornish have no difficulty, perhaps time has overcome it, as it might in a race of Frenchmen after speaking English for centuries.

There is another very common phrase, viz: "How be'ee?" for, How are you? this is only, "How be ye?" making the *y* an *i* which in the Cornish dialect is pronounced like *e*. This is more common in the west after passing St. Austell. As we advance eastwards we find that the word *yiew* (you) is a very representative expression and increasingly so as we travel towards the Tamar where there is no obvious difference between the dialects of Devon and Cornwall.

The Devon dialect drives back the Cornish from the east of the County.

Near the Tamar we hear the people saying "How are yiew?" or "How be yiew" the word *yiew* being spoken with a curious twist of the mouth; also the expressions referred to already, viz: "Semmee" or "Semmee to me" for "I think."

There also, we hear people saying *her* for *she* as "Ther her gothe."

In all shades of the Cornish dialect it is very common to use *he* for *it* but the miner generally says *et* for *it* as in this expression "He'eve a dun et" for "He has done it" and *a* for *he*, thus: "Iss a ded" i.e. "Yes he did." It is rare, if ever, that in the dialect the adjective is used *after* the noun. There is a favourite expression in the west, and one of endearment when speaking to a little child. It is "cheel-vean or cheeld-vean," meaning "child little."

It is singular that the Cornish do not often place the adjective after the noun; in speaking their ancient language they commonly did so.

In order to form some idea of the pronunciation, the following examples are given, and, making due allowance for differences in the Cornish dialect, may do sufficiently well.

The Alphabet as Spoken in Ordinary English, and in the Cornish Dialect.

	English.	*Cornish.*
a	ai	aa
b	bee	bee
c	see	zee
d	dee	dey
e	ee	ai
f	ef	aaf
g	jee	jee
h	aitch	aatch
i	i or eye	i or eye
j	jay	jaa
k	kay	kaa
l	el	ael
m	em	ame
n	en	ane
o	o	o
p	pee	pey
q	cue	koo or kiew
r	ar	ar
s	ess	ess
t	tee	tay
u	u or you	oo or yiew
v	vee	vey
w	double u	double yew
x	eks	ex
y	wy	whye
z	zed	zad
&c.	et cetera	ampassy, also passy

The numerals are pronounced just as follows: 1, Wawn; 2, Tew or dew; 3, Dree; 4, Fower, or vower; 5, Vyve; 6, Zix; 7, Zebb'n; 8, Ite; 9, Nyne; 10, Tane; 11, Levv'n, or Lebb'n; 12, Twaelve; &c.

Conjugation of the Auxiliary and Neuter Verb To Be, in the Cornish Dialect.

INDICATIVE MOOD.

Present Tense.

Singular.	*Plural.*
1.—I be.	1.—We be.
2.—Thee airt, or thee'rt.	2.—Yew be.
3.—A es, she es, et es.	3.—Thay be.

Imperfect Tense.

Singular.	*Plural.*
1.—I waz.	1.—We waz.
2.—Thee, or Yew waz.	2.—Yew waz.
3.—A waz.	3.—Thay waz.

Perfect Tense.

Singular.	*Plural.*
1.—I haave a ben.	1.—We haave, or wee've a ben.
2.—Thee'st a ben.	2.—Yew haave, or you've a ben.
3.—A haave a ben.	3.—Thay haave, or thay've a ben.

Pluperfect Tense.

Singular.	*Plural.*
1.—I haad a ben.	1.—We haad a ben.
2.—Thee haad, or theed a ben.	2.—Yew haad a ben.
3.—A haad a ben.	3.—Thay haad a ben.

First Future Tense.

Singular.	*Plural.*
1.—I shaal, or shul be.	1.—We shaal, shul, or wol be.
2.—Thee shust, wust, or wol be.	2.—Yew shaal, shul, or wol be.
3.—A shaal, or wol be.	3.—Thay shaal, shul, or wol be.

Second Future Tense.

Singular.	*Plural.*
1.—I shaal, or shul a ben.	1.—We shul a ben.
2.—Theelt a ben.	2.—Yew wol a ben.
3.—A wol a ben.	3.—Thay wol a ben.

IMPERATIVE MOOD.

Singular.	*Plural.*
1.—Lemmé, or laiv ma be.	1.—Laiv us be.
2.—Be tha.	2.—Be yew, or be'ee.
3.—Lett'n, or laiv'n be.	3.—Lett'm, or laiv'm be.

POTENTIAL MOOD.

Present Tense.

Singular.	*Plural.*
1.—I may, or caan be.	1.—We may, or caan be.
2.—Thee mayst, wust or cust be.	2.—Yew may, or caan be.
3.—A may, or caan be.	3.—Thay may, or caan be.

Imperfect Tense.

Singular.

1.—I might, cud, wud, or shud be.

2.—Thee mights, cudst, wudst, or shudst be.

3.—A might, cud, wud, or shud be.

Plural.

1.—We might, cud, wud, or shud be.

2.—Yew might, cud, wud, or shud be.

3.—Thay might, cud, wud, or shud be.

Perfect Tense.

Singular.

1.—I may, or caan a ben.

2.—Thee mayst, wust or cust a ben.

3.—A may, or caan a ben.

Plural.

1.—We may, or caan a ben.

2.—Yew may, or caan a ben.

3.—Thay may, or caan a ben.

Pluperfect Tense.

Singular.

1.—I might, cud, wud, or shud a ben.

2.—Thee mights, cudst, wudst, or shudst, a ben.

3.—A might, cud, wud, or shud a ben.

Plural.

1.—We might, cud, wud, or shud a ben.

2.—Yew might, cud, wud, or shud a ben.

3.—Thay might, cud, wud, or shud a ben.

SUBJUNCTIVE MOOD.

Present Tense.

Singular.

1.—Ef I be.

2.—Ef thee be, or airt, or thee'rt.

3.—Ef a be, or a es.

Plural.

1.—Ef we be.

2.—Ef yew be.

3.—Ef thay be.

Imperfect Tense.

Singular.	*Plural.*
1.—Ef I waz.	1.—Ef we waz.
2.—Ef tha, or thee waz.	2.—Ef yew waz.
3.—Ef a waz.	3.—Ef thay waz.

The remaining Tenses are in accordance with similar ones in the previous moods.

INFINITIVE MOOD.

Present Tense. To be. *Perfect Tense.* To haave a ben.

Participles.

Present, Bein. *Perfect*, Ben.

Compound Perfect, Haavin, or hevvin a ben.

SHORT SPECIMENS OF THE CORNISH DIALECT.

It is beyond the scope of this book to make long extracts from Cornish writers of tales, and not very necessary, because the reader can so easily obtain original books full of the dialect.

What is here quoted will only be just sufficient to give some idea of what the Cornish dialect is like. The reader should remember how the letters are pronounced in reading the following from Tregellas's story, called "California."

"And so Isaac, you have been fortunate in California, have you? Iss, why how fortinate! I have had putty good speed theere, and a good many good little sturts. Well, as you may say, I have done well-a-fine. But 'twas coose work theere I 'suree. My brother Tom was out theere weth me, and we lived like pigs a'most, we ded a'most, both of us; that es to say, for the time you knaw. Aw, my dear! sich sour maggoty bread, and sich ratten stinkin biskies, and sich sour belly-vengeance beer, when we could git any.

And then the soort of a house we lived in wasn't better then a cow-house, what we righted up weth trees and sich like; and as for our bed, Aw, my dear! 'twas nothin' but strawy traade and leaves, and like that; and all the waater we had to drink was the saame as we washed the gowld dowst in, and 'twas always puddled. Aw, loar! the owld gipsies what do live 'pon hedgyboors and that soort of mait, was more betterer off then we wor as regaard to livin'. Why we'd awnly wann laarge soort of saucepan to booil everything in, and baake too, and we had no spoons but two, what Tom and I maade out of two sticks."

In the following example the words are spelt more in accordance with sound. It is from the story called, "Visit to Lunnun" by "Uncle Jan Treenoodle."

"Dost thee knaw, soas, I've ben op te Lunnun Church
 town?
A vine passel uv things I zeed theere te put down,
Wer I sliced into slivers ze theen as a straw,
I cudd'n tell tha haaf tha braave theengs as I zaw.
Whay, now, what do'ee theenk? thaive got temberin
 rooads,
Which es vitty at times, but for quilkins an tooads;
Puor spoort for tom-toddies, or a padgité pooe;
An whan et do cum, cheel, but a bit uv a skew,
Why tha rain et do maake em so slippy, and slottery,
'Tes no wawnder thay hosses, do git stogged, or trot awry.
Then tha 'Cabs' as they caals 'em, keeps pootin about,
Like a Angleditch twisten etselve en an out,
An thay 'Busses uv which then plaise sure theere's a mort,
Skeyes about like tha bilers uv ingines en spooart.
Wale cheel, as fur tha shops, I wer quite in a maze,
'Fath I ne'er zeed sich booties en oal ma boorn daays.

Theere es sum weth out-wenders as laarge as tha housen
Oal prink'd op se pridy, weth theere picters, an cloasen.
An then, ef I ever! sich vine tummals uv cloam,
Thay maakes a scat-marchant uv thay spaars op te hom.
Fur tha maaids thee mayst zee too, sich nackins an gownds,
An sich aperns an coats; I'd as lieve as tew pounds,
That ma wive baan't slocked en thicky noshuns te zee,
Fur ma vangings wud look scoy an wisht ef so be.
She've jist caal'd ma a cropeing timdoodle i'facks!
'Caas uv cuyn I ded gev her less than she ded axe.
Then plaise sure, theere's no caase te be creenin or dreulin,
Be bedoled weth tha rhoomatiz, roadlin or pulin.
Fur theere's doctirs as pomstirs oal soarts uv desaises,
Theer't palcht op quite braave-like whenever thee plaises.
What's tha odds, ef theer't scat oal abroad? 'tes a pity,
But en few hours' vallee, theer't flam-new an vitty."

THE INVITATION. *(A Parody.)*

Az wance down Lemon Street I strayed,
A leetle while agoan,
I mit a putty lukkin maaid,
A waalkin oal aloan.

My dear! Naow woll'ee haa a chaht?
Tha aivnin es sa vine,
Ses she, I caa'nt agree to thaht,
Becaase, 'tes haaf paste nyne.

Aw! haaf paste nyne; my dear, yew'm wrong,
Plais shore, yew caan't be right,
Be thikky clock I cum along,
'Twas awnly haaf paste ite.

Cum weth ma, soas! Naow do'ee cum,
We'el waalk abaout tha plaace;
She sweeng'd her aarm, an lukkin glum,
She scat ma in tha faace.

BILLY TELLING THE NEWS TO YOUNG FARMER KESSELL. *(A Parody.)*

Kessell.—Hullaw Billy! How be'ee? How es oal hom?

Billy.—Bad, shore nuff. T'howl magpie es dade.

Kessell.—Aw! Ee's dade, es a? How cum that te be?

Billy.—A ovver-ait hesselve, a ded.

Kessell.—Ded a? What waz et a ait?

Billy.—Hoss-flesh, tell a cudd'n clunk no moar.

Kessell.—How cum a te git that soort uv mait?

Billy.—Maister's hosses.

Kessell.—Thay baen't dade be'um?

Billy.—Iss, oal awin te haard wurk.

Kessell.—What haard wurk do'ee main?

Billy.—Thay putt'em te draa waater.

Kessell.—What vur?

Billy.—Te put tha vire out weth.

Kessell.—Vire! what vire?

Billy.—Doant'ee knaw; Way Maister's houz es oal a burn down

Kessell.—Vaather's houz a burn down! How waz et?

Billy.—Thay gashly owld lanturns ded et, I de theenk.

Kessell.—Lanturns! what be'ee taalkin abaout? whane waz et?

Billy.—That theere time whane we was berrin yewer poar mawther.

Kessell.—Mawther! Es she dade?

Billy.—Iss, and nevvur spok no moar aafter thaht.

Kessell.—Aafter what?

Billy.—Aafter ower owld maister dide.

Kessell.—Es vaather dade too?

Billy.—Iss, a tuk to es bade direkly a was towld?

Kessell.—Towld! what waz a towld?

Billy.—Desmal newas, plais shore.

Kessell.—Aw loar! what wisht newas waz et?

Billy.—Wale ef yew must knaw I'le tell'ee, Tha Bank's a brok'.

Kessell.—Aw, dear! Aw, dear! Thickky es tha wishtest theeng uv oal. We shul oal be scat, evvery wawn uv us.

In the following story the writer has endeavoured to show that the Cornish Dialect is as capable of pathos as of fun. The dialect put into the mouths of Richard and Betty is a specimen of what may be heard near St. Austell.

RICHARD AND BETTY AT ST. AUSTELL FEAST.

(A Parody.)

Wawn day laast week I caaled inta owld Spletfigs fur te buy a bit a bacon, whane who shud I mit but my owld swithart Betty Polglaze; she stopp'd oal to waunce an zaid, "Way Rechard es that yew,?" an I zaid "Iss, 'tes me shore nuff," an she zaid "Rechard be'ee cummin te St. Austell Faist temorra?" an I zaid "No—I ded'n knaw,

I might praps," an Betty laffed; an thane I zaid "I wud," an zo I maade op me mind te go te St. Austell Faist. Nex mornin I got out a bade, an put on me clain things an a noo pair uv lace-ops what I boft in te town laast maarket day.

Thay waz Cordivan letther, an thay draad me vit zo that I cud haardly cloppy along. Howsumevvur whane I cum inte town I zeed Betty in her faether's doar-way, an tew chaps hangin awu, wawn wawn zide, an tha t'other tha other, an I ded feel oal ovver in a putty way. Aw! Massy! I'de a nation good mind te give aich uvv'um a good clout onder tha ear, fur Betty she ded'n take no notice, zo I glaazed at her, but she ded'n mind, an thane I gived her a bit of a titch in tha aelbaw, an thane she zaid "Way Rechard es that yew?" an I zaid "Iss 'tes shore nuff," an she zaid, "Rechard woll'ee cum in an set down a bit?" and I zaid "Iss I wud" an zo I ded, an I waalked in; an whane I cum in I found a fine passel uv people inside, lots uv 'um, an Betty zaid, "Rechard, woll'ee haave a liddl drap a sumthin?" an I zaid, "Iss thenk'ee," an I ded, an a nice liddl drap et waz, an I laffed, an waz feelin cumfurtable like, very cumfurtable; an Betty zaid, "Rechard woll'ee zing a bit uv a zong? and I zaid "Iss I wud way oal me hart," an zo I ded.

Aw! I caal te mind very wale that thikky waz tha fust zong I zing'd te Betty, an she zaid, "Yew'l zing wawn moar, want'ee?" an I zaid, "Iss, that I wud," an zo I ded, an turn'd to an zing'd wance moar.

Aw, dear! Thikky waz tha laast zong evvur I ded zing te poar Betty.

Et waz gittin laate an zo I zaid, "Betty, 'tes time fur me te go hom," an she zaid, "whanever yew de wish Rechard," an I zaid, "Woll'ee cum an ze ma paart uv tha way hom, Betty?" an she zaid she wud, an zo she ded, an cum along way me oal tha way down te tha bottom uv tha town; an thane I lukked at Betty an I zaid "Betty give us a kess, now woll'ee?" an she zaid "Iss she wud," an she ded too, an she gived me a kess.

"Wale, Betty, thee'st lemm'ee cum an ze'ee te-morra night?" an she zaid "'tes jist as yew de wish Rechard" an zoon aefter I staerted fur hom, an got inte bade.

Tha aivnin aefter that, I went te mit Betty. Ite a'clock! an Betty wadd'n cum—Nyno a'clock! an no Betty—tane a'clock, an no Betty—lebb'n, twaelve a'clock, an no Betty; zo I zaid to meselv, 'tes sa well te go hom as stay heer, an zo I ded, an nex mornin I heerd that poar Betty waz tuk very bad, very bad shore nuff, an that she sent word fur me te cum; zo I went, an zeed poar Betty, an she zaid, "Rechard, ef so be that I waz te die, yew'l go te me berrin want'ee?" an I zaid, "I dedn't knaw what te zay"—"praps"—an thane I zaid, "I wud," an I ded, an I waalked behind tha coffin zingin hymns oal tha way, fur poar Betty dide—Iss she ded—an I de nevvur go inside St. Austell berrin-groun wethout I de drap a tear in mind uv poar Betty Polglaze.

WORDS IN THE CORNISH DIALECT

Compared with several which are found in the writing of Chaucer.

(Chaucer was born A.D. 1328, and died A.D. 1400.)

The following are some common words as spoken in Cornwall. Without asserting that all are correctly compared, yet taken as a whole, they seem very familiar to a Cornishman, as he meets with them in the quaint old English verse of Chaucer.

It is not contended that similar words are never used elsewhere; only that they are not now so pronounced by the educated classes in Cornwall, and that while found in Chaucer's writings, such words also form a portion of the Cornish dialect.

As is well known, many old words in Spenser, and in Shakspere, are still used in Cornwall, but they are few compared with those to be found in Chaucer.

The form of English which first reached Cornwall when the ancient language was passing away, was apparently that of Chaucer, which, after his death, at last passed the banks of the Tamar, and spread gradually towards the west.

As the language changed, influenced as it must have been by such writers as Spenser, Shakspere, &c., so in succession, wave after wave of English passed from the east into Cornwall, each wave modifying the dialect spoken by the Cornish during the long period of the decay of the ancient Celtic tongue of the County.

As a Cornishman, one often feels "at home" in reading some parts of Chaucer, especially the "Coke's Tale of Gamelyn," thus, the following verse, when read in Cornish fashion, does not seem to have been written 500 years ago :—

> "As they were eting and drinking
> Of the best *wele and fine*,
> Then said *the t'on to the t'other*
> This is yonge Gamelyn."

In the following comparisons, the ordinary English word is first given in black letter ("**Advise**"), then the Cornish form of it in *ITALICS*, and for each some quotations by way of illustration. Thus the reader will be enabled to judge for himself.

The *spelling* in the extracts from Chaucer, is that given in "The Complete Edition of the Poets of Great Britain" published by John and Arthur Arch, of London, and Bell, Bradfute and Mundell of Edinburgh. The following is the

LIST OF WORDS COMPARED WITH SOME IN CHAUCER, VIZ :—

Advise. *AVISE.*

> "Now be well *avysed* ageyne to-morowe day,
> Then shalt thou have thy jugement, ther is no more to say."
> (*The Merchant's Second Tale.*)

> "And so much the more that thou art nat wise,
> And cans't nat me of no maner *avise*." (*Ibid.*)

Afraid. *AFERED.*

"Was in a bush, that no man might him se,
For sore *afered* of his deth was he."

(*Canterbury Tales.*)

Alas! *ALAAS!* (so pronounced.)

"Thus herte mine! for Antenor *alas!*
But how shull ye doen in this wofull *caas.*"

(*Troilus & Creseide.*)

"What shall I doon, my Pandarus *Alas!*
Sens that there is no remedy in this *caas.*"

(*Ibid.*)

Are. *AAR.* (so pronounced.)

"That it n'ill as the moeble fare,
Of whiche thei first delivered *are.*"

(*Romaunt of the Rose.*)

Ask. *AX.*

"You lovers *axe* I now this question,
Who hath the werse, Arcite or Palamon?"

(*The Knight's Tale.*)

"Under the mone that may wane and waxe,
And for my werk right nothing wol I *axe.*"

(*The Doctour's Tale.*)

Asked. *AXED.*

"If that he *axed* after Nicholas."

(*The Miller's Tale.*)

"And gan to bord ageyn and *axed* him in game,
Sith thou art our fadir who is then our dame?"

(*The Merchant's Second Tale.*)

Asking. *AXING.*

"I you forgeve this trespas every del,
And they him sware his *axing* fayr and wel."

(*The Canterbury Tales.*)

Bailiffs. *BAILIVES.*

"These joly knights and *bailives*
These nonnis and these burgeis wives."
(*Romaunt of the Rose.*)

Bark. *BERK.* (also pronounced baark.)

"And to *berk* as doith an hound and sey Baw baw."
(*Merchant's Second Tale.*)

Beasts. *BAISTIS.*

"Of faire wethir and tempestis,
Of qualme, of folke, and of *bestis.*"
(*The House of Fame.*)

Before. *AFORE.*

"Thou must pass through the hall, but tary nat I rede,
For thou shult fynd a dur up right *afore* thyn hede."
(*Merchant's Second Tale.*)

"For as the seven sages had *afore* declarid."
(*Ibid*)

"What should Mercie do but Trespas go *afore*,
But Trespas, Mercie woll be litill store."
(*Chaucer's Ballads.*)

Between. *BETWIX.*

"Every man to other will seyne,
That *betwyx* you is somme synne."
(*Romance of the Lyfe of Ipomydon.*)

"This was the forward pleinly for t'endite,
Betwixen Theseus and him Arcite." (*Ibid*).

Black. *BLAKE.* (pronounced blaak.)

"Of lambe skynnys hevy and *blake*,
It was full olde I undertake."
(*Romaunt of the Rose.*)

"As soon as poverté ginneth take,
With mantil and with wedis *blake*."
(*Ibid.*)

"An hat upon his hed with frenges *blake*,
Sire, quod the Sumpnour, haile and wel atake."
(*The Frere's Tale.*)

"Have here a light and loke on all these *blake*,
But oftin gan the hert to glad, and quake."
(*Troilus and Creseide.*)

Brass. *BRAZ.*

"I found that on the wall there was
Thus written on a table of *bras*."
(*The House of Fame.*)

"Toke out his blacke trompe of *bras*,
That foulir then the devill was." (*Ibid.*)

Bull. *BULL.* (The *u* pronounced as in *dull*, the same also in the word *bullocks.*)

"For of the Pope I have the *bull*,
I ne hold not my wittis dull."

Busy. *BESY.*

"The *besy* larke the messenger of day,
Salewith in hire song the morwe gray."
(*Canterbury Tales.*)

"And while he *besy* was this fendly wretch,
This false chanon, the foule fend him fetch."
(*The Chanone's Yeomannes Tale.*)

Busily. *BESILY.*

"Gan I beholdin *besily*,
And I wol tel you redily." (*Romaunt of the Rose.*)

Carry. *CARY.*

"And said twise by Saint Mary,
Thou art a noyous thinge to *cary*."
(*The House of Fame.*)

Case. *CAAS.*

"But if it be in certaine *caas*."
(*Romaunt of the Rose.*)

"But thei would hatin you *parcaas*,
If that ye fillin in ther laas." (*Ibid.*)

"That 'till a lover longith in this *caas*."
(*Troilus and Creseide.*)

"That ben his frendis in such manir *caas*."
(*Ibid.*)

"I tuck'd up, with arowes in ther *caas*."
(*Legend of Dido.*)

Chest. *CHIST.*

"And eke of brotherhed, if that thee list,
I have gold and silver lying in my *chist.*"

(*The Frere's Tale.*)

Cóntrary. *CONTRÁRY.*

"Away fro truth it doth so varie,
That to gode love it is *contrárie.*"

(*Romaunt of the Rose.*)

Crisp. *CRIPS.*

"As writeth th'on in the Apocalyps,
Her here that was owndie and *crips.*"

(*House of Fame.*)

Danger. *DAUNGER.* (also pronounced daanger.)

"Wythout more *daunger.*"

(*The Merchant's Second Tale.*)

Dark. *DERK.* (also pronounced daark.)

"N'iste wher she was for it was *derk,*
But faire and wel she crept in by the clerk."

(*The Reve's Tale.*)

"The shadowe makith her bemes merke,
And her hornis to shewin *derke.*"

(*Romaunt of the Rose.*)

Darkness. *DERKNESS.*

"For thre dayis incessantly the *derkness* among them was."

(*The Merchant's Tale.*)

"For fere of night so hatith the *derknesse.*"

(*The Legend of Good Women.*)

Deaf. *DEFE.* (deef.)

"For that I rent out of his book a lefe,
That of the stroke myn ere wex all *defe.*"

(*The Wif of Bathe's prologue.*)

"Why that I rent out of his book a lefe,
For which he smote me so that I was *defe.*"

(*Ibid.*)

Drove. *DROV or DROFF.*

"And *droffe* all his brother's men,
Right sone on an hepe."

(*The Coke's Tale of Gamelyn.*)

Dwale. *DWALE.*

"Ther n'as no more ; nedeth hem no *dwale*,
This miller hath so wisly bibbed ale."

(*The Reve's Tale.*)

Ease. *AISE.* (ese.)

"And said, I love the both and preise,
Sens that thine answere doth me *ese*."

Else. *ELS or ELLES.*

"Have we nat *els* now for to think oppon."

(*The Merchant's Second Tale.*)

"For she desirid nothinge *elles*,
In certain, as the boke us telles."

(*The House of Fame.*)

Far. *FER.* (or Fur, also Ver).

"As *fer* as that the day beginneth dawe."

(*The Monke's Tale.*)

"As *ferre* as I have remembraunce."

(*The Romaunt of the Rose.*)

Fast. *FASTE or FAASTE.*

"Then now in our tyme ; for all thing doith waste,
Saff vile and cursid lyving, that growith all to *faste*."

Four. *FOWER.* (also Vower.)

"With other *fower* I dare well saie,
That nevir woll be toke awaie."

(*Romaunt of the Rose.*)

Fringes. *FRENGES.*

"An hat upon his hed with *frenges* blake,
Sire, quod the Sumpnour, haile and wel atake."

(*The Frere's Tale.*)

Full. *FULL.* (the *u* as in *dull.*)

"Now is the mone yong and of light dulle,
Ere he come home it will be at the *fulle.*"

(The Remedie of Love.)

Full time. *ALL TIME.*

"Lo Grenwich, there many a shrew is inne,
It were *al time* thy tale to begin."

(The Reve's Prologue.)

Further. *FORTHER FORE.* (or Vorthervore.)

"*Forther for* they wer aftir sent, and was their charge."

(The Merchant's Second Tale.)

Gave. *GOV or GOFF, also GAV.*

"He toke to the one staff,
And beginning to worke wele,
And gode strokes he gaff."

(Coke's Tale of Gamelyn.)

Glad. *GLADE or GLAAD.*

"But God that alle made,
That I shold sittin here fasting,
And othir men make *glade.*"

(Coke's Tale of Gamelyn.)

"So shortly to conclude, the marriage was made,
Betwene hir and Beryn, many a man to *glade.*"

(The Merchant's Second Tale.)

Goes. *GOATH or GOTH.*

"Ther stomblen stedes strong and down *goth* all,
He rolleth under foot as doth a ball."

(The Knight's Tale.)

Gown. *GOWND.*

"When Machyn wept sore and brought his fadir's *gownd,*
And gaf hym the same knyff oppon the see strond."

(The Merchant's Second Tale.)

Had. *HADE.* (pronounced *haad.*)

"She of her love graunt to him made,
Sir Mirthe her by the fingir *hade.*"

(Romaunt of the Rose.)

"Upon the woundis that he *hade*,
Thorough the eye, in my herte made."

(Romaunt of the Rose.)

Haul. *HALE.*

"And cast over a perch, and *hale* along my throte."

(Merchant's Second Tale.)

Have. *HAAVE.*

"And yet I had levir, as God my soule save,
Se thes wondir pleys then all the good I *have.*"

(Merchant's Second Tale.)

"And if that wickid Deth him *have*,
I woll go with him in his grave."

(Romaunt of the Rose.)

Home. *HOM.*

"If that I walke or play unto his hous,
Thou comest *hom* as dronken as a mous."

(Wife of Bathe's Prologue.)

If it happen so. *IF SO BE.* (pro. Ef so be.)

"And *if so be* that thou my lady win,
And sle me in this wode, ther I am in."

(Canterbury Tales.)

"*If so be* that thou ne mayst not,
Thin owen conseil hide."

(The Tale of Melibeus.)

"Be queinte or torned in another place,
If so be thou wolt not do me grace."

(The Knighte's Tale.)

Is. *BE.*

"I trowe his habitation *be* there."

(The Pardoner's Tale.)

Fey. *IS FEY.* (By my fey.)

"For he shal tell a tale by my *fey*,
Although it be not worth a botel hey."

(The Manciple's Prologue.)

Kep-kep-kep. (The call for a horse to come of his own accord, as used in Cornwall, and supposed to be not *now* used in any other County.)

"With *Kepe-kepe;* stand, stand, jossa warderere,
Or whistle thou, and I shal *kepe* him here."

(The Reve's Tale.)

Keys. *KAYS.*

"Adam toke the *kaies* and lat
Gamelyn out anon."

(The Coke's Tale of Gamelyn.)

"The opened and shet, and went hir wey,
And forth with hem, they caried the *kay*."

(The Chanone's Yemanne's Tale.)

"And if that bokis were awaie,
I lorné were of all remenbraunce the *kaie*."

(The Legend of good women.)

Kiss. *KESSE.*

"For would she of her gentilnesse,
Withoutin more me onis *kesse*."

(The Romaunt of the Rose.)

Laugh. *LOFF.* (Lawgh.)

"The burgeyses gon to *lawgh*."

(The Merchant's Second Tale.)

Lend. *LEN or LENE.*

"I n'ere but lost; and therefore I you prey,
Lene me this summe, or elles mote I dey."

(The Shipmanne's Tale.)

"Beseching him to *lene* a certain
Of gold and he wold quite it him again."

(The Chanone's Yemanne's Tale.)

"*Lene* me a marke, quod he, but dayes three,
And at my day I wol it quiten thee."

(Ibid.)

Mad. *MAZED.*

"Thyn help, quod Beryn; lewde fole,
Thow art more then *masid*,
Dres the to the shippis ward with thy crown yrasid."

(The Merchant's Second Tale.)

Master. *MAISTER.*

"Sire Knight (quod he) my *maister* and my lord,
Now draweth cutte for that is min accord."

(The Canterbury Tales.)

"But at the last his *maister* him bethought,
Upon a day whan he his paper sought."

(The Coke's Tale.)

"And afterward he said unto the Frere,
Tel forth your tale min owen *maister* dere."

(The Frere's Prologue.)

Merchant. *MARCHANT.*

"Yit nethirles yf thy hert be so inly set,
For to be a *Marchaunt*, for nothing woll I let."

(The Merchant's Second Tale.)

"Though he be chapman or *marchaunt*,
And have of golde many besaunt."

(The Romaunt of the Rose.)

Merchandise. *MARCHANDISE.*

"Of my *marchandise*, such as he to-fore had seyn."

(The Merchant's Second Tale.)

"Or that he wold bergeyn eny *marchandise*,
And right doith these marchandis in the same wise."

(Ibid.)

Myself. *MYSELVE.*

"It passeth not ten days or twelve,
But it was tolde right to *myselve.*"

(*The Romaunt of the Rose.*)

Nature. *NATUR.*

"Geffrey was right myghty, and wele his age did bere,
For *natur* was more substantiall when tho dayis wer."

(*The Merchant's Second Tale.*)

Needle. *NIDILL.*

"And gan this *nidill* threde anone."

(*The Romaunt of the Rose.*)

Near to. *N'ISTE.*

"And *n'iste* wher she was, for it was derk."

(*The Reve's Tale.*)

Neither. *NETHIR.*

"For comfort *nethir* counsaill of my men have I noon."

(*The Merchant's Second Tale.*)

Nonce. *NONES.*

"Adam seidë yong Gamelyn,
Y blissid be thy bones,
That is a rightë gode counsaile,
Y givin for the *nones.*"

(*The Coke's Tale of Gamelyn.*)

None. *NOAN.*

"All was for naught, for still as stone,
He lay; and word ne spoke he *none.*"

(*Chaucer's Dream.*)

Not. *NAT.*

"Geffry was so nigh com that Beryn myght *nat* fle."

(*The Merchant's Second Tale.*)

"Naie, certainly, it shall *nat* be."

(*The Romaunt of the Rose.*)

Number. *NOMBER.*

"Of my diseses there is no *nomber*,
Daungir and shame me encomber."

(The Romaunt of the Rose.)

Own. *OWEN.* (Oan).

"And sayd, this is a short conclusion,
Your *owen* mouth by your confession."

(The Canterbury Tales.)

"Ne spaireth not min *owen* maister dere."

(The Frere's Tale.)

Pass. *PAAS.*

"Wherefore er I woll ferthir gone or *paas*,
Yet efte I the beseche and fully saie,
That privité go with us in this caas."

(Troilus and Creseide.)

Place. *PLASE.* (plaas.)

"And rid so forth talkying a soft esy pase,
Homward to his *plase* ther that Rame was."

Pour. *POWER.* (poure.)

"The selfe daie or that verry houre,
That I on hem began to *poure*."

(The House of Fame.)

Round. *ROUN.*

"Wherefore they gon *roune*."

(The Merchant's Second Tale.)

Run. *RENNE or REN.*

"Which that I herde *renne* faste by."

(The Romaunt of the Rose.)

"And doen his lose so widé *renne*,
That all quicke we shouldin him brenne."

(Ibid.)

"For pitee *renneth* sone in gentil herte,
And though he first for ire quoke and sterte."

(The Knighte's Tale.)

"And many a yere as it passed henne,
Sin that my tappe of lif beganne to *renne.*"

(The Reve's Prologue.)

"The wif came leping inward at a *renne,*
She sayd Alas! youre hors goth to the fenne."

(The Reve's Tale.)

Scatter. *SCATER.*

"And som are *scatered* all the shore aboute,
Som lepen into the roof withouten doute."

(The Chanone's Yemanne's Tale.)

Self. *SELVE.*

"It passith not ten daies or twelve,
But it was tolde right to my *selve.*"

(The Romaunt of the Rose.)

Shall. *SHUL.*

"And ye *shul* both anon unto me swere,
That never mo ye *shul* my contree dere."

(The Knighte's Tale.)

"Ne never *shul* have, terme of all hir lives."

(The Frere's Tale.)

"Bring eke with you a boile or elles a panne
Ful of water, and ye *shul* wel see thanne."

(Ibid.)

Should. *SHUDDE.* (shud.)

"He knew not Caton, for his wit was rude,
That bade a man *shudde* wedde his similitude."

(The Miller's Tale.)

Shut. *SHETTE.* (shet.)

"This Nicholas his dore faste *shette,*
And doun the carpenter by him he sette."

(The Miller's Tale.)

"Voideth your man, and let him be thereout,
And *shet* the dore, while we ben about."

(The Chanone's Yemanne's Tale.)

"Of man ne woman forth right plaine,
But *shette* her one eye for disdaine."

(The Romaunt of the Rose.)

"Tho were the gates *shette*, and cried was loude,
Do now your devoir, yonge knightes proude."

(The Knighte's Tale.)

"And on the Monday whan it drew to night,
He *shette* his dore, withouten candell light."

(The Miller's Tale.)

Small. *SMALE.* (smaal.)

"And *smale* foules maken melodie."

(The Canterbury Tales.)

"This goddesse on an hart ful heye sete,
With *smale* houndes all about hire fete."

(Ibid.)

" - - - - - - - Wol ye here the Tale?
Ovide, amonges other thinges *smale*."

(The Wif of Bath's Tale.)

"Leteth your othes bothe gret and *smale*,
But, Sires, now wol I tell you forth my tale."

(The Pardonere's Tale.)

"How Sire Thopas with sides *smale*,
Priking over hill and dale."

(The Rime of Sire Thopas.)

"The mavis and the nightingale,
And othir joly birdis *smale*."

(The Romaunt of the Rose.)

"Turn over the leef, and chese another tale,
For he shal find ynow bothe grete and *smale*."

(The Pardonere's Tale.)

Smart. *SMERT.*

"For many a man so hard is of his herte,
He may not wepe although him sore *smerte*."

(Canterbury Tales.)

Some. *SOM.*

"And *som* man wold out of his prison fayn,
That in his house is of his meynie slain."

(Canterbury Tales.)

"That by *som* aventure or *som* tretee."

(Ibid.)

"*Som* in his bed, *som* in the depe see,
Som in the large feld, as ye may see."

(The Knighte's Tale.)

Soul. *SOULE.* (sowl.)

"As God my *soule* save."

(The Merchant's Second Tale.)

Sound. *SOUN.*

"This man complinin with a pitous *soun*,
For even like without addicioun."

(The Complainte of the Blacke Knighte.)

"Of 'hem that makin blodie *soun*,
In trumpe, beme, and clarioun."

(The House of Fame.)

Standeth. *STONDETH.*

"And is so grow in yeris that LX yeer ago,
He sawe nat for age; and yit it *stondith* so."

(The Merchant's Second Tale.)

Step. *STAP.*

"And cried, out-and-harrowe! and nere hym gan to *stap*."

(The Merchant's Second Tale.)

"And would fayn have voidit and outward gan to *stapp*,
But Machaigne arose, and sesid by the lapp."

(Ibid.)

Sudden. *SODEN.* (soaden.)

"But feir and soft wyth ese homward they her led,
For her *soden* sekenes ful sore they were adred."

(The Merchant's Second Tale.)

Suddenly. *SODENLY.*

"O! word, for pure anguysh that he toke *sodenly*."

(The Merchant's Second Tale.)

"And songen all the roundel lustily,
Into a studie he fell *sodenly*."

(The Knighte's Tale.)

Swift. *SWIFF.*

"Beryn made a *swyff* pase; ther myght no man him let."

(The Merchant's Second Tale.)

Swoon. *SWOUN.*

"Or of aught elles, fledde were out of toune,
Adoune he fell all sodainly in *swoune*."

(Troilus and Creseide.)

Tackling. *TAKELING.*

"They made their *takelyng* redy, and wend the sail acros."

(The Merchant's Second Tale.)

Than. *THEN.*

"Se the wondir pleys *then* all the good I have."

(The Merchant's Second Tale.)

The other. *THE T'OTHER.*

"*The t'other* sette on erth, and fast began to fle."

(Coke's Tale of Gamelyn.)

"Should do *the t'odir's* bidding."

(The Merchant's Second Tale.)

There. *THEER and THER.*

"And aspyed reddy yf ye fynd me *there* (theer),
In the meen while I woll abyde here."

(The Merchant's Second Tale.)

"And so them thought betir and leve their good *ther*,
Then abyde ther oppon and have more fere."

(Ibid.)

Throat. *THROTT.*

"And yknet fast with a riding knot,
And cast over a perch, and hale along my *throte.*"

(The Merchant's Second Tale.)

Torment. *TOURMENT, TURMENT.*

"And eke with peine that love me yeveth also,
That doubleth all my *tourment* and my wo."

(The Canterbury Tales.)

"For she is so grete *turment.*"

(The Romaunt of the Rose.)

"For *turment* that he had, so wery he was and fente,
And to God above thus he made his pleynt."

(The Merchant's Second Tale.)

Treason. *TRAISON.*

"He that purchasid the *traison*,
Of Roulande and of Olivere."

(The Dreme of Chaucer.)

Truly. *TREWELY.*

A! quod this sumpnour, benedicite, what say ye?
I wend ye were a yeman *trewely.*"

(The Frere's Tale.)

"Bur *trewely*, min owen maister dere."

(The Pardoner's Tale.)

Twice. *TWISE.*

"Now (quod Pandare) er houris *twise* twelve,
He shal the ese unwist of it himselve."

(Troilus & Creseide.)

"I have herd saie eke times *twise* twelve,
He is a fole that woll foryete him selve."

(Ibid.)

Upon. *OPPON.*

"When he saw the pangis of deth comyng so fast,
Oppon his wife Agea almost his hert to brast."

(The Merchant's Second Tale.)

"Fawnus *oppon* a dey, when Beryn cam at eve,
Was set *oppon* a purpose to make his son leve."
(The Merchant's Second Tale.)

Was. *WAAS.* (also waz.)

"And rid so forth talkyng; a soft esy pase,
Homward to his plase ther that Rame *was*."
(The Merchant's Second Tale.)

"Thus they talkid to eche othir tyl they com into the plase,
And wer yentrid in the hall, ther the steward *was*."
(Ibid.)

We. *US.*

"Wherefore *us* ought as wel."
(The Tale of Melibeus.)

Weary. *WERRY.*

"We environn bothe londe and se,
With all the worlde *werryin* we."
(The Romaunt of the Rose.)

"*Wery* and wet, as bestis in the rain,
Cometh sely John, and with him cometh Alein."
(The Reve's Tale.)

When. *WHAN.*

"Withouten any lenger tarying,
A morwe *whan* the day began to spring."

"Doth to the ladies *whan* the from him wente,
But shortly for to telle is min entente."
(The Canterbury Tales.)

"*Whan* that the time shall be."
(The Coke's Tale of Gamelyn.)

Where. *WHER.*

"*Wher* as this lady romed to and fro,
And with that sight hire beautie hurt him so."
(The Knighte's Tale.)

While. *WHILES.*

"*Whils* that I here stond."

(*The Merchant's Second Tale.*)

Will. *WOL.* (or wul.)

"And after *wol* I tell of our viage,
And all the remenant of our pilgrimage."

(*The Canterbury Tales.*)

"And thus he thoughte wel that every man,
Wol helpe himself in love, if that he can."

(*Ibid.*)

"Till we be fast, and than we *wol* hem shewe,
Wel may that be a proverbe of a shrewe."

(*The Wif of Bathe's Prologue.*)

Wonder. *WAUNDER.*

"Of whom thou hast grete fere and *wonder*,
And dwellinge with the god of thonder."

(*The House of Fame.*)

Wore. *WERED.*

"Of fustian he *wered* a gipon,
Alle besmotred with his habergeon."

(*The Canterbury Tales.*)

"Upon his hede he *wered* of laurer grene,
A gerlond fresshe and lusty for to sene."

(*The Knighte's Tale.*)

Wouldest. *WUST.*

"Where me be wo o mightie God! thou *woste*."

Wound. *WOUNDE.* (wownde.)

"But cruil day, so welaway the stounde,
For whiche hem thought thei felin deth'is *wounde*."

(*Troilus and Crescide.*)

"And how Hipomédon in a litil stounde,
Was dreint, and dedde, Parthenope of *wound*."

(*Ibid.*)

"That to my foe that gave my herte a *wounde*,
And namily there were none may be founde."

(The Complaint of the Blacke Knighte.)

Wrestling. *WRASTLING.*

"*Wrastlen* by veray force and veray might,
With any yong man, were he never so wight."

(The Monke's Tale.)

"That was so doughti a champion,
In *wrastling* and in fight."

(The Coke's Tale of Gamelyn.)

"Y cryid a *wrastling*." *(Ibid.)*

Yet. *YIT.*

"And met nevir man *yit*, that me coud tell with mowth."

(The Merchant's Second Tale.)

Yock. *YOXETH.* (Yuck, to try and swallow when the mouth is empty, to hiccough.)

"He *yoxeth*, and he speketh thurgh the nose,
As he were on the quakke, or on the pose."

(The Reve's Tale.)

You. *YEW.*

"A! Sir be *yew* that man? of *yew* I have y herd,
Gentill Sir, doutith nat, no be nothing aferd."

(The Merchant's Second Tale.)

COMMON ENGLISH WORDS IN THE CORNISH DIALECT.

Many ordinary English words, although not exactly dialectic, are much changed, and differently pronounced in the Cornish dialect, and as we meet with them in reading Cornish tales, such words, being *in situ*, often arrest the attention by their peculiar quaintness, and force.

Hundreds of English words are so "handled" by the Cornish, that it is difficult to say whether such words should, or should not, be included in a Glossary.

It may not be amiss to make a list of some of them, and although the catalogue could be much lengthened, the following may suffice. To extend it would be of no great use, and certainly tedious for perusal. The selection of words in the following list will illustrate to some extent the peculiarities of the dialect.

CORNISH.	*ENGLISH.*
Aant or Un...	*Aunt*
Abroad ...	*Wide open*
Afore ...	*Before*
Aise ...	*Ease*
Anatomy ...	*Skeleton*
Anend ...	*On end*
Antic ...	*Fool*
Apern ...	*Apron*
Apernt ...	*Apron*
Apsen ...	*Aspen*
Arg, Argy, Argyfy ...	*Argue*
Arter or Aafter	*After*

CORNISH.	ENGLISH.
Athurt	... *Athwart*
Atween	... *Between*
Atwixt	... *Betwixt*
Avore	... *Before*
Awnly	... *Only*
Ax	.. *Ask*
Baan't	... *Am not*
Bait	... *Beat*
Bakester	... *Baker*
Bankrout	... *Bankrupt*
Beel	... *Bill*
Beel	... *Beak*
Belk	... *Belch*
Belve	... *Bellow*
Berrin	... *Funeral*
Bestest	.. *Best*
Betterfit	... *More suitable*
Bettermost	... *Best*
Billees	... *Bellows*
Bilt	... *Belt*
Bind	... *Band*
Bine	... *Bind*
B'law	... *Believe*
Blawed	... *Blowed*
Boalin	... *Boiling*
Boft	... *Bought*
Bould	... *Bold*

CORNISH.	ENGLISH.
Brether	... *Brother*
Brik	... *Break*
Broft	... *Brought*
Brudge	... *Bridge*
Buts	... *Bots*
Bye	... *Lonely*
Caalin	... *Calling*
Caan't	.. *Cannot*
Capp'n	... *Captain*
Cause	... *Because*
Cause	... *Case*
Chacks	... *Cheeks*
Chainy	... *China*
Chait	.. *Cheat*
Cheeld	... *Child*
Chelder	... *Children*
Cheldern	... *Children*
Cheen	... *Chine*
Chimbly	... *Chimney*
Chimley	... *Chimney*
Ching	... *Chin*
Choorin	... *Charing*
Chow	... *Chew*
Chuck	.. *Choke*
Ch'town	... *Churchtown*
Clain	... *Clean*
Claps	... *Clasp*

CORNISH.	*ENGLISH.*
Clath	... *Cloth*
Clem	... *Climb*
Coin	... *Corner*
Coose	... *Coarse*
Coose	... *Course*
Crabbit	... *Crabbed*
Crack	.. *Blow*
Craw	... *Crop*
Crepple	... *Cripple*
Crids	... *Curds*
Criddle	... *Curdle*
Critch	... *Crutch*
Croom	... *Crumb*
Crougin	... *Crouching*
Cruds	... *Curds*
Cruddle	... *Curdle*
Cruel fine	... *Very fine*
Crully	... *Curly*
Cud	... *Quid*
Cussn't	... *Cannot*
Dafter	... *Daughter*
Dail	... *Deal*
Datch	... *Thatch*
Derk	... *Dark*
Deef	... *Deaf*
Dishclout	... *Dishcloth*
Drane	... *Drone*

CORNISH.	*ENGLISH.*
Drule	... *Drivel*
Dryth	... *Dryness*
Dung	... *Manure*
Dung	... *Mud*
Eerth	... *Earth*
Emperent	... *Impudent*
Ent	... *Empty*
Enties	... *Empties*
Faather	... *Father*
Faist	... *Feast*
Fetterlock	... *Fetlock*
Filth	... *Fulness*
Find	... *Provide*
Fine and	... *Very*
Fitty	... *Proper*
Flannin	... *Flannel*
Flick	... *Fling*
Full drive	... *Fast driven*
Fur	... *Far*
Fur	... *For*
Furder	... *Further*
Furrin	... *Foreign*
Fust	... *First*
Gashly	... *Ghastly*
Girts	... *Groats*
Go abroad	... *Dissolve*
Gone poor	... *Tainted*

CORNISH.	ENGLISH.
Gone poor	*Sour*
do.	*Decayed*
Goodness	*Fat*
Gov	*Gave*
Gwain	*Going*
Gress	*Grease*
Gripe	*Ditch*
Gurt	*Great*
Haaf	*Half*
Hack	*Dig*
Haps	*Hasp*
Harve	*Harrow*
Heed	*Hide*
Hollin	*Shouting*
Holt	*Grasp*
Holm	*Holly*
Hom or hum	*Home*
Homly	*Homely*
Homward	*Homeward*
Honey-sweet	*Sweet as honey*
Hong	*Hang*
Howsumever	*However*
Howsumdever	*However*
Housen	*Houses*
Hunk	*Hunch*
Hungry	*Greedy*
Innerd	*Inward*

CORNISH.	ENGLISH.
Innerds	*Intestines*
Insye	*Inside*
Janders	*Jaundice*
Joice	*Juice*
Kail	*Keel*
Keem	*Comb* (*v.*)
Kep or kip	*Cap*
Kit	*Kin*
Kivver	*Cover*
Knack	*Knock*
Knawed	*Knew*
Knitster	*Knitter*
Lafs	*Laths*
Lank	*Flank*
Lappy	*Lap* (*v.*)
Lash down	*Throw down*
Laurer	*Laurel*
Liard	*Liar*
Lick	*Smear* (*v.*)
Licks	*Leeks*
Lights	*Lungs*
Loff	*Laugh*
Lookin	*Expecting*
Maa	*Maw*
Maake hum	*Shut*
Make hom	*Shut*
Mash	*Marsh*

CORNISH.	ENGLISH.
Maun	... *Maund*
Mawther	... *Mother*
Maxims	... *Whims*
Moyle	... *Mule*
Mait	... *Meat*
Mait	... *Flesh*
Maity	... *Fleshy*
Maunge	... *Munch*
Meddick	... *Emetic*
Moral	... *Likeness*
Munge	... *Munch*
Musicianer	... *Musician*
Naet	... *Night*
Nawl	... *Awl*
Nawse	... *Nose*
Nevvy	... *Nephew*
Niddle	... *Needle*
Noaise	... *Noise*
Norra	... *Neither*
Nuther	.. *Neither*
Oddit	... *Adit*
Oft	... *Ought*
Ool	... *Wool*
Ood	... *Wood*
Oogly	... *Ugly*
Oppon	... *Upon*
Orry	... *Either*

CORNISH.	ENGLISH.
Outlander	... *Foreigner*
Ovver	... *Over*
Ovvergone	... *Exhausted*
Pame	.. *Palm*
Pankin	... *Panting*
Passel	... *Many*
Passel	... *Much*
Passel	... *A lot*
Pass'n	... *Parson*
Peart	... *Brisk*
Peart	... *Pert*
'Pere	... *Appear*
Peasen	... *Peas*
Peeth	... *Pith*
Peethy	... *Witty*
Pella	... *Pillow*
Pennerd	... *Pennyworth*
Petch	... *Pitch*
Piecen	... *Patch* (*v.*)
Pilcher	... *Pilchard*
Pin	... *Hip*
Pitched	... *Taken root*
Poam	... *Pummel*
Poor	... *Tainted*
Poss	... *Post*
Portmantle	... *Portmanteau*
Pots	... *Bowels*

CORNISH.		ENGLISH.
Powdered	...	*Corned*
Prentis	..	*Apprentice*
Progue	..	*Probe*
Proper	...	*Handsome*
Pult	...	*Pulse*
Put hom	...	*Shut*
Putcher	...	*Pitcher*
Putty	...	*Pretty*
Rabbin	...	*Robin*
Remlet	...	*Remnant*
Rish	...	*Rush*
Rossum	...	*Rosin*
Rowl	...	*Roll*
Rub	...	*Rob*
Rud	...	*Red*
Ruggy	...	*Rugged*
Ruggy	...	*Rubbly*
Ruttlin	...	*Rattling*
Sample	...	*Supple*
Sample	...	*Soft*
Say	...	*Sea*
Scrunch	...	*Crunch*
Skerd	...	*Abraded*
Shale	...	*Scale*
Sharps	...	*Shafts*
Shanks	...	*Spokes*
Shellard	...	*Shillings-worth*

CORNISH.		ENGLISH.
Sherd	...	*Shard*
Shoul	...	*Shovel*
Skivver	..	*Skewer*
Slat	...	*Slate*
Slish	...	*Slice*
Sliver	...	*Slice*
Slone	...	*Sloe*
Smert	...	*Smart*
Sodger	...	*Soldier*
Soils	...	*Seals*
Sond	...	*Sand*
Sonny	..	*Son*
Soun	...	*Sound*
Sound	...	*Swoon*
Soundin	...	*Fainting*
Spare	...	*Slow*
Sperrits	...	*Spirits*
Sperrits	...	*Courage*
Spore	...	*Spur*
Squinny	...	*Squint* (v.)
Splat	...	*Spot*
Staarch	...	*Starch*
Stap	...	*Step*
Stirrage	...	*Hubbub*
Stuffle	...	*Stifle*
Sturch	...	*Starch*
Sturt	...	*Start*

CORNISH.	ENGLISH.
Survey	... *Auction*
Swoun	... *Swoon*
Swound	... *Swoon*
Swoundin	... *Fainting*
Sye or Zye	... *Scythe*
Taw	... *Tow*
Teel	... *Plant* (*v.*)
Tell	... *Count* (*v.*)
Tend	... *Attend* (*v.*)
Thikky	... *That*
Thoft	... *Thought* (*v.*)
Trikle	... *Treacle*
Trist	... *Trust* (*v.*)
Truckle	... *Trundle*
Turmets	... *Turnips*
Twiggle	... *Wriggle*
Ubb'n	... *Oven*
Vaather	... *Father*
Veet or Vit	... *Feet*
Vitty	... *Proper*
Vut	... *Foot*
Walvin	.. *Wallowing*
Waps	... *Wasp*
Way	... *The reason (why)*
Wered	... *Wore*
Whap	... *Whop*
Whichy	... *Which*
Widdy	... *Widow*
Widdy-man	... *Widower*
Widdy-woman	*Widow*
Winder	... *Window*
Wust?	... *Will you?*
Wust	... *Worst*
Wuth	... *Worth*
Yaller	... *Yellow*
Yowlin	... *Howling*
Zad	... *Sad*
Zad	... *Zed* (*Z.*)

ON THE GLOSSARY OF CORNISH PROVINCIAL WORDS.

Although some of the words contained in the following glossary are in use in other parts beyond Cornwall, yet, taken as a whole, they may be said to represent the provincialisms peculiar to the County.

No doubt there are many omissions, and some words may be thought to scarcely deserve a place in the list.

To know with certainty what to admit, or what to exclude, requires a knowledge of most of the dialects of the Kingdom, but the simple rule, which has been followed here, is to include such words as are not generally spoken by the educated classes in Cornwall, and so are considered as fairly belonging to the provincial dialect of the County.

The following is an example of words common to another district besides Cornwall, notwithstanding this, such words are also claimed as belonging to the Cornish dialect.

Latham, in his book on the English Language, (3rd Ed. p. 561) alludes to English dialects not in conformity with the mother tongue, and says, " that among the most remarkable is what may be called "Little England beyond Wales." "In Pembrokeshire and Glamorganshire the language is English rather than Welsh."

In the following list are words collected by the Revd. J. Collins, and included in the "Transactions" of the Philological Society, No. 93. (see Latham.) The following is a selection compared with Cornish provincial words.

PEMBROKE.	*CORNWALL.*	
Angletouch...	Angleditch, or Angletwitch.	... Earthworm.
Brandis ...	Brandis	... Iron stand for a pot or kettle.
Cloam ...	Cloam or Clome...	Earthenware.
Clit ...	Clib	... To stick together.
Dreshel ...	Drashel	... A flail.
Eddish ...	Arrish	... Corn stubble.
Evil ...	Evil, Eval or Heeval	... A three-pronged dungfork.
Foust ...	Foust	... To tumble.
Hamrach ...	Hames	... Straw horse-collar.
Nesseltrip ...	Nessel-bird	... The smallest pig in a litter; in Cornwall, the youngest in a family.
Ovice ...	Ovvice	... Eaves of a building.
Peert ...	Peert	... Lively, brisk.
Quat ...	Quat	... To press down, to flatten.
Reremouse...	Airymouse	... The bat.
Suant ...	Suant	.. Regular, in order.
Want ...	Want	... A mole.
Weest ...	Wisht	... Lonely, desolate.

These resemblances between words in South West Wales, and Cornwall, point to the inter-communication by sea, because, in journeying by land, the traveller passes through districts in which such words are not used.

The writer, being a native of central Cornwall, will be found to have spelt many words which are not exactly so pronounced in other parts of the County; it has been explained how the Cornish dialect varies between the Tamar and the Land's End, yet it is hoped that the spelling and the meanings are not very different from what we find in other.districts. There are various ways of spelling provincial words, and as each writer is guided by his hearing the spelling of a great many of them must be phonetic.

Young Cornish people appear to be unaware how rapidly their language is altering because of so much more travelling and intercourse, therefore it may be of some interest, if not use to collect all the provincial words which the writer can remember, or glean from other scources; without so doing it would be impossible that a glossary could ever be completed or rendered useful.

Like two colours, the Miner's dialect and that of the Husbandman shade off into each other; this shading is more or less intensified in different places, and the dialectic words are being continually scattered, or intermingled by the constant movements of the Cornish population.

Western people coming eastwards, and Eastern people going westwards, must therefore keep up a continual interchange of Western and Eastern dialect.

For the sake of simplicity and uniformity, the writer has made this attempt to compile *one* glossary for the whole County.

He is convinced that such a method, if it can be perfected, will be found to be more useful and practical, notwithstanding the wide difference in dialect between the extreme ends of the County.

The names and authorities, so far as they can be ascertained, are given in the reference table at the end of the glossary.

Wherever words are quoted they are signified by initials or names to each of them.

The rest of the glossary not so initialed consists of words known to the writer.

A large number of Rabelaisque words could be added but for obvious reasons they are entirely omitted.

GLOSSARY

OF

CORNISH PROVINCIAL WORDS.

Abear. To bear. (In Spenser.) Always used negatively in the Cornish dialect as, "I caan't *abear* te do et."

Abroad. Wide open, as, "the door is abroad," also, mistaken, as, "he's all abroad there."

Addle-pool. A cess-pool. In Celtic Cornish it is *atal*, refuse, waste; and *pol*, a pond, a pool, stagnant water, a miry place, mire, mud, slime; a well, a pit.

Adventurer. A shareholder. As in a mine, &c.

Afered. Afraid.

> "Of his visage children were sore *afered.*" *Chaucer.*
>
> "Were thou *afered* of her eye?" *Gower.*

Afty or **Aafty, Arter** or **Aarter.** Various forms of the name Arthur.

Agar. Ugly. This is a Celtic Cornish word and spelt *hager*, meaning ugly, deformed, rough, foul, evil, naughty, fierce, cruel.

Agáte. "All agáte," i.e., full of expectation, all eye and ear, on the *qui vive.*

Agist, Aginst, or **Agin.** Against. *(Ageins. Chaucer.)*

Aglets. The berries of the hawthorn (haws); also called *aglen* and *awglen*. *Cratægus oxyacantha.*

Agnail. A whitlow; from *Ange-nail*, i.e., pain-nail.

Ailer, or **Heller.** See *Hailer*.

Airy-mouse. The bat. The boys call to it thus,

> "Airymouse! Airymouse! fly over my head,
> And you shall have a crust of bread,
> And when I brew, and when I bake,
> You shall have a piece of my wedding cake."
>
> *(Couch's History of Polperro.)*

Aitch-piece. The catch or tongue of a buckle. M.A.C.

Ake. A groove in a stone for a rope or iron band, secured so as to be used as an anchor. W.N.

Aketha! Forsooth! U.J.T.

Alley. The allis shad. *Alosa vulgaris.* C.

Alleys. Boys best marbles of white stone, or of china. Used mostly as taws.

Allsanders. Called *skit* or *skeet* by boys who made squirts of the stems. *Smyrnium olusatrum.* C.

Amenuts. Almonds. U.J.T.

Ampassy, also **Passy.** Terms meaning *et cætera*, (&c.)

Anan? or **Nan?** What? What do you say? *Nan* is also used in Kent.

Anatomy. A skeleton. See **'Natomy.**

Ancell. A steelyard. *The Cornishman.*

Anék. "Crying anék." This crying of *anék* is a harvest ceremony, probably of very great antiquity. The *a* is pronounced like *a* in *mate;* the accent is very strong on *nek.* There are some variations in "crying anék." This is how the writer remembers it:

The reaper, with his reaping hook, (it was thought a shame to cut wheat with any other tool) having cut a last handful of wheat, held and waved it high over his head, as with a loud and joyful voice he cried,

"I have et, I have et, I have et,"

on which the other harvesters standing around shouted,

"What have'e?, What have'e?, What have'e?

and then arose the triumphant cry,

Anék, Anék, Anék.—Hooraa!

Lhuyd (Archœologia) says, *Anaic* (Irish) means "save (thou) me." It would seem that when a Cornishman cries Anék, anék, anék—Hooraa!" its equivalent in English is

Saved, saved, saved—Hurrah!

A full account of this ceremony is given in R. Hunt's "Romances of the West of England."

Angallish. Gallows-like. Vicious.

Angleditch. Earthworm. Also called Angle-twitch, and Angle-touch. Carew calls it Tag-worm.

In Devonshire it is Angle-dog, and Angle-twitch.
(*Angeltwecca.* Ang. Saxon.)

Anker. A small cask or keg of about four gallons, used for brandy.

The ankers which contained smuggled brandy used to be cut in two, and so, many of the Cornish provided themselves with tubs. "Free-traders"* imported their "moonshine" in such ankers when the nights were dark.

See **Moonshine.**

Anointed. Used thus, "you anointed vellan," i.e., "you confounded rascal."

Antic. A good humoured fool. "Such an antic."

Anyst, or **Anist.** Close by, near to.

Appledrane. A wasp. *Callington.*

Apple-bird. A chaffinch. *Polwhele.*

Appurtenances. See **Purtens.**

Apsen. The aspen tree.

Apty-cock. A sharp little fellow. *W. Briton.*

Ardar. A plough. This is a Celtic Cornish word, in which language we have *Dên ardar,* a ploughman.

Arear! Oh, strange! Wonderful! from the Celtic Cornish *Reâ,* meaning the same.

Arg, or **Agyfy.** To argue, to dispute.

Arrant. An errand. *(Arande. Chaucer.)*

Arrant boy. An errand boy.

Arrish. Stubble land after the corn has been cut. *Errish* in Devon, *Ersh* in Sussex.

Arrish-geese. Stubble fed geese.

---

* Smugglers.

Arrish-mow. A round pile of corn sheaves, about ten feet high ending with a cone, crowned by a single sheaf. Raised in the fields for fear of rain before the corn is carried.

Arry. Any. **Arry wawn.** i.e., any-one.

A-sam. Partly open, as of a door. "The door's a-sam."

Ascrode. Astride. C.

Ass. This animal has several names in Cornwall, viz: Ass, Donkey, Jackass, Neddy, Negger, Dicky; Moguz and Peter Moguz, in Callington; King, in Redruth. *Asen* and *Rounsan* are Celtic Cornish for ass.

Ass-neger. A silly fellow, a fool. U.J.T.

Brewer, in his "Dicty. of Phrase and Fable," spells it *assinego*, and calls it a Portuguese word.

"Thou hast no more brain than I have in mine elbows; an *assinego* may tutor thee."

Troilus and Cressida.

Atal. (Pronounced *attle.)* Mine rubbish, refuse, or waste. A Celtic Cornish word. It has even been said that this is a Phœnician word.

Atal Sarazin. The offcasts of the Saracens, old works supposed to have been worked by them.

Keigwin, quoted by Pryce in his Cornish English Vocabulary.

Atween. Between. "Right atween the two."

"Her loose long yellow locks, like golden wire,
Sprinkled with perl, and perling flowr's *atween*." *Spenser.*

Audit. An adit. *Carew.*

Aunt or **Un.** These words are often used instead of Mrs.— in speaking of an aged Cornishwoman, even though not related to the speaker. See **Uncle.**

Avise. Advise. "I caan't avise et." The same word is in Chaucer.

> "Of warre and of battaile he was full *avise.*"
>
> *P. Langloft's Chron.*

Aw! Oh! **Aw! Jimmery!** Oh! Gemini!

Awner's 'Count. At the expense of the "adventurers."

Ax. Ask. "Ax en," i.e., Ask him.

Axed out. Having had the banns called in church. U.J.T.

Aye facks! Yes faith! yes indeed! see, I'facks, &c.

Azue. When a cow is dry, that is, ceases to yield milk, she is said to be "azue," or "gone to zue." The Celtic Cornish for *dry,* is *zeh.*

Bace. Prisoner's bace (or base.) A game so called. It is an ancient pastime mentioned in the records of Edward 3rd. (1327 to 1377.) *Toone.*

> "So ran they all as they had been at *bace,*
> They being chased, that did others chase."
>
> *Spenser's Fairy Queen.*
>
> "The country *base.*" *Shakspere in Cymbeline.*

Babby-rags. Small bits. C.F.

Back-jouster. An itinerant fish-dealer who carries the fish in a *cawal*, or basket, on the back. See **Cowal** and **Jowder**. *Mousehole.*

Backlet, or **Backside.** The yard, or court behind a house.

Backsyfore, or **Backsyforsy.** The hind part before.

Bagganet. Bayonet.

Bal. A mine. Celtic Cornish *balas*, to dig, to delve, and *bal*, a pick, a mattock, a shovel.

Bal. Loud talking or chattering, "Hould tha bâl, dew," "Hould yer bal," i.e., Do cease talking, hold your tongue.

Bal. To thump or thrash any one, "Gibb'n a good balin," "Bal'én well."

Balin. (Pronounced bah-lin.) A thrashing. Also, crying or blubbering,

"What be'ee balin about?"

Beal, bealo, Saxon, meaning, misery, misfortune, and in Celtic Cornish, *bal*, a plague, or pestilence.

"The one side must have *bale*."

Shakspere in Coriolanus.

Also poison, as

"For light she hated as the deadly *bale*."

Spenser's Fairy Queen.

Bal-maid, Bal-girl, Bal-maiden. A girl who works on the surface at a mine.

Balch. A stout bit of cord, a rope.

Bal-dag. To bespatter with mine slime. M.A.C.

Balk. Timber squared as imported.

Balscat. A cross patch, a termagant.

Balshag. A very shaggy flannel used in mines.

Ball-eyed. Wall-eyed.

Ballymuck. An ill constructed thing, as a "ballymuck of a dock." *The Cornishman.*

Bally-rag. Violent or coarse abuse.

Bandeleer. A wooden toy like a thin flat reel, moved by a string to wind and unwind. M.A.C.

Banes. Beans.

Banger, or **Banging.** Big, very large.

Banister. The baluster of a staircase.

Bankers. Seat cushions.

Bannel. The plant known as broom. In Celtic Cornish it is *banal* and *banathel.* *Cytisus Scoparius.*

Bare-ridged. "Riding bare-ridged," i.e., riding without a saddle.

Bargain. A contract for certain work in a mine, claywork, &c.

Barker. A whetstone. C.

Barker's knee. Hunt, in his "Romances of the west of England," says that the fairies called buccas, or knockers, once left all thelr tools on Barker's knee. The knee was so injured that it continued stiff ever after. "As stiff as Barker's knee" became a proverb. Who Barker was is not stated.

Barm or **Burm.** Yeast. It is *burm* in Celtic Cornish, and *berme* in Chaucer.

"And sometimes makes the drink to bear no *barm*."
Shakspere in the Midsummer Night's Dream.

Barragon, or **Barracan.** Fustian. H.R.C.

Barrow. A sepulchral mound.

Barwell, or **Barvil.** A fisherman's leathern apron. W.P. by W.N.

In Celtic Cornish, *barvas,* means a cod-fish.

Bāsting. A beating or thrashing. "Thee'lt git a putty bāsting." *Baston* (Spanish) a stick.

Basting. A kind of light or loose sewing, or stitching.

"In the swete seson that lefe is,
With a thred *bāsting* my slevis."
Chaucer's Romaunt of the Rose.

Bawk. A shy, as of a horse; clumsiness, as "he made a bawk (muddle) of it"; a jeer, as "he made a bawk at me"; hindrance, objection, as "he's sure to make a bawk about it."

Bazzom. Blue, purple.

Bazzomy. Bluish, purplish. Mostly used of the skin, face, and especially the lips.

Beagle, or **Bagle.** A troublesome person. "Beagle it"! or "Ad beagle it"! i.e., "bother it." M.A.C.

Beam or **Bine.** A band, a binder, as of a rope of straw, hay, &c.

Bean. A withy band. C.

Bee-butt. A bee-hive. *Butt*, a beehive, is a Celtic Cornish word.

Bee-skip. A bee-hive. M.A.C.
Bee-*skib*? *Skiber* is Celtic Cornish for, a *large* room.

Beat, or **Bete.** Turf cut and dried, for burning at home, or in the fields.

Beat burrows. Heaps of dry turf collected for burning on the open ground. Also used of the burrows when burnt.

Beat-burning. The firing of dried turf for the sake of the ashes as manure. *Bete* (Saxon) to make fires. "To bete fires." *Chaucer.*

Beauty. Used as a term of contempt, thus, "that beauty!" or thus, "you'm a putty beauty!"

Becker. A species of bream. C.

Bed-ale. Christening or lying in ale. *Polwhele.*

Bedman. A sexton. C.
Bedh is Celtic Cornish for, a grave.

Bedoled. Overdone by grief or pain—see **Dowlin.**

Bed-tye. A feather bed—see **Tye.**

Bedwaddled, or **Betwattled.** Bewildered, confused. W.T.A.P.

Beety. To mend fishing nets.

Beheemed. Sickly. M.A.C.

Bell-metal. A brass pot or crock used for boiling fruits for preserves or jams.

Belly-tember. Good and solid food.

Belvin. Blubbering, weeping aloud; also, howling, as, "Belvin (or howling) like Tregagle."

Bender. A big thing, as, "What a bender!" also a great lie, as, "that's a bender," i.e., that's a "thundering" lie.

Berrin. A funeral. "How was it you wasn't to Betsey's *berrin?* It was a bootiful corps, one solid scab all ovver. We had a pleasant arternoon, and a fine rig in the evenin." *Near Bodmin.* *W. Hicks.*

Besom. A broom; also, heath, viz., that used for making brooms. See **Griglan** or **Grig.**

Beth. Be ye, or, "be'ee"; are you, or, "arre'e"; *Beth* in Chaucer also.

Bettermost. The best of anything. The upper hand, or advantage gained over another, as, "I got the bettermost of him."

Betwattled. See **Bedwaddled.**

Beverage. A weak drink, as that of the weak cider made from the apple cake of the cider press by adding water. See **Pimpey.**

Bevering, or **Bivvering.** Quivering, trembling, or shaking with cold. Also the peculiar quivering of an infant's under jaw when yawning.

Bezibd. "It is not allotted me." R.H.
"'Tis not bezib'd," i.e., fortuned. *Carew.*

Bib. A small fish; a blind. M.A.C.

Biddix. A double digging tool, one end pointed, the other flattened.

Bilders. *Heraclium sphondilium.* Cut as fodder for pigs. Couch *(Hist. of Polperro)* thinks that this name, in other parts of Cornwall, is applied to the poisonous hemlock, water-drop-wort. *Ænanthe.*

Billis, Billez, Billees. Bellows; *(belous, Chaucer.)*

Bishop. The fish *Cottus scorpius.* C.

Biscan. A finger glove of leather, used by the harvest women, particularly in support of a wounded finger. *Polwhele.*

This is a Celtic Cornish word, and is also written *besgan* and *veskin.* *(Bis,* a finger, and *Bisgan,* a thimble. *Pryce.)* See **Veskin.**

Biskey, Biskeys. Biscuit, biscuits.

Bits. Scraps of beef, liver, &c., sold by the lump as "bits" for a "false roast," or a fry. This name is also given to a green tender herb resembling spinach and used for pies, or, as "greens."

Bitter-weed. An unruly, mischievous person; "She's a bitter weed."

Blaad, Vlaad, or **Flaad.** See **Blawed.**

Blackhead. A boil. *Furunculus.*

Black-jack. Sulphuret of Zinc. Blende.

Black-strap. Gin and treacle; Bad wine for poor and lowly guests. J. W.

Black tin. Tin ore fit for the smelting or blowing house.

Black-wine toddy. Port wine negus.

Black-worm. The black beetle of the kitchen, &c.

Blamed, or **Blame.** "Well, I'm blamed ef I knaw." "Blame me ef I doan't." (The word *blowed* is also used thus.) It seems a mild form of swearing.

Blast. A sudden inflammation of an eye. "A blast in the eye."

Blawed. Quite out of breath.

Blawed. Also, **Blaad, Vlaad,** and **Flaad.** Terms used of cows which have eaten too largely of grass, causing meteorism.

Blinch. To catch a glimpse of. C.

Blind-buck-a-davy. Blind-man's buff. C.

Blind-nettle. A stingless nettle. *Galeopsis.*

Blink. A small light or flame. "There isn't a blink of fire.

Blobber, or **Blob.** A large bubble. A vesication as from a blister; "all in great blobbers."

Bloody sea-dock. The *Lapathum marinum sanguineum.* *Borlase.*

Bloody-warriors. Wall flowers. (The red crane's bill. M.A.C.)

Blood-sucker. The sea anemone. M.A.C.

Blooth. Blossom, *(Carew)*; *Blath*, Gaelic; *Blodon*, Celtic Cornish; *Bluthe*, German.

Blowing-house. A place for melting tin. So called from a fire or blast perpetually kept by a large bellows turned by a water wheel.

Blowing tin. Melting tin ore in the blowing-house.

Blowser. One employed in a seine boat, in the pilchard fishery.

Blubber. A large jelly-fish. Sting-blubber.

Blue-poll. A kind of salmon. C.

Board-em. An old fashioned round game of cards. The players may be from two to eight persons. M.A.C.

Bob. The great beam of a mine pumping engine.

Bobbery. A fuss, a row, an uproar.

Bobble. A pebble. C.

A ground swell of the sea. M.A.C.

Bobble. To bob up and down.

Boilin, or **Boailin.** "The whole boilin," i.e., the whole lot of them. The whole "crew."

Bock. See **Bawk.**

Boist, or **Busthious.** See **Boostis.**

Bolt. A stone-built drain. M.A.C.

Bon-crab. The female of the edible crab. *Platycarcinus pagurus.* C.

Boo, or **Booey.** A louse. "Oh! another great booey!" In Celtic Cornish *boawhoe.* *Pryce.*

Boobish. Lubberly, *Carew.* In Celtic Cornish, *boba,* a blockhead, a booby.

Boobus, Booba, or **Boobun.** A wick for a small lamp. *Newlyn.*

Booley, or **Bulley.** A boy's very large marble.

Boosterin. Hard and hot work. "'Tes boosterin work," i.e., "a sweating job." In Celtic Cornish, *boys* means heavy, weighty.

Boostis, or **Boistous.** Fat, corpulent. In Celtic Cornish *boys* means meat, food. "He is getting quite boostis."

Boozy. Intoxicated. "Always boozy." *Boos,* Celtic Cornish, to drink to excess.

Boryer. A borer, an iron bar with a wedged shaped end, for boring holes in rocks for the powder in blasting.

Boss. The master or manager. *Callington.*

Boots and Shoes. The columbine. C.
The flowers of monkshood. *Aconitum napellus.*

Botany bay. The Hydrangea.

Botham. A wheal, or lump caused by a blow. *Polwhele.*

Bothem. Fever-few. The herb so called.

Bottom-pie. Potatoes and pork baked on a thick layer of dough. W.N.

Bottoms. Valleys, old stream works, stents.

Boulter. A long fishing line, with short branches and many hooks. *Carew.*

Bounds. Tin bounds are parcels of land marked out by small pits, about a foot deep and wide, at the angles of the ground. Straight lines from pit to pit fix the boundary.

Bounders. The holders of tin bounds.

Bowerly. Good-looking, handsome. "Eve's a fine, bowerly maid." *Mrs. Parr's Adam & Eve.*

Bowgie or **Bougie.** A sheep's house, or shed for cattle. M.A.C.

The Celtic Cornish word is *boudi*, and Lhuyd gives *boudzi deves*, a sheep-fold. *Boudi* was anciently *bouti* from the old word *bou*, a cow, and *ti* or *ty* a house.

Bowings. The large joints, especially the knees. "I've got such pains in my bowings."

Bowjouler. A place in a fishing boat for hauling the footline through. W.F.P.

Bowldacious. Brazen, impudent, "you bowldacious hussy."

Boxing Harry. A commercial room phrase, used of one who shirked the cost of dining with his fellows at the inn. Doing so was "boxing Harry." A term also used elsewhere.

Boys' love. The herb Southernwood, also called by the very proper name "Maidens' delight."

Braave. First rate, very well, capital. This is a very representative word in the Cornish dialect. "He's gittin on braave," i.e., very well. How be'ee? "Braave thenk'ee," and so on. Spenser used the word *brave* for what is not only valiant and good, but fine and spruce.

Braa set-up. A row, a fuss.

Brace. The mouth of a shaft. W.N.

Braggashans. Bragging. U.J.T.

Braggety. Mottled. Often used of the skin of a baby's limbs, "See what braggety legs he's got."

Braging. Raging. M.A.C. A corruption of *raging*, or perhaps, from *bridzhan* or *bredion*, Celtic Cornish, to boil.

Brandis. An iron triangular stand with three short legs for resting the crock, kettle, &c., on, over the fire.

Brash. An eruption on the skin.

Breach. Coarse, furzy, and heathy ground on which the turf has been cut and burnt. *Tonkin.*

Breachy. Brackish, saltish.

Breedy. To make a fishing net.

Breeming, or **Briming.** A phosphorescent shining, or sparkling of the sea at night, when agitated by steam-paddles, &c. *Briming, Couch. Briny, Carew.*

Breez, or **Browse.** Small-coal, broken wood-fuel, and such-like. In Celtic Cornish *browsian*, means crumbs, fragments; and *brosy* to destroy.

Breal, or **Breel.** A mackerel. B.V.

Bren, or **Brend.** To frown, to wrinkle the brow.

Brik, or **Brek.** A break, a rent. *Brike,* Chaucer.

Brink. The gill of a fish. *W. Noye.*

Briny. See **Breeming.**

Brit. Small fish, about half the length of a sprat.

Brithil, or **Breithal.** A mackerel. Also a name for a trout. It is a Celtic Cornish word. From *brith,* mottled. *Brilli,* mackerel.

Broil. The back of a lode. "The lode has its top covered over with a parcel of loose (more or less mineral) stones and earth . . . . . this in Cornwall we call the broil of the lode." *Borlase's Natl. Hist.*

Brood. Impurities mixed with ore. M.A.C.

Broom-swike. A twig of heath broom.

Brose of het. Very hot, perspiring copiously. "I'm in a brose of het." See **Bulderin.**

Broth, or **Brath.** The Cornish say, "I'll have a *few* broth."

Browse, or **Bruss.** A thicket. See **Breez.**

Brown-wort. Fig-wort. *Scrophularia nodosa.*

Browthy. A term for light and spongy bread. M.A.C.

Brythall. A trout. H.R.C. See **Brithil.**

Bubble and squeak. Cold potatoes and cabbage, mixed, chopped, and fried. Elsewhere the same phrase is used for cold boiled *meat* and greens fried. The meat *bubbled* in the boiler, and *squeaked* in the frying pan. *Brewer.*

Buck. A kind of minute fungus? infesting ill-kept dairies. It is called "the buck" and the dairy contents become spoilt by it. *Buchar* is Celtic Cornish for, bucked milk, sour milk. *Pryce.*

Also a name given to the spittle fly. M.A.C.

Bucking. Breaking up the ore into small pieces.

Buckle to. To set about anything in earnest.

Buckle up to. To defy or "show fight," also, to court.

Bucha, or **Bucca,** and **Bucha-boo.** A ghost, hobgoblin, or scare-crow. *Bucca* is a Celtic Cornish word for ghost.

Buck-horn. Whiting salted and dried. C. (*Buckthorn.* M.A.C.)

Bucky-how. A boy's game resembling "touch timber." M.A.C.

Buddle. A mining term. It is "a pit seven feet long," three wide, and two deep, for washing the ore in. *Borlase.* In Celtic Cornish *buddal,* to buddle, to drown. *Pryce.*

Buddle. A bubble.

Buddling. Washing ore.

Bud-picker. A bullfinch. *Polwhele.*

Buffiehead. A thickhead, a fool. "Yew gashly bufflehead."

Bulderin. Hot and perspiring. (*Boldering,* lowering weather. *Polwhele.*)

Bulgranack. The pool, or bull toad in sea rock pools. H.R.C.

Bulk-headed fool. Said of one "who is always running his head against a wall." H.R.C.

Bulgranade. Stickleback. M.A.C.

Bulhorn. A snail. This is a Celtic Cornish word.

Bulk. See **Bunch.**

Bulk or **Belk.** To belch; (*Bulk*, to toss as by the horns of a cow.) M.A.C. Also see **Bulking.**

Bulking. Piling up pilchards in regular order against the walls of a cellar; with salt between each layer.

Bulley. See **Booley.**

Bullum. The fruit of the bullace shrub. (Bolas tree. *Chaucer.*) *Prunus insititia.*

Bultys. See **Boulter.**

Bum. A blow. This is a Celtic Cornish word. **To bum.** "I *bummed* my head right against the door.

Bumfoozle. To humbug, to mystify.

Bunch. A mass of ore in a lode.

Bunch. To butt at, or toss with the horns, as with a ram, or a cow. Children playing and running "head on," cry out, "I'll bunch'ee, I'll bunch'ee."

Bunchy. A lode is so called when the ore is irregularly distributed in it.

Bunken, or **Bumpkin.** A piece of iron projecting from the bow of a boat, to which the jib is fastened. W.N.

Bunker headed. "Bunker headed fools." *Gwinear.* T.C.

Bunt. The concavity of a sail, or of a fishing net.

Bunting. Sifting flour.

Burm. The Celtic Cornish word for, barm, or yeast.

Burn. "A burn of hake." 21 hakes. *Mousehole.* Also, a pile of furze, a rick of hay.

Burranet. The shell-drake. M.A.C.

Burrow. See **Barrow.**

Bush. An apparatus formed of two hoops at right angles, covered with white calico; used for signalling the position of a school of pilchards.

Bushing corn. Beating out corn into a barrel by threshing bunches of it against the side of the barrel. No flail is used.

Busken or **Busk.** The "breast bone" of an old-fashioned stays. Formerly of wood, or whalebone, about two feet long, and two inches wide!

Busker. An "out and out" fisherman who dares all weathers.

Busthious. See **Boostis.**

Buss. A yearling calf still sucking. C.

Bussa calf. A calf which in time weans itself. *Polwhele.*

Bussa-head, or **Buzza-head.** A thick-head, an empty fool. From the Celtic Cornish *Buzza* a pan. A poor *brain-pan.*

Busy. What demands all ones time, or energy. Thus, It will busy all the time, i.e., *take* all the time. "It will busy all he can rise to pay it." "It will busy all he can do to finish it in time." *Bysy* is a Celtic Cornish word and means, diligent; and *besy*, needful.

But. Buttock of beef.

But. To sprain, or put out of joint.

But-gap. A hedge of pitched turf. *Polwhele.*

Butt. A two-wheeled cart. This is a Celtic Cornish word still used in Devon and Cornwall.

Butter and Eggs. The double yellow daffodils.

Butter-dock. Burdock. *Arctium lappa.*

Butty. A comrade, a "chum." W.T.A.P.

Buzza, or **Bussa.** A coarse earthenware pan, or jar.

Buzzy, or **Bussy milk.** First milk after the cow has calved.

Caaled. Called or cryed by the town cryer.

Cab. A mess, anything wet, sticky, or dirty.

Cab-a-rouse. This is in seamen's language, to pull together at a cable shouting and singing. (A gall or callous. H.R.C.) See **Caperhouse.**

Cabby. Wet, or sticky and dirty.

Cabbed, Cabbed up, Cabbled, or **Cabagled.** Terms used of anything which has been messed or dirtied by handling, &c.

Cabobble. To mystify, to deceive. "T'ull niver do for'ee to try to cabobble Uncle Zibedee." *Mrs. Parr's Adam & Eve.*

Caboolen stones. (W.F.P. and B.V.) See **Minnies.**

Caddle. To do household work in an untidy and irregular manner.

Caddler. One who "caddles about the house," i.e., working but messing.

Cader. A small frame of wood on which a fisherman keeps his line. *Polwhele. (Cantor, Penzance.* M.A.C.)

Caff. Refuse of any kind, rubbishy stuff.

Cage. A set, as "a cage of teeth."

Cagged. Annoyed, vexed.

Cag Mag. Tough old geese; food which none can relish. (Gaelic and Welsh, *cag magu. Brewer.)* In Celtic Cornish *cagal* means rubbish, dirt. *Borlase.*

Cake. A fool, a poor thing. "A regular cake." Brewer derives it from the Greek word *kakos,* bad.

Cal. Tungstate of Iron.

Calcar. The lesser weaver, or sting fish. The lance fish. *Sennen.* H.R.C.

Call-out. To have the banns called in Church. U.J.T.

Calve's snout. The snap-dragon. *Antirrhinum minus. Borlase.*

Cam or **Cand.** Flour spar.

Camels. Chamomile flowers.

Canker. The Celtic Cornish name for a crab-fish. It also means the rust in corn. (*Kankar. Borlase.*)

Cannis. To toss about carelessly. C.

Cant. A fall. *Polwhele.* "A *cant* of a way," i.e., a long way. W.N.

Capel or **Cockle.** Shorl.

Caper-longer. The razor shell fish. *Tonkin.* The shell fish *pinna ingens.* C.

Cappen, or **Capp'n.** Captain, or head man of a mine, claywork, &c. Grass-capp'n is the term used for one who is manager "at grass," i.e., on the surface.

Caperhouse, or **Caprouse.** Uproar, row, confusion; a "kick up," a "jolly row."

Carbona, or **Carbonas.** An accumulation of rich ore in a mine, a "house" of ore.

Care. The mountain ash. *Pyrus aucuparia.* C.

Carn or **Cairn.** A heap of stones. A sepulchral mound of stones. A rock. *Carn* is Celtic Cornish.

Carney. To wheedle, to keep caressing, and calling another *cara,* (dear). *Brewer.*

Carrots. Nickname for a person with red hair.

Casabully. Winter cress. *Polwhele.*

Casling. Prematurely born, a castling.

Cat-lap. Derisive term for insipid fluid drink.

Catch up. To lighten up, as of a fire; to dry up, as of clothes, &c. Also thus, "catching" (changeable) weather.

Cat-in-the-pan. "He turned cat in the pan," i.e., he proved himself a traitor. Also a play of head over heels round a bar while still holding on.

Cats and dogs. The catkins of the willow.

Cauch. A mess. This is a Celtic Cornish word for ordure, manure, dung.

Cauchy. Messy, dirty, sloppy.

Caudle. A mess, a muddle.

Caudler. One who messes and muddles. An improvident person; a foolish spendthrift.

Caulk. A "drop" of liquor. "I've had a bit of a *caulk* but not a drop more." *Mrs. Parr's Adam & Eve.*

Caunter. A cross-handed blow.

Cawed. A sheep affected with the rot. C.

Chackin, or Chackt. Very thirsty, very dry in the throat." "I'm chackin with thirst."

Chacks. The cheeks. "I'll scat your chacks, that I will, you gashly great bufflehead."

Chad. A small fish like a bream.

Chad. "To put a *chad*," i.e., a turn of a rope in the horse's mouth. *J. H. Nankivell.*

Chakky cheese. The fruit of the common mallow. C. See **Cheeses.**

Chall. A cowhouse.

Champion lode. Principal or leading lode.

Chamy. (Pronounced Chah-me). The profile of a toothless person, when it falls in at the mouth, gives the appearance called chamy.

Chape. The catch of anything, as of a buckle, or the hook of a scabbard. The tip of a scabbard.

Chaunt or **Chaunty.** To scold, to mutter, to prate. M. A. C.

Cheel or **Cheeld.** Child. **Cheldern.** Children.

Cheel-vean. Little child. Often used as a term of endearment. *Vean*, Celtic Cornish for little.

Cheeldin. In labour with child, also pregnant. "The *childing* autumn," i.e., the pregnant autumn.

Shakspere in the Midsummer Night's Dream.

(*Chylded.* Brought forth.) *Spenser.*

Cheens or **Cheins.** The loins, the small of the back; *cheim* is Celtic Cornish for back.

Cheening. Sprouting in the dark, as of potatoes in a dark cellar.

Cherk or **Chark.** A cinder, a piece of charcoal. *Chirk, Callington.*

Cheeses. Seed vessels of the mallow. Chuck-cheeses. (Chukky-cheeses. F.C.)

Cheese et. Stop it, i.e., Dont go on quarrelling so. *Callington.*

Chet. A newly born cat. This is a Celtic Cornish word. Kittens born in May used to be drowned, that month being thought unhealthy and unlucky. "May chets bad luck begets."

Cheevy. Thin, miserable looking. M.A.C.

Chewidden day. "(*Jeu-whydn,* Cornish.) White Thursday. That is one clear week before Christmas day, it being the day on which black tin or ore was first turned into white tin, or metal." U.J.T.

Chick. To crouch down. To "chicky down." (The sitting *œstrum* in hens. C.)

Chicker. The wheatear. *Polwhele.* Also chick-chack. (*Chick-chacker.* M.A.C.)

Chiff-chaff. The white-throat. *Sylvia hippolais.* *Ogilvie.*

Childermas day. Innocents' day.

Chill. A small earthenware lamp. Anciently in use.

Chimbley. A chimney. *Shimbla* in Celtic Cornish.

Chipper. The cross-bill. M.A.C.

Chitter. Thin. **Chitter-face.** The face thin and furrowed. C.

Chitterlings. The shirt frills of former days. M.A.C.

Chives. A kind of small onions, called also, chive garlic. *Ogilvie.* Used cut up to flavour broth. *Allium shœnoprasum.*

Chivvels. Another name for chives. Q.V. See **Cives.**

Chivvy. A row, an uproar, a fuss.

Chod. A stew. A "stodge." Q.V.

Choog, or **Choogy.** A pig. **Choogy-pig.** A little pig.

Choog-choog-choog. A cry inviting the pigs to meals. (Chee-ah. *Bottrell.*)

Choust. A cheat. **To choust,** to cheat.

Chorus. A carouse, a feast.

Chorusing. Feasting. "A grand chorusing." *Crowst* is Celtic Cornish, for luncheon.

Chores. Household jobs. "A few chores."

Chowter. Fish dealer. See **Jowder.**

Chuck. The fat beneath the chin, the "double chin," so called. "He is very big about the chuck."

Chuck. The throat or swallow.

Chuck-children. The allis shad. C. (Choke-children.) So called because the fish is full of bones.

Chuck-sheep. A term of offence, and contempt. "Ah! you old chuck-sheep."

Chucklehead. A booby.

Church-ale. "A feast in commemoration of the dedication of a church."

Church-town. (Pronounced ch'town.) A hamlet, a village, or a town near the church; even a city, thus, "Lunnun ch'town."

Cider-pound. Cider-press.

Cives. A species of very small leek, growing in tufts, used like chives for flavouring broth.

Clabby. Wet and sticky. See **Cabby.**

Clack. Much noise, a great deal of talking. "Hould your clack, do." See **Clap.**

Clacker. A woman's tongue, a rattle, a pump valve. "The clacker of a mill," i.e., the noise and rattle of it. "Your tongue goes like the clacker of a mill." See **Clap.**

Clain, or **Clain-off.** Very well, perfectly, quite. "A ait et clain-awf," i.e., he ait the whole of it. "A ded that clain-awf," i.e., he did that perfectly.

> "Let's hew his limbs 'till they be *clean* consumed."
> *Shakspere in Titus Andronicus.*

Clam. A tree, or plank used as a bridge across a stream. *Polwhele.* The star fish *Asterias glacialis.* C.

Clammed. Out of health. *Polwhele.* Half-starved, as, "Better *clam* than go to the Union." *Brewer.* *Clamdere* is Celtic Cornish for to faint away, to swoon.

Clap. Prating. "Hould yer clap." It is a Celtic Cornish word.

Clappin. Throbbing, as in pain. See **Loppin.**

Church-hay. The churchyard, or close.

Clavel. The impost on a square headed window, door, or chimney. C.

Clay dues. The holder of a china clay sett pays from 3/- to 3/6 per ton on clay sent or sold out of the works, as dues to the land-owner.

Clay maidens. Girls employed in china-clay works, generally as "scrapers." They remove the outside sand, &c., from the dried clay. See **Clay pans.**

Clay pans. Shallow places from 50 to 80 feet square and about 18 inches deep. The floors being covered with sand, the semi-fluid clay from the "clay pit" is poured or pumped into them, so as to filter off and evaporate the water, until the clay is firm enough to be cut out in square blocks, to be further dried in the sun. The process is now generally superseded by the **Dry.** Q.V.

Clay pit. A large water-tight pit, about 8 feet deep and from 40 to 80 feet square. The china clay held suspended in water is allowed to deposit in such a pit, the clear water running away. See **Clay pans.**

Clay sett. A portion of land containing a bed of "clay," (i.e., granite in a decomposed soft form) marked out for raising, washing, or preparing china or porcelain clay.

Clay stopes. The place, or pit where the decomposed granite is dug up and "washed" so as to separate the sand and mica from the pure porcelain or china clay.

Clays, or **Clayers.** Boys marbles made of brown clay fired.

Clecky. See **Cloppy.**

Clem, or **Clember.** To climb, or mount up, "clem op," i.e., climb up.

Clem, or **Clemmin.** Very thirsty. See **Chackin.**

Clems. Fish and potatoes fried together. M.A.C.

Clemmed. Simply adhering, as plate glass to plate glass, or as do the leaves of a new book. Were anything like gum, &c., put between, then things would be said to be *cligged*, or *clibbed* together. See **Clibby** and **Cliggy.** "Clemmed" is a term also used of a period in the *œstrum* of dogs.

Clever. Very well, doing very well, in good health. "How are you?" "Clever thank'ee." "How are you getting on?" "Clever shore nuff."

Clibby, or **Cliggy.** Anything wet, sticky or adhesive, as entrails, wet untanned skins, gum, tar, treacle, birdlime, &c. "My fingers are clibbed (or cligged together." *Clybye* is a Celtic Cornish word and means, to wet, or moisten. *Glybye,* or *glibbie,* is also Celtic Cornish, and means the same as *clybye.*

Click. A sharp quick blow. See **Clip.**

Click-handed, or **Clicky-handed.** Left-handed. From the Celtic Cornish word *cledhec,* left-handed.

Clickpaw or **Clicky-paw.** Left-handed.

Cliders. See **Clyders.**

Clidgy. Same as **Clibby** or **Cliggy.** Sticky.

Clidgy. Sugar stick. Toffy.

Clink. A town or parish blackhole for tramps and rogues.

The word *clink* is old and known outside Cornwall. The writer when a boy knew no other name for a blackhole. *Clink* is giving place to the term "the lock up." The derivation is obscure. Dr. Johnson says "*clink* is perhaps softened from *clank*, or corrupted from *click*."

Clicket (in old French *cliquet*) means a key, or instrument to open a door.

> "Save he himself for the smale wicket
> He bare alway of a silver *clicket*."
>
> *Chaucer's Merchant's Tale.*

Compare *clink* with the Latin *clingo*, to encompass. (In *Festus, Minshew.*)

Clip or **Click.** A fillip, or light quick blow. "I'll giv'ee a clip in the ear." Also, a short, snappish way of speaking, as, "She's very clip."

Clip. To turn the earth for a crop.

Clisty. See **Clusty.**

Clitter. A clatter, a confused noise, a fuss.

Cloam, or **Clome.** Earthenware. This word is also used in Pembrokeshire, &c.

Cloamin. Made of "cloam." Q.V. A stupid person is called "a cloamin fellow."

Cloamers. Boys' clay marbles. See **Clays.**

Clob. A lump of earth, or clay. Also **Cob.** Q.V.; Coarse clay and straw mixed, for building a *cob* wall.

Clobbed. Begrimed. Dirty clothes, or utensils are said to be "clobbed with dirt."

Clobbed up. Choked, as thus of a man's pipe stem, "it is clobbed up."

Clock. The crop, or maw.

Clodgy. Sticky like pitch, or birdlime.

Clop, or Cloppy. To walk lame, to limp along.

Cloppy. Lame. In Celtic Cornish *cloppec* and *clof* mean, lame, crippled. *(Kloppek. Borlase.)*

Clopper. One who halts, or limps in walking. "A blinker and a clopper were never caught in a good trick." A hard old saying.

Clopping. Walking lame. "Clopping along."

Close. Reticent, reserved. "He is always very close."

Clouching. Without character, not to be believed. *St. Buryan.*

Clout. A blow, a slap. "I'll giv'ee a clout under the ear." This is a Celtic Cornish word.

Cluck, Clucky, Clucky down. To lower the body to a very stooping posture; sitting on the heels and bending the neck very much, is a posture comparable to that of a barn door fowl, "clucking," i.e., sitting flat down with the head lowered. Lhuyd gives

Keliock as Celtic Cornish for a *cock*, a name probably originating from the sound *cluk* which the bird makes. (*Clutty*. W.F.P.)

Clubbish. Rough and brutal in manner.

Clum. Benumbed with cold. "My hands are clum with the cold."

Clump. An extra sole to a boot, or shoe.

Clunk. To swallow. This is a Celtic Cornish word. (*Klunk. Borlase.*)

Clunker. The "swallow," or fauces. The uvula.

Clushy in. To draw nearer together, as in sitting on a form. To nestle closer together. (*Clouch*, gathered together. *Spenser.*)

Clusty, or **Clisty.** Close grained, or "heavy," as "clusty potatoes."

Cluit. A hurdle of rods wattled together. *Polwhele.* A crate, a wattled gate. *Williams.* It is Celtic Cornish.

Clut. "A gap in a hedge. To fall with a *clut*, i.e., to fall in a heap." M.A.C. (*Clut* in Celtic Cornish, a clout.)

Clutchy. Sticky. The same as **Clodgy.** Q.V.

Clyders, or **Clythers.** The rough bed-straw. *Galium aparine.* C. In Celtic Cornish *Gledh* means chickweed. (*Clivers, cleavers*, goose-grass. H.R.C.

Clyne. A sea bird's feast. *M. Dunn, Mevagissey.*

Co. This curious word has opposite meanings according to its use, as "*Go* at once, co." "*Come* at once, co." *Co* is a Celtic Cornish word and means the memory, remembrance; also *cof*, and *ko*.

Coady. Sheep with diseased livers are coady. *Stratton.*

Coanse, Cawnse, or **Scoanes.** The stones, or pavement. U.J.T.

Coanse-way. A paved path-way.

Cob. A thump, a blow. Also the top locks of a horse's mane. (Welsh *cob* or *cop*, a tuft.)

Cob. A mixture of coarse brown clayey earth, and straw, for building a *cob* wall.

Cobba. A simpleton. M.A.C. **Cobbe.** A bungler. R.H. (A cobbler. *Dryden.*)

Cobber. A bruiser of tin.

Cobbing. Breaking up the ore into small pieces with a "cobbing hammer." Also, a thrashing, as "He deserves a good cobbing." In Celtic Cornish *dho cob*, to break, or bruise.

Cob-nuts. Hazel nuts. Also, a game so called played with nuts. (Cock-haw. *Polwhele.*)

Cobshans. Money or savings. U.J.T.

Cockle. Capel or Caple. Schorl.

Cockle up. To buckle, or curl up.

Cockle up to. To confront in a defiant manner.

Cockle-bells, or **Cockle-buttons.** The burrs of the Burdock. *Arctium lappa.* Icicles are called Cockle-bells.

Cock-a-hoop. Full of hope and intent. "All cock-a-hoop."

Cock haw. A boy's game with hazel nuts.

Cock-hedge. A thorn hedge trimmed. M.A.C.

Cockly-bread. "To make cockly-bread," i.e., to turn head over heels in bed. M.A.C.

Cocky. Pert and conceited.

Codgers' end. Shoemakers' wax ends. (Coajer's-end, cobler's-wax. U.J.T.

Codgy wax. Cobler's wax.

Codnor. "Cognomen for stewing." T.W.S.

Coffins. Old surface mining excavations, often opened into by mining *up* from below. E.N.
(*Koffen.* "The hollow of an open mine." *Whitaker.*) In Celtic Cornish *cofor* means a chest, a coffer; Welch, *côf*, a hollow trunk; Armoric, *cufer*; Irish *cofra.* *Williams.*

Coining tin. "The large blocks of tin being brought to a coinage town, the officers appointed by the Duke of Cornwall, assayed it by taking off a piece of one of the under corners of the block of about a pound weight, partly by cutting, and partly by breaking;

and if well purified, stamped the face of the block with the impression of the seal of the Duchy." This was "coining" the tin, after which it became "merchandable," and not before. *Borlase.*

Cold roste. This expression has been used by one of our earliest writers in this way. "A beggarie little town of cold roste." Is this last the sense in which it is used in connection with the sean pilchard fishery? *The Cornishman,* 1881.

Colp. A thump, a cuff. (A short rope used for carrying sheaves. M.A.C.)

Colpas. A prop to a lever. M.A.C.)

Collaring or **Collar.** The top boarding of a mine shaft.

Colloping. A good thrashing or beating.

Collybran. Summer lightning. The smut in corn. *Uredo segetum,* a blight in corn. In Celtic Cornish *colbran,* lightning.

Collywobbles. Rumbling and flatulence inside the body. *Borborygmi.*

Come-by-chance. Anything obtained fortuitously.

Come-upping. A flogging. M.A.C.

Comfortable. Agreeable, obliging. "A very "*comfortable* man."

Comical-tempered. Cross, ill-tempered.

Condiddle. To diddle, cheat, or impose upon.

Condudles. Childish, stupid notions.

Conger-douce. Conger split, and dried without salt. *Tonkin.*

Confloption. A great flurry.

Conkerbell, Cockabell, or **Cockerbell.** An icicle.

Continny. To continue. "Yew was always a bootiful buoy (boy) my dear, and so yew still *continnies.* *Near Bodmin.*

Cooche-handed. Left-handed. *Stratton.*

Cooler or **Cool.** A large salting tub.

Coom (or **Coomb.**) A valley. *Borlase's Celtic Cornish Vocabulary.*

Copperfinch. The chaffinch.

Cop. The tuft on a fowl's head. In Welsh *cob* or *cop,* a tuft.

Coppies. Fowls with a tuft of feathers on each of their heads are so named.

Core, or **Coor.** Eight hours work. Three cores in the twenty four hours.

Coose. "In coose," i.e., of course, provided that.

Coot. A thump. A Celtic Cornish word. **Cootin.** A thrashing.

Coranting. Frisking, jumping about, gambolling.

Corn-crake. The land-rail.

Cornish diamonds. Crystals of quartz, "of a fine clear water but some are yellow, brown, cloudy, opake, white, green, purple, black. The black is very rare, and called by Linnæus *nitrum quartzosum nigrum*, or "*Morion.*" *Borlase's Natural History.*

Cornish organ. The bellows.

Cornish pies. These are various, toothsome, and wholesome. Some are peculiar. It is a moot question which is the better, a Cornish pie or a Cornish pasty. Here is a list of a few pies :— *

1. Squab pie.
2. Fishy pie.
3. Star-gazing pie.
4. Conger pie.
5. Parsley pie.
6. Herby pie.
7. Lamb-y pie.
8. Piggy pie.
9. Nattlin pie.
10. Muggety pie.
11. Likkey pie.
12. Tetty pie.
13. Giblet pie.
14. Taddago pie.
15. Bottom pie.
16. Sour-sab pie, &c.

They say that the Devil would not venture into Cornwall, fearing that the Cornish might put *him* into a pie. They use pepper instead.

Cornish. "To Cornish together," i.e., several persons to use only one glass like "a loving cup."

Cornish hair. The rough wool of ancient Cornish sheep. *Carew.*

---

* The composition of these pies is given, for the most part, in this Glossary.

Cornish hug. A powerful wrestling grip, very effectual if it can be made.

Corrat. "Pert, impudent, sharp in rejoinder." "As corrat as Crocker's mare." *East Cornwall Provb.* C.

Corrosy. An old family feud. *Polwhele.* (*Coreesy, Corrizee.* M.A.C.)

Corve. A floating crab box. *Captn. H. Richards, Prussia Cove.*

Corwich. The crab *Maia squinado.* C.

Cos'sened. Hammered into shape and newly steeled. H.R.C.

Costan. A basket for straw and brambles. M.A.C.

Cothan. A stratum of sandy earth and small stones, so called by tinners "wherein the sand-tin is usually found about a foot and a half above the karn." *Borlase.*

Country. The ground itself, especially used of that about or near an excavation.

Countryman's treacle. Garlic. The Hundred of Stratton in Queen Elizabeth's time was remarkable for its plenty of garlic, "the Countryman's treacle, says Carew, which they vent not only in Cornwall but in many other places."

Cousin-jacky. A local term of contempt.

Cover-slut. Any clothing "slipped on" to hide untidiness beneath.

Cow. A windlass with a cowl shaped top to supply air in a mine. M.A.C.

Cowal. A fish-basket used by fish-jowders, and carried on the back. This is from the Celtic Cornish *cawal*, *cauwal*, or *cowal*, a hamper, a basket.

Cow-flops. Wild parsnips.

Cowl. A fish bladder. B.V.

Cowshern. Cow-dung.

Cowsherny. A term descriptive of the colour of the sea when it looks olive-green, or turbid as if coloured with cow-dung. C.

Cowsy, or **Coosy.** To chat. This is from the Celtic Cornish *cows* or *caws*, to speak, or talk. *Causen*, (*Spenser*), to argue or debate.

Coxy. See **Cocky.**

Crake, or **Craak.** To croak, to quaver in speaking, or singing. *Crake* and *crakel* are Chaucer's words.

Craake. A croaker, a querulous, fretting person. "She's a regular craake."

Craakin. Always fretting and complaining, also continual and melancholy chatter. "Te's wisht to hear her craakin hour by hour."

Craaky. Hoarse, and shaky. Used of the voice.

Cracky. Half mad. "Flighty."

Crame. To creep. "To crame down." In Celtic Cornish *cramia* means to creep, and *cramyas*, creeping.

Cram. A "white" lie. "That's a cram," i.e., that's a likely story. Also, to crumple, as "Don't cram it."

Crammer. A big lie. "What a crammer!"

Cran. "A cran of herrings," i.e., 800 herrings.

Cravel. "A wood cravel in a chimney." (?)

Crawn. A dried sheep's skin. *Davy, Zennor.*

Crease. The ridge tiles of a roof.

Creem or **Crim.** A creeping, trembling, shuddering feeling, as from fear. Also a shiver, as from cold.

Creem. To squeeze, crush, or press.

Creeming. Shivering with cold, shaking with fear. "I'm creeming all over."

Creener. A fretful complaining person.

Creening. Complaining, fretting, as if "bad all over." "She's always creening," i.e., always talking about her ailments.

Crellas. British hut circles. "An excavation in a bank, roofed over to serve for an outhouse." *Bottrall.*

Cresser. A small fish resembling a bream, but more red. H.A.C.

Creeved. Underdone. M.A.C. In Celtic Cornish *criv* means crude, raw. *Pryce.*

Crib. A small meal, or lunch. "I've just had a crib." A crust of bread. **Cribs.** Fragments of food.

Cribber. A pilferer; a small eater. "He's but a cribber."

Cribbage face. A thin wrinkled face.

Cricks. Dry hedgewood. *Polwhele.*

Cricket. A low three legged stool.

Crickly. Frail, rickety.

Cricklin. Breaking down from overweight, also, stooping in walking. "Cricklin along."

Cripse. To craze, or injure the edges of anything brittle, as of glass or china.

Crim. A crumb. A little bit of anything.

Crissy-crossy. Criss-cross.

Crock. A three legged iron pot used in cooking.

Crogen. A shell. It is a Celtic Cornish word. (*Croggans* limpet shells. M.A.C.)

Cromlech. (pro. krom'lek.) A term applied to ancient Celtic constructions consisting of a large flat stone supported on three or more other stones set on end. Once supposed to be altars but now judged to be ancient British tombs. This is a Celtic word derived from *lêk*, a flat stone, and *krum*, crooked, and according to Borlase, *Cromlech* means literally, a crooked flat rock, or stone.

Crooks. Great wooden hooks used saddle fashion on horses, donkeys, and mules, for carrying goods. Also called pannier-crooks.

Croom. A small bit, a short time. "Give us a croom." "Wait a croom."

Croony. Foolish, imbecile.

Cropin, or **Cropeing.** Stingy, miserly, like "an old hunks."

Crouging. Crouching, shuffling. "Crouging along."

Crow, or **Crou.** A hut, a hovel, a sty. This is a Celtic Cornish word.

Crowd. "A wooden hoop covered with sheep skin used for taking up corn." *Davy, Zennor.*

Crowd. A fiddle. **Crowder.** A fiddler. **Crowdy.** To play the fiddle. *Crowd* and *Crowder* are Celtic Cornish words.

Crowst or **Crouse.** A luncheon, a feed. This is a Celtic Cornish word. (*Croust. Pryce*).

Crowning. An inquest.

Crow-sheaf. The crown or topmost sheaf of an arrish mow.

Cruddy, Crudded, or **Cruddled.** Curdled.

Cruel shaape. "In a cruel shaape," i.e., in a terrible mess.

Crulley-head. Curley head. (*Crull*, curled, *Chaucer.*) *Kryllia:*, curled, in Celtic Cornish.

Crum. Crooked, bent, curved. This is a Celtic Cornish word. It also means chilled, or cramped, as "my hands are *crum* with the cold."

Crum-a-grackle. Perplexity, bother, "Here's a pretty crum-a-grackle." St. Just. T.C.

Crummet. A very little bit. A crumb.

Crumpling. A wrinkled apple.

Crunk. To croak like a raven. F.C.

Cuckhold dock. The Burdock. *Arctium majus.* (Cuckle dock. C.)

Cuckoo, or **Guckoo spit.** A frothy little mass like spittle, seen on bushes, as on furze, rosemary, &c. Caused by an insect to be found in the middle of it. (*The Cicadia spumaria.* C.)

Cud. A quid of Tobacco.

Cuckoo, or **Guckoo flowers.** Wild hyacinths.

Cudgelling. A game at fencing with stout sticks, or cudgels. The man who first "brought blood" was declared the victor.

Cue. An ox-shoe. An iron heel for a boot, or shoe.

Culch. Oyster spat. C.

Culiack. A good-for-nothing person. *Davy, Zennor.*

Culver-hound. The lesser spotted dog-fish. C.

Cunner pots. See **Weelys.**

Cuny. Mildewed. M.A.C.

Curl. A carol, as sung at Christmas. In Celtic Cornish *Karol,* a choir, a song.

Curls. Glands. "The curls (i.e. glands) of the neck."

Custis. A battle-door or nearly circular shaped flat piece of hard wood, with a handle about ten inches long, used at school to slap the boys hands, &c. The punishment itself was also called "the custis," or "having the custis."

Cuttit. Sharp in reply. Pert, impudent. C.

Cyphers. See **Sives,** or **Chives.** *(Cipeolon).*

Daark, or **Derk.** Blind. "Th'ould man es daark an 'most totelin" i.e., the old man is blind and nearly imbecile.

Dab. A thump, a blow, as "Gibb'n a dab"; also a thrust, as "he dabbed it right in my eye"; also a lump of anything, as "a dab of butter"; also a clever, or skilful person, as "he's quite a dab at it."

Dabbety fay! An exclamation meaning, "Give us faith. H.R.C.

Daffer. Crockery ware, as the tea things, &c. *Polwhele.*

Dag. An axe used by miners. (A hatchet. *Callington).*

Daggens. Sprinkled heavily, showing a good crop; something plentiful. T.W.S. Also, **Daggins,** lots.

Daggin. Longing to do a thing, ready for it; as, "He's daggin for it." Also draggling; weighted down (i.e. daggin) with fruit.

Daggin. Draggling. "Daggin in the mud."

Dame-ku. A jack snipe. R.H.B.

Dandy-go-russet. Term used of faded clothing; also, an ancient wig which has done good service.

Dane. "Red headed Dane" a sneering term. M.A.C. See **Carrots.**

Daps or **Dops.** Likeness, or image of. "The very daps."

Dash-an-darras. The dram, or "stirrup cup" for the parting guest. *Polwhele.*

Datch. Thatch.

Datcher. A thatcher. "This is the weather for ducks and datchers."

Davvered. Faded, looking old and worn.

Day-berry. Wild gooseberry. M.A.C.

Deads. Rubble or loose rubbish and broken stones in a mine, and containing no metal. *Borlase.*

Dealsey, or **Delseed.** A fir cone. M.A.C.

Deaf, or **Defe nettle.** See **Blind-nettle.**

Deef, Defe, or **Deve.** Hollow, decayed, as a "deef" nut. It is also used thus in the North of England. There is a term also, "defe as a haddock," meaning, very deaf.

Delbord. The nurse hound. *Squalus canicula.* N.E.C.

Denneck, or **Redanneck.** Piper, or Ellick, names applied to a species of tub fish. W.F.P.

Derry. "A putty derry." "Kicking up a putty derry." In Celtic Cornish *deray* means a deed, an exploit.

Devil. An eval. *q.v.*

Devil's bit, or **Devil's button.** Blue scabious. M.A.C.

Dew-snail. A slug. *Limax agrestis.*

Dido. A row a fuss. "Kicking up a putty dido." *Callington.*

Dicky. One of the names for an ass. Used also in Yorkshire. See **Ass.** Also, a sham bosom, or "false-front" to a shirt. A half shirt.

Dijey. A small farm, or homestead. *Bottrall.*

Dig. To scratch, as when itching. "Don't dig your head like that." Also, a blow,or poke, as with the elbow. "A dig in the ribs."

Dinky. Tiny, very small, a mere mite.

Dinged. Reiterated. "He dinged it into my ears from morning to night."

Dilly-dally. To do anything in a slow, lazy manner.

Dinyan. A little corner. M.A.C.

Dippa. A small pit. A mining term. A Celtic Cornish word.

Dippers. In the catching of pilchards the boats which attend for the purpose of conveying the fish from the tuck-net to the shore are termed *dippers.* *Dr. Paris.*

Dish. A gallon of black tin. *Carew.* Also, the landlord's share in the produce of a mine.

Dishwasher. The wagtail.

Disle, or **Dicel.** The thistle, especially the "Milky dicel" (so called by boys) for feeding rabbits. (*Sonchus oleraceus.* C.)

Doat figs. Broad-figs. U.J.T.

Dob, or Dab. To throw, or fling. As, "he dobbed a great stone at me."

Dobbet. A short, stumpy little person.

Dock. The crupper of a saddle. Also used in Devonshire.

Docy. Pretty, charming, or neat in person. "A docy little maid." "She is very docy."

Dogga. The dog-fish. *Acanthius vulgaris.* C.

Doggetin along. Plodding along in walking. A "dog trot" pace.

Dogg along. To drag along.

Doggle. To totter in walking, as does a child, "dogglin along."

Dole. Mine dues. A lot of ore.

Doldrums. In low spirits, "In the doldrums."

Dollop. A lump of anything, thus, "a dollop of fat."

Dollymop. A vulgar flirt.

Dollymoppin. Flirting with the girls.

Dooda. A stupid person. M.A.C.

Doodle. To diddle, to cheat.

Dormant. Melancholly, sad, gloomy. "A dormant house," i.e., a gloomy house. "Feeling dormant," i.e., melancholly or sad. Used in the same sense as *wisht.* *q.v.*

Dorymouse. The dormouse.

Dossity. Spirit, activity. C. (A corruption of Audacity). 'Dacity.

Dot-and-go-one. A term used of a lame person. Skittering, sliddering, stapping, straking; stumping, stanking, and fooching along; craming, and clopping, like a clouching ould tôtle, goes thickky-there poor ould "dot-and-go-one."

Douse. To throw a thing down violently. To lower, as, "douse the sail." To thrash, or beat, as, "give him a good dousing." To pay, as, "come douse out your money." To throw water over anyone, "to give him a dousing."

Douse, or **Doust.** A blow, or thump.

Dousse, or **Doust.** The husks of winnowed corn. Poor people used it to stuff their pillows and bed-ties.

Doust. To pelt. As in throwing stones at one.

Douster. A fall, "a regler douster."

Doustin. A thrashing.

Dover. An uproar, a row, a great fuss. "There's dover," or, "There's dover to pay."

Dow. A cross old woman. *Gwinear.* T.C.

Dowl, Dool, or **Dolley.** To toll a large bell.

Dowlin pain. A dull, persistent pain.

Down-danted. Depressed in spirits. Discouraged, "down in the mouth."

Down souce. A sudden fall of anything, as, "down it came souce." Also, as in speaking very plainly, "I told him down souce."

Dowser. One who uses the dowsing rod.

Dowsing-rod. A forked branch of hazel used for discovering a mineral lode. Now laughed at as useless, and *dowsing* considered as silly and superstitious. Divining rod.

Drabbit! Drat it! "Aw! Drabbit the ole scrubbin."
Mrs. Parr's Adam & Eve.

Draft, or **Draff.** Brewers' grains. Used as food for pigs. Chaucer uses the word *draf*, meaning "things thrown away as unfit for man's food."

Dram. A swathe of cut corn. *Bottrall.*

Drang. A narrow place, passage, trench, gutter, or drain.

Dranged up. See **Dringed up.**

Drash. To thrash as of corn, to thump or beat. To dash a thing violently down. Also, to shut or open violently. "He drashed open the door."

Drashel. A flail.

Drasher. A thrasher of corn. (In Celtic Cornish it is *drushier;* or *drusher. Borlase.)*

Drashin. Thrashing corn. Also beating, or flogging.

Draw-bucket. A bucket with a rope to draw water up a well.

Draxel, or **Drexel.** The threshold. *(Dreckstool. Polwhele.)*

Drazac, or **Drazackin.** Slow, stupid, dull.

Dredge corn. A mixed crop of barley, oats and wheat. C.

Dredge wheat. A bearded wheat, used to be sown in coarse land. *Tonkin.*

Dredgy ore. Inferior mineral. *Borlase.*

Dreshel. See **Drashel.**

Dressel, or **Dresshel.** See **Draxel.**

Dribbs, or **Driffs.** Small quantities of anything.

Drift. A trench cut in the ground resembling a channel dug to convey water to a mill-wheel.

Drilsy. A low, murmuring, and monotonous sound, or hum.

Dring. A crush of people, "a regular dring." Also, a narrow place. See **Drang.**

Dringed up. Crowded up together. Generally used of people in a crowded room, or vehicle. Soiled, as with dirt at the bottom of a dress.

Dripshan. Mother's milk. Spirits. M.A.C.

Driving nets. Nets drawn after the boats, fastened only at one end, in the meshes of which fish are caught as they try to pass through.

Droke. A wrinkle, a furrow, a passage. M.A.C.

Droll-teller. An itinerant story-teller, news-monger, and fiddler, who travelled from town to town, and village to village. There were two such in Cornwall as late as 1829. H.

Droolin. Drivelling, as with an infant, or an idiot.

Droozenhead. A stupid, dull person.

Droozlin. Stupid, dull, mournful. (In Celtic Cornish *dreuesy* means mournful, lamentable. *Pryce.)*

Drover. A fishing boat used in taking fish with a driving net. Usually called *driving* boat.

Druckshar. A small solid wheel. M.A.C.

Drug. To drag, as "drug the wheel." The word *drugge* is used by Chaucer for *drag.*

Druggister. A druggist. Now elegantly called "A pharmaceutical chemist."

Drule, or **Drool.** Drivel.

Drumblin. Stupid, obtuse.

Drum. To flog. **Drumming.** Flogging. "Gibb'n a good drumming."

Drusy. In most veins (lodes) there is a central line or fissure . . . . . formed by the close apposition and occasional union of two crystallized or as they may be called, *drusy* surfaces. *Dr. Paris.*

Dry. The name given to a long, low building, (from 100 to 150 feet long), with a tall chimney at one end and a coal-burning furnace at the other. There are flues beneath the tiled floor. On the hot floor the semi-liquid china clay is dried and rendered fit for shipment. This mode of drying Clay has been used about 20 or 30 years.

Dryer. A dram or "nip" of spirit after drinking beer. "We had fower pints of beer, and haaf a noggin of rum for a *dryer.*" *J. T. Tregellas.*

Duffan. "An egotistical hypocrite." "A regular duffan."

Duffed. Struck. E.N.

Duffy. An outspoken person. *Bottrall.*

Dug. A push, a thrust, a poke. A "dig."

Duggle. See **Doggle.**

Dule. Comfort. *Carew.*

Dull of hearing. "*Hard* of hearing."

Dum-dolly. A mishapen marble. M.A.C.

Dummets, or **Dimmets.** Twilight. "Between the two lights."

Dumbledory, Dumbledore, Dumbledrone, Drumbledrain, and **Dumbledrane.** Different names for a drone. (In Celtic Cornish *drane* means "a thorne, a bryer, a bramble." *Pryce.)*

Dungin'. Manuring. **Dunged.** Manured. Messed or dirtied. "I'll have ivy graw oal roun' the tower," says the passon. "And so you shall, my dear," says the churchwarden; and when the passon was gone he beginned to put some in; a Trura man looked in and seed un, and thoft he was *dungin'* the tower to maake un graw." *J. T. Tregellas.*

Durgy or **Dourgy.** A short, stout person. M.A.C. It is a Celtic Cornish word and also means a small turf hedge. *Pryce.*

Durk, or **Dark.** Blind.

Durn. The door post. The side post of a door or gate. *Dorn,* Celtic Cornish, the door post.

Duty. The estimated work done by a mine steam-engine. The amount of duty is registered and issued on "duty papers."

Dwalder. To speak tediously and confusedly. C.

Dwaling. A dreamy, sleepy manner of muttering. It is often said of a sick person that he has been "dwaling all night." Angl. Sax. *dwelian.* (*Dwale,* a sleeping draught. *Chaucer.*)

Ear-bosoms or **Ear-busses.** The glands of the throat. When swollen it is said, "My ear-bosoms are down." The orifices behind the gills of a conger.

Ear-buzz, or **Ear-buzzer.** The spinning, or brown Cock-chafer. The Oakwebb. Boys make the insect spin or "buzz" by putting a pin in its tail.

Ear-wig. A millipede kind of insect. It is an old belief in Cornwall, that if an earwig crept into the ear, deafness would be caused.

Easement. Relief. (Esement, *Chaucer.*)

Easy. Feeble minded. Silly.

Eaving. See **Heaving.**

Edge on. To egg on, to incite.

Eggy-hot, or **Egg-hot.** Hot beer with eggs, and sugar beaten up. Sometimes flavoured with rum.

Ekky-mowl. The titmouse.

Elbow-crookin. Tippling.

Elbow grease. Work or labour in doing a thing well. "Give it more elbow grease."

Elecompanie. A tomtit. *Polwhele.*

Element. The atmosphere, the sky.

Elleck. The gurnard. *Trigla cuculus.* C. See **Illek.**

Emmut. In the eye of the wind, i.e., in the *emmut* (or brunt) of it. *Polwhele.*

Empidenter. More impudent. "He's moar empidenter then I caan suffer."

Ena, mena, out. A row of children stood facing another child, and the latter, pointing to each in succession, said these words in an ordinary voice, except the word "out," which was shouted.

> "Ena, mena, mona, mite,
> Bascalora, bora, bite,
> Hugga, bucca, bau;
> Eggs, butter, cheese, bread,
> Stick, stock, stone dead,—**Out.**"

The moment "out" was said, the one on whom this word fell had to quit the row; and so *seriatim*, repeating the above words each time.

In West Cornwall according to M.A.C. the following are the words used:—

"Ena, mena, mona, mi,
Pasca, lara, bona, (or bora,) bi,
Elke, belke, boh,
Eggs, butter, cheese, bread,
Stick, stack, stone dead."

In the game of Blindman's Buff.

"Among the many evidences that furnish the philologist with the proof that a once powerful people existed in our midst are those "wandering words" that flit through the atmosphere of our every-day lives. At first their indistinctness adds nothing to their beauty; but, after a careful scrutiny, their roughness wears away, and amidst an accumulation of what is seemingly unreal and unsatisfactory, we begin to discover something that eventually will repay us for the labour we have bestowed upon them. There is—so to speak—nothing too common, nothing too mean, nothing so out of the everyday working of our lives, that will not lead us to a successful issue. A bit of bronze, a battered flint, a broken bussa, a single word or expression,—each carries us back to a period when manners, dress, domestic appliances, and the prevalence of a now forgotten tongue were scattered up and down our land; and which differ from the England and the English in every essential of the present day.

For instance, who would surmise that the talismanic words uttered by our children in their innocent games have come down to us very nearly as perfect as when spoken by the Ancient Briton; but with an opposite and widely different meaning? The only degree of likeness that lies between them now is that where the child of the present day escapes a certain kind of juvenile punishment the retention of the word originally meant DEATH in a most cruel and barbarous way.

The couplet, as near as I can bring it to orthographical standing, will read thus:

"Ena, mena, bora—mi—
Kisca, lara, mora—di."

The force of habit is so strong in our modes of actions,—of seeing, hearing, and doing,—that the endless repetition of those seemingly childish words has taken no further hold on us than the generality of such nursery twaddle would. In this instance the case ought to be widely different; for this is a veritable phrase of great antiquity—"*the excommunication of a human being, preparatory to that victim's death.*"

The analysis of the two lines in question will show that a double meaning was clearly involved; the first line laying a ban on the then chief articles of food, or life-producing elements, *eggs*, *butter*, *bread;* the second, or judicial, line foreshadowing death by *beating*, or, as the line clearly enough expresses it, "*beaten to death by sticks.*" *Mi* and *di* are the old British ordinals, and stand for *first* and *second;* therefore, the twofold principle would make it appear as if the criminal not only suffered the deprivation at home of home comforts but that death followed with unerring severity."

T. W.S. in the 'Cornishman' on "Wandering words."

Engine-stack. The lofty chimney of a mine-engine house.

Epiphany. A name applied in west Cornwall to the *Cuscuta Epithymum*, abundantly growing amongst the furze, "winding its spiral structure in all directions and producing from its reddish hue a beautful contrast." *Dr. Paris.*

Epping-stock. See **Hepping-stock.**

Erish, or **Errish.** See **Arrish.**

Ettaw. A shackle used to fasten two chains, so as to make one. *Mousehole.* W.F.P.

Eval, Hevval, Yewal, Yewl, or **Devil.** A dung-fork with three prongs has these different names.

Ever, or **Aiver.** See **Heaver.**

Eving, or **Eaving.** See **Heaving.**

Evet, Ebbet, or **Emmet.** A newt.

Fackle, or **Feckle.** An acute inflamation in the foot. M.A.C.

Fadé. (Faddy). To go. As at Helstone on Furry day.

Fadé tune. The furry-song tune as played at Helstone on the 8th of May. The music of it is given in Dr. Paris's "Guide to Mount's Bay and Land's End," p. 222; in "Specimens of Cornish Provincial Dialect," by Uncle Jan Trenoodle, pp. 106-7-8, and also in other books on Cornwall.

Fadging along. Walking along. Getting on, prospering.

Fadge. To suit, or fit. "How will it fadge?" i.e., how will it suit, fit, or answer. Angl. Sax. *fegan.*

"I'll have thy advice and if it *fadge* thou shalt eat."
Mother Bombie, 1594.

"You see how matters *fadge*." *The Merry Devil of Edmonton.*

Fadgy. "How do'ee *fadgy*?" i.e., how do you get on?

Fagot. A Cornish wrestler who has bargained *not* to win, is said to have "sold his back," and he is contemptuously called a fagot. It is also a name of contempt and anger for an impudent girl, or "hussy." "Ah! you fagot!"

Fair-a-Mo. Pig fair in November at St. Ives. M.A.C.

Fairmaid, fumade, or **fermade.** Names for a cured (formerly smoked) pilchard. Pilchards "when caught, used to be preserved by smoking,"..... "therefore denominated *fumadoes* by the Italians to whom then, as now, we principally sold them, and which are still denominated *fumadoes* by the very populace of Cornwall, even when they are now preserved by pressing." *Whitaker's ancient Cathedral of Cornwall,* Vol. 2, pp, 248, 249. "Fumadoes were perhaps the *gerres* of Pliny." *Camden.*

"They carry them" into Spayne, Italie, Venice, and divers places within the straytes, where they are very vendible, and in those partes tooke name *fumados* for that *they are dried in the smoake.*" (Norden, A.D. 1584).

Fair play! Fair play! Make a ring! A favourite Cornish cry when there is a fight, or a strife for mastery.

When Cornishmen fought, or cudgelled, or wrestled, they did so generously, and like men, and very often for the sake of prowess without a sign of rancour. They did not, two, three or four together, fall on a single man, or, kick or strike him when he was down, nor did they like cowards pull out their knives, or revolvers, but they used the weapons (and good ones too) with which nature had provided them. In their quarrels they were rough enough, but they were not typical of the modern "rough," on the contrary, in their quiet moments there were no men more civil, and good natured.

When the writer was a youth, it was common to see a fight in the street on a market day. The constable would be sometimes present, apparently to keep order. The men first shook hands, then set to, and again shook hands at the finish.

Then both parties adjourned to an inn, smoked a pipe, drank ale, settled about the next trial in fisticuffs, and finished by singing a song or two to the tune of "the old hundred."

A celebrated preacher once said that he did not see why the Devil should have the best tunes, and those men thought conversely. Yet they were very kindly, worked hard, lived hard, and stood by one another like bricks in a strong wall, veritably like "One and all."

Once when the writer had lost his way on a wild moor, late at night, one of such men rose from bed and guided him in safety away from the mine shafts. A reward for the trouble was evidently quite unlooked for, and it would have given offence to have pressed it. The writer merely records the facts as known to him. These Cornishmen gave hard blows, and what is harder, they learnt how to take them. With all their roughness they were better men than Pecksniff, or Mawworm; but times are changed, and we are changed with them. So much the better. But how much?

Fairy. A weasel. C.

Falky. A long-stemmed plant. *Halliwell.*

Fal-the-ral. Nonsense.

Fallows. Risers to a cart, to make it hold more.

Fang, or **Vang.** To get, to seize. (*Fong, Saxon*).

Fangings, or **Vangings.** Earnings, winnings.

Fantads. Rediculous notions.

Fardle. A burthen. *Fardel, Chaucer.* It is *fardel* in Celtic Cornish.

Fare nuts. Earth nuts. Ground nuts.

Farthing of land. Thirty acres of land. *Halliwell.*

Fawt. Fault. This is a Celtic Cornish word.

Fay. Faith. *Iss fay!* Yes faith! Fay in Chaucer. *Fey* and *fay* are Celtic Cornish words.

Feather-bow. The plant fever-few.

Feather-bog. A quagmire. M.A.C.

Feather-tye. A feather bed.

Feebs, or **Feeps.** Pitch and toss. M.A.C.

Fellon. Alveolar abscess. A cattle disease.

Fellon-herb. Chickweed. M.A.C. *Felen* is Celtic Cornish for wormwood. (The mouse-ear hawk weed. C.)

Fer. Far. *Fer, Chaucer.*

Fernig. See **Furnig.**

Fern-webb. A small brown beetle used in fishing. (**Fernicock.** M.A.C.) *Melorontha horticola.*

Fescue, or **Vester.** A pointer for teaching children to read. *Polwhele.* *Vester* is a Celtic Cornish word meaning master.

Fetch. To reach to, arrive at, or get to; as, "fetch it down," "hard work to fetch hom."

Few. Some. Curiously used thus, "I'll have a few broth." Also used thus in Yorkshire.

Figs. Raisons are so called in Cornwall. In Celtic Cornish, *figes ledan*, broadfigs; *figes an houl*, raisins.

Figgy-duff. Dough, suet, and raisins, mixed and baked in the shape of a pasty. Also called figgy-hobbin.

Figgy pudden. Plum pudding. *Fig* pudding is more correct than *plum* pudding. In Celtic Cornish *figes an houl* means figs of the sun, raisins.

Filth. "A filth," i.e., a dirty slut. Also, a bellyfull. "I've had my filth."

Fingers. The depth of a hole for blasting rock is measured by a miner placing his fingers against the borer in the hole. "There's three more fingers to bore."

Fire-tail. The red-start. M.A.C.

Firk. v. To tease roughly by hand. F.C.

Fish-fag. Female fish-dealer. A fish-wife.

Fish-jousting. Hawking fish.

Fitchered. Baulked. "Used by miners when some difficulty occurs in boring a hole for blasting."

Garland.

Fitch, Fitcher, or **Fichet.** A polecat.

Fitty, or **Vitty.** Suitable, proper, well adapted.

Fish-jowster, Fish-jowder, or **Fish-chowter.** Names for an itinerant fish dealer. One who carries a cowal of fish on the back is also called a back-jouster.

Five-stones. A boy's game with five small stones, placed on the palm of the hand and then tossed up together a few inches high so as to be caught by a quick turn on the back of the same hand. He who thus catches the greatest number, after a series of such turns, wins the game.

Flair. Pig's kidney fat. M.A.C. *Flair* in Celtic Cornish means a smell, a stink.

Flaad. See **Blawed.**

Flam. A flame. This is a Celtic Cornish word: *flambe* in *Chaucer.*

Flam-new. Quite new.

Flap. A flash, "a flap of lightning."

Flip. A fillip, or slight quick blow.

Flaygerry. Frolicsome.

Fleeting. Guttering of a candle.

Flickets, or **Vlickets.** Flushes, blushes.

Flink. A pert, or insolent kind of deportment. "She's in one of her flinks again."

Flip-jack. A rude fire place. M.A.C.

Flisk. A large tooth comb. M.A.C.

Flookan. "*(An a flaw,* a cut), it being a parcel of ground which calleth off one part of a lode from another." *Borlase.*

Flop. A slap.

Flop-down. To sit, or drop suddenly down on a seat, or the floor.

Flopper. An under petticoat. *Polwhele.*

Flora-day. See **Furry-day.**

Floor of tin. A stratum of tin ore as it lies in alluvial deposit. As in a stream work.

Flosh. To flush, or well wash with water, as in washing a courtlage.

Flote ore. Seaweed. *Carew.*

Floury milk. Hasty pudding. See **Whitepot.**

Floury. Mealy, as a floury potatoe.

Flox. To agitate, or shake up fluid, as in a barrel which is partly filled.

Flummox. To cheat, deceive, or impose upon. "Regularly flummoxed!"

Flush, or **Flushed.** Full fledged.

Flushet. A stream dam.

Fly-by-night. A silly, thoughtless, restive girl.

Flying mare. A wrestling term.

Foacer. There are two such, viz: liquid, and solid. The solid one is a good lump of plain pudding before cutting the joint, so as to take off the edge of a sharp hunger. The liquid one is a large basin of broth before dinner, so as to damp, or rather, whet the appetite of young folks. Such domestic tricks have been done once too often. A boy, in desperation at the sight of so much broth, when asked to say "grace," cried out, "Oh! deliver us from this ocean of broth, and land us safely upon the little island of mutton!" The following was often said, "Woll'ee haa a *foacer*, cheeld?"

Foacin. Pushing, striving. "Doant'ee be so foacin."

Foathy, or **Forethy.** Forwards, intrusive. "She's very foathy."

Fogans, or **Foogans.** A kind of cake. U.J.T.

Folyer. See **Volyer.**

Foot of tin. Two gallons of tin ore. *Carew.*

Footway shaft. The shaft by which miners go down to their work in a mine.

Foo-ty. Mincing, affected, ridiculous in manner. "Such footy ways"

Fooch. Upon occasion, as, "it will do upon a fooch;" a pretence, "it is a poor fooch;" also, a shove, "I gov'n a fooch."

Fooch. To poke in the way, as, "what arr'ee foochin about?"

Foochy. Maladroit, stupid, clumsy in method, or manner.

Fooching along. Pushing along, getting on tolerably well.

Fore-right. See **Vore-right.**

Forrel. The cover of a book. *Forel* is the name of a kind of parchment for the cover of books.

Forth-and-back. Shuffling and vaccillating in manner.

Fouse. To handle carelessly, or crumple.

Fouster. To work hard, to bustle about.

Foxy. When china-clay contains much oxide of iron, there is produced a reddish tint when it is burnt. This spoils the pure white colour, and this reddish tint gives to the clay the term "foxy."

Frape. To bind tightly. "Lor ! how she es fraped in about the waist," i.e., tight laced.

Frange. To spread out like a fan. M.A.C.

Free-fish. Fish so called in contra-distinction to shell-fish. *Carew.*

Freath. A gap in a wattled hedge. C.

Frith. A wattled hedge or gate. *Dr. Bannister.*

Frickets. See **Flickets.**

Fringle. A kitchen grate. M.A.C.

Fuggan. A pork pasty. See **Hoggan.**

Full-drive. Fully driven. (*Ful-drive,* Chaucer).

Fulling. That which well satisfies hunger. "And good fulling traade et was."

Fulsome. Food too fat, rich, or sweet. "It is as fat and *fulsome.*" *Shakspere.*

Fumade. See **Fairmaid.**

Furr. v. To pull the ears. "I'll furr your ears, you rascal."

Fuzz. Furze. Gorse.

Fuzz-chet. The stone-chatter.

Fuzz-kite. The ring tailed kite. M.A.C.

Fuzzy-pig. The hedge-hog.

Furnig, Fernig, or **Furniggy.** To outwit, deceive, or cheat.

Furry-song. The song of the Furry-day, for which consult Cornish Histories. It is noticed here because of the words "with Halantow, Rumbelow!" which by Polwhele are written thus, "With Halantow, Jolly rumble O." Sir John Stoddart in his learned treatise on "Grammar" in the Encyclopœdia Metropolitana, says, "But the old Scottish and English "Heve and How," and "Rumbelow," is singular enough to be cited:—

> "With hey and how! rohumbelow!
> The young folk wer full bold."
>
> *Peblis to the Play.*

> "They rowede hard, and sungge ther too,
> With Heuelow! and rumbeloo."
>
> *Richard Cœur de Lion.*

> "Your maryners shall synge arowe,
> Hey how! and rumbylowe."
>
> *Squyre of lowe degree.*

Furry day. A Cornish custom from time immemorial, is to hold a festival on the 8th of May at Helstone. Anciently at Penryn on the 3rd of May; at the Lizard, near the beginning of the century, on the 1st of May; and also in the parish of Sithney.

Drew's Hist. of Cornwall.

It is generally supposed that this was an institution of pagan origin, designed to celebrate the return of spring.

Polwhele says, that to suppose Furry to be a corruption of Flora "is a vulgar error." "Furry is derived from the old Cornish word *Fer*, a fair or jubilee." It is not correct therefore to call it Flora day, it should be Furry day. It is sometimes called Faddy day, or as Whitaker spells it, *Fadi* day.

Beal (Britain and the Gael) speaks of Davies as referring to old Briton rites, in the words of the Bards, and by a quotation from Greek poetry. "Ruddy was the sea beach, and the circular revolution was performed by the attendance of the white bands in graceful extravagance, when the assembled train were dancing and singing in cadence with garlands, and ivy branches on the brow."

"On Ida's mountain with his mighty mother,
Young Bacchus led the frantic train;
And through the echoing woods the rattling timbrels sound.
Then the Curetes clashed their sounding arms,
And raised with joyful voice the song,
While the shrill pipe resounded to the praise of Cybele,
And the gay satyrs tripped in jocund dance, &c."

Beal says, (p. 85), "In the month of May, a memorial of something like this, yet lingers in an ancient Cornish town." Whitaker says in a letter to Polwhele, (Polwhele's Biographical Sketches in Cornwall, vol. 3, p. 97), "When . . . . . you derive Furry from *Fer* (Cornish) a fair, and now suppose the *Fair-o* of the song to confirm your conjecture; I thoroughly concur with you. . . . . Only I never considered *Fer* (Cornish) as the word "whence (comes) the Latin *Feria*."

The Latin is the original term, and the Cornish only a derivative from it, *Fer* (Cornish) being the same with *Foire* (Irish) and so forming *Fair-o* or *Furry* in pronunciation.

Gaby. A fool.

Gad. A short, wedge-like mining tool, used with a hammer in splitting rock, &c. *Gedn* and *gad* are Celtic Cornish for a wedge.

Gaddle. To drink greedily with haste. "She gaddled it up in no time."

Gaert, or **Gurt.** Great. "A gaert maur o' fuzz," i.e., a great root or stump of furze.

Gait, or **Gate.** Manner, habit, or way. W.T.A.P. *Gate, Chaucer.* "What a gate you have of doing it!"
Wadebridge.

Gake, Gaake, or **Geke.** To stare about. "What be'ee gaakin about?"

Gale. An ox. U.J.T. A childless man. *Garland.* An impotent bull. C.

Galliganter. A hulking, big woman. "She is a regular galliganter." This word, (galliganter) is from Galligantus, the name of "the giant who lived with Hocus-Pocus, the conjuror—Jack the Giant-killer blew the magic horn, and both the giant and conjuror were overthrown."
Nursery Tale of Jack the Giant-killer.

Gallivanter. An incurable flirt.

Gallivanting. "Running about with the girls." Flirting.

Gallus-row. "A gallow's row." (A word perhaps from the hanging scenes at Newgate prison). A great fuss, or outcry. There is a singular resemblance between these words and the Celtic Cornish word *galar*, sorrow, grief, lamentation; *galarow* in the plural number. Also the verb *galarow*, to weep for, to bewail, to lament. *Galarow* reminds one of the old word Harow ! an exclamation, (see Chaucer), or *arowe*, as in the old line,

"Your maryners shall synge *arowe.*"

Squyre of lowe degree.

Gambers. "By gambers !" (An exclamation).

Gambrel. A spreader for the feet of an animal recently killed. (The hock. C.)

Gammuts. Frolic, fun, play. "You're up to your gammuts again."

Gange, or Ginge. To gange a hook is to arm it and the snood with a fine brass or copper wire, twisted round to prevent its being bitten off by the fish.

Garbage. The skimmings of salt, filth and congulated oil from pilchards, which are prepared to be put into hogsheads.

Gashly. Ghastly, horrible, ugly, disagreeable. "A gashly wound." "A gashly looking thing." "A gashly temper." "You gashly bufflehead."

Gathorn. A mine spirit, or phantom. M.A.C.

Gaully grounds. Ground full of springs of water.

Carew.

Gaupuses. Fools, idiots. "The gaupuses have sooked it all in," i.e., The fools have believed it all.

Mrs. Parr's Adam & Eve.

Gaver. Crayfish. *Polwhele.*

Gawk, Gawky, Gawkum, or **Geck.** A stupid, clumsy fellow." "The most notorious *geck.*" *Shakspere.* *Goky* and *Gukky* are Celtic Cornish words meaning foolish, silly, absurd.

Gays. Child's playthings. M.A.C.

Geagled. Draggled, dirtied. *Geagle* is Celtic Cornish for dirty, filthy.

Geese or **Geez.** A saddle-girth.

Geeze-dance. See **Guise-dance.**

Gerrick. A whistler fish; sea pike. (*Garfish.* C.)

Giblets. Nickname for a thin, lanky, bony person.

Gidge. "Oh! my gidge." An exclamation. M.A.C.

Gifts. Term used for the white spots seen on the finger nails.

> "A gift on the thumb is sure to come,
> A gift on the finger is sure to linger."

Giglot. A giddy, flighty young girl, or woman. This is a Celtic Cornish word, and means, a foolish laughter, a wanton girl. "Away with those giglots too." "A giglot wench," "a wanton giglot." *Shakspere.*

Gill. A pint of black tin. *Carew.*

Ging. A whip to make a top spin. C.

Giss, or **Geist.** Hemp girdle, a saddlecloth. M.A.C. Gru-*gis* or Gri-*gis* is Celtic Cornish for a girdle, a belt.

Giving. Thawing, bedewing. When stones become wet by change of temperature, they say "the stones are giving." See **Heaving.**

Giz-dance, or **Geez-dance.** See **Guise-dance.** Applied to the Christmas play.

Gladdy. The yellow-hammer. C.

Glân. "The bank of a river." *Polwhele. Glân* is a Celtic Cornish word, meaning, the bank, the side, or the brink of a river. The side of anything.

Glawer. The fish *Morrhua minuta.* N.E.C.

Glaws. Dried cow-dung, formerly used for fuel. *Tonkin.* It should be spelt *glose* or *gloas,* which is the Celtic Cornish for "dried cow-dung, (used as fuel.") *("Ha glose tha leskye."* And dry dung to burn. *Pryce.)*

Glaze. To stare hard at anything, or person. "What be'ee glazin at?"

Glen-ader. The cast skin of an adder, sometimes worn as an amulet. H.R.C. *Nader* is Celtic Cornish for adder, viper, snake.

Glidder. Glaze, or varnish, like white of egg, gum, &c.

Gliddery. Shiny, as the surface of a cake, or bunn when varnished with white of egg. Also, slippery.

Glint. To glance at, to catch a sight of. *Glent, Chaucer.*

Glumps. Sulks. "He's got the glumps." "He's in the glumps."

Glumpy. Sulky. *(Glombe,* Saxon, to look gloomy).

Glumped up. Sitting apart in the "sulks."

Gluthening up. Gathering into rain. "A common expression in Meneg." *Polwhele. Gluth, Glut* or *Glit* is Celtic Cornish for dew, a hoar frost, a rime.

Goad. Half a square yard of land.

Gob. A mass of expectorated phlegm. *(Gobbet,* a morsel, a bit, *Chaucer).*

Go-a-gooding. Poor old women of Polperro "go-a-gooding," travelling the parish over to collect materials for the Christmas cake, and pudding. C.

Goal. Slow, heavy pain. "A goalin pain." In Celtic Cornish *gelar* or *galar* means anguish.

Go-by-the-ground. A short little person.

God's cow. The lady-bird, (an insect). *Callington.*

Goffans. See **Coffins.**

Goggling for gapes. Looking foolishly amazed.

Goil. Cuttle fish. (C.) *Sepia officinalis.*

Golden chain. Bunches, or rather the natural rows of laburnum flowers.

Golles. By Golles! An exclamation. Hercules was worshipped by the name of Golion or Goles; one of the gates of a city in Spain was dedicated to Goles. Hence we discover the meaning of the oath of the common people of Cornwall. Aye and of gentlemen, when they say "By Golles!" i.e., "By Hercules." *Hogg's Fab. Hist. of Cornwall,* note p. 444.

Gommock. A fool.

Gone poor. Decayed, tainted, turned sour.

Gone to lie. Said of corn, or grass beaten down by rough weather.

Gone round land. Dead. **Gone dead.** Dead.

Good carne. Good rocks for fishing near. *Tonkin.*

Goodness. The richness, or fatness in food.

Goodspoon. A young brat. A "ne'er do well." J.W. *Lostwithiel.*

Goody. To prosper, to thrive. "Its sure to goody."

Goog. A cliff cavern. N.E.C.

Gook. A bonnet shade like the peak of a boy's cap, generally blue. Also, a bend in the neck, from an awkward habit of leaning the head down, and thrusting the face forwards. "He's got such a gook."

Goonhillies. A celebrated breed of small horses formerly bred on the Goonhilly downs in Cornwall. Norden, in his "Topographical and Historical description of Cornwall," and whose survey, says the Editor of the edition of 1728, was probably taken in 1584, states that, "There is a kinde of naggs bredd upon a mountanous and spatious peece of grounde, called Goon-hillye, lyinge betweene the sea coaste and Helston; which are the hardeste naggs and bestes of travaile for their bones within this kingdome, resembling in body for quantitie, and in goodnes of mettle, the Galloway naggs."

Goose-chick. A gosling. A symbol of exhaustion. "As weak as a goose-chick."

Gorry, or **Gurrie.** A large wicker flasket with a long handle on each side, and carried like a sedan chair.

Gorseddan. A place of elevation, whence it has been said, the Druids pronounced their decrees. *Gorsedd* is Celtic Cornish for a seat of judgment.

Goss. A tall reed growing in marshy places, or in shallow ponds. The boys used to make arrows of the stems. *Arundo phragmites.*

Goss. A fuss, a perplexity. M.A.C.

Goss. Moor, or wood *(cos).* *Dr. Bannister.*

Goss-moor. Great *(mawr)* moor *(cors)*; or wood *(cos)* moor. *Dr. Bannister.*

Gossawk. A lubber, a blundering fellow. "For loke how that a *goshauke* tyreth (feeds)." *Chaucer.*

Gothhomm, or **Gosshomm.** An expression of contempt, as if to say, "Go home," "Get away," "Get out, you fools." In Celtic Cornish *Gothoam* (Pryce), means fools. The word is curiously similar to gothhomm.

Gowk, or **Gook.** Somewhat like a Quaker's bonnet in shape, with a "curtain" behind. It is of large size. Worn by mine, clay-work, and country girls, or women.

Gozzan, or **Gossan.** This is Celtic Cornish for rust, the rusty ochre of Iron. Also, the course, bed, broil, or back of a lode. Hence, "keenly gozzan," i.e., a promising lode.

Gozzan. An old, rusty, scratch wig.

Grab. Very sour.

Grafted. Coated, or loaded with dirt. "Your nails are grafted with dirt."

Grail. A three-pronged fish spear. M.A.C.

Grainy. Sour-tempered, close-fisted, proud. "A grainy ould chap."

Grambler. A stony place. M.A.C.

Grammer-sow. See **Sow-pig.**

Gramfer, or **Granfer.** Grandfather.

Grange. See **Grunge.**

Grass. The surface at a mine, a miner's term. "Gone to grass," i.e., come up out of the mine.

Graving clouds. Clouds moving contrary to the wind below them. A sign of storm.

Grebe. A handful, a small portion.

Green sauce. The dock sorrel. *Rumex acetosa.* See **Sour-sauce, Sour-sabs,** and **Sour-sops.**

Greet. Dry earth.

Greet-board. The earth board of a plough.

Greglan. See **Griglan.**

Grend. A twist or kink in a chain. *Mousehole.*

Grendin-stone. Grinding stone.

Grey. A badger. *Polwhele.*

Grey-bird. The song thrush.

Gribble. The part of the tree for grafting on. C.

Griddlin. Sitting "hanging over" the fire, and so warming nose and knees together.

Griglan, or **Grig.** Heath, or ling. (At St. Agnes heath flowers are called "browth of the griglans." H). Celtic Cornish words, *Grig,* heath; *griglans,* sticky heath. *Borlase.*

Griggan. A grass-hopper. M.A.C.

Gripe. The ditch along the foot of a hedge.

Gripy. Greedy, stingy, miserly.

Grishens. See **Growshans.**

Grizzle. To grin. *Grisla* is a Celtic Cornish word, and means to grin like a dog, and *a grisla,* grinning. "What be'ee grizzlin at?" "You ould grizzla."

Grobman. A bream two thirds grown. *Polwhele.*

Grock. To pull, to tweak; as to pull the hair up over the ears. H.R.C.

Groot. The same as **Greet.** Q.V. *Callington.*

Growan. Soft granite-like ground. Also, a name for granite. Celtic Cornish, *grow,* gravel or sand; or *grean,* gravel.

Growder. A soft kind of decomposed granite used for scouring.

Growts, grownds, grudgings, growshans, grooshans, or **grishens.** Terms used of coffee grounds, dregs or sediment in a cup of tea, &c. Probably derived from the Celtic Cornish word *grow,* sand.

Groyne. A seal. M.A.C.

Grunge, or **Grange.** To grind the teeth, to make a grinding sound in chewing.

Guag. Rubbish is so called by shoaders. *Tonkin.* A Celtic Cornish word. Pryce says "when the tinners hole into a piece of ground, which has been wrought before, though filled up again, they call it *holing in gwag.*"

Guff. See **Caff.**

Guinea-pigs. Small white cowrie shells.

Guis. "An old sow that hath had many pigs." *Polwhele.* It is a Celtic Cornish word.

Guise-dance. A kind of carnival or *bal-masqué* at Christmas.

Polwhele calls it the *guise* or *disguise* dance, for so the Cornish pronounce *guise* (geez). "This dance answers to the 'mummers' of Devon, and the morrice dancers of Oxfordshire," &c. In Celtic Cornish *ges,* means mockery, a jest.

Gulge. To drink to excess.

Gur. The shanny fish. C.

Gurt. A gutter. *Callington.*

Gurgo, or **Gurgy.** A low hedge, or rough fence. *Gur* in Celtic Cornish means an end, an extremity, and *ge,* a fence.

Gurgoes. Long narrow lanes. W.F.P. In Celtic Cornish *gur*, end, extremity; and *go*, a particle used with words to denote a progress towards. *Williams.*

Gurrie. A handbarrow for fish; a wicker basket with handles as in a sedan chair.

Gut. A narrow gap, trench, or passage.

Guts. A contemptuous term for a glutton.

Gwaith. "The breast hook of a boat." M.A.C.

Gweans. See **Queens.**

Gwenders, or Wonders. A tingling or stinging of the extremities from cold. In Celtic Cornish *gwan* means a sting.

Haaf saved. Half witted. See **Half baked.**

Hadgy-boor. See **Hedgy-boar.**

Haestis, or Hastis. Hurriedly, hastily, impatiently.

Haestis-go-thurra. The diarrhœa.

Hag. A mist.

Hager. Ugly, deformed, rough, foul, evil, fierce, cruel. This is a Celtic Cornish word. See **Agar.**

Hailer. A thief's confederate. "The hailer is as bad as the stailer" (stealer).

Hair-pitched. Bald. *Newlyn.* T.C.

Haivery. Miserly, greedy of money, envious. From the Celtic Cornish *avi*, *avey*, or *avy*, spite, envy, discord.

Hale. To haul, drag, or pull. "Hal'en op," i.e., pull him up.

> "Hither *hale* the misbelieving Moor."
> "I'll *hale* the dauphin headlong from his throne."
>
> *Shakspere.*

Halish. (Pale. M.A.C.) Ailing, weak.

Half-baked, or **Haaf saved.** Said of one who is silly, and stupid.

Hallyhoe. The skipper fish.

Hall Monday. The day before Shrove Tuesday. See **Nicka-nan night.**

Halvan. Refuse of the ore after spalling. *Tonkin.*

Halvaner. One who receives half the produce for his labour. E.N.

Hall-nut. Hazel nut.

Hallan-tide. All saints' day.

Haly-caly. To throw things to be scrambled for. M.A.C.

Hame. A circle of straw rope. A straw horse-collar. (A hame is used to fasten the fore leg of a sheep to prevent him from breaking fence. C.)

Hange. (Pronounced, hanjh). See **Head and Hange.**

Hanges, or **Hange.** The heart, liver, and lights of a sheep. Those with the head are called "Head and hange," or "head and hinge," (or hinges.)

Hardah. Elvan rock. C.

Hard-head. The refuse of tin after smelting. The plantain. J.W.

Hard-heads. Centaury. *Centaurea nigra.*

Hare's meat. The common wood sorrel. *Oxalis acetosella.*

Harve. To harrow. **Harve.** A harrow.

Hatter-flitter. A jack-snipe. M.A.C.

Hauen. Haven. *Carew.*

Havage. Family origin, or stock. "He comes of a bad havage."

Hayned up. Land left to grow a crop of grass for hay.

Haysing. Poaching. C.

Haybands. About 50 or 60 years ago, countrymen in wet weather "wore haybands," i.e., ropes of hay coiled closely round each leg to keep it dry. Mackintosh was not known then. ("Haybands up to his knees." *Tregellas).*

Head and Hange, or **Head and Hinges.** The head, lungs, liver, and heart of an animal.

Heaps. Thus said of an egotist, "He thinks *heaps* of himself."

Heaver, or **Hayver.** A grass seed. *Lolium perenne.*

Heaving, Haiving, or **Eaving.** The stones (large slate stones) becoming wet from change of temperature, are *heaving.* Also said of ice beginning to thaw. See **Un-eave** and **Giving.**

Heavy. Close grained, as *heavy* bread, &c.

Heel-tap. The leather heel of a boot, or shoe. Also, the metal shield, or "scute" of the heel of a boot, or shoe. Also, the last few drops of a glass of grog. **To heel-tap,** to repair the heel of a shoe, or boot.

Hedgy-boar, or **Hadgy-boor.** A hedgehog.

Hellier, Heller, or **Healer.** A slater of roofs.

Helling. A slated roof.

Helling-stone. A slate stone used for roofs.

Henderment, or **Handerment.** Obstruction, delay, hindrance.

Hepping-stock, or **Hipping-stock.** An erection, or stand of three or four steps, for more easily mounting a horse. In Lancashire it is called Horse-block, or Horse-stone.

Herby-pie. A pie made of spinach, bits (a herb so called very much like spinach), parsley, mustard-cress, pepper-cress, young onions, and lettuce, with some slices of bacon, and a little milk. Seasoned with pepper and salt.

Herring-bairn. A sprat. C.

Hevah. See **Hubba** and **Hevah.**

Hevval, or **Hewal.** See **Eval.**

Hez. A swarm of bees. (Also *glez*). *Polwhele.*

Hick-mal. See **Ekky-mowl.**

Hiding. A thrashing. A "tanning."

Higher-quarter people. People from the uplands near a town. *St. Austell.*

Hile. The beard of corn.

Hilla, or **Hillah.** The nightmare. *Borlase.* It is a Celtic Cornish word.

Hippety-hop, or **Hippety-hoppety,** A jumping kind of walk or gait.

Hoase. Forbear. *Carew.*

Hobbies. A kind of hawk. *Carew.*

Hobbin, or **Hobban.** Dough, raisins, and fat, baked in the form of a pasty; also called **Figgy-duff,** Q.V.

Hobble. A band for the legs of animals to prevent their breaking fence or running away.

Hobbler. An unlicensed pilot. Two or three men own a boat, so as to tow a vessel in with a rope. They share the *hobbles,* or profits between them.

Hobbelers. This so spelt by Hals, is, he says, the name given to the men and horses posted on the Cornish beacons, to give notice on any alarm of the approach of an enemy. On the beacon was a pile of wood, or barrel of pitch elevated on a pole, and fired in the night; or in daytime a smoke was raised from some combustible matter.

Hoddy-mandoddy. A simpleton. U.J.T. (*Hodmadod, N. of England*).

Hoggan, or **Fuggan.** A pork pasty. A tinner's pasty. *Hogen,* Celtic Cornish. *Pryce.*

Hogget. A two year old ewe. **Hog lamb.** A sheep under a year old.

Holidays. Parts left untouched in dusting. "Don't leave any holidays."

Hollibubber. One who earns his living out of the refuse of the slate quarries at Delabole. C.

Holla-pot. See **Tom-holla.**

Holm. The holly-tree.

Holm-scritch. The missel-thrush. C.

Holt, or **Holster.** A lurking place, a place of concealment. A place of rendezvous. (*Hulstred, Saxon,* hidden).

Honey-pin. A peculiar sweet apple. *Bottrell.*

Hood, or **Ood.** Wood.

Hoop. The bullfinch. C.

Hopps. Small bits, as, "Hopps of gold." *Carew.*

Hooraa! Wurraa! or **Wurraw!** Hurrah! or Huzza! A word common to many nations. Jewish, *hosanna;* Old French, *huzzer,* (to shout aloud); Dutch, *husschen;* Russian, *hoera* and *hoezee. Hurrar* is a corruption of *Tur-aie* (Thor aid), a battle cry of the Northmen. *Wace, "Chronicle." (Brewer's Dicty).*

Hootin. Blubbering, "Stop tha hootin', dew."

Hooze, or **Hoozy.** Hoarse. *Hoz,* Celtic Cornish.

Hooze, or **Hoost.** A bronchial disease in cattle.

Hoozle-pipe. See **Oozle.**

Hoppety bed. A game, hopscotch. In playing it, a figure like the diagram is marked out on the ground, on a space about 9 or 10 feet long, and about 4 feet wide. The figures are for explanation.

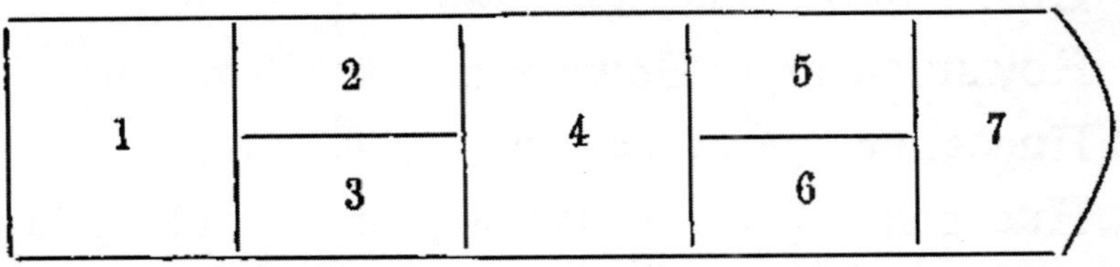

A small stone being placed at No. 1, the player, standing on one foot, has to tip the stone, in hopping, from bed to bed, as numbered. If the stone go beyond the next space, or over the line, or, if the player cease to stand on one leg, he is "out." (Pan bed. *Truro).*

Horn-fish. The gar-fish. *Borlase.*

Horny-wink. Plover, (in the east); slugs, (in the west). *Dr. Bannister.*

Horny-winky. A toad. *H. J. Royal Instit. of Cornwall.*

Horny-winky. Desolate, outlandish, as of a place fit only for "horny-winks and lap-wings." J.W.

Hosen. Stockings. In Celtic Cornish, *hosan*, a stocking.

Housey. *Ennui* from too much confinement in the house, "feeling housey."

Hoss in the lode. When a piece of "dead," ground (matrix) is found in an expansive form in the lode, they say "the lode have taken hoss," (horse). E.N.

Horse adder. The horse fly, the dragon fly.

Housen. This old plural form for *houses* is nearly obsolete.

Hov. Heave. In Spenser, *Hove.*

Howsumever, or **Howsomdever.** Howsoever.

Huccaner. A wood corner. M.A.C.

Hucksen. The knuckles, or joints. "Muck up to the hucksen."

Hubba! and **Hevah!** "Great excitement prevailed here (St. Mawes). The cry of Hubba! rang through the town, and quantities of pilchards were reported to be passing through the stems. The seines were soon manned and pulled with all possible speed."

Cornishman, Oct. 13, 1881.

"The welcome sound of Hevah! was heard at St. Ives yesterday, and the boats on the look-out for pilchards were instantly on the alert."

Western Morning News, Oct. 14, 1881.

These words, Hubba and Hevah, require a little notice. *Hubba* is wrong, it should be *Ubba* as written in ancient manuscripts. It is a Celtic Cornish word, meaning, in this place, here. In *Ubba* we seem to have the sound of the word Hubbub. Anciently *Ubba* was written *Ubma,* and still more anciently it was *omma,* in which we have some of the sound of the word *hum,* a continued sound, or murmur.

Hevah by the change of a letter would be *heuah* or *hewah,* just as we find *Eval* to be pronounced *Yeul* or *Yewl* and *Yewal,* words for a three-pronged dung-fork.

In *heuah* we seem to have the sound of *hue* as in "Hue and cry."

Whether the origin of the word **Hevah**! can be traced to **Evoe**! is not very clear, yet the following quotation by Beal (Britain and the Gael) may be interesting to the reader.

"Strabo (born about A.D. 19), speaks of an island near Britain, where sacrifice was offered to *Ceres and Proserpine*, in the same manner as at Samothrace; and in the words of Dionysius Perieg, (lines 1225, 1228), or of his translator," it is said,

> "As the Bistonians on Apsinthus banks
> Shout to the clamorous Eiraphiates;
> Or, as the Indians on dark-rolling Ganges,
> Hold revels to Dionysos the noisy,
> So do the British women shout **Evoe**!

Finally, it may be observed that *ubba* is also written *uppa* (but pronounced *oopa)* a word or outcry also meaning, in this place, here. See **Uppa, uppa, holye.**

Hud, or Hull. A shell, as of a nut, &c. In Celtic Cornish *hudha,* to cover, to hide.

Hud. The dry crust or scrab on a sore.

Huel. A mine, a work. *Hwel, wheal, wheyl, whel,* and *whyl* are Celtic Cornish for the same.

Huer. A man stationed on some look-out place near the sea to give notice of the position of a shoal of pilchards. Dr. Paris, in describing the Pilchard fishery. *(Guide to Mount's Bay and the Land's End,* note, p. 150), says that Tunny-fish were caught by a similar process in the Archipelago. "Ascendebat quidam (Anglice the *Huer*, Græce *Thunoscopos)* in ultum promontorium, unde Thunnorum gregem speculeretur, quo viso, signum piscatoribus dabat, qui ratibus totum gregem includebant." Vide Blomfield's Notes on the Persæ of Eschylus, p. 148. The seine was as familiar to the Athenians, as the Pilchard fishery is to the inhabitants of Cornwall; and it is said that Eschylus took great delight in witnessing it," and they had a "huer" who did exactly as in Cornwall.

Hummock. A stout, unwieldy woman. M.A.C.

Hurle. A filament. *Ourlen,* silk in Celtic Cornish.

Hurling. A game of throwing or hurling a silvered or silver-gilt ball, played by two opposing parties, each striving to get the ball to a goal. An especial game at St. Columb. This is one of the manly and exciting games for which Cornwall is deservedly famous.

Hurling-ball motto. The ball is a round piece of timber about three inches diameter, covered with plated silver, sometimes gilt. It had usually a motto in the Cornish tongue alluding to the pastime, as, "*Guare wheag yw guare teag,*" i.e., fair play is good play. A ball at Paul had this motto, "*Paul Tuz, whek Gware Tek heb ate buz Henwis,* 1704." In English thus, "Paul men, fair play, without hatred, is sweet play." *Lake's Parochial Hist. of Cornwall.*

Hurrisome. Hasty. See **Haestis.**

Hurts, or **Herts.** Whorts, whortleberries. See **Whorts.**

Huscen. Scolded. T.W.S.

Iles. Flukes. *Distoma Hepatica.* The cause of the rot in sheep. Also the name given to a plant, *Rosa solis,* by eating which it was supposed the disease was caused. *Tonkin.* The *plant* is not injurious until it becomes infested with the ova of the "fluke."

Illek. The gurnard fish. *Carew.* See **Elleck.**

Ill-wished. Bewitched.

Inchin. Encroaching inch by inch. Boys cried out at play, "No inchin, no inchin."

Ingrossers. Persons who bought wheat at eighteen gallons the bushel, and delivered the same at sixteen gallons the bushel. *Carew.*

Ire. Iron.

Ishan. The dust, (douse) or husks from winnowed corn. F.W.P. It is a Celtic Cornish word and spelt *ision,* or *usion,* meaning, chaff, or husks of corn.

Iss. Yes. "Iss a es," i.e., Yes he is.

Issterday. Yesterday.

I-facks! Yes faith! In the north of England I-fakins!

Iss fath! Iss fay! or **Iss fey!** Yes sure! *Fay* and *Fey* are Celtic Cornish words meaning, faith.

> "Whether sayest thou this in earnest or in play!
> Nay, quod Arcite, in earnest by my *fay.*" *Chaucer.*
>
> "By my *fay.*" *The London Prodigal.*

(Ru'm fay! or (Re-'m) "*Rum fey,*" by my faith, is also Celtic Cornish).

Jack. Almost if not quite disused in Cornwall. The well known name of the machine for turning a spit in roasting; worked by a weight with pullies, by which the spit was turned round

Jack Harry's lights. Phantom lights preceding a storm, superstitiously thought to take the form of the vessel doomed to be lost.

Jack-o-lent. A dirty, slovenly fellow. C.

Jack with the lantern. Will-o-the-wisp. *Ignis fatnus.*

Jacky. Too much Black Jack or Blende in the ore. "For the ore was waik and *jacky* in the stoan.

Tregellas.

Jacky-ralph. A wrasse. M.A.C.

Jaffle. A handful. See **Yaffle.**

Jail, or **Jaale.** To walk fast. "Jailing along."

Jaller, or **Jallishy buff.** Yellow. See **Yaller.**

Jan-jansy. Two-faced. M.A.C. Janus-like.

Jelly-flower. Gilly-flower, the stock. *Gilofre, Chaucer.*

Jews' ears. Some kinds of fungi. C.

Jews' fish. The halibut, *hippoglossus vulgaris.* Called the Jews' fish because of its being a favourite part of their diet. (At Plymouth in the first half of the century the brill was always called the halibut).

(*The Cornishman,* 1882).

Jews' house. A very ancient smelting place for tin.

Polwhele.

Jews' pieces. Very ancient blocks of tin. *Polwhele.*

Jews' works. Very ancient stream-works "are now stiled, Jews' works, and were used to be stiled in Cornwall "*attal sarazin,*" or the leavings of the Saracens." Q.V. *Polwhele.*

Jick, or **Juck; Yux, Yuck,** or **Yock, Yex,** (**Yoxe** *Saxon, and in Chaucer).* To hiccough. See **Yock** or **Yuck.**

Jiggety-jig. A jog-trot style of travelling in a shaky vehicle, "gwain jiggety-jig."

Jigging. A process of sifting the ore from the refuse in a tub, or tank of water.

Jimmery chry! An exclamation of surprise. Can it be believed?! In Celtic Cornish we have *krysy*, to believe, to have faith in.

Jinny-ninny. A simpleton.

Jinny-quick, or **Jenny-quick.** Italian irons. When a woman wants to "do" her caps and collars, she calls for the Jinny-quick.

Joan the Wad. The name of one of the fairies. *Wad*, Celtic Cornish, a forefather.

John-jaick. A snail. *Callington.*

Jonnick. "That's jonnick," i.e., that's jolly.

Josing. Scolding. "Jawing."

Joustin. Shaking. "A good joustin."

Jowder, jowter, chowder, and **jouster.** An itinerant fish-dealer who carries the fish on the back in a *cowal* (Q.V.) Also called *back-jouster* (Q.V.) In later years a donkey cart has been much used instead.

Jowds, or **Jowders.** Pieces, bits. "Tes scat oal to jowders," i.e., It is broken all to pieces.

Jowlin. A dull, gnawing pain is so called, as "I've a jowlin tooth ache."

Juck. See **Jick,** and **Yock,** or **Yuck.**

Jumpin. Thus used, "a jumpin little scamp." A little humbugging fellow is a "jumpin" or a "rumpin" fellow. A term of contempt.

Jung. Young. *Jungk,* Celtic Cornish, young.

Junket. New (or raw) milk fresh from the cow, curdled by rennet. Clotted cream is laid on the top, and the whole flavoured with nutmeg and rum. Elsewhere junket means a cheese cake, a sweet-meat, properly made of curd. The word is the Italian *giuncate* (curd, or cream cheese), so called because carried on junk or bull rushes *(giunco).* *Brewer.*

"You know there want no *junkets* at the feast."
Shakspere "Taming of the Shrew."

Just alive. Mining term, meaning a small appearance of ore in the stone.

Jyst. A joist or beam. *Jyst* and *gyst* are Celtic Cornish words for a beam.

Kager, Keggas, or **Kai-yer.** Wild parsnip, wild carrot. H.R.C. The ancient Cornish called hemlock *kegas.*

Kan Kayers. Two or three confederates who unite to undervalue, or make fictitious offers, and praise anything they wish to sell; tricksters. *Bottrell.*

Karn, or **Carn.** The solid, hard, or rocky ground. See **Carn.**

Katty-ball. A child's ball for playing with.

Keamy. Mould on a liquid surface.

Kayer. A coarse sieve for winnowing corn. M.A.C.

Keddened, (or **Cabagged,** B.V.) Covered over with mud or dust. W.F.P. *Kaggled.* H.R.C. (See **Geagled.**)

Keels, or **Kails.** Skittles. Ninepins.

Keel-alley, or **Kail-alley.** A place for playing at ninepins or skittles.

Keem. To comb, as of the hair.

Keeming comb. A small-tooth comb. M.A.C.

Keenly. Promising in appearance, as of a lode. "Keenly gozzan." Also, clever, as, "he did that putty keenly."

Keenly-gozzan. See **Keenly.**

Keggled. See **Geagled.**

Keg-nail, or **Kag-nail.** An ill shaped toe or finger nail. A thickened toe-nail.

Keeve, or **Kieve.** A great tub, or vat; also, a potatoe *cave*, i.e., a place where potatoes are heaped and buried with earth. Perhaps *cave* mispronounced, in this sense.

Kelter. "In good kelter," i.e., in good condition, as of cattle.

Kendle teening. Candle lighting time. To tine, or teen, is to light, as "teen the candle."

Kenack. A worm. (A weakly child. W.C.B.) *Kinak, Borlase.* It is Celtic Cornish.

Kennin. A white cloudy spot on the cornea, like a thin film. (**Kennel.** M.A.C.) *Ken* is a Celtic Cornish word meaning the peel, or skin of anything.

Kennin herb. A plant, the decoction of which is used for the cure of a *kennin. Polwhele* says it is Crow-foot. *Ranunculus.*

Keeping company. Phrase used of lovers after "popping the question."

Keep on, keeping on, or **keeping on keeping on.** Idiomatic phrases used of a scold who won't cease talking. Also used of a bully.

Kep-kep-kep. A call to make a horse come near one. (See back for this in "*The words compared with Chaucer.*")

Kern. To curdle.

Kerned. Concreted. "He has also seen gold kerned about spar," that is, fixed and concreted on the quartz. *Borlase.*

Kerning. Term used of corn as it ripens after the period of blossoming.

Kert. A cart. It is a Celtic Cornish word. Also *caart.*

Kib. v. To repair, as of a hedge, with thorns, &c.

Kibbed. Ground fenced off with bushes, furze, &c. *Polwhele.*

Kibble. An iron mine bucket, used up and down a mine shaft. (*Kibbal*, a bucket, a little tub). *Borlase.* A Celtic Cornish word.

Kibby heels. Sore heels. Heels with chilblains on them.

Kick and sprawl. The courage and power to resist. "If people tried to hand him over to any one, he would soon let them see that he had some *kick and sprawl* in him."

Kicker. A small mizen used by fishing boats. W.F.P.

Kicklish. Ticklish. A dangerous state, or position. A delicate or difficult job, as, "a kicklish job," "he is standing in a kicklish place."

Kicky. To stammer.

Kiddaw. The guillem. A sea bird. M.A.C.

Kiddliwink, Kidleywink, Kiddle-a-wink, and **Tiddly-wink.** These are names for a beer-house. The term Kiddle (*kettle*)-a-wink is perhaps the correct term. At a conversazione at Laregan in 1881, Mr. F. Holman gave the origin of the word thus. "At the time the name arose the beershops were not all kept by honest dames, for they were then fond of keeping a little smuggled brandy which was put in the kettle, so as to deceive the officers of the law, and those who were in the secret, when they came into the room, and wanted some of the brandy, would *wink at the kettle.* Hence arose the term "Kettle and wink," or Kidley-wink." *Cornishman, Nov.* 17, 1881.

Kiddle, Kiddly, or **Kiddlin.** To be engaged about various little jobs. "Always kiddlin about."

Kidge. To stick, to unite, to "chum" together.

Kidney. To agree together, to be *chums* together, to confederate, as, "they kidney together very well." (**Kidge.** M.A.C.)

Kiggal. A spindle. *Bottrell.* This is a Celtic Cornish word, spelt *Kygel* or *Kigel,* and meaning a distaff.

Killas. Clay slate, the "schist" of the geologists.

Killeck. A stone used as an anchor for punts. W.F.P.

Killi-more. Earth-nuts. *Halliwell.* Grove-nuts. *Polwhele.* *Kelli* or *Killi* is a Celtic Cornish word meaning a grove, and *mor* berries. *Moran,* a berry.

Kimbly. Couch, in his History of Polperro, says that "at weddings it was formerly the custom when the party set out for church, for one person to be sent before with a piece of bread or cake in his or her hand, (a woman was usually selected) and this was presented to the first person met in the procession. The gift was called the "kimbly," and was also given at births to the person who brought the first news to those interested in the new arrival." Kimbly was also given to the one who brought first news in the smuggling times. "If us catches sight of 'em (smugglers) comin in we'll rin down and tell the news, and you shall have *kimbly* for telling it."

Mrs. Parr's Adam & Eve.

Kings. The name used at Redruth for donkeys. *Corn. Telegraph* 1879. An ill applied name to so patient an animal.

Kip. A small net used to hang vegatables in. W.C.B.

Kipes. See **Giblets.**

Kipper. A male salmon. C.

Kiskey. "A dried brittle stem." "A withered *kiskey* of a man" M.A.C.

Kist-vean. A Celtic stone built chest or burial place. It is Celtic Cornish and reads literally *chest little.*

Kit. A smear. **To kit.** To dab. *Halliwell.*

Kit. Kith or kin "I'll turn out the whole kit," i.e., the whole lot of them. In Celtic Cornish *keth*, the common people; also, *chet*, a companion, a fellow.

Kitey. Flighty, hair-brained, impulsive.

Kittens. The kidneys.

Kittereen. A primitive omnibus. "The *Kit-tereen* was a car that ran between Penzance and Truro, set up by Christopher Treen," (Kit Treen.) J.W.

Kitting. Stealing ore. **To kitt.** To steal ore.

Kitty-bags. Coarse cloths bound round the legs of labourers to keep them dry. They used also to wear straw or hay rope coiled round the legs as a protection in rough weather. See **Hay-bands.**

Kivver. A cover. *Kevere, Chaucer.*

Knacked. Stopped working, said of a mine; also to dissuade, as, "I've a knacked that out uv hes hade."

Knap. The top, or summit of a hill.

Knick. To cheat.

"Hes stoanin wights and temberin scaales,
I'm sure they air but smaal,
Beware of Moases Tonkyn,
Or he will *knick* ee oal." *J. T. Tregellas.*

Knot cow. A cow without horns, having a little knot or knob on the head instead of them.

Knuckle down. To submit, to yield, to "give in."

Ko. See **Co.**

Koffen. See **Coffins.**

Lace. A rood, or perch of land. M.A.C.

Lace. This is a Celtic Cornish word meaning to lick or slap; to throw about; to cudgel; to lash. Pronounced *lak* in the old Cornish, as, "*me ath lak,*" I will lace thee.

Laggen. V. To splash in the water. *Mousehole.*

Lagging. Dragging in the mud, also **Ligging.** Q.V.

Laister. The yellow water-iris. M.A.C.

Lake. Used of a sea cove, as Gwavas lake. (A brook is so called at Lostwithiel. J.W.)

Lambs' legs. The snivel of a child's neglected nose.

Lambs' tails. The blossoms of the crack willow. *Salix fragilis.*

Lamb-y or **Lammy-pie.** "*Lammy* pie isn't made of *lamb*"! as the name would imply. The following tale will explain. It is fully given in Warner's Tour through Cornwall in 1809. "A Cockney who had a mind to see the world, strayed down as far as St. Ives, where he entered an inn and called for supper. Have you any beef for a steak? No! Any veal for a cutlet? No! Any mutton for a chop? No! What! no meat! No please your honour, except a nice *lammy-pie*, which was baked to day. The Cockney licked his lips at the prospect of a cold *lamb-pie*, and ordered it up. Hunger was his sauce; he ate heartily, and relished his meal exceedingly. He passed the night in horrors, but had no idea they arose from the indigestible quality of his supper, till the next morning, when he was about to mount his horse. 'Well Sir,' said the ostler, seeing he was a stranger, 'how did you like missuses *lammy-pie* last night? Excellent,' replied he, 'twas the best *lamb* I ever tasted. Lord love ye,' returned John, 'it was not *that; lammy-pie* isn't made of *lamb.* Why what the devil was it then? exclaimed the horrified traveller. 'Why our poor *kiddy*, to be sure,' returned the other, 'who *died* yesterday," This dainty dish is obsolete.

Lamper. A lamprey.

Lampered. Mottled, stained. "Lampered all over with dirt."

Lannard. A kind of hawk. *Carew.*

Lantern fish. The *solea lævis* or *Arnoglossus*, so called because it is a very transparent sole.

Lap, or **Lop.** To throb, as in pain. (*Lap,* to beat. *Garland.*)

Lap, or **Cat-lap.** Tasteless, insipid fluid, or drink.

Lappy. To lap.

Lappior. A dancer. This is a Celtic Cornish word.

Larrence. (St. Lawrence). "He is as lazy as Larrence."

Larrikins. Mischievious young fellows, larkers. "Mischievious larrikins who pull the young trees down." *The Cornishman.*

Lashin, or **Lasher.** A very large thing, a lot or plenty.

Lash. To throw anything down violently, as "he lashed it down." To pour, as of rain.

Lash. Bait cut from the tail of a mackerel. C.

Lasking. Keeping near the coast, a fisherman's term. B.V. *Mousehole.*

Latteen, Lattin, or **Lattice.** Names for tin-plate.

Lattice. The vegatable lettuce.

Lattis. A milk-pail. *Penwith, in the Antiquary.* Probably from *lait,* which besides being the French for milk, is also a Celtic Cornish word, and it is "the old orthography of *leyth* or *lĕth* as written in the "Ordinalia." *Williams's Cornish Dicty.*

Launder, or **Lander.** A water shute of a building.

Lauch. A sloppy mess, any ill combined liquid food. Beef tea and treacle, would be a *lauch* if mixed.

Lawn, or **Lawen.** "A large open mine-work in the back of a lode left in a dangerous state."

Towednack. T.C.

Leaping-stock. See **Hepping-stock.**

Leary, or **Lairy.** Faint and hungry, sinking from want of food. In use in Devon and Dorset. In Wiltshire they say *leer*, (empty.)

Leasing. Picking stones. *Polwhele.*
Gleaning. C.

Leat. An artificial channel for a stream, as of water for a mill.

Leavers, or **Lavers.** Marsh Iris. Name probably from *levar*, Celtic Cornish, a book.

Lemon plant. The verbena.

Lent-lillies. Daffodils.

Lerrick. To flap about, "lerriking about."

Lerrup, or **Lerruper.** A slut. "A regular lerrup." A trollop.

Lerrupin. Trolloping. Also, something very big. "a lerrupin great turnip."

Lerrups. Rags, tatters, "all to lerrups."

Lerrups, or **Lirrups.** See **Bits.**

Lester-cock. A floating contrivance with a small sail to carry a "boulter" seawards in fishing. *Carew.* In Celtic Cornish *lester* means a ship, and *coc*, a boat.

Let. Hindrance, hesitation, delay. **To let.** to hinder, to stop or impede. This word was in use in Cornwall many centuries ago, although not Celtic; being the old English *let*, as in the following, "*Hep na moy let*," i.e., without any further delay.

Letterputch. A dirty untidy person; also a short hornpipe dance, but more with the heels than the toes. In Lancashire it is called *Letherty-patch.* An idle person stands on one's doorstep, hands in pockets, and every now and then kicks up his heels to this dance. Those within, annoyed at the sound cry out, "there goes letherty-patch again with his, rat-tat, rat-tat, ratty-tatty, rat-tat-tat. Also spelt *letterpooch*, and *lutterpouch.*

Leu, Lew, Leuth, or **Lewth.** (Synonymous). A sheltered place. It also means concealment, as "He's lying lew" i.e., lying hid, or "out of the way." *Hleo*, Celtic Cornish, sheltered.

Leustre. To plan. M.A.C.

Level. An adit.

Libbety-lat. The name of a game for children. M.A.C.

Libbings. "The webs of a waterfowl's feet." M.A.C.

Lick. A wipe of the face with a wet corner of a towel. "I've just given my face a lick."

Lide. The month of March. C.

Lidden. An oft told tale. "Harping on one string," always telling the same old story, "that old lidden again." *Leden,* Chaucer. *Ledden,* Spenser. In the North of England it means noise, din.

Lie. "Gone to lie" is said of grass or corn beaten down by rough weather. Also "The wind is gone to lie," i.e., it is become calm.

Lifting clome. Tippling, guzzling.

Lig, or Liggan. A deposit, as of seaweed, a detritus of dead leaves. *Ligge,* to lie down. *Chaucer. Lig* or *Liggen,* to lie. *Spenser.*

Lig, or Liggan. A kind of sea weed. M.A.C.
A manure formed of leaf deposit. C.

Liggy. Muddy, mucky, damp.

Ligging. Dragging along and smearing with mud; very wet, drizzly, as of the weather.

Lights. The lungs. "Rising of the lights" a phrase used of a choking feeling in the throat.

Likky pie. Pie of leeks, with bacon, and an egg or two broken over the hot contents.

Lilly-bangers. The "cup and dice" were so called at Penzance. M.A.C.

Lilly-banger stalls. "Until within the last 20 years it was the custom in Penzance on Easter Monday to bring out tables before the doors, on which were placed thick ginger-bread cakes with raisins in them, cups and saucers, &c., to be raffled for with *lilly-bangers*," and the stalls were thus named. M.A.C.

Limb, or **Lemb.** There is a curious use of this word, thus, "My face is my best limb." Also, a young brat, imp, hussy, or termagant. "She's a regular lemb." A she-devil.

Lime-kill. Lime kiln. "Which is hateful to me as the reek of a *lime-kill*."

Shakspere in the Merry Wives of Windsor.

Linsing, or **Linching.** A severe thrashing.

Ling. Anything very tough is said to be "as tough as old ling."

Linhay. An outhouse, or shed, with a lean-to roof and an open front.

Lintern. A lintel.

Lipsy. A lisping. "He speaks all lipsy."

Listin. The selvedge of cloth. Woven and used for hearthrugs, mats, &c. In Celtic Cornish *lysten,* a towel, a napkin.

Listing. Aching, throbbing with pain.

Living stream. A course or stratum of stones impregnated with tin. *Borlase.*

Loader. A double shaped apple.

Lob. "A stone tied to the end of a fishing line, to keep it fast when thrown from the rock." C.

Lobba, Loaber, Lubba. An awkward fellow, a lubber. U.J.T.

Locking bone. The hip joint. See **Pin** and **Whirlbone.**

Locus. Sweet stuff, sugar stick. See **Clidgy.**

Lodden or **Plodden.** A pool. M.A.C.

Lodes. Mineral veins. Most lodes, says Pryce, (*Mineralogia Cornubiensis*) are named from the minerals contained in them. He divides lodes into twelve different kinds as under.

1.—Gossan lode.	7.—Crystal lode.
2.—Peach lode.	8.—Killas lode.
3.—Scovan lode.	9.—Mundick lode.
4.—Caple lode.	10.—Black-jack lode.
5.—Pryan lode.	11.—Flookan lode.
6.—Quartz lode.	12.—Grouan lode.

To notice each separately would exceed the limits of this book. The following is characteristic.

"What's a caunter lode, Uncle Henney?" "Why thee'rt old enuff and ugly enuff, Old Tom, to knaw what a caunter lode es as well as I do." "Well, so I thoft I ded too," says Old Tom, "till I heer'd our boy Jacky readin in the *Mining Journal* that a caunter lode ded run north and south." "Then a couldn't be a caunter," says Uncle Henney, "but a cross-coose running right athurt, for a caunter is slanting, or caunting a east and west lode, and that is the meaning of a caunter lode, for suppose there is a east and west lode, and another lode running north-east and south-west—slanting the east and west lode—the north-east and south-west lode is a caunter, and that's all that can be said about'n I reckon," says Uncle Henncy; "and I say so too," says old Tom; "and I say," says Jan Tenby, "that lots of they larned men going about now a day don't know a caunter lode from a cross-coose, or a true tinker from Old Joe H—y's tinker." *From the "Cornishman."*

Lode-plot. A lode that underlies very fast; or horizontal, and may be rather called a *flat* lode. *Pryce.*

Lofty-tin. Rich, massive, rough tin ore, and not so weak or imperceptible in the stone, or in powder on the shovel. *Pryce.*

Logan rock. A logging rock. A rock so nicely balanced as to rock easily. Hence the name of the celebrated Logan rock. In Celtic Cornish, *logan*, shaking.

Loggers, or **Lugs.** The ears. M.A.C.

Long-cripple. A lizard. M.A.C. "In Devonshire, a snake." J.W. The slow worm or deaf adder of authors. *Borlase.*

Long-nose. The sea pike, the garfish.

Long oyster. The sea crayfish. *Polwhele.*

Long-stone. A tall (granite) stone, either monumental, directing, or boundary. Many such, of great antiquity, are still standing. In Celtic Cornish *maen heir*, battle stone, or *maen hir*, long stone. *Heir*, battle; *hir*, long.

Loobs. A Celtic Cornish mining term. The tin slime or sludge of the after leavings in washing tin. The slime "leavings."

Looby weather. Muggy weather. From the Celtic Cornish *loob,* slime, sludge.

Looch, or **Loach.** See **Lauch.** *Looch,* filth, refuse. *Hayle.* T.C.

Lootal. A tawdry gadabout. T.C.

Loppard, or **Lopper.** A lame person.

Loppety lop. A hopping, or lame-like movement, moving like a rabbit is to go "loppety lop."

Lopping. Throbbing with pain. "Its lopping very bad;" also walking lame, "lopping along."

Lop-lolly, Lob-lolly, or **Lobba.** A fag, a factotum; a lazy fellow.

Lords and Ladies. The common Arum or Cuckow pint. *Arum maculatum.*

Lost-slovan. From the Celtic Cornish *lost,* a tail, a rump. Commonly *low*-slovan. The beginning of an adit through the tail or end; that part which lies open like a trench before they drive underground. *Pryce.*

Louggy. Tired. *G. E. in the "Cornishman."*

Louning. Long, lank, thin. C.

Louster, or **Loustry.** To work hard. "He who can't scheme must louster."

Loustering. "A loustering man," i.e., a well-grown powerful man. "Loustering work," very hard work.

Love-entangle. The fennel flower. *Polwhele.*

Lubber-cocks. Turkey cocks. (**Lubber-leets.** M.A.C.)

Lucky-bone. The knuckle-bone of a leg of mutton.

Lud. "Sent all of a *lud,*" struck all of a heap. W.N.

Lugg. Undergrowth of weed, clover, &c., among corn.

Lug-worm. A salt-water worm, used for bait in fishing. Beach worm.

Lump. To resign oneself to what is inevitable. "If you don't like it you must lump it."

Lurk, or **Lurgy.** Laziness.
"Fever *lurk,* neither play nor work." *Brewer.*

Lurker. The small boat which attends the other boats in pilchard seining. The boat in which the master seiner goes.

Mabyers. Chickens, young fowls. In Celtic Cornish *mab* (filius) a son.

Maggots. Whims. "Such maggots!"

Maggoty pie. A mag-pie.

Maggy-owler, or **Maggy-owla.** The goat moth. *Cossus ligniperda.*

Mahogany. Gin sweetened with treacle.

Maidens' delight. See **Boys' love.**

Maiden Elder. The elder of the wood, or in Celtic Cornish *Scau-an-Câz.* The *Sambucus humilis* of Ray. *Borlase.*

Mait. To feed, "go and mait the pigs."

Mair. Sheaves of corn put "longitudinally, about 18 feet in length by 12 feet deep," because of very uncertain weather. *St. Levan.* H.R.C.

Mait banes. Broad beans. *Callington.*

Magpies. (Sayings about them.)

"One for *sorrow*; two for mirth,
Three for a wedding; four for a *birth.*"

Couch, Polperro.

"One for *anger*; two for mirth,
Three for a wedding; four for *death.*"

St. Austell.

Make-wise. A substitute, a pretence, a "make believe."

Making wise. Pretending to do a thing.

Male. The fish shanny, *Blennius pholis.* C.

Malkin. A rag mop for clearing the ashes from an oven. A dirty person.

Manshun bread. Small bun shaped loaves, mauchets. M.A.C.

Man-engine. A machine used in deep mines, to bring the miners up or down the shaft, and to avoid the fatigue of using the ladders. Although differently constructed it serves as a "lift" for the men. Invented about 40 or 50 years ago.

Marchant May's little summer. A fine autumn.

Marinade. A term used of fish cured or cooked in a particular way in vinegar, with bayleaves and spice. "Marinaded pilchards."

Marlion. A kind of hawk. *Carew.* (*Merlion*, a merlin, a sort of hawk. *Chaucer.*)

Mashes. Large quantities, lots, as, "Mashes of mait." (meat.)

Massy! Aw! massy! Exclamations, just as Mercy! or Grammercy! (*Mascie*, by my faith. *Chaucer.*)

Maunge. To chew noisily, to munch. (*Monche*, *Chaucer.*)

Maur. See **Mor** or **More.** A root.

Maw. "A sugary maw." See **Wad.**

May-bee. A cockchafer. M.A.C.

May-bird. The whimbrel. C.

Mayburn. A kind of bird. *Marburan* (?) is Celtic Cornish for a Raven.

May-games. Frolics, tricks, practical jokes.

Máy-gemmin. Frolicsome, silly, childish. "Such máygemmin ways."

Maazlin. Knocked foolish. T.W.S.

Mazed. Greatly bewildered, downright mad.

Maazedish, or **Maazedy.** Maddish.

Mazed antic. A wild, crazy, foolish person.

Mazegary, Mazegerry, or **Mazejerry.** Crazy, half mad.

Mazejerry pattick, or **Mazegerry pattick.** A mad simpleton. U.J.T.

Meader. A mower. *Polwhele. Meder* is a Celtic Cornish word, and means a reaper, a mower.

Meara-geeks. Noisy or obstinate people.

Hals (A.D. 1736) says, "*Camborne*, signifies an arched burne, or well-pit of water .... to which young people, and some of the elder sort, make frequent visits .... in order to wash and besprinkle themselves, out of an opinion of its great virtue and sanctity, forsooth!"

Those sprinkled "are called by the inhabitants *merrasicks.* These again by others are called *mearagaks*, alias *moragiks;* that is to say, persons straying, rash, fond, obstinate." In Celtic Cornish *gycke* or *gyc* means noise; and *mêre*, much.

Meas. "A meas of herrings," i.e., 505 herrings.

Meat-earth. The natural soil or surface of the land. "A load of good meat earth."

Meddick. An emetic. *Medhec* is a Celtic Cornish word, and means a physician. Also *medhecnaid*, physic.

Melliers. The axles of the frame used in washing ores.

Mên-an-tol. A holed stone. (See Cornish History.) In Celtic Cornish, *maen*, stone, and *toll*, a hole, a perforation.

Mêneolas. A fisherman's original kind of wooden box stove, "filled with clay and stones" on which to cook. W.F.P. Mênolas. H.R.C. In Celtic Cornish, *mâen*, stone; and *olas*, a hearth, i.e., hearthstone.

Mên scryfa. An inscribed stone (See Cornish History.) In Celtic Cornish, *mâen*, stone; and *screfa*, to write.

Merle. A chain link. M.A.C.

Mermaid's purses. Brown, purse-shaped cases often found on the sea beach.

Merry-dancers. The Northern lights. *Aurora borealis.* So called because of their undulatory motion.

Merryman. The clown at a Circus or Theatre.

Merry sole. The French sole-(fish.)

Meryan. An ant. W.F.P. (*Meryan* is a plural noun and means, ants. *Murrian* is the true Celtic Cornish plural for ants; and *murrianen* or *menwionen*, for an ant.)

Metheglin. Mead. Honey and water boiled together and fermented and flavoured with spice. This is the name used in Cornwall; *mead* was almost an unknown word there. It is a Celtic Cornish word from *medh*, mead, or *meith*, whey, and *whegol* or *huegol*, all sweet.

As if to say, "the all sweet mead," or whey. In Wales they call it *mezyglen.*

In Sanscrit are the words *madhu, mada, mad,* to intoxicate, which compare with *mead* (or medh.)

Mewed. "Scattered by fright." T.C. *Sennen.*

Mews. Moss. W.T.A.P.

Mica. In the china clay works this is the name given to the coarser, or inferior clay, which is deposited in the mica pits. The finer clay, held in suspension in water, passes on into the large "clay pit." It is the washing away of this "mica," that makes the rivers look like milk. In reality "mica" contains a very large proportion of porcelain clay, and therefore is often saved, and sold at a lower price.

Mica-pits. The clay in the *stopes,* (Q.V.), held in suspension by water, having deposited the sand, flows into shallow, narrow, but long pits; as the clay fluid passes slowly on, the mica deposits in these *mica pits,* and the pure clay passes as it leaves these pits into the *clay-pit.* (Q.V.)

Michy. (Pro. *Mit-chee.)* See **Minching,** or **Miching.** Also **Minch** or **Mich.**

Midjans and jowds. Shreds and tatters.

Midgets, or **Midjans.** Small pieces, or bits.

Midgetty-morrows. The fidgets. M.A.C.

Midgetty por, Miggal conpore, Migglecum-pore. Synonymous words for uproar.

Mimsey, or **Minny.** A minnow (fish). *Menow, minow,* and *minys* are Celtic Cornish words, and mean little, small.

Minch, or **Mich.** To play the truant. In Gloucestershire they say *mooch.*

Mincher, or **Micher.** A truant.

Minching, or **Miching.** Playing the truant.
"Marry! this is *miching* Mallecho." *Hamlet.*

Milky-dicels, or **disles.** Thistles used for rabbits' food.

Milprev. The Druids' or serpents' egg. *Lhuyd.* The *ovum anguinum* of Pliny. From the Celtic Cornish *mil,* a thousand; and *prêv,* a reptile. It was a common belief in Cornwall, about 1700, that the glass beads which are frequently found in Cornwall, and Wales, and called by the Welsh *glain neidyr,* were the work of snakes; and it is a common belief now in Wales, that on a certain day of the year an immense number of snakes come together and make these beads with the foam of their mouths. This agrees substantially with Pliny's account, and has descended from the Druids.

Williams' Cor. Dicty.

Milsey, Milcy, or **Milchy.** Corn injured by damp undergoes a change, and becomes milsey. The bread made from it has a doughy consistence, and a peculiar taste, and is called milsey or *ropy* bread.

Minnies. Stones fastened to stout cords, or small ropes, are used to prevent pilchards from escaping, by plunging such stones (or minnies) constantly in the gap by which the fish may escape from the seine net.

Miracle plays. Sacred dramas which were acted anciently in a "round" (Q.V.) In Celtic Cornish they were called *Guaré meers* or Great plays, and *Guaré mirkl* or Miracle plays. The place of acting was called *pluen an guaré.* (*Gwaré.* Williams).

Missment. A mistake, an error.

Mix-medley. A jumble, "all sorts together."

Miz-maze. Confusion, perplexity. "We are all in a miz-maze."

'Moast. Almost, nearly, well nigh. "Et's moast dun," i.e., it's nearly done.

Mock. The apple cheese (Q.V.) from the cider press. *Polwhele.*

Mock, or **Mott.** A large block of wood, such as is used for a Christmas fire.

Mocket. A bib to an apron to keep the dress clean.

Mogust, or **Moguz.** The ass. *Callington.*

Mole. The fish rock goby. C.

Mollish's land. A game played by girls. One stood in the middle of the street, while the others rushing across had to be caught by her.

Mood. A mucous, or jelly-like matter formed in fluids. Linseed tea when too thick is a *mood.* (Vegetable sap. C.) Also a name for the Pancreas of an animal. A substance formed in vinegar is a mood (or **Mother** Q.V.)

Moonshine. Smuggled brandy was so called. "Woll'ee haa a drop uv moonshine?"

Moor-house. A hut belonging to a mine for the shelter of workmen, and keeping their implements. *Borlase.*

Moorstone. Granite so called as being "scattered over our hills." *Borlase.* The term is used now of granite from any source.

Mop. In the game called Mop and hide away, (i.e., Hide and Seek) the Mop is the one who has to stand with the face covered by the hands, facing a wall, or in a corner, waiting to seek those who have hidden away. Doing this as the mop, is called mopping.

Mor, More, or **Maur.** The root, stump, or bole of a plant, or tree.

Mor. The guillemot. C.

Moral. See **Daps.** The very image of. Likeness.

Mord, or **Mort.** The fat of the pig from which lard is melted out. It is also used for *lard.*

Morion. See **Cornish Diamonds.**

Mort. A lot, a large quantity as a "mort of money." This word is used in Kent, &c.

Moth. See **Mews.** F.C.

Mother, or **Mood.** A soft jelly-like matter formed in a fluid, as in vinegar.

Mott. See **Mock.** Generally used of a large root of a tree.

Mousey-pasty. An article of diet, with which little children who wetted their beds were threatened, "There now, you bad child, I'll give you some mousey pasty."

Mowhay. The rick-yard.

Muggets. Sheep's or calf's entrails.

Muggety-pie. A pie of sheep's, sometimes calf's entrails, flavoured with parsley, pepper, and salt, and enriched with cream.

Mugwort. A plant, *artemisia vulgaris,* often used to make tea for a bad cold, or taken as a tonic.

Mule. To knead dough, to bespatter with mud. C. To work hard.

Mumchance. By mere accident, "twas a mumchance."

Mun. Decayed fish, used for manure. M.A.C. In mining, any fusible metal. *Pryce.*

Mundic. Pyrites, Marcasite.

Munger, or **Mungar.** A straw horse collar. *Polwhele.* It is a Celtic Cornish word.

Mur. The guillemot.

Murs. Mice. *Polwhele.*

Mured. Squeezed, forced, or thrust against a wall. *Mur* a wall (French). *Mured* enclosed. *Spenser.*

Murely. Nearly, almost, well nigh. U.J.T. In Celtic Cornish. *mur*, much.

Murfles. Freckles. **Murfled** or **Murfly.** freckled.

Murgy or **Morgye.** A dog fish. An ill looking wench. It is Celtic Cornish and spelt *morgi* by Pryce.

Murrick. A sloven. R.J.C.

Mute. The hybrid between an ass and a mare. C.

Mutting. Moody. Silent and sulky. (Mute-ing?)

My Ivers! An exclamation of surprise. (My vernos! M.A.C.)

Nacked. See **Knacked.**

Nacker. The wheatear. *Saxicola œnanthe.* C.

Nackin, Nacken, or **Nacker.** Handkerchief.

Nagging pain. A dull, persistent pain.

Nag-ridden. Troubled with the nightmare.

Nail-spring. The splitting of the skin at the root of a finger-nail, or a small splinter of the nail itself.

Naked-jack. A crock-dumpling. *Callington.*

'Nan. See **Anan.**

Nanny-viper. A caterpillar. M.A.C.

Nash. Pale, weak, chilly. M.A.C.

Natey. "Streaky" meat or flesh. C.

Nation. Very, very big, very good, as, "a nation big horse," "a nation good job," "'tis nation nice."

'Natomy. A skeleton. Very slight and wasted in person, "a mere 'natomy." Anatomy.

Nattlin pie. A pie made of pigs' entrails.

Nattlins. Pigs' entrails. Those not used for the skins of sausages are sometimes fried, "fried nattlins."

Neaps. Turnips.

Neck. "Crying the neck." See **Anek.**

Neddy. See **Ass.**

Neflin. Newfoundland cod. M.A.C.

Nepperkin. Half a gill. U.J.T.

Nessel. A snood of twisted twine fastened to the hook. C.

Nessel-bird. The smallest of a brood. A woman's youngest child. A petted child. It is *nessel-trip* in Pembrokeshire, and *nestling* or *nessel-cock* in the North of England.

Nessel-taker. A fisherman's contrivance for making a nessel. C.

Nettle. When one is stung by a nettle an old rhyme is thrice repeated, meanwhile rubbing the part stung with a dock leaf. This custom is very old, and was noticed by Chaucer 500 years ago.

"But canst thou play at racket to and fro?
Nettle in, dock out; now this now that Pandure.'
Chaucer.

"Is this my in dock out nettle?"
Dissembler's besides women, P. O. Moore.

The following are the forms used,

"Out nettle, in dock,
Dock shall have a new smock,"

also thus, "Out nettle, in dock,
Nettle nettle stung me."

and simply thus, "In dock, out nettle."

New-fang or **New-vang.** Any new fancy, enterprise, or operation. The term is generally applied satirically as "that's one of his new-fangs." (*Newefangel*, desirous of new things. *Chaucer.*)

Nibby-gibby. Narrowly escaped; nicely missed. C.

Nice chance. Nearly, "a close shave," all but.

Nick. Knack, or skill in doing a thing.

Nick. To overreach, to deceive, to cheat.

Nicka-nan night. "The night preceding Shrove Tuesday is so called in Cornwall, because boys play impish tricks and practical jokes on the unwary."
Borlase.

Nickers, Nuggies, Knockers. See **Piskey.**

Nickety-knock. Throbbing, palpitating, tapping, "my heart's gwain nickety-knock."

Niddil, or **Neele.** A needle. (*Nidill, Chaucer.*)

Niffed. Tiffed, vexed, in a pet, "put out."

Niggur, or **Neggur.** See **Ass.** *(Onager, Latin.)*

Night-crow. A species of owl, rare in Cornwall. "I take it to be the fern-owl of Shropshire, called churn-owl in Yorkshire, from the noise it makes when it flies. The goat-sucker, the *Crapimulgus* of Ray." *Borlase.*

Night-rere. A woman's nightcap.

Night-riders. Piskey (Fairy) people who have been riding Tom (the name of a horse) again. H.

Nipped. Vexed, "Her's nipped about somethin." *Mrs. Parr's Adam & Eve.*

Nimpingale. A whitlow.

Nog-head, Noggle-head, or **Noggy.** A young fool. Tir na *nog,* in Irish means, "the land of youths."

Noggy. A blockhead. *Garland.*

Nones, or **Noance.** Nonce, for the present call, or occasion. *Nones* in *Chaucer.*

Nool. To thump, or beat. **Nooling,** a thrashing.

Nope. A bullfinch. *Borlase.*

Nort. Nothing. "What's good for nort comes to no hort." (Hurt or harm.)

Nosey. Impertinent, intrusive.

Nowle. Noddle. Used satirically. *Noule,* the crown of the head. *Spenser.*

Nub. A knob. "A nub of sugar."

Nuddick, or **Niddick.** The nape of the neck. *Nuddic* is a Celtic Cornish word.

Null. A dry crust. M.A.C.

Nurly. Sulky. T.C.

Nuttall or **Nut-hall.** The hazel bush.

Nyst. Near to, nearly, "all but."

Oak-mask, or **Oak-mass.** Acorns.

Oal-the-wor. In the fashion. "Hoods be oal the wor, and bunnets be wered wai a dep." (Heard said near Bodmin.)

Off his chump. Insane. *Callington.*

Ogôs. Cliff caves. *Polwhele. Ogo* is a Celtic Cornish word for a cave. See **Vugg,** a cavern.

Oilet. A frying pan, a gridiron. It is a Celtic Cornish word.

Okum-sniffey. A hot and nice little glass of grog. "Woll'ee haa a drap uv okum-sniffey?"

Old men. This term is applied to those who were mining in ancient days; perhaps centuries ago. In this way it does not mean *aged* men.

Old men's backs. Old workings in a mine. When old workings are explored or worked again, miners say, "they are scratching the old men's backs."

Old men's workings, or **Learys.** The remains of old mining, and stream works, done anciently by Cornish Miners.

Ollick, or **Hollick.** *House leek.* "House leek, used to be grown on house roofs, from the notion that it warded off lightning."

Brewer's Dict. of Phrase and Fable.

Oliphant. Elephant. It is a Celtic Cornish word.

Oodel-doodel. Helter-skelter. "And runned off oodel-doodel."

Oost. See **Hooze.** *Jern in the Cornishman.*

Oozle, or Oozle-pipe. The windpipe.

Ore-dresser. One who superintends the dressing operations of a mine, and is called the captain of the "floors," also "grass captain." E.N.

Ore-plot. The place for depositing the dressed ore.

Oreweed Sea weed. See **Flote-ore.**

Orrel. A raised wooden porch or balcony of a house above the cellar, and approached by outside steps.

Organs, or **Orgal.** Penny royal. *Mentha pulegium.* much used for "organ tay," (tea).

Orts. Leavings, scraps, fragments, as of food, &c. This word is always plural. "The fractions of her faith, *orts* of her love" *Shakspere.*

"Thou son of crumbs and *orts.*" *B. Johnson.*

Outlander. A foreigner.

Out of Core. Working "out of core," i.e., employing the spare time after the regular period of work.

Out-winder. A bow window.

Overgone. "Done up," exhausted, fatigued.

Overlooked. Bewitched, under the influence of the "evil eye." "Thou wast o'erlooked."

Shakspere, in the Merry Wives of Windsor.

Ovice, or **Ovvice.** The eaves of a house.

Over nigh. Near to, close up to. "Ovver nigh by the doar."

Owners, or **Awners.** See **Adventurers.**

Padal, or **Padel.** A dish, a pan. It is a Celtic Cornish word.

Paddick, or **Pattick.** A small brown pitcher holding one or two quarts.

Paddle. A weeding tool with a long handle and a narrow blade.

Padgy-paw, Pagety-paw, Paget-e-poo, or **Padzher-pou.** Names for a newt, eft, lizard. In Celtic Cornish *padzar* means four, and *paw* a foot. Literally, four-footed.

Pair. A company of men working together on the same bargain, pitch, or take, in a mine.

Palch, Palchy, Palched. Broken down in health, very frail and delicate in constitution. The writer has often heard it used thus, "He is very palchy." "He is very much palched." *Palch* is a Celtic Cornish word and means, weak, sickly, amending, poorly.

Pallace. A cellar for the balking (bulking) of pilchards. In Celtic Cornish, *palas,* means to dig or delve. The word probably meant originally, a place dug out. (Pallace is by Phillips derived from *pallicia*, pales or paled fences. In Devonshire it means a storehouse; in Totness, "a landing place enclosed but not roofed in," according to a Lease granted by the corporation of Totness in 1703. *Brewer's Dicty.*)

Pan bed. See **Hoppety bed.**

Panes. Parsnips. This is a Celtic Cornish word, *panan*, a parsnip, *panes*, or *panez*, parsnips.

Pannier-crooks. See **Crooks.**

Pan-crock. A large, brown, earthen pan.

Panshion. A milk pan. M.A.C.

Park. An enclosure, a field. *Parc* is a Celtic Cornish word for the same.

Parrick. A little jug. T.W.S.

Pasher. A clumsy workman. T.C.

Patch-hook. A bill-hook. M.A.C.

Pattic. A simpleton, a fool.

Pawse. A cold that runs at the nose. *Polwhele.* From the Celtic Cornish *paz* or *pas*, a cough.

Peach. Chlorite. A bluish green soft stone. A lode of this stone is called "a Peachy lode."

Peart. Brisk, lively. (*Peark, Spenser.*)

Peas. The hard roe of fishes.

Peson, or Paisen. Pease. This is the old plural form. In Celtic Cornish *pes* means pease, pulse. *Peson. Chaucer.*

Pedalincan. The great cuttle fish. H.R.C.

Pednan. Small pieces of turf. *Davy, Zennor.*

Pedn-paley. The tom-tit. (Blue-tit. M.A.C.) This is a Celtic Cornish word, *pedn*, a head; *paly*, satin, or velvet.

Pedn-borbas. Cods' head. B.V. Celtic Cornish. (Pedn barvas. *Pryce.)*

Peecher. A bait, an allurement. B.V.

Peel. A pillow. *Polwhele. Pilwe*, Saxon.

Pelf or **Pilf, Pelfy** or **Pilfy.** See **Pluff,** and **Pluffy.**

Pelt. In a pet, passion, or hurry. "Back he comes in a reg'lar pelt."

Peendy, or **Pindy.** Tainted. Used of animal food going, or gone bad.

Peeth. A well. M.A.C. (Wit; **Peethy,** witty).

Prize. See **Pize.** *Peise. Chaucer.*

Peizen, or **Pizen.** Weights. **Peizer.** a weigher.

Pellar. A conjurer, a cunning man.

Pellow-bere, or **Pillow-bere.** A pillow case. *Pelwe-bere. Chaucer.*

Pelch, or **Pilch.** A three cornered clout, or napkin used for infants. Brewer, (Dicty. of Phrases) calls it "The *flannel* napkin of an infant." Saxon, *pylche*, a skin coat. *Pilche, Chaucer.*

Penny-cake. The leaves of navel-wort. Children pluck and string them to resemble a pile of pennies.

Pezac. A pilchard with a broken back. W.C.B. In Celtic Cornish *pesach* means rotten.

Piffed. Slightly affronted, or vexed. See **Tiffed.**

Pigol, or **Piggal.** A pick-axe. A large hoe for cutting turf. *Pigol* is a Celtic Cornish word.

Piggy-pie. See **Taddago pie.** *Piggy*-pie is not exactly *pork*-pie as generally made, and is now probably an obsolete dainty, just as is *Lamby,* or *Lammy*-pie.

Piggy-whidden. Piggy-wiggy, or the smallest pig of the litter. The little *white* pig. In Celtic Cornish *whidn, gwiden,* or *gwyn,* white.

Pig's-crow. A Pig-sty. *Crow,* is Celtic Cornish and means a hovel, hut, sty.

Pile. A lot, a plenty, as "a pile of money."

Pilcher. Pilchard. The *Clupea pilchardus* of naturalists. They call pilchards *gipsy herrings* in Scotland. As is well known pilchards are taken in immense quantities on the Cornish coast, large shoals sometimes make their appearance on the Southern coast of Ireland, and about 90 years ago, a tolerably good fishery was there carried on. Pilchards are also taken off the French coasts but not in large quantities. These fish also frequent the coast of Spain, but not in great numbers as on the Cornish coast. "The merchantes that do deale in this commoditie of pilchards, as doe divers Londoners, vent them in sundrie places. In Fraunce they utter their *pickled* pilchardes, now not known but in domestic use, and suche as they pack in hogsheades and other caske, wher they are receyved as a verie welcome reliefe to the sea coaste of that kingdome, and from the coaste revented to their great profit in the inland townes.

All this trade into France is now gone. The *dryed* ware they carrye into Spain, Italie, Venice, and divers places within the Straytes. "Norden, A.D 1584, quoted by Whitaker (Anc. Cath. of Cornw. Vol. 2, p. 249, note.") (In Celtic Cornish, *Hernan* and *Llean*, a pilchard; *Herne*, pilchards; and *Allec*, herrings, pilchards. *Borlase.)*

Piler. "A farm instrument used to pound or cut the beards from barley in winnowing." B.V.

Piliers. Tufts of long grass, rushes, &c. M.A.C. The name seems derived from the hillocky appearance of large tufts of grass or rushes. *Pil* in Celtic Cornish means a hillock.

Pill. A pool, a creek.

Pillas, Pillis, or **Pellas.** Naked oats, bald, bare, or naked oats without husks. *Dr. Paris. Avena nuda. Piles,* or *Pilez* in Celtic Cornish means bare, bald. Also called Pill-corn. *(Pilled,* or *piled,* bald. *Chaucer.)* Polwhele, (A.D. 1803), says of it that "it is still used in several places," and describes it as a "small yellow grain . . . and for fattening calves accounted superior to any other nourishment."

Pillion. The tin which remains in the scoria or slags after it is first smelted, which must be separated and re-melted. *Pryce.*

Pillum, Pillem, or **Pilm.** Dust. *Pilm* is a Celtic Cornish word, and means according to Pryce, "dust flying like flour."

Pil-jack, or **Piliack.** A low, mean fellow. *Davy, Zennor.*

Pimpey. A weak cider made by adding water to the apple "cheese." Q.V. It is also called "beverage." Q.V.

Pin, or **Pin-bone.** The hip. The hip-joint. *Pen-clun* is the Celtic Cornish word for the hip-joint. *Pen* the head, and *clun*, the hip, or haunch.

Pinnick, or **Punick.** An undergrown weakly child. Puny.

Pinnickin. Very small and weakly. "What a poor pinnickin child!"

Pinni-menny. This was, (and is now by a few) the name given to the little chapel-well near Trenance bridge, St. Austell. Young people wanting to know their fortune, dropped pins into the well and "wished." *Menny*, or *Mynny*, in Celtic Cornish means, to will, to wish.

Bernard Quaritch, in a review of Elton's "Origins of English History," says, "There is ample proof that the pin is not a mere offering to the spirit of the well, such as a rag, a pebble, or a small coin might be, but is flung in by way of curse, to injure the person who is present in the mind at the time the pin is thrown in. It is a companion superstition to that of sticking pins into a wax image, an animal's heart, an orange, or an apple, which is prevalent over a great part of the world. A pin is, speaking mythologically, a deadly thing, perhaps because it is a spear or dagger in miniature; a prick from one is more dangerous than from a needle or a splinter of wood, because it gives the sufferer the 'evil humours' of the person who has carried it on his person. In Iceland, if there is any fear that a dead person's spirit will walk, pins are driven into the soles of the corpse's feet.

Pin-tail. A person who is very small and narrow in the hips.

Pip. A disease among chicken.

Pipe, or **Bunny of ore.** A great collection of ore without any vein coming into, or going from it.

Pryce.

Piran. Intoxicated. "He was Piran last night." This is a slander on St. Piran, who is traditionally said to have died drunk, yet, says Carew, "if legend lye not he lived 200 years and died at Piran."

Piran broad-cloth. The rush mats made there.

Tonkin.

Pirl. To whirl, twirl, or twist around.

Piskey. A fairy. The common clothes moth is also so called from some old superstition. In Robt. Hunt's delightful book, "The Romances of the West of

England," are names of the various kinds of fairies, viz: 1.—The small people. 2.—The Spriggans. 3.—The Piskies or Pigseys. 4.—The Buccas, Bockles, or Knockers. 5.—The Browneys. (*Pisky* is Celtic Cornish for Fairy. *Borlase.*).

Piskey feet or **Pixies' feet.** See **Pysgy pows.**

Piskey-led. Said of one bewildered, confused, or who has lost his way. "He's like anybody piskey-led."

Piskey-stool. A mushroom.

Pit-work. The part of the mine machinery which is placed in the shafts or levels. E.N.

Pitch. A bargain of work in a mine.

Pitch, pitch, butterfly! An invocation by which children hope to catch a butterfly, thus "Pitch, pitch, butterfly, down low, down low."

Pitch to. To set about a thing in real earnest.

Pitch-haired, or **Pitchy-haired.** A rough staring coat, as of a horse in cold weather.

Pitch up to. To make advances, as in "making love."

Pize, Pise, Peize, or **Peise.** To weigh. In Cornwall it means generally, to estimate or guess the weight of a thing by holding it in the hand, as "I've a pized et," i.e., I have handled it, or lifted it so as to *judge* the weight. *Peise. Chaucer.* (**Peysen, peisen,** weights. M.A.C.)

Planchin, or **Planchen.** A plank or wood floor. In "Arden of Feversham" is this expression "Whilst on the *planchers.*" In Celtic Cornish *planken,* or *plynken,* means a plank, a board.

Plashet, or **Ploshet** A moist, watery place. A quagmire.

Plat. A plot, or small piece of ground. (In Celtic Cornish, *plat* means flat, also in Chaucer.)

Platted down. Flattened down, pressed down.

Plat-footed. Flat-footed, splay-footed. *Plat or platte. Chaucer. Plat* is a Celtic Cornish word meaning flat, *splay.*

Plethan. To braid, or plait. *Polwhele.* (In Celtic Cornish it is *plegye).*

Pliskin. An egg-shell. A Celtic Cornish word. *Polwhele.*

Plod, or **plad.** Plaid, or check-pattern.

Plosh. A puddle, a messy, dirty place. *Plos* is a Celtic Cornish word for dirt, filth, &c.

Plosher. A half grown bream. M.A.C.

Ploshy. Splashy, sloppy, wet and miry. In Celtic Cornish *plosec,* foul, filthy.

Pluff, Pelf, or **Pilf.** Fine, or broken fragments of fur, feathers, &c. Also the fur or *fine* hairy coat of an animal, as of a hare, &c. In Celtic Cornish *pluven* means a feather, a pen, *pliv* or *plûv,* feathers, and *plufoc,* a bolster.

Pluff, Pluffy, or **Ploffy.** Soft and spongy like a dried up turnip. "Feeling pluffy" means poorly, "out of sorts."

Plum. Anything soft and springy, as a pillow, cushion, &c., also leavened, as "the dough is plum."

A Cornishman would not say mud was plum, yet if he fell on it he would say that "he fell plum," To "fall plum" is understood as contrary to "fall hard."

"To plum up," is to swell up like leavened dough which is then said to be "plum" or "light." "To plum up" also means the resumption of the former state after pressure is removed, as of a pillow which "plums up" again. The shaking up of a bed, or a pillow, is to "plum up," the bed, or pillow, i.e., render them soft. The word *plum* meaning elsewhere £100,000, or a "nice plum," was formerly spelt *plumb*, and refers to one who is, "pretty well off for *tin*." Tin by the ancient Romans was called *plumbum album*. *Pluman* is the Celtic Cornish word for the *fruit* plum, and *plom* or *plobm* for lead.

Plummin. The yeast mixed with the flour for leavening, is called so.

Poam. To pummel, to thump, to beat, "poamén well," (*Paume*, the palm of the hand. *Chaucer*.)

Poaming. A pummelling.

Pock. A push, a shove. *Poc*, or *Pock* is Celtic Cornish. See *Poot*.

Poddlin. Poking about, meddling.

Podar. Mundic, pyrites. In Celtic Cornish *podar* means rotten, corrupt; mundic; ugly.

Borlase's Corn. Vocab.

"Upon the first discovery of Copper ore, says Dr. Paris, the miner to whom its nature was entirely unknown gave it the name of poder *(podar)*; and it will hardly be credited in these times, when it is stated that he regarded it not only as useless, but upon its appearance was actually induced to abandon the mine, the common expression upon such an occasion was that *the ore came in and spoilt the tin.*"

The writer when a boy used to hear aged men speak of copper ore (thought to be *podar* or mundic) having been used to mend the roads.

"About the year 1735, says Dr. Paris, Mr. Coster, mineralogist of Bristol, observed this said *podar* among the heaps of rubbish, and seeing that the miners were wholly unacquainted with its value . . . . . . he entered into a contract to buy all he could get, and no doubt he found it a profitable transaction."

Podge. A short fat person, "quite a podge."

Podgy. Short, thick, and fat.

Pókemen. Stupid, clumsy, "such pókemen ways," (**Podging.** M.A.C.)

Poldavy. A very coarsely woven linen cloth. Sail cloth was formerly called *Powle-davies.*

Polled. Beheaded, used of fish. *Polwhele.*

Pollet, or **Polleck.** A crooked stick, knobbed at one end. W.F.P. **Polyn.** A stick. B.V.

Polrumptions. Uprorious, restive.

Pomster. A quack. In Celtic Cornish it is spelt *ponster,* meaning quackery, giving improper medicines.

Poochin. Shoving, poking in the way. "What be'ee poochin like that vur?" (Potch. *Shakspere.)*

Poochy, or **Poochy-mouth.** The lips very prominent and thick.

Pooching. Making a mouth at any one.

Pook. A heap of hay, or turf. It is a Celtic Cornish word.

Pooled. Splitting granite "is effected by applying several wedges to holes cut, or *pooled* as it is termed, in the surface of the stone, at a distance of three or four inches from each other." *Dr. Paris.*

Poor. Tainted, turned sour, decayed, rotten.

Poor as a coot. In great poverty. *(Coot,* the bird *Fulica atra.)*

Poor tipple. Small beer and such like drink.

Poot. To thump, to kick. This is a Celtic Cornish word, as also, *pook* and *pouk.*

Pop and touse. A general row. All sorts of oaths. In Celtic Cornish *pop,* every; and *tos,* to swear.

Pop-docks, or **Poppies.** The fox-glove. *Digitalis purpurea. (Corn*-poppy is the name for the common *red* poppy.)

Pope. A puffin. M.A.C.

Popple, or **Bobble.** A pebble.

Por, or **Poar.** Hurry, fuss, agitation. "What a poar you'm in!"

Porbeagle. A small kind of shark. *Borlase.*

Porf. A pool of stagnant water. M.A.C.

Porvan. A rush wick for a lamp. M.A.C.

Posh. Phlegm oppressing the breathing. *Polwhele. Pose. Chaucer.* In Celtic Cornish *pos* means heavy.

Poss, poss up, or **possed up.** To stand up, to "stick up," leaning against a wall or a post. "Theer a stonds possed op, lookin like a vool." **Pos.** A post, is Celtic Cornish.

Post groats. "In the time of Henry 8th there were two coinages (of tin) in a year, viz; at Midsummer and Michaelmas, but two more were added at Christmas and Ladyday for the conveniency of tinners, for which they paid as an acknowledgment four pence for every hundred of white tin then coined." The *duty* to the Duke of Cornwall being four shillings for every hundred weight of tin coined. *Borlase.* See **Coining tin.**

Powdered. Slightly sprinkled with salt, corned.

Pots. The bowels; wooden panniers for carrying manure on an animal's back, *dung pots.*

Pot-crooks. The second form in learning to write, next to making strokes. Pot-hooks.

Pot grouan. Soft granite-like ground in which it is easy to drive an adit. *Pryce.*

Pot-ground. A miner's term for loose ground.

Pot-guidn. White pudding. *Polwhele.* It is Celtic Cornish. *Pot,* pudding; *guidn,* white.

Power. A great deal, a great number, as "a power of good," "a power of people."

Power. The fish *Gadus minutus.* C.

Preedy. On an even balance, as with a scales. C.

Preedy. Easily, creditably. "Putty preedy."

Preventive men. Coast guard men.

Preventive station. Coast guard station.

Pride of the country. A miner's term. "When ore is found near the surface, at a level where it is rarely met with, and in great abundance and very rich; also when a bunch of ore is found out of a lode like stones scattered in a quarry, they say, "It is the pride of the country." *Pryce.*

Pridy, or **Preedy.** Proud, handsome.

Prid-prad, Priden-prall. See **Pednpaley.**

Prill. v. To mix, to turn off sour, to get tipsy or half drunk.

Prill. A small bit, or quantity.

Prilled, or **Prill.** Half drunk. "He's prilled."

Prilling a sample. Giving a false sample of the ore. E.N.

Prince-town college. A facetious name for Dartmoor prison.

Prinked up, or **Prinkt up.** Dressed up in fine clothes. "Dressed to the nines." *Prankt,* Spenser.

Prinking along. Walking in an affected manner.

Prong. A silver fork; a hay fork.

Proper. Prim, handsome. "Being so *proper.*"
Shakspere in King Lear.

Proud flesh. Overgrowth of the flesh in a healing wound.

Prophecy table. For casting the matrimonial horoscope.

IN CORNWALL.	*ELSEWHERE.*
Tinker.	Soldier.
Tailor.	Sailor.
Soldier.	Tinker.
Sailor.	Tailor.
Rich man.	*Gentleman.*
Poor man.	Apothecary.
Apothecary.	*Ploughman.*
Thief.	Thief.

Pryan lode. A flookan lode, as a soft clayey vein of tin. In Celtic Cornish *pryan* or *prian* means, clayey ground.

Pudlock. A short beam for supporting the planks of a scaffold. One end in the wall, the other tied to the scaffold pole.

Pullan. This is a Celtic Cornish word, meaning a pit, a pond. (A salt water pool. M.A.C.)

Pull-cronack. A small fish found in salt water pools; bully-cods, the shanny. M.A.C. *Pul*, or *pol*, is Celtic Cornish for pond, &c., but *cronec* means a toad. See **Bulgranack.**

Pul-rose. The wheel-pit. This is a Celtic Cornish word; *pul* or *pol*, a pit, &c., and *ros*, a wheel. Spelt *Poul-roz* by Pryce; and *Pol-roz* by Borlase.

Punick. See **Pinnick.**

Punnion-end, or **Punkin-end.** The gable end of a house.

Pure, or **Pūr.** Very, quite. This is a Celtic Cornish word. (*Pure*, mere, very. *Chaucer.*) "He's pure and fat," i.e., He's very fat.

Purgy. Thick in stature, fat, as "a purgy little chap," "a purgy pig."

Purl. Watch, "on the purl," i.e., on the watch. *Polwhele.*

Purser. The financial agent for a mine.

Purt. A niff, a tiff. "He has taken a purt." C.

Purt'ns, Purtens, or **Portens.** The heart, liver, and lungs of an animal.

Purvan. Shreds of cloth. W.F.P. **Purvans.** B.V. See **Porvan.**

Put going. Murdered.

Put hom, home or **hum.** Shut or close, as "put hom the door."

Pye. Blocks of tin when formerly adulterated by lumps or pieces of iron being enclosed in the centre, were called *pye*. *Tonkin.* They say that by the old Stannary laws a person convicted of this fraud was made to swallow three spoonfuls of melted tin. It was a certain cure.

Pysgy-pows, or **Pixies' feet.** "Ridge-tiles are placed on houses in West Cornwall, having a round knob on them. The people say they are for the pixies to dance on; and that if you omit to place one for their amusement they will turn the milk sour." *W. C. Borlase, in the Western Antiquary.*

Quab. Sickly, infirm. *Garland.* (*Quad* or *quade*, bad, and also *quappe* to tremble, to quake, are in Chaucer.)

Quaddlin. A semi-imbecile, stupid manner.

Quaff. (Pron. quaif.) To puff up. M.A.C.

Quaiffed, or **Quatted.** Satisfied, full. M.A.C.

Quail. To wither. **Quailed.** Withered, as in speaking of flowers.

Quailing. A sinking sensation in the stomach.

Qualk. A heavy fall. "I came down with a qualk."

Quarantine. A bright red apple.

Quarry, or **Quarrel.** A pane, or square of glass.

Quat. To squat, to flop down, to flatten down.

Quandáry. Perplexity, uncertainly, in a wandering state of mind. In Celtic Cornish *quandré* means, to walk about, to wander; but this is borrowed from the English.

Quârey. "When a lode or stratum breaks in large hard rocks, being jointed as it were, it is called a *quârey* lode or stratum, from its joiuts or *quâres.*" *Pryce.*

Queedy. Shrewd. M.A.C. Perhaps from the Celtic Cornish *quethé*, to work or labour at.

Queens, or **Gweans.** Scallops. (Perriwinkles. *Bottrell.*)

Queer. A mining term. "A queer of ground." A square piece of ground. (?) *St. Just.* See **Quârey.**

Quiddles. Foolish fancies.

Quiddlin. Same as **Quaddlin.** Q.V.

Quignogs. Rediculous fancies, or conceits.

Quilkin, Quilkey, or **Quilkquin.** A frog. See **Wilkin.** In Celtic Cornish it is *kwilken, guilkin,* or *cuilcen.*

Quillaway, or **Quailaway.** A stye, or small abscess on the eyelid. *Hordeolum.*

Quillet. Three leaved grass, clover. *Bottrell.*

Quilter. Flutter, flurry, agitation of mind. "She was all in a quilter."

Quilting. A severe thrashing.

Quinted. Animals over filled with food are quinted.

Quishin. A cushion. This word is in Chaucer.

Quoit. A broad thin stone or rock. It is a Celtic Cornish word. The Cromlech at Lanyon is called the "Giant's quoit." The large table stone resembling a *discus* or quoit.

Quoits. A game played with roundish but flat stones, thrown at a mark or place. Once very common. (*Quoit* or *Koeten*, in Celtic Cornish, means a broad thin stone, or rock. *Borlase.*)

Rab. Granite rubble.

Rabban. Miner's term for a "yellowish dry stone resembling gossan." *Pryce.*

Rabbet et! or Od Rabbet et! An exclamation, as if to say, "Confound it."

Rabble. An iron rake for stirring and skimming off copper ore in calcination and melting. *Pryce.*

Rabblerash. A dirty, noisy mob. "The great unwashed." Rubbishy stuff.

Rabble-fish. Inferior fishes.

Race. To place things in a row. Also, to string things together, as "a race of onions."

Race. A go cart. M.A.C.

Radgell. An excavated tunnel. *The W. Briton.*

Rafe or Raffe. To tear or rend.

Raff, or Raffle. Poor stuff, anything scrappy and inferior.

Raffain. Raff. **Raffain ore.** Poor ore of no value. *Pryce.*

Ram-cat. A "Tom" cat.

Rames. The skeleton, as, "the rames of a goose." J.W. *Lostwithiel.*

Rag. A large, irregular, slate roofing stone.

Rag-pump. A chain pump.

Ramper. Playful. *Callington.*

Ramping. In great pain, as a "ramping tooth ache"; also raging. "A *ramping* lion rushed suddenly."
Spenser's Faery Queene.

Ramping and roving. In a state of almost unbearable pain.

Randigall. A long, rambling story.

Randivooze. A resort; also, an uproar, "a putty randivooze up there." (*Rendezvous.* French.)

Ranter's jace. A "wild goose" errand. A rambling hunt, or search, or chase.

Ranter go round. An old fashioned game of cards so called. M.A.C.

Rany. A ridge of rocks which is bare at half-tide. C.

Ranny. A wren.

"Those who kill a robin, or a wren,
Will never prosper, boy or man."

Rap and rind. "By hook or crook." F.C.

Rare. Flesh, meat, underdone. Half raw; any eatable thing early in the season is *rare.* See **Rear.**

Rash. Brittle, as applied to wood; or crisp, as of vegetables.

Raunin, or **Raunish.** Hungry, ravenous. He's got a raunin appetite." (Spenser used the word *royne,* to bite or gnaw.)

Raw-milk. The milk as it comes from the cow.

Raw-ream, or **Raw-cream.** The cream of milk not scalded.

Reamer. A flat, perforated, shovel like skimmer, for removing clotted cream from "scalded" milk.

Rear. Early. (So used also by Milton and Shakspere. *Polwhele.)*

Red-knot wheat. So called from the colour of the joints and husks. *Tonkin.*

Red-rabb. Red killas. *Pryce.*

Reed. The unbruised stalks of corn, so called in the mass.

Reeming. Stretching and yawning together.

Reen. A steep hill side. M.A.C.

Reese, or **Reeze.** Overripe, ripe corn shedding the grains is said to reese. M.A.C.

Reeving. Sifting so as to separate various sized grains from each other.

Ridar. A sieve, a riddle. *(Ridar a kazher.)* A sieve is still called a *casier. Pryce.*

Riders, or **"The riders."** Circus equestrians.

Rig, or **Rigs.** Fun, frolic, uproar, fuss.

Riggle, or **Riddle.** To poke up, or to stir up the fire, also to rattle out, as, "Riggle up the fire," "Riggle out the fire.".

Ringle. To ring, to tinkle.

Rise in the back. To work upwards towards the surface in mining.

Rising of the lights. An hysterical or choking feeling in the throat. A ball in the throat. *Globus hystericus.*

Roaring. Blubbering. Crying aloud with tears.

Robin's alight. A game of forfeits played before the fire, by whirling a burning stick around. It is so moved and passed from one to another. The one who last holds it as the fire in the stick goes out, pays the forfeit.

Rock basins. Round, or oval cavities of various sizes on the surface of granite rocks. Most rock basins are on a level, some on a sloping, and a very few on a perpendicular face of the rock. These basins are formed by the gradual action of water long resting on the rock in little pools, causing disintegration in the form of a more or less shallow basin. Some basins are so artificial in appearance, that antiquaries have thought them wrought out so as to be pools of lustration. Some of these basins may have been altered, but they are almost entirely of natural formation, whatever their Druidical uses may have been.

"Quid magis est saxo durum,—Quid mollius unda,
Dura tamen moli saxa cavantur aqua." *Ovid.*

Rode. Gumption, sense, nouse.

Rodeling, Roodling, or **Rodeless.** Hesitating and uncertain in manner, vaccillating, maundering and stupid. A dull stupid way of speaking, "Such roodling ways!" In the Armoric language *rodella* means, to turn or wind about.

Rod-shaft. The engine-shaft in a mine, in which are the rods of the pumping gear.

Roper's news. News not new, being stale. East Cornwall saying. C.

Ropy. A term applied to bread made with milsey flour. See **Milsey.**

Rouan. The name of a good cider apple grown in the Lizard district. *Rouan* is Celtic for *Roman.*

Rory-tory. Anything vulgar in design, or colour. Tawdry.

Round or **Roundago.** An ancient circle of stones or earth. "It is said the priests (Druids) danced within an enclosure of stones, moving sideways in imitation of the dragon, or serpent. This means they danced within a "round" of which there are remains in Cornwall." *Hogg's Fab. Hist. of Cornwall.*

Polwhele describes it thus—"*Roundago,* a circle of stones standing erect or piled in a wall-like form without mortar. Stone circles, originally pagan, were probably used by the Christian Cornish for their miracle plays and dances." Polwhele (Hist. of Cornwall, vol. 2. p. 84.) also says that the *rounds* were "probably places of meeting of the general stannary assemblies," (in the same manner Crockern Torr in Dartmoor was the seat of assembly for the tinners of Devon; and the place of *general* assembly for the tinners *both* of Devon and Cornwall was Heugston Hill.")

Rounders. A game of bat and ball, somewhat like cricket, but with only one batting place, from which there are three stations to run round by, before reaching the batting place again.

Round robin. The angler fish. C.

Roup. To drink, or gulp down fluid in a noisy manner.

Rouse-about. See **Stiracoose.**

Routing out. Turning out the holes and corners, cleaning up.

Roving. In great pain. "A roving toothacke." Also used thus, "roving mad."

Row. Rough. "He loked wel *rowe.*" *Chaucer,*

Row. Refuse from the ore stamping mills. E.N.

Row-hound. The fish *Squalus canicula.* C.

Row-tin. The large grained rough tin. *Borlase.*

Rud. Red. In Celtic Cornish *rudh.*

Rudge. A partridge. *Polwhele.*

Rouser. Something big, or resounding.

Ruddock. A robin red-breast. Called also Rabbin, and Rabbin-redbreast. (Ruddock. *Chaucer.*) In Celtic Cornish it is *Ruddoc. Rydhic,* means reddish, in this tongue.

Ruinate. Ruined, overthrown. Spenser used this word.

Rumbustious. Noisy, cantankerous.

Rummage. Rubbish, odds and ends, a rubbishy lot of things. Confusion or disorder.

Rummet. Dandriff. See **Scruff.** "The child's head is full of rummet."

Rumped up. Feeling cold and miserable, "rumped up with the cold." See **Scrumped up.**

Rumpy. Anything coarse and uneven, as of cotton &c.

Rumpin. The same as **Jumpin.** Q.V.

Run. A mining term meaning a fall of loose ground after an excavation.

Runner. A round towel on a roller.

Runky. Hoarse, wheezy breathing. In Celtic Cornish *renkia* means, to snore, to snort.

Running ground. Loose, sandy, or soft ground, which falls in just as fast as it is excavated

Runnin. (Rennet. M.A.C.) Melted fat.

Running-wound. A wound discharging matter.

Rush, or **Rish.** "Beginning a new rush," i.e., turning over a new leaf, commencing a fresh score.

Russell's wagon. "As big as Russell's wagon." A saying. This was a huge wagon for the conveyance of goods and passengers, drawn by 6, 8, even 10 great horses, with tinkling bells. It took nearly a fortnight, (50 years ago) to go from Cornwall to

London. Passengers sometimes slept in it on their own bedding, and made their wills before starting. The writer's own father has made wills for such travellers.

Rustring comb. Dressing comb. A flinking comb.

Ruttlin. The sound of phlegm rattling in the bronchial tubes.

Ruxler, or **Wroxler.** A restless fidgety person, one continually shifting about, as on a seat.

Sabby. Soft and wet.

Saim, or **Seym.** Train oil, fat, grease. Celtic Cornish words.

Sam, or **Zam.** Half-heated. **A Sam oven,** is one half-hot after bread has been baked in it. "Tell the baker to bake the biskeys (biscuits) in the sam oven."

Sammy-Dawkin. A thickhead. A Padstow illustration of incapacity. "A regular Sammy Dawkin."

Sampling. Testing the worth of the ores of a mine.

Sample. Soft, pliant.

Sampler. A small square of canvas on which girls stitched letters and figures; one who tests the value of mineral ores.

Sampson. A drink of cider, brandy, and a little water, with sugar. M.A.C.

Sam-sawdered, or **Sam-sodden.** Anything ill cooked, and insipid, especially if tepid, or "half hot."

Sang, or **Zang.** A small sheaf such as that of a gleaner. C.

Sape, or **Sapey.** See **Zape.**

Saracens. "The Jews therefore denominated themselves, and were denominated by the Britons of Cornwall *Saracens*, as the genuine progeny of Sarah."
Origin of Arianism, pp. 329 . . 325, *quoted by Polwhele.*

Save-all. A large apron to cover and protect a child's dress.

Sawen. See **Zawn.**

Say-fencibles. Sea-fencibles. The old coast-guard.

Scabby-gullion, (B.V.) or **Scabby-gulyun.** (W.F.P.) A stew of cut up meat and potatoes.

Scad. The horse mackerel. The shad. *Borlase.*

Scal, or **Scale.** See **Schale.**

Scald cream. Clotted or clouted cream.

Scald milk. Milk which has been heated and deprived of the clotted cream.

Scalpions. Dry salt fish, as salt whiting. H.

Scaly. Grumpy, ill-tempered, miserly.

Scammed. See **Trowled.**

Scamp. To do work badly, or with inferior, or scanty materials.

Scarf. A joint. **Scarfe.** To join. They are Celtic Cornish words, "My a'n *scarf* yn ta wharé." I will soon join it well.

Scarlet runners. Kidney-bean plants.

Scat. A slap. "I'll giv'ee a scat in the faace;" a sharp frost, as, "a scat of frost;" diarrhœa; anything burst or broken open. *Scat* is a Celtic Cornish word and means a buffet, a box, a blow.

Scat. v. To slap, to break, to smash, to be bankrupt.

Scat-marchant. One who has failed in business. It was formerly a term of great contempt, and the boys even mobbed a scat-marchant. *Now* he is "white-washed" not mobbed.

Scat abroad. Burst open, smashed, "Tes oal scat abroad." **A scat to,** a "set to," or quarrel.

Scaval-an-gow. Chattering, confused talking. *Scaval-an-gow* (Cornish) the bench of lies. U.J.T. *Scavel* is Celtic Cornish for, a bench, a stool, and *gow*, a falsehood, a lie.

Scavarnoeck, Skavarnak, or **Scovarnog.** Celtic Cornish names for a hare. *Scovarnog* is the oldest form of the word. (*Long eared,* still used in Cornwall. *Polwhele.*)

Scaw. Elder or *scaw* trees. **Scawen.** An elder tree. *Scaw* and *scawen* are Celtic Cornish words.

Scawsy-buds. Elder flowers.

Schale. A scale, as a "schale of earth," or earth slide in an excavation.

Sclum, Sclow, or **Scrow.** To sclaw, to scratch, as "the cat will sclum you," also used thus, "Ah! you old sclum-cat." i.e., you old spite.

Scoad, or Scud. To spill, to shed, to pour, to scatter.

Scoce. To exchange, to barter. C.

Scoanes. The pavement, the stones. See **Coanse.** U.J.T.

Scollucks. Refuse of a slate quarry. *Delabole.* C.

Scollops. The remains of pig's "**mord.**" Q.V. from which the fat has been melted out. Also called scollop fat, and "*scrolls.*"

Scouring-geard. A soft china-stone granite used as sand for scouring, or for whitening floors. M.A.C.

Scovan lode. A tin lode. Only in contra-distinction to all other lodes. *Pryce.*

Scove. Tin stuff so rich and pure, that it needs but little cleansing. *Pryce.*

Scovy. Looking smeared and blotchy, as a badly or unevenly painted surface.

Scoy. Thin, poor, as applied to silks or stuffs; small, insignificant, "for my wages would look scoy." U.J.T. Perhaps from the Celtic Cornish *skez,* a shade, a shadow. In Manx, *scaa.*

Scrabble. To scramble.

Scragged. Strangled.

Scranny. To scramble, to contend, to strive. In Celtic Cornish it is *scornye.*

Scranching, Scrunching. Crushing a hard substance between the teeth.

Screech. A short sudden blaze. "Some tam fuzz for a screech."

Screech like a whit-neck. To make a great outcry.

Screed. A scrip, or very small bit. Also a very thin person. "Looking like a screed."

Screedle. To cower over the fire. U.J.T. See **Gridddle.**

Screw. The shrew or field mouse. C.

Scriff-scraff. Rummage, a lot of trumpery things.

Scrimp, or **Scrimpy.** Scant, scanty,

Scrinkt. Screwed. U.J.T.

Scrinking, or **Scrinked up.** Peeping about with (screwed up) half-closed eyes, and puckered mouth. In Celtic Cornish, *scryncye,* means to snarl, to grin.

Scrip. To escape. *Carew.* "He will never scrip it."

Scritch. A crutch.

Scroached, Scrawed, or **Scrowled.** Scorched or broiled, as "scroached pilchards." Before being scroached, they are split, half dried, peppered, and salted.

Scrolls. See **Scollops.**

Scrolled. Same as **Scroached.** Q.V.

Scrow. See **Sclum.**

Scrowl. "When a lode is interrupted and cut off by a *cross-gossan*, it may sometimes be found again by the tendency of some loose stones of the true lode in the body of the *gossan*, i.e., *a scrowl*." *Pryce.*

Scrowling. Scratching.

Scrouge, Scrudge, or **Scrooge.** To squeeze, as in a crowd, to crowd together. (*scruze*, squeeze out, press out. *Spenser.*) "We cud haardly scrouge room for to stond in the fair."

Scruff. Dandriff. See **Rummet.**

Scruff. The nape of the neck. The scrag.

Sruff. v. To scuffle, to struggle. "We scruffed together."

Scruffy. Rough and scaly.

Scruffy-head. A head full of dandriff. A term also of contempt, "old scruffy-head."

Scrumped, or **Scrumped up.** The same as **shrumped,** and **rumped.** Q.V. In Celtic Cornish we have the word *scruth* meaning, a shiver.

Scry. The report of the approach of a body of fish, as pilchards. *Leland.* C. In Celtic Cornish we have *scrymba*, an outcry.

Scub-maw A "mess" of food," anything not cooked in an orthodox manner. Scraps, pieces, **orts.** Q.V.

Scud. To spill, see **Scoad;** to crust over as does a sore. **To scud over.** To scab over.

Scud. The dry crust or scab of a sore.

Scudder. See **Skitter.**

Scuffler. An agricultural implement for breaking up the clods after ploughing. *Callington.*

Scule, Scool, or **School.** A shoal or large body of fish swimming together.

Scullions. Onions. T.W.S.

Scute. The metal shield *(scutum, Latin)* of the heel or toe of a boot or shoe.

Sea-adder. The pipe-fish.

Seam or **Zeam.** A cart or wagon-load of hay, manure, &c.

Seam of tin. A horse load, viz: two small sacks of black tin. *Pryce.*

Searge. A sieve. *Pryce.*

Seech, or **Sych.** Seech, "the rush of sea waves inundating the streets at high tides." *Bond's Hist. of Looe. Sych,* "the edge or foaming border of a wave as it runs up a harbour, or on the land." *Couch.* Lhuyd says that in the Armoric language *gulab a sych* means, wet and dry. *Sech* or *Sych,* dry, in Celtic Cornish.

Seed-lup, or **Seed-lip.** A sower's box or basket for holding the seed while sowing.

Seine, or **Sean.** A pilchard net many hundreds of feet long. See **Stop net.**

Seine boats. In seining for pilchards three boats are employed, viz: two large ones and a small one; each large boat containing seven men, and in the small one are the master-seiner, another man, and two boys. The "Seine-boat" and the "Follower" are the names by which the two large boats are distinguished, and the small one is called the "Lurker."

Semmee. It seems to me. This and the expression, "I seem," for, I think, is common along both banks of the Tamar, &c.

Sett. Ground within the bounds of which a mine, or a clay-work &c., may be worked.

Seven-sleeper, or **Sound-sleeper.** A speckled moth (Ermine moth,) is so called in Cornwall.

Seym. Grease, train oil. This is a Celtic Cornish word. (*Saim. Borlase.*)

Shacky. Shacky-fish. A small fish found in salt water pools, also called Goby and Shoky fish.

Shag. The cormorant or sea raven. "As wet as a shag." *Shagga. Polwhele.*

Shale-stone, or **Shellstone.** Slate stone.

Shallal. A serenade of kettles and pans.

Shámedy. Confused and ashamed.

Shammel. "A stage of boards used in old 'coffins' before shafts were in common use. So they now call any stage of boards for shovelling of ore or 'deads' (rubble) upon, a shammel." *Pryce.* See **Coffins.**

Shammels. Stopes. A mining term.

Shammel-whim. An engine for drawing the ore up over an inclined plane.

Shammel-working. "A method of working by an open mine where .... they followed the lode as far and to as great a depth as they were able to pursue it." *Polwhele.*

Shammick. A low, mean, shuffling fellow.

Shammick. To cheat, to act with low cunning.

Shanny. The fish *Blennius pholis.* C.

Shape, or **Shaape.** A bad state or condition. "Here's a putty shaape!" i.e., Here's a mess! "What a shaape you'm in!" i.e., What a mess!

Shenagrum. Rum, sugar, and lemon with hot beer. M.A.C.

Sheevo. "Such a sheevo." A form of the word *chivvy* meaning a fuss or row.

Shell-apple. The cross-bill. *Tonkin.*

Shell-stone. A slate stone. In Devon, shindle-stone.

Shift. A form of displacement in a lode in which it has become disjointed. E.N.

Shigged. Cheated. T.C. "Shigged out."

Shiner. A sweet-heart. W.T.A.P.

Shivver. One of the bars of a gate.

Shodes, or **Shoads.** Scattered or dispersed parts from the "broil" (Q.V.) of a neighbouring mineral lode. (Perhaps from *shutten*, to pour forth. *Borlase.)*

Shoaders. Miners engaged in shoading.

Shoading. Sinking pits and trying for the lode.

Shoading heaps. Heaps from pits in the search for lodes. E.N.

Shoading pits. Pits dug in the search for a lode.

Shogg. To make a sifting movement, as in washing ore in water. *Carew.*

Shong. A broken mesh. B.V.

Short bob. A short, black or well seasoned clay pipe.

Shot. A fish closely resembling a trout. *Carew.*

Shrimmed. Chilled. U.J.T.

Shrumped, or **Shrumped up.** Shivering with cold.

Shuffer. Full, stout, well. T.C.

Shune. Strange. *Carew.*

Shute. A channel of wood or iron for conveying a small stream of water. Also, the watering place where the women fill their pitchers from the "shute." Also, a small stream of water running from a shute or channel.

Shut-hom. To close, as "shut-hom the door."

Shutting or **Shooting ground.** Hard ground or rock requiring powder for blasting it.

Sich. Such. It was also used by Spenser.

Sigger, or **Sigure.** To leak. H.R.C. In Celtic Cornish *siger* means hollow, full of holes.

Sight. A large number or quantity, as "a sight of people," "a sight of money."

"Where is so huge a syght of mony." *Acolastus* 1540.

Simmee, and **I sim.** See **Semmee.**

Sissling. Moving uneasily in sleep. *Garland.*

Sives. See **Cives.**

Skainer. One who runs fast is said "to run like a skainer."

Skal. Calling out. "You great skal." A term of abuse. *Newlyn.* T.C.

Skatereens. Shivereens, all in pieces.

Skawd. See **Scud.** Spilt, scattered. *Callington.*

Sky-blue. Milk and water mixed.

Skedgwith, or **Skerrish.** Privet. M.A.C.

Skeer. See **Skitter.** To skim a stone on the water.

Skeer. To skitter or skutter. Q.V.

Skeerin. Fluttering, flying about.

Skeese, Skeyze, Skeyce, or **Scouse.** To frisk about, to run fast. In Celtic Cornish *skesy* means, to get free, to escape.

Skellet, or **Skillet.** A brass pot with three short legs and a flattish handle, all of one casting.

Skeeny. A sharp and gusty wind. C.

Sker, or **Skeer.** To scrape or scramble down a place. "To come scraping down." To rub against. To abrade, as "Ive skerred my hand."

Skerret, or **Skivet.** (C.) See **Skibbet.**

Skerrish. Privet. C. See **Skedgwith.**

Skerrimudge. It is not used of a *scaramouch*, or buffoon, in Cornwall, but is the name of a toy of a grotesquely human shape, the limbs of which are moved by a string so as to make strange antics.

Skerry-werry. A slight active person. "We seed little skerry-werry cut by Rawe's door." *J. T. Tregellas.*

Skew. Thick drizzling rain. U.J.T. A driving mist. C. Probably from the Celtic Cornish word *kuaz*, a shower of rain. (**To skew,** to shun. *Carew.)*

Skibbet, Skivet, or **Skerret.** A small box fixed in one end of a larger one. "Look in the box and you'll find it in the skibbet."

Skiddery. See **Skittery.**

Skimp. To scamp. Q.V.

Skimpings. The lightest and poorest part of the tin ore in the dressing of it.

Skipper, or **Hopper.** A kind of insect infesting hams.

Skirt, or **Skeert.** Short.

Skirtings. The diaphragm of an animal.

Skit. A syringe, a squirt.

Skit. The name given to a plant by boys who cut out portions of the hollow stems to make *skits.* (Also called Alexanders, or Allsanders. *Smyrnium olusatrum.* C.)

Skit. A mine pump used to raise water from a small depth. It is like a ship's pump. *Pryce.*

Skit, or **Skeet.** To squirt. Also a mode or trick of expectorating by forcing out the saliva suddenly between the closed teeth at one of the corners of the mouth.

Skitter. A track on ice or frozen snow for sliding (not skating) on.

Skitter. One who slides. To skitter, (or *skutter*) a stone, is to make it hop and skim along the surface of water, to make "ducks and drakes."

Skittery. Slippery, like ice, &c.

Skivet. See **Skibbet.**

Skove. The tinners say of a rich lode "'tis all *skove,* or *scove*; pure and clean. Celtic Cornish. *Pryce.*

Skuat, or **Skuit.** A legacy, a windfall. "A skuat of money."

Slack. Impudent talking. "Jaw." "Hold your slack."

Slack, or **Slacket.** Slight, thin.

Sladdocks. A cleaving and splitting tool for slate.

Slag. Misty rain, sleet. M.A.C.

Slam. To slap. (To trump, "I'll slam that card." M.A.C.)

Slams, Scrams. Scraps of meat. M.A.C.

Slappin. Stalwart, big. "A slappin fellow."

Slatter-cum-drash. Uproar, confusion. "Knocking every thing about."

Sleepy. A peculiar state of decay, as "sleepy wood" with a kind of white dry rot. Also used of linen when mildewed, or spotted by being kept too long damp. Also, stupid. "A sleepy-headed fellow."

Sleuchin. Shambling, slouching. "A great sleuchin fellow."

Slew, or **Slewed.** Twisted or canted round, or aside.

Slewed. Intoxicated. "He's slewed."

Sliddery. Slippery. (*Slider, Chaucer.*)

Sligering, or **Slaggering.** (g. soft). A great row. T.C.

Slim. Giving food too hot, "slims" the teeth. *Polwhele.*

Sling. A dram. **Slingers.** Invited guests. *Garland.*

Slingers. Kettle broth made of boiling water, bread, salt, and pepper, with sometimes a little butter. *Callington.*

Slintrim. An incline. M.A.C. In Celtic Cornish *slyntya* means, to slide, to glide along.

Slip. A young pig. Also, the outside cover of a pillow or a bolster. A pillow-slip, also, bolster case.

Slock. To entice, to tempt, to induce, as when one boy slocks another to steal apples, or as with an unwilling dog, "slocke'n along." (To pilfer, to give privately. *Polwhele.)*

Slocking bone. See **Locking bone.**

Slocking stone. Pryce calls it *(Mineralogia Cornubiensis)* "a tempting, inducing, or rich stone of ore." Some miners produce good stones of ore, which induce those concerned to proceed, until they expend much money perhaps, and at last find the mine good for nothing, so, likewise there have been some instances of miners, who have deceived their employers by bringing them "slocking stones" from other mines pretending they were found in the mine they worked in, the meaning of which imposition is obvious."

Slocum. A lagging, stupid, lazy fellow. "Come along old slocum."

Slones. The fruit of the black thorn. Sloes.

Slosh. To flush with, or splash water about.

Sloshy. Wet and muddy.

Slotter. A wet, dirty mess. **To slotter.** To make a mess.

Slottery. In Celtic Cornish it is spelt *slotteree* and means, rainy weather, foul and dirty, muddy; as "slottery weather," "slottery roads."

Slow cripple. A blind-worm. A slow-worm.

Slow-six-legged walkers. Lice. *Carew.*

Slummock. A dirty, slatternly woman.

Slump. A careless workwoman. M.A.C.

Slydom. Cunning.

Small tin. Smaals, the miners call it. Finely powdered tin-stuff. See **Floran** *(in the Addenda.)*

Smeech, or **Smitch.** A strong suffocating smell, as of burnt bones, feathers, &c.

Smicket. A smock, a chemise, a shift. A woman's under garment.

Smulk. A drunken dirty woman. M.A.C.

Snaggle. A snag, or large and ill-formed tooth. "Snaggly teeth," i,e., very irregular or ill-shaped teeth. Such are sometimes named "great snaggles."

Snead. The handle of a scythe. C.

Sneg. A small snail. C.

Sneivy. Low, mean, sneaking, cunning. "He's a sneivy fellow."

Sniffy. Supercilious. One who "cocks her (or his) nose" at anything.

Snifting clack. A valve in the old Cornish steam-engine, so called because of the noise it made in working. *Pryce.*

Snip, or **Snippet.** A little bit.

Snite. A snipe. C. *Snit* is the Celtic Cornish word.

Snob. The nasal secretion.

Snoogly sot. Well fitted, as with clothes. *Callington.*

Snuff. "To be snuff," affronted. *Polwhele.* See **Sniffy.**

Soas. This curious word is often used, and in various ways. It appears to be a wheedling or coaxing expression, as "Woll'ee, soas?" i.e., Now will you? "Do'ee, soas," i.e., Come now, do; and so on. It may be compared with the word **Ko** or **Co**. Q.V. (Neighbour, friend, companion. U.J.T.) (In Celtic Cornish *mar sose*, if thou art. (?) *Pryce.)*

Soaked. Bread not baked enough is said to be not well soaked.

Sodger. A red-herring. Soldier.

Sog. A sleep. A nap, drowsiness, numbness. "I've just had a bit of a sog." It is a Celtic Cornish word.

Sog. To doze, to have a short sleep.

Soggy. Quaggy, moist, marshy. In Celtic Cornish *sog* means, moist, wet.

Soller, or **Saller.** *(Pryce,* Corn. vocab. *solarium* vel *solium.* From the Latin.) In Celtic Cornish it is *soler,* meaning, a ground room, an entry, a gallery, a stage of boards in a mine; or *sel,* a foundation, base, or groundwork.

"A *saller* in a mine is a stage or gallery of boards for men to stand on and roll away broken stuff in wheel-barrows ...... There is also another kind of *saller* in an adit, being boards laid hollow on its bottom, by means of which air is conveyed under feet to the workmen ..... In a foot-way shaft the *saller* is the floor for a ladder to rest upon." *Pryce.*

So-long! Good bye! Adieu! (Heard in Looe and Wadebridge). W.T.A.P.

Some-clip. Very nice and particular. *Callington.* "He's some clip."

Soodling. Comforting, fondling, caressing, flattering. "Such soodling ways!" In Celtic Cornish *soth* means to flatter, but this is from the old English.

Soons. Amulets, charms. M.A.C. In Celtic Cornish *sona* means, to sanctify, to consecrate, to charm. Also, *soné*.

Sory. C. See **Scry.**

Sound-sleeper. See **Seven-sleeper.**

Sound. To swoon, to faint away. "Did your brother tell you says Rosalind how I counterfeited to *sound* when he showed me your handkerchief?"

Shakspere in "As you like it."

Soundy away. See **Zoundy away.**

Sour-sauce, Sour sabs, or **Sour sops.** The common sorrel. *Rumex acetosa,* also called Green-sauce.

Sour as a rig. Very ill-tempered. *Callington.* "Bless her when she is *riggish.*" *Antony and Cleopatra. Rig* anciently meant strumpet.

Sour-sab pie. A pie made with the most juicy leaves, and tender stems of the "Common Sorrel," *Rumex acetosa.* Eaten with sugar and cream. The writer once made an experimental *pasty* of the

Common Sorrel, and it was quite as good as some kinds of Rhubarb. Some mention is made of this plant in the Flora Medica, where it is said, "The leaves are refrigerent and diuretic, ... and taken in large quantities as *food* will be found of considerable efficacy. In some parts of France it is cultivated as an edible vegetable, and the natives of Wermeland, on the confines of Sweden, in seasons of great scarcity, form it into bread, and that it is not unsalutary."

Souse. To fall, sit, or bump suddenly down. "Down he came, souse."

Sow-pig, or **Grammar-sow.** The wood-louse.

Sowdling. Burly, ungainly. M.A.C.

Soyl. A seal. The sea calf. *Carew.*

Spading. Cutting turf in large thin slices with a great cross-handled spade.

Spal, or **Spale.** A fine for lost time, or absence from work. Amercement. Forfeiture. It is spâl in Celtic Cornish.

Spaliard. A pickman; a working tinner. *Pryce.*

Spalier, or **Spalyer.** Espalier.

Spalled, or **Spaaled.** Fined for absence or lost time in working.

Spalliers, or **Spadiards.** Miners so called from their spades. (Spalliers, *Polwhele.*)

Spalling. Breaking large stones of ore, &c. See **Cobbing.**

Spalls. Small chips of metal or stone. Stonecutters often say, "I've got a spall in my eye."

Spanjar, or **Span.** A tether. M.A.C.

Spanker. A large thing.

Spankin. Big, very large.

Spar. Quartz. "In Cornwall all the white, opake, common hard stone is called spar; erroneusly it must be owned for it is quartz."

Borlase's Natl. Histy.

Sparables. Sprigs; very small, short, headless nails, used for the soles of boots and shoes. (Hob-nails. *Dr. Bannister.*)

Sparable pie. A quaint term meaning anything unpalateable, as thus to a boy, "I'll give you some sparable pie."

Spare. Slow. "A very spare job."

Sparrow. A wooden rod or skewer, used by thatchers to secure the thatch.

Spar stone. Quartz.

Speed. Luck. "I had very poor speed."

Speedy. To hurry, to quicken. In Celtic Cornish it is *spedye,* to succeed, to hasten; *ta spedye,* to speed well. (See Borlase's Cornish Vocaby.)

Speedy ground. See **Teary ground.**

Spell. See **Stem.**

Spence. A store-room for wine, or victuals. "And hadden him into the *spense.*" *Chaucer.* In Celtic Cornish *spens* means a buttery.

Spend. v. To break ground. *Halliwell.*

Spiffy. Choice, neat, "natty," "spicy."

Spikkety, or Spekkety. Spotted, as a "spikkety hen." In Celtic Cornish *spekkiur* means, spotted, speckled. "A man in a spikkety jacket was theere."

Spiller. A long fishing line with many hooks, also a ground line.

Spinning-drone. A brown cock-chafer, or oak-web.

Spise. To ooze, or flow gently out.

Splat, or Splot. A plot, or small piece of ground. A spot, or blot, as of ink.

Splatty. Spotty, pimply, uneven in colour, covered with smears or blots. "All splatty."

Split and blout. To make a great fuss. *Callington.*

Splitting along. Going very fast.

Split-fig. A very stingy person. Nickname for a grocer who would cut a raisin in two, rather than give overweight. "Ould splet-fig."

Splot. See **Splat.**

Spoom. Scum, froth. *Spoum* in Celtic Cornish.

Spraggety. Mottled.

Spraggling. A sprawling, ill-drawn design is "spraggling" or "loud."

Sprawl. A disease of young ducks. They lose their strength and seem as if "*they could hardly sprawl.*" See **Sproil.**

Sprayed. Face, or hands roughened by cold.

Spraying. An east wind is "a very *spraying* wind."

Spriggan. A fairy. See **Piskey.**

Sprigly. Split, or split up, as of a wart when growing much cracked or split. "A sprigly wart."

Springle. A trap for snaring birds. A little wicker work, (made of a slight willow rod), about eight or ten inches long, and shaped like a battledoor, is pinned to the ground at the broad end. At the apex, a notch is cut for a button or catch. Across the apex an arched short rod, called the bridge, is stuck at both ends into the ground. A willow rod is stuck into the ground about three feet off, having at the top a line ending in a slip noose. The noose is passed under the bridge, and laid on the wicker, the rod being bent down and secured by a button near the noose, to the bridge and the wicker. Bait is placed on the wicker, a bird hopping on it releases the button, the rod flies back, and the bird is caught by the running noose.

Sproil, or **Sprawl.** Energy, strength. "I haven't got a bit of sproil." **To sprawl,** as, "I can hardly sprawl," i.e., scarcely stand or move.

Sproosen. An untidy, ungartered woman. M.A.C.

Sprouncey. Cheerful, jolly, slightly intoxicated.

Spry. Wide awake. "All alive." Spruce.

Spud. A young brat. Also, a garden tool used in cutting up weeds.

Spudder. A fuss, a bother. "What a spudder!"

Spuds. Small potatoes. W.T.A.P.

Spuke. An instrument spiked on to a pig's snout. The transverse bar, on which is a small roller, prevents the animal from grubbing.

Spur. A short time at work. A "nip" or small glass of spirit. "Something short."

Spurticles. Spectacles. "Where's my spurticles?"

Squab, or **Squadge.** A shove, a squeeze.

Squabbed. Pressed, or crushed.

Squab pie. A pie of apples, mutton, and an onion or two, seasoned with sugar, pepper, and salt.

Squadged. Squeezed, crushed, as of fruit, &c., injured by pressure.

Squard. A rent or tear. *Squerd* in Celtic Cornish.

Squarded. Torn, crushed in like a broken bandbox. In Celtic Cornish *squardye* means to tear, to rend, to break to pieces.

Squat. Pressed, flattened, burst. In Celtic Cornish *squattya* means to pluck, to tear to pieces, to hew.

Squat. A miner's term. "The *squat* of a lode," a broad heap. *Pryce.* In Celtic Cornish *squat,* suddenly, as when a lode has suddenly enlarged.

Squeeze. An old frump. A cross old maid. "A regular old patch," "an old squeeze."

Squiddle. A squirt. **Squiddling.** Squirting.

Squiddles. Diarrhœa.

Squinge grub. A small shrivelled pippin. "She's a regular old squinge grub." *Newquay.*

Squinny. To squint.

"Dost thou *squinny* at me?" *Shakspere.*

Squinny-eyed. A person whose eyes are habitually half closed. A squinter.

Squitch. A twitch, a jerk. In Celtic Cornish this word is spelt *squych* and means the same thing.

Squitchems. The jumps, the jerks, "the fidgets." From the Celtic Cornish *squych.* See **Squitch.**

Stacey-jar. A quart stone bottle. M.A.C.

Stack. The term used of *one* chimney, especially of a lofty one, as the engine *stack* of a mine engine-house.

Stag. A young cock.

Stagged, or **Stogged.** Stuck in the mud. In Celtic Cornish *stagen,* means a lake, a pool.

St. Agnes tôtle. A stupid old fool.

Stam-bang. Plump down. "Slap down."

Stamps, Stompses. Stamping or ore crushing mills.

Standard. A wrestling term. He who has thrown two men becomes a standard for the future contests in the ring.

Stand sam. "To stand sam," i.e., to stand treat, to pay for all, to bear the charge. This phrase is not peculiar to Cornwall only. It is noticed here because in Celtic Cornish, *sam* means a burden, a *charge.*

Stank. A mess, a muddle, a scrape. "We'em in a putty stank now." *Stanc* is Celtic Cornish for a pool, a pond.

Stank. To walk along, to step, to tread upon. "He's stankin' along at a putty rate." "What be'ee stankin' 'pon my toes vur you g'eat bufflehead?"

Stannary Laws, Stannaries, and **Stannary Courts.** "Are laws, præcincts, customs and courts peculiar only to tinners and tin mines." *Pryce.*

Stare. A starling.

Stares. Irregular spots or blotches. "It is full of stares."

Star-gazing, Staare-gaaze, Starry-gazy, or **Staring pie.** A pie made of leeks and pilchards. Sometimes without leeks. The noses or heads of the fish show through a hole in the crust. Hence the name.

Starving, or **Steeving.** Suffering from the cold. In Celtic Cornish *stervys*, or *sterys*, to catch cold, to be very cold.

Stash. "There now, *stash it* there, i.e., Don't say another word. *Mrs. Parr's Adam & Eve.*

Stave. To move quickly and noisily. To knock down. U.J.T.

Staver. A busybody. "A regular staver." One who is always in a fuss.

Steeve. To knock down. "I steeved down three to waunce;" "And a catched up a shoul for to steeve ma outright."

Steeved. Stowed, forced down, broken in.

Stem. A period of work, or of time, a job. A day's work. A double stem is to work six hours extra.

Stemming. Turn by turn, taking your turn. Spelt *stemmyn* in Borlase's Vocabulary of Celtic Cornish words. "To work out his stemmyn," i.e., to do his share of the work.

Stempel. A slant beam used in a mine for supporting certain places. *Pryce.*

Stent, or **Stents.** Rubble left by tin streamers in their workings. Such places are called stent bottoms. In Celtic Cornish *stener*, a tinner, *stean*, tin.

'Stent. The limit or boundary of a bargain or pitch or sett in mining, It is the word *extent* shortened. "That is the 'stent of it.

Stew. Fuss, ill-temper, row. "What a stew you're in!"

Stewer. A raised dust. Warmth or closeness of the air of a room. "What a stewer you're making!" "Kicking up a dust." In Celtic Cornish *steuys*, warm.

Steyne. A large brown salting pan or pot. *Stên*, a milk-pail, in Celtic Cornish.

Stickings. The last of a cow's milk. M.A.C.

Stickler. One who is on watch in the wrestling ring to see fair play.

Stiddle, or **Stoodle.** The pole to which an ox is tied in the stall. See **Studdle.**

Stile. A flat iron. M.A.C.

Sting-blubber. The sea nettle. See **Blubber.**

Stingdum. The fish *Cottus scorpius.* C.

Stint. To impregnate. C.

Stiracoose. A bustling, energetic woman.

Stirrage. Commotion, fuss, movement.

Stock. A large block or log of wood. The "Christmas stock" of Cornwall is the "yule-block" of the North of England. *Stoc* in Celtic Cornish.

Stodge. Food when very "thick and slab," is so called in contempt. "What stodge!"

Stogged. See **Stagged.**

Stoiting. The leaping of a shoal of fish. C.

Stool-crab. The male edible crab. C.

Stope. A step. "When a sumph (sump) or pit is sunk down in a lode, they break and work it away as it were in stairs or steps, one man following another, and breaking the ground which . . . . is called stopeing; and that height or step which each man breaks, is called a stope. Likewise, hewing away the lode overhead, is 'stopeing in the back.'" *Pryce.*

Stopes. Mining term for a stull, winze, or rise. In the Clay-work district it means the face of the clay-pit. "A good stopes," i.e., a good deep body of clay.

Stope-a-back. A mining operation. E.N. See **Stope.**

Stop net, or **Stop seine.** The great, or principal seine net used to enclose a shoal of pilchards. It is often 1600 feet long, and about 60 feet broad. One edge is supplied with corks to float it, the other with leaden weights to sink it. When "shot," for a shoal of pilchards, it surrounds them circularly like a wall, and the "tuck-net" is used to remove the fish from it. See **Tuck-net.**

Stound. A sudden and great pain.

Strake, or **Strêke.** A small *tye* or *gounce* for washing the fine ore *stuff*, as in streaming tin. *Pryce.* The term *strakes* is used of the *mica pits,* (Q.V.) or long shallow places in a clay-work. The clay water runs slowly along them as it deposits *mica* (Q.V.) In Celtic Cornish, *strêk,* a stream.

Strake, or **Strakey.** To steal marbles. M.A.C.

Straking along. Walking slowly, sauntering. In Celtic Cornish *strechye* means, to stop, to stay, to tarry.

Stram. A falsehood.

Stram. To slam, or shut anything violently.

Stram-bang, or **Slam-bang.** All of a sudden, in a noisy manner.

Strammer. A big lie, a large thing, a tall stout woman. "What a strammer!"

Stramming. Telling "awful lies," telling "thundering" lies.

Strange. Half mad, delirious, "talking quite strange."

Strap, or **Strop.** A bit of string. A small cord. (*Strop,* Armoric. *Borlase.*)

Strat. To abort. "Strat veal." C.

Straw mot. A single straw.

Stream of tin. Loose stones containing tin "when found together in great numbers making one continued course from one to ten feet deep, which we call a stream." *Borlase's Nat. Histy.*

Streams. Strains, as "streams of music."

Streamer. A tinner who works in a stream work, searching for, or washing tin ore.

Streaming. Washing tin-ore in a stream work; also, dipping washed linen in the "blueing" water, or rinsing it in clean water.

Stream-work. A place for the raising and washing of surface or alluvial tin ore.

Stretcher. An exaggeration, a lie. "What a stretcher!"

Strike. v. To anoint, to apply any unguent by smearing it on a diseased surface.

Strike. Eight gallons measure, or Winchester bushel.

Strike, Streeck, or Strik. "To let a man down in the shaft by the windlass, and if he calls up to the men above ground to '*streeck,*' they let him go further down." *Pryce.* From the Celtic Cornish word *stric,* active, nimble, swift.

String. A thin vein or lode of ore is so called.

String course. See **String.**

Stringy. Term used of vegetables when too old and fibrous.

Stroil. Strength. *Polwhele.* See **Sproil.**

Stroil. A weedy growth of coarse grass, sedge, &c. In Celtic Cornish, *strail elester,* means, a mat of sedge or rushes.

Strome. A streak. **Stromy.** Streaky.

Strother, or Stroth. Hurry, fuss. "What's all the stroth about?"

Strove. To force or compel an unwilling belief. "He strove me down to a lie."

Strow, or Strawl. A litter; confusion, row, disturbance, or turmoil. (**Strove.** U.J.T.)

Strub. To steal. As, to strub an orchard, i.e., steal the apples.

Strunty. Misty, foggy. M.A.C.

Stub. To grub or dig up the roots, as of furze, &c. "Stubbing furze."

Stubbard, or Stubbet. A kind of apple.

Studdle. A timber support of the "deads" in a mine. "As if a studdle had broke and the 'deads' were set a running." *Borlase's Celtic Cornish Vocaby.*

Stuffle. To stifle, to suffocate, as with smoke.

Stugg. A large brown earthenware vesssel. See **Steyne.**

Stuggy, or **Sturgy.** Short and fat.

Stull. A place to receive ore. E.N. This is a Celtic Cornish word and means in that language, a rafter or style. In a mine, timber placed in the backs of levels and covered with boards, or small poles to support rubbish, is called a *stull. Astull*, or *astel* in Celtic Cornish means "a stage of boards."

Stumpy. To walk, to hobble. "Stumping along."

Sturt. A run of good luck. A beginning of work,

Suant, Zuant, or **Suent.** Going smoothly, regularly, or without much friction or obstruction. There is another meaning, thus, if a tobacco pipe were nearly chooked it would be said "Et doan't draa zuant." Also thus, a thirsty man drinks eagerly and on putting down the glass may say, "Ah! that's suant." Also of sowing seed in a regular manner, thus, "Thaim zawed zuant."

Subsist, or **'Sist.** Money paid a miner in advance, or on account.

Sucked stone. "A honey-combed porous stone." *Pryce.* See **Swimming stone.**

Sugary candy. When the boots or shoes creak, they say there is sugary candy in them.

Sugary quartz. A very crumbly or pulverulent quartz, closely like white sugar.

Sump. Bottom of a mine shaft. (Sumph. *Pryce.)*

Sumpmen. Men who sink mine shafts.

Sumps. Pits made at the bottom of the mine for the water, or for trying in depth beyond the general workings. *Borlase.*

Sunbeams. The air-floating webs of the gossamer spider.

Survey. A public sale, an auction. Letting work in a mine.

Suss, or **Sess.** See **Zess.** *Sus,* Latin, a sow.

Swabstick. A mining tool.

Swaising, or **Whazing.** Swinging, as of the arms in walking. M.A.C. *Swegh,* a Saxon word, means, a violent motion, swaying.

Swallet. A gulph or chasm. *Pryce.*

Swap. A gadfly. M.A.C.

Swarr. Swathe, "a good swarr of hay."

Swealed, or **Swailed.** In the Cornish dialect, means, scorched and crumpled, as of parchment by heat. *Swelt,* (Spenser) burnt.

Swellack. The redwing. See **Whinnard.** *Suellak* in Celtic Cornish. *Polwhele.*

Swike. A twig of heath. M.A.C. See **Griglan.**

Swimming-stone. A stone formerly found at Nancothan Copper mine near Redruth. It consists of laminæ as thin as paper, intersecting each other in all directions. The stone is thus so cellular that it will float on water. It is of a yellow gossan colour and seems like a light kind of *lapis calaminaris.*

Borlase's Natl. Histy.

Swipes. A thin, poor alcoholic drink. Small beer.

Sŷch. See **Seech.**

Sye, or **Zye.** A scythe.

Tab, Tabbun, or **Tubban.** A piece of turf. In Celtic Cornish *tabm* means, a piece, a morsel.

Tabm. Celtic Cornish for a piece of bread and butter. ("Still used in Cornwall." *Polwhele.*)

Tacking. Clapping, as of the hands. Also, a punishment for a child, "I'll give'ee a good tacking!"

Taddago pie. A pie made of prematurely born veers.

Tadly-oodly. Tipsy. "He's all tádly-oodly."

Taer. A fuss, a row, great excitement. "Vaather's in a putty taer." In Celtic Cornish *taer* means, potent, powerful, rude.

Taering round. Making a fuss, being in a passion. "He was in a taering passion."

Taering. Rushing, or running about. Making a great clatter, or rumpus.

Tag. The tail end of a rump of beef. M.A.C.

Tag-worm. Earthworm. See **Angleditch.**

Tailings. The last or refuse ore.

Tailors needles. *Scandix pecten veneris.* C.

Tail-on-end. Full of expectation.

Tail-pipe. To tie a kettle to a dog's tail.

Take. A bargain of work in a mine.

Take a heave. A mineral lode is said to "take a heave" when a "fault" has shifted or broken its course.

Taken horse or **Hoss.** See **Hoss in the lode.**

Taking. Great excitement, trouble, or commotion. "Great pity is, he be in such *taking*."

Spenser in the Shepherd's Calendar.

Taking Day. "An old custom, about the origin of which history tells us nothing, is still duly observed at Crowan.

Annually, on the Sunday evening previous to Praze-an-beeble fair, large numbers of the young folk repair to the parish Church, and, at the conclusion of the service, they hasten to Clowance Park, where still larger crowds assemble, collected chiefly from Leedstown, Carnhell-green, Nancegollan, Black Rock, and Praze. Here the sterner sex select their partners for the forthcoming fair; and, as it not unfrequently happens that the generous proposals are not accepted, a tussle ensues, to the intense merriment of passing spectators.

Many a happy wedding has resulted from the opportunity afforded for selection on "Taking Day" in Clowance Park. *The Cornishman.*

Talch. Bran. It is a Celtic Cornish word.

Talafat. "A raised alcove for a bed." M.A.C.

Tallack. A garret. *Polwhele.* (Tallic. *Pryce.*)

Tallet. A stable loft. In Celtic Cornish *tallic* means, that which is placed high, a garret.

Tam. It is a Celtic Cornish word, and means, a morsel, a piece, a jot, a bit. *Tame furze,* i.e., short furze. *Carew.*

Tamlyn. A miner's tool. U.J.T.

Tamp. To beat or ram down, as of powder into a hole in blasting rocks.

Tamping. Material used in blasting.

Tamping iron. A tool for ramming down blasting materials in a hole for blasting.

Tammy. A straining sieve.

Tammy cloth. A loosely woven tissue for a straining cloth.

Tang. See **Twang.**

Tantra-bobus, or **Tantrum-bobus.** Term applied to a noisy, playful child. "Oh! you tantrabobus!"

Tap. The sole of a boot or shoe. Also the iron (or other metal) "scute" of the heel, "heel tap." **To tap,** i.e., to sole a shoe or boot.

Tarve. v. To fuss about in a rage.

Tarving. Struggling, storming, agitating. "Tarving about."

Taunt. Pert. "High and mighty." Saucy.

Tay-dish. A tea cup. "A dish of tay."

Teary. Soft, like dough. C.

Teary, or **Tary-ground.** Ground which, in mining, is easily dug out, because of its numerous small joints or fissures.

Teat. A draught of wind. M.A.C.

Teating. Whistling of the wind. M.A.C.

Teel. To plant or sow. To set or "teel a trap." To be obstinately bent on doing something, as "he's teeled for it," i.e., "he's ripe for it."

Teeled. Buried in the grave. Planted.

Teem. To pour out, i.e., "to teem out."

Teem. To ladle out water (in mining) by means of a bowl or scoop. To bale out.

Teen, Tend, or **Tine.** To light, as "teen the candle." "*Tine* the fierce lightning." *Milton.*

Teen. To close. "I hav'nt teened my eye. C.

Teening time. Twilight, candle lighting time.

Tend. To kindle, or set a light to. C.

Tend. v. To provide, to supply. "One boy *tended* the stones as the other threw them at the apples."

Tender. A waiter, as at an inn, or at a gentleman's dinner table. "Ev'ry Tender what's theere, my dears, is a rail gen'leman to look upon, mostly passons I reckon, or they've got their cloos, and they're like 'em too 'bout their throtts."

The "Queen's washing day" by Tregellas.

Tender-box. Tinder box. A metal box with a cover containing charred rags on which a spark from flint and steel increased so as to light a sulphur match. Superseded by lucifer matches in 1834.

Tern. A bittern. "Crying like a tern." M.A.C.

Tetties, Taties, Tates. Potatoes.

Tetty-hobbin. Potato cake. *Callington.*

Tetty-hoggan. Potato pasty. *Callington.* *Hogen* in Celtic Cornish means a pork pasty. *Pryce.*

Tetty-rattle. Cornish stew.

Thew. Threaten. *Carew.*

Thikky, Thekka, Thikky there. That, as "thikky man," i.e., that man. (In Celtic Cornish *thĕk* means *the. Pryce.)*

Thickee and thuckee. This and that. "Some caan't abide *thickee,* and t'other man caan't tich *thuckee.*" *Mrs. Parr's Adam and Eve.*

Thirl, or Thurl. Thin, wan, hollow-eyed. "He's looking quite thirl." "I'm feeling very thirl."

Throstel. A thrush. *Throstel. Chaucer.*

Throyting. Cutting little chips from a stick. *Carew.*

Thrashel. See **Drashel.**

Thraw to un. To persevere, to stick at it. "Thraw to un, for theer't sure to have a bundle of a lode very soon."

Thunder-axes. "There are also taken up in such works, (stream-works) certaine little tooles of brasse (bronze) which some term *thunder-axes.*" These are the *celts* so well known to the antiquary.

Thunder and lightning. Bread spread with clotted cream, and treacle over it.

Thunder-planet. In sultry weather they used to say, "there is a thunder planet in the air."

Thurt eyed. Said of one who squints.

Thumb-beam, or **Thumb-bine.** A twisted band of straw formed coil by coil off the thumb. Used formerly by countrymen, coiled round the legs to keep them dry.

Ticketing day. A term used of the days on which tin and copper ore are sold, "upon which days attend the Agents for the ores to be sold, and those of various Companies who having previously sampled the ores through their Assayers, produce a sealed ticket of the price they will give for ore; and he whose ticket is highest, takes the ore on the part of the Company for whom he acts." *Dr. Paris.* In this way the sale of £20,000, or more, in value of ore, is often concluded in an hour or two. This system has been inpractice about 150 years.

Tic-tac-Mollard. A game of "Ducks and Drakes." M.A.C.

Tiching. "Setting up turves to dry, to prepare for fuel." *Grose.*

Tidden. Tender, painful (mentally). Hard to put up with. "It came somewhat *tidden* to him." *Gulval.* T.C.

Tiddies. Teats. *Tethan* in Celtic Cornish for teat or udder.

Tiddy, or **Titty.** A teat, human milk. *Tidi* and *tethan* are Celtic Cornish for breast, pap, or teat.

Tiddy bit. A little piece.

Tiddliwink. A beerhouse. See **Kiddliwink.**

Tiddly. To do the lighter kind of household work. "What can you do? said a mistress to the maid. "I can louster and fouster, but I caan't tiddly," said she. W.T.A.P.

Tidy. Good, smart, intelligent. "A tidy house," "a tidy dinner," "a tidy sort of a chap."

Tie, or **Tye.** A feather bed. Also used of beds otherwise stuffed, as with "douse." Also called bed-tie.

Tie. A large wooden trough used for washing ore.

Tifles, Tiffles, or **Tifflens.** Small thready fragments. "Your dress is covered with tifles."

Tifle out, or **Tiffle out.** To unravel thready material or tissue.

Tifling. Fraying out. "tifling it out."

Tig, or **Tiggy.** A children's game played by several of them, there being one at each station. They interchange places. If in running from one station to the other a player be touched by the "Tig" (who is so called) the one touched becomes *tig* instead, and so on. This game is elswhere called *Tag.*

Tight. A tight blow, i.e., a sharp blow, also (as elswhere) drunk. "He's tight."

Timbal. A mining tool. M.A.C.

Timberin, or **Temberin.** Wooden.

Timberin hill. The staircase, or road to bed. "'Tis time for you to go up temberin hill."

Timdoodle. A silly fellow.

Timmersome. Timid, nervous.

Tin-glass. A name for bismuth. *Borlase.*

Tine. A tooth of a harrow. C. **To tine.** (The same as *to teen*), to light, as of a candle.

Ting. To tie up together.

Tinged up. Tied up. "I shaan't be tinged up to he." "Doant'ee come tinging aafter me."
J. R. Netherton.

Tink. A chaffinch.

Tinker after. Courting, making up to, feeling a fondness for.

Tinner. The water wagtail. *Bottrell.*

Tin bounds. Marked out land in which to search for and stream tin.

Tinner. A workman in search for, or employed in the washing of tin in a streamwork.

Tinners. "All Cornish miners." *Pryce.* (1790.)

Tin mine. A mine in which tin ore is dug from the tin lode.

Tin-stuff. Black tin. The miners use the term tin-*stuff* for tin, and copper-*ore* for copper when in a mineral state.

Tin-work. A stream work. Q.V.

Tippy. Smart, handsome, "quite the thing." "A tippy pair of boots."

Titch pipe, or **Touch pipe.** A habit with miners of having a short smoke during worktime, "titch pipe a croom."

Toad-in-the-hole. Meat with batter around it baked in a dish.

Toas, or **Toze.** To shake or toss the wet tin to and fro in a kieve or vat, with water, to cleanse and dress it. *Pryce.*

Toasts. "One and all." "Fish, tin, and copper." "Hakes and Tates." "No scads nor rays." "No staring pies."

Toat. The whole lot. "The whole toat of them."

Todge. See **Stodge.**

Toit or **Toitish.** Pert, saucy, or impudent.

Tokened to. Betrothed.

Tollur. A man who inspects and superintends tin-bounds; so called because "bounds" are terminated by holes cut in the earth which must be renewed, and visited once a year; or because he receives the tolls or dues of the lord of the soil. *Borlase.* (In Celtic Cornish *toll* or *doll* a hole).

Tom-holla. A noisy, rude fellow.

Tom-horry. A sea bird. The common name of two or three species of *skua.* C.

Tommy-tailor. The crane fly, or Daddy-long-legs. *(Tipula.)*

Tommy-toddy, or **Tom-toddy.** The tadpole.

"Like a tommy-toddy
All head and no body."

Tom toddy. "A game in which each person in succession has to drink a glass of beer or spirits, on the top of which a piece of lighted candle has been put, whilst the others sing

" *Tom-toddy* es coom hoam, coom hoam;
Tom-toddy es coom hoam
Weth hes eyes burnt, and hes nawse burnt
And hes eyelids burnt also.
Tom-toddy es," &c. *Uncle Jan Trenoodle.*

Tom-trot. Sweet stuff. Toffy, hard-bake.

Tongue-tabbas, or **Tongue-tab.** A chattering old scold.

Tongue-pad. A pratler, a chatterer, a very talkative person.

Tonnell, or **tunnell.** A great tub or task. *Polwhele.* *Tonnel* is Celtic Cornish for cask.

Tootledum pattick. A great simpleton.

Toppy. The bush of hair brushed straight up from the forehead. Very common about 50 years ago with men and boys.

Top-cliff. Half a gallon of black tin. *Carew.*

Tor. A pile of rocks, or a huge rock, generally crowning a hill of granite. The word is Celtic Cornish and means, a prominence, a bulge, the swell of a mountain, a mountain, a tower or high place.

Tormentor. An agricultural implement for breaking up the clods of a ploughed field.

Tose. To pull wool. **Tosing.** A process of pulling or preparing wool. M.A.C.

Tot. A dram, or "nip" of spirit, "a *tot* of liquor."

Tōtle. A stupid silly fellow.

Totelin, or **Totelish.** Both senile and imbecile. "A poor toteling old man."

Toucher. A close hit or miss. "That was a toucher."

Touch-wood. Wood in a peculiar state of decay. A sort of dry rot, as in dead, but still standing trees.

Tosh. A large bunch, as of flowers. M.A.C.

Touse. Fuss, row, uproar, hurry. "Making such a touse." (*Tos*, he swore, in Celtic Cornish.)

Touser. A large coarse apron for kitchen use. (*Touzier* in Armoric, a table-cloth).

Tousing. Working briskly, bustling about.

Towan, Towin, Tewen, Tuan, or **Tûyn.** These are Celtic Cornish words for a dune or heap of sand. Many places are called by this name whose situation answers to this etymology, as Towan Porth, Pentuan, &c. *Lhuyd* (Archeologia p. 220) says it means a hillock, and *Gwavas* applies the term to a plain, a green, or level place. "The spots, says *Polwhele*, most favourable to our sheep are those were the sands are scarcely covered with the sod, the green hillocks or levels of our downs in the vicinity of the sea. We call them *towans*."

Town of trees. A grove near a dwelling-house.

Town-place. The farm yard, a hamlet.

Towze. To pull about in a rough manner.

Toytish, or **Toit.** Pert, snappish.

Toze. To walk fast. **Tozing along.** Going along in a hurry. M.A.C.

Traade. Physic. "Doctors' traade." Anything nauseous, i.e. "poor traade." Synonymous with "stuff," "poor stuff," i.e., "poor traade."

Traapse. To gad about. "Traapseing about in the mud."

Trammel. A fishing net. (*Tramels,* nets. *Spenser.*)

Trawy. A trough. T.C.

Treesing. Idling. M.A.C.

Tregagle, or **Tregeagle.** A legendary personage. The name is used thus "Howling like Tregagle." *See the Legend in Corn. Histy.*

Treloobing. Washing the *loobs*, Q.V., or slime tin, &c., so as to save the fine ore, which sinks to the bottom. *Loob*, Celtic Cornish, slime, sludge.

Tremmin. Good, very nice, pleasant. "Good for sore eyes," i.e., good to see. "Now I call that, tremmin." In Celtic Cornish *tremyn* means, sight, look, aspect.

Trester. A beam. "Put in a good big trester." In Celtic Cornish, *troster*, a beam, a rafter, and *tresters*, beams, rafters.

Trestrem. Bait cut up for the hooks. *F. W. P., Mousehole.*

Tribet. A trivet. A stand or support having three legs, or feet. An andiron. It is a Celtic Cornish word.

Tribute. The share or share price by contract, of ore raised, claimed by the miner.

Tributers. Miners who work for "tribute," (Q.V.), i.e., undertake to raise ore from the lode at a percentage in the pound sterling, on the value of the ore brought to "grass."

Triddling. Trifling, talking nonsense. *Garland.*

Trig. To put on the drag to a wheel. To set up or support with a prop, "to trig it up." To trip up. If falling, a lad would say he had "trigged his foot."

Trig. Shellfish are so called at Helford, and many other places in Cornwall. *Polwhele.* (*Treage,* The muscle (fish). *Borlase.*) Celtic Cornish.

Trikle. Treacle. (*Triacle. Chaucer.*)

Troach. To step along, to tread upon, to trample on.

Troachers. Itinerant dealers or pedlers. So called because they *troach* (trot) about the country.

Troaching. Trudging, plodding along, walking about. (Hawking vegetables. M.A.C.) Treading upon. "Troaching about all day long."

Troddler. Just "going off," one just learning to walk, "a little troddler."

Troil. A feast. (A short row on the sea. M.A.C.)

Troil. A tinner's feast. (Also called a *duggle. Pryce.*)

Troll foot. See **Trowled.**

Troll footed. One who has club feet.

Trone. A small furrow, or narrow trench.

Trool. To turn round or run, as does a small wheel, or roll like a ball. See **Truckle.**

Trot. The bed of a river. *Polwhele.*

Trot. **"An old trot."** A moping, cross, and wretched old woman, a covetous person, an old miser. From *troth,* Celtic Cornish, poor, wretched.

Trowled, or **Trolled.** Turned or twisted down, as of the heel of a shoe. Also a deformity of the foot (talipes), "a trowled foot." Also sprained, as, "I've trowled my foot."

Troy-town. "Like Troy-town," i.e., confusion, litter; intricacy of roads or streets.

Truck. Trash. "What truck!" *Troc* in Celtic Cornish means, evil, harm.

Truckle. A very small wheel or roller.

Truckle. To roll along, or around as a small wheel, or as a ball.

Truff. Trout. H.R.C. *Trud* in Celtic Cornish, but borrowed from the Latin *trutta*, a trout.

Trug. To trudge.

Trundle. A salting pan. *Callington.*

Trunk. A mining tool. E.N.

Trunking. One of the processes in tin dressing. E.N.

Tub. The fish. *Trigla hirundo.* C. Red Gurnard.

Tubbans. Clods of earth. **Tabs.** Q.V.

Tubbal. A miner's tool.

Tubbut. Short and thick. See **Dobbet.**

Tuck. Chuck, as "a tuck under the chin." Also an operation in seining pilchards.

Tucker. One who works in a fulling-mill.

Tuck in. A good large meal, a blow-out. "I've had a regular good tuck in."

Tucking. Working in a fulling-mill. Also an operation with a tuck-net in the taking of pilchards by removing the fish enclosed in the large stop-net.

Tucking-mill. A fulling-mill.

Tuck-net. A fishing net used in the taking of pilchards which have been enclosed by the seine, or stop-net.

Tummals. Lots, heaps, quantities of any thing. "Tummals of meat." *Tomals* in Celtic Cornish, for the same.

Tulky, or **Tulgy.** A slovenly woman. M.A.C.

Tun-tree, or **Tuntry.** The pole of an ox-wagon.

Turned ugly (oogly). Loss of temper, very cross, or sulky. "He's turned oogly."

Tut. A footstool. A stupid person. M.A.C.

Tutmen. Men who work in a mine by the piece, such as sinking shafts, driving adits, &c., at so much per fathom.

Tutwork. Work in a mine done at a certain price, as by the fathom, &c.

Twang, or **Tang.** A peculiar taste or flavour.

Twingle. To twist and wriggle like a worm on a hook. Also to tingle as from cold.

Twister. A difficult job, "that's a twister."

Tye. An adit or drain. A Celtic Cornish word formerly in use about St. Austell. *Tonkin.* Also a bed. See **Bed-tye.**

Tye. "The same as *strêk*, (or strake) but worked with a smaller stream of water." *Pryce.*

Tyor. A thatcher, or hellier (slater). *Polwhele.* It is a Celtic Cornish word.

Udjiack. "A small moveable block of wood used by builders in fitting the planks of a boat." B.V.

Ugly, or **Oogly.** Morose, ill-tempered.

"Esna lukkin oogly ovver et!"

Uncle. This word, like *aunt* (Q.V.), is very often used instead of Mr., in speaking to, or of an aged Cornishman, although not related to the speaker.

Underground captain. The person who overlooks miners at work down in the mine.

Uneave, To thaw. *Polwhele.* Heaving, eaving, and giving, are synonymous words. Chaucer used *yeve* for *give*, and the true word seems to be *yeaving.* It is now used without the prefix *un.* See **Heaving,** and **Giving.**

Únkid Gloomy, lonely, dull, uncanny.

Unlusty. Unwieldy, very fat.

Unream. To skim off the clotted or clouted cream from the surface of the scalded milk with a *reamer.* (Q.V.)

Un-tifled. Frayed out, unravelled or frayed by wear; used of tissues.

Uppa, uppa, holye! (Pronounced *oopa, oopa, holly*). When the writer was a boy the following were the words used in the boy's game of fox-hunting. When the hounds (the boys) were "at fault" the leader cried out to the missing "fox" in these words,

"Uppa, uppa, holye,
If you don't speak,
My dogs shan't folly (follow)."

The first line is Celtic Cornish, *uppa* meaning, in this place, here, and *holye*, to follow, to come after, to watch. This is a "cry" in two languages, and the only one (except perhaps **Ena Mena**, Q.V.) of the kind known to the writer. It is probably very old, and when, long ago, Cornish boys hunted together, some of them perhaps could only speak their native Celtic tongue, while others among them knew both English and Cornish. See **Hubba** and **Hevah.**

Uprose, or **Uprosed.** Churched, as with women after childbed.

Urge. To retch, or strain in vomiting.

Vady. Musty. Damp. (*Vaded*, gone. *Spenser.*)

Vag-ends. Fag ends, scraps, remnants.

Vally. Value, worth, price.

Valsen. Fresh water eels. *Carew.*

Vamp. A sock, or short stocking.

Vamp. To put a new foot to a stocking.

Vamping. A tippler's trick. Tipplers who desire to make the most of *one* glass of grog, first drink a little, then add some spirit, then sip again, next add some more water, then drink again, and so are repeating the trick known as vamping. In a way it *is* putting a new foot to a stocking.

Vang. A notion, or conceit, "one of his new vangs."

Vang. To get, to earn.

"Vang thee that." *The London Prodigal.*

Vangings. Earnings, winnings. See **Fangings.**

Vang-tooth. The eye-tooth. (*Wang*, Saxon).

Vanning. Trying a sample of tin ore by washing it on a shovel.

Vargood. "A spar about 23 feet long used as a bow-line to the foresail of our fishing boats." W.F.P.

Veak. A whitlow. C. **Veach.** M.A.C.

Vean. Little. "Cheeld vean," little child. It is Celtic Cornish. Also *vyan.*

Veer. A young, or sucking pig. (In Celtic Cornish *verres* means a boar pig. *Pryce.)*

Vellon. See **Fellon.**

Vellum-broken. Ruptured, *(hernia)*. Suffering from hydrocele.

Venom. A gathered, or inflamed finger. A whitlow.

Veôr. Great. A Celtic Cornish word, also written *vor, veur* and *meur.*

Veskin. See **Biscan.**

Vester. See **Fescue.**

Vestry. The smiling of infants in their sleep. M.A.C.

Victor-nuts. Hazelnuts. M.A.C.

Vistes, or **Veestes.** The fists.

"But I'll tame the ould deval afore et es long,
Ef I caan't wai ma veestes, I will wai ma tongue."

Vinny, or **Vinnied.** Turned sour. "The beer is gone vinny." Mouldy, as of cheese.

Vinney, or **Vinnewed ore.** "Copper ore that has a blue or green spume, or efflorescence upon it like verdigris." *Pryce.*

Virgin ore. Malleable or native copper. So called because of its purity.

Visnan, or **Vidnan.** A sand lance, a sand eel. M.A.C.

Visgay, or **Visgie.** A digging tool, a kind of mattock. *Callington.*

Vitty. See **Fitty.**

Vlaad. See **Blawed.**

Vlicker. "Flicker," or blush.

Vlickets. Hot flushes, blushes.

Vlicker up. To blush, or flush violently. "She vlickered up all over, "i.e.," Her face was all on fire."

Voace-put. Something done for the occasion, or, under great necessity, or compulsion. "Twas a voace-put aafter oal."

Voider. A baby's clothes-basket.

Vogget. To hop on one leg. C.

Volyer, or **Vollier.** The second seine boat in pilchard fishing. It carries the tuck-net. Also called **Folyer,** or **Follower.**

Vooch, and **Voochy.** See **Fooch,** and **Foochy.**

Vore. A furrow. *For* or *for* in Celtic Cornish, a way.

Vore-heap. A wrestling grip or hitch.

Vore-right, or **Fore-right.** A straight-forward, blunt, or brusque manner of speaking. The coarse ground, "entire grain," (corn) made into bread is called "vore-right," or "forth-right" bread.

Vorethy, or **Voathy.** See **Foathy,** or **Forethy.**

Vorver. A horse way. In Celtic Cornish *vor, vordh,* or *for,* a way, and *verh,* (a mutation of *merh*) a horse.

Voryer. The fowls' or hens' path, or way. From the Celtic Cornish *vor,* a way; *yer,* hens, (*yar,* a hen).

Vrape. See **Frape.**

Vugg, or **Voog.** A natural cavity in a mine often found beautifully crusted with minerals. There are various names in Celtic Cornish for a cave or cavern, viz., *vooga, vou, vugga, vug, vugh, hugo, fogo, fogou, fou, googoo, ogov,* and *ogo.*

Vurry-cloth, or **Furry-cloth.** An oval piece of red cloth about 3 inches by 2 inches, placed over the fontanel of a new-born babe before putting on a cap. This custom of the vurry-cloth was in use about 40 or 50 years ago. Poor women begged the red cloth of tailors to use for this purpose. The custom is obsolete or very rare now. Perhaps from the Celtic Cornish *fur*, sage, prudent. Sage-woman's cloth. *Bodmin.*

Wack. Allowance, *quantum.* "He looks like a fellow who can take his *wack.*"

Wad. A small bunch, or bundle of hay, straw, &c. The "rubber" used by french-polishers is called a "wad." Also, bread, butter, and sugar in a tied rag, for infants to suck. This is called a "sugary wad."

Waiter. A tea tray.

Wagel. A grey gull. M.A.C.

Wambling. Rumbling in the stomach. Feeling sick and faint. See **Wimbly-wambly.**

Wang. To hang about in a tiresome manner. M.A.C.

Want. A mole. **Want-hill.** Mole-hill.

Warming stone. A name formerly given to a kind of stone, which when once heated retains the heat a great while. Called by Charlton, *Lapis schistos duriss: et solidissimus.* (Borlase's Natl. Histy.)

Warn. To warrant, as "I'll warn'ee," i.e., I'll warrant you.

Watercase. A plant resembling watercress, but the leaves are not so round, and it has a more stinging taste. (*Helosciadum nodiflorum.* C.)

Wattery. Faint and hungry, "I'm feeling very wattery."

Watty, or **Wat.** A name for a hare. So called from his long ears or *wattles.* *Brewer.*

"By this poor *Wat*, far off upon a hill
Stands on his hinder legs, with listening ear."
Shakspere in "Venus and Adonis."

Way. The "reason why." "That is the *way* I did it," i.e., That is *why* I did it.

Way. "In a way." Disturbed in mind. Angry. "Mawther's in a putty way." See **Taer, Taking. Touse,** and **Por.**

Ware East. Ware West. Cries in hurling for the goal. *Carew.* (*Ware* or *Whare,* Celtic Cornish for quickly, soon, at once.)

Wear, or **wor.** Fashion. See **Oal tha wor.** "It is not the *wear.*" *Shakspere.*

Wedgin day. A day set apart by miners for repairing tools, &c. E.N.

Weelyes. (weelys) Crab or lobster pots. *Tonkin.*

Wee's nest. A mare's nest.

"Why dost thou laugh?
What mare's nest hast thou found?"
Beaumont and Fletcher, "Bonduca," v. 2.

In Cornwall they say, "you have found a wee's nest and are laughing over the *eggs.*" *Brewer.*

Wee-wow. A rocking unsteady motion. Wobbling about.

Weet. To pull. ("I'll weet thy loggers." M.A.C.)

Weet. To pull the hair. W.F.P.

Weet-snob. It was a sight to see the cobbler's face as he pulled his hog's bristle and waxed thread, when we boys used to flatten our noses against his window. How he "glazed," when we called out "Weet snob! If I hear anybody say weet snob! I'll weet snob him!" Those boys! (Weet was pronounced *wheet.)* *St. Columb.*

Weeting. (A thrashing. M.A.C.) Pulling anyone about.

Weeth. A field. **Weethans.** Small fields. M.A.C.

Well-a-fine. "That's all well-a-fine." "That's all very well." "Very well considering." Middling.

Wettle. An infant's inside flannel.

Whap. Whop, a blow. *Whaf* is Celtic Cornish for a blow.

Wheal. A mine, a work. See **Huel.** It is a Celtic Cornish word. Also spelt *whel*, *wheyl*, and *whyl*.

Whelk, or **Whilk.** See **Quillaway.**

Whelve, or **Whilve.** "To turn a hollow vessel upside down." C.

Whiffing. A fishing term. Trailing a fishing line with baited hook after a boat.

Whim, or **Whem.** A large hollow drum with a perpendicular axis, and a powerful transverse beam, worked by one or two horses walking round and round in a circle. The rotation of the drum with the rope coiled round it causes the kibble to ascend or decend in a shaft. It used to be said that the inventor of the "whim" was asked what he was doing. He replied that he had a "whim" in his head. This is an improbable tale as in Celtic Cornish *wimblen* means, whirling, and such is the action of the machine.

Whinnard. The redwing. Also called **Swellack.** Q.V.

Whinnard. Used of one who is looking very cold. "Looking like a whinnard."

Whipsidery. A machine for raising ore. M.A.C.

Whip-and-go. A near miss, a near chance, all but, "'Twas whip-and-go to get there in time."

Whip-and-while. Every now and then, occasionally.

Whip-the-cat. A tailor who works in private houses, and who is paid by the day.

Whisky. An old name for a gig.

Whistercuff. A box on the ear.

Whip-tree. The whipple-tree of a carriage.

Whirl. The hip joint. "I've got such a pain in my whirl."

Whirl-bone. The round head of the hip-bone. The hip-bone.

White-livered. Cowardly. "Lily-livered." "A lily-livered action taking knave." *Shakspere.* This term, white-livered, was formerly used of a man who had married three or four times.

Whit-neck. A white-throated weasel. E.N.

White-pot, or **Whitpot.** A dish made of milk, flour, and treacle, with a slice of bread on the surface, baked; also milk and flour with sugar or treacle, boiled. *Pot* is Celtic Cornish for *pudding.* ("To keep well filled with thrifty fare, as *white-pot,* buttermilk, and curds." *Hudibras.)*

Whitsul. Milk, sour milk, cheese, curds, butter, and such like as come from the cow. *Carew.*

White tin. The *metal* tin, in contra-distinction to the *ore,* or black tin.

White-witch. A quack, cheat, and dealer in charms, &c. One who trades on the superstitions of the ignorant.

Whiz. A fussy person, "a dreadful old whiz."

Whizzy. Giddy. "Head gwain roun'."

Whizzing about. Fussing about, whirling.

Whizzy-gig. A whirligig.

Whurts, or **Hurts.** Whortleberries or Hurtleberries.

Widdles. Whims, silly conceits.

Widdershins. From north to south, through east. M.A.C.

Widdy-widdy-way. The following is said in starting children for a race.

> "Widdy, widdy, way,
> Is a very pretty play,
> Once, twice, three times,
> And all run away." Off.

Wiff. A small tippet or cape. "Go and put on your wiff."

Wildfire, or **Weeldfire.** Erysipelas.

Wild lead. See **Mock lead.**

Willen. A beetle. This is spelt *hwillaen* in Celtic Cornish by *Pryce; Huilan* by *Borlase.*

Wilkin, or **Wilkey.** A frog. See **Quilkey,** and **Quilkin.**

Wilver. The pot, or "baker" under which country bread is baked in burning wood ashes; called a "baking kettle" in Devonshire.

Wimbly-wambly. Feeling sick and giddy. "I'm all wimbly-wambly."

Windle. A spindle.

Wind-mow. A rick made in the open field.

Winds. A windlass. *Pryce.*

Windspur broach. "A crooked stick thrust into each end of a thatch to secure the windspur rope." H.R.C.

Windspur rope. A rope to keep the top of a hay-stack safe from the wind.

Wingarly. Faint, sick. *Borlase.*

Wingery. "Oozing, shiny, as tainted meat." M.A.C.

Winky. Very quickly, "like winky," i.e., in a moment, in the twinkling of an eye.

Winnick. To over-reach, to deceive, to cheat. "I'll winnick him."

Wint, or **Windt.** A whirling, wheel-like machine for twisting straw rope. (**Wink.** c.)

Winze. In mining, a small shaft sunk from one level to another for the purpose of ventilation. *Ogilvie.* A small shaft with a windlass. M.A.C. A communication between two mine galleries by a partial shaft in the intervals between the two great shafts. *Dr. Paris.*

Wisht, or **Whisht.** Melancholy, dismal, sad, "'Tes whisht, i.e., 'tis sad. "I am feeling quite whisht," i.e., I am very low in spirits. "'Tes whisht weather," i.e., Very rough weather. "He's a whisht poor workman," i.e., He's a stupid workman. "'Tes whisht poor traade," i.e., It is very nauseous. (*Weest* in Pembroke.)

Wol, or **Wull.** Will.

"I *wol* not tellen God's privitie." *Chaucer.*

Wonders. See **Gwenders.** c.

Wood tin. Tin ore having a structural resemblance to wood.

Woodwall. The green wood-pecker. c.

Wormals. Lumps in the skin of an animal from the presence of larvæ therein. (*Wornal.* c.)

Worms. "Poor old worms," i.e., poor old souls, (old people). Poor worms! Poor dear worms! i.e., poor little souls, (children.)

Wownd. A wound. Used thus in rhyme by Spenser.

"The myrrhe sweete bleeding to the bitter *wound*,
The fruitfull olive, and the platane *round*."

Faery Queene.

Wriggle, or **Wiggle.** See **Riggle.**

Wrinkle. A dodge, a trick, a cunning suggestion. In Celtic Cornish *wrynch*, a trick. (Also used elsewhere). "I've put him up to a wrinkle or two."

Wrinkles. Periwinkles.

Wroth. A fish known as Conner, or sea Carp. *Tonkin.*

Wroxler. See **Ruxler.**

Wurraw! See **Hooraa!**

Yaffer, or **Yeffer.** Heifer.

Yafful. A handful.

Yaller, or **Yalla.** Yellow.

Yap. A short snapping bark of a dog.

Yaw. Ewe.

Yellow janders. The jaundice.

Yes. A Cornishman has a way of answering "yes" which cannot be written, or spelt. It is thus done. The teeth a little apart, and the mouth rounded, a sudden and sibilant inspiration is made. The sound so produced is meant for "yes," and is equivalent to a nod. In Buckinghamshire they did not understand it!

Yet. A gate. "Wull'ee opp'n the yet?" It is a Celtic Cornish word.

Yewl. A dung-fork. See **Eval.** *Callington.*

Yock, Yerk, or **Yolk.** The greasy impurity of a sheep's fleece. C.

Yock, or **Yuck.** To hiccough. Trying to swallow when the mouth is empty, is called "giving a yock." *Yeox. Saxon. Yoxe. Chaucer.*

Zacky. See **Cousin-Jacky.**

Zam. See Sam.

Zam-zodden, or **Zam-zoddered.** See **Sam-sawdered.**

Zang. See Sang.

Zape, or **Zapy.** A blockhead, a fool.

Záwkemin, or **Záwkin.** Stupid, thickheaded.

Zawker. A dull stupid fellow.

Zawn. A hole in the cliff through which the sea passes. (A cave where the tide flows in. *Dr. Bannister.*) Spelt *Sawan* by *Polwhele* and *Pryce.* Borlase says *Zawn* is Celtic Cornish for a creek.

Zeer. Worn out, aged, withered, sere. (*Sere,* dry, *Chaucer.*)

Zess, or **Sess.** A great fat woman. From the Latin *sus,* a sow, a pig, a hog.

Zew. "To work alongside a lode before breaking it down." *Garland.* From the Celtic Cornish *sewe* or *sewye,* to follow, to pursue.

Zighyr. "When a very small slow stream of water issues through a cranny under-ground, it is said to be *Zighyr* or *Sigger.*" In Celtic Cornish *sigyr* means, sluggish, lazy.

Zog. See **Sog.**

Zoggy. See **Soggy.**

Zoundy away, or **Soundy away.** To faint, to sink down, convulsed with laughter. "I towld'n a story 'bout a swemmin grendin-stoan an a ded zoundy, **zoundy, z-o-u-n-d-y** away, wai lawfin."

Zukky. To smart. "I'd make un zukky." *Camborne.*

Zwealed. See **Swealed.**

ADDENDA.

Alive. When a mineral lode is rich in tin, copper, &c., it is said to be *alive,* in contra-distinction to *deads.* Q.V.

Angelmaine. The Monk fish, *squatina angelus.* C. (Mevagissey.)

Astull. "An arch or ceiling of boards over the men's heads in a mine, to save them from the falling stones, rocks, or scales of the lode or its walls." *Pryce.* It is *astel* in Celtic Cornish, meaning, a board, a plank. See **Stull.**

Back of the lode. That part of it which is uppermost or nearest to the surface of the earth.

Bottoms in fork. When the deepest parts of a mine are freed by a pumping engine from the accumulated water, miners say, "The bottoms are in fork, or, "She (the mine) is in fork." Pumping up the water is "forking" it. The engine is "in fork (see *Pryce)* when it has done its pumping.

Bunny. A sudden enlargement or bunch of ore in a lode. *Pryce.* Perhaps this word is from *ben,* Celtic Cornish for, butt end.

Burden, Over-burden, or **Top-burden.** The rubble or dead ground which overlies a stratum of tin-ore, &c. In china clay works it is the top ground, from the surface to the bed of clay which lies below.

Cakka-man-áh, or **Akka-mannáa.** Human fœces. Perhaps from the Celtic Cornish *cac*, ordure. (Williams, *Corn. Dicty.*, gives for it in "Welsh, *câch.* Armoric, *câch.* Irish, *cac.* Gaelic, *cac.* Manx, *cuch.* Sanscrit, *cakan.* Greek, *kakké.* Dutch, *kak.* Spanish and Portuguese, *caca.*") Latin, *caco.* v.

Cappenin, or **Capp'nin.** Overbearing or domineering. "Don't come capp'nin over me."

Casier. A sieve. In Celtic Cornish, *kazer.*

Caunter lode. See **Lodes.**

Cómmercin. Conversing, chattering. "Whatever is all the cómmercin about?"

"Looks commercing with the skies." *Milton.*

Comreesing. Fleeting, sliding away. *Polwhele.* From the Celtic Cornish *rees*, to fleet, or slide away.

Costean or **Costeaning pits.** "Shallow pits to trace or find tin." *Pryce.* In Celtic Cornish *cothas*, to find, (*Borlase*) *stean*, tin.

Crawn. A dried sheep's skin. *Davy, Zennor.* In Celtic Cornish *croin*, a skin.

Cross-course. (Pro. cross-coose.) Cross bar, cross-gossan, cross-lode. "Is either a vein of a metallic nature, a cross-gossan, or else a soft earth, clay, or flookan like a vein, which unheads and intersects the true lode." *Pryce.* See **Lodes.**

Dilluer, or **Dillueing sieve.** A horse-hair sieve used in washing the fine ore stuff, as in streaming tin. *Pryce.* From the Celtic Cornish *dilleugh* or *dylyer*, to let go, to let fly, to send away.

Down-park. An enclosed down, or Common. See **Park.**

Dowst. Dust. (See **Douse.**) From *dowstoll*, Celtic Cornish, all to pieces.

Drift. In mining "is the level that the men drive underground from one shaft to another, or north and south out of the lode, in which, only one man at a time can work, it being but a working big, and about five or six feet high." *Pryce.*

Driggoe, or **Drigger.** The lowest of the tier of pumps of a water-engine. *Pryce.* The word is a form of *trig* or *trigger*, that which props up, or supports.

Duggle. A tinner's feast. Also called a **Troil.** *Pryce.*

Elvan. "A very hard close grained stone." *Pryce.* *Elven* in Celtic Cornish means, a spark of fire; as if the name were applied to stone hard enough to strike fire.

Fang. (See **Fangings,** or **Vangings.** Takings, earnings, winnings. Also **New-fang.**) Craik (*English Literature, and Language, p.* 87) quotes the following Semi-Saxon line.

"On *fang* bring hegilich with the in Godes riche." i.e. *Take,* bring him quickly with thee into God's kingdom. This written use of the word dates about, or before A.D. 1264, and no doubt it was in oral use much earlier.

Fast. The solid, unmoved ground, or rock, in mining is called "the fast" or "fast ground."

Floran. Very fine tin-stuff. (**Flour tin.**) *Pryce.*

Fork, Forking, In fork. See **Bottoms in fork.**

Gatchers. The after-leavings of tin ore. *Pryce.* See **Loobs.**

Gibb'n Camborne. "Give him Camborne." A threat of punishment used by Cornish rowdies. See **Meara-geeks.**

Gollop. To gollop up. To gobble up, to eat ravenously. "He golloped up the whole of it in no time."

Gollop. A lump, as of food. Same as **Dollop.** Q.V.

Gounce. See **Strake.**

Grass Capp'n. Grass Captain is the one who superintends the men, &c., working "at grass" i.e., on the surface of a mine.

Gulph of ore. When a part of a lode proves very rich, miners say they have a "gulph of ore."

Gunnies. "Means breadth or width. A single gunnies is three feet wide; a gunnies and a half is four feet and a half; and a double gunnies is six feet wide. The former vaults or cavities that were dug in a mine, are termed 'the old gunnies;' and if they are full of water, they are sometimes called 'gunnies of water,' yet more commonly, 'a house of water."

Pryce.

Hooler. A bundle of blunt borers. A mining term.

"*The Cornishman.*"

House. See **Gunnies,** and **Turn-house.**

House of water. See **Gunnies.**

Hulk. An old mine excavation. *Pryce.*

Jew. A name given to a black field-beetle. Because it exudes a bloody or pinkish froth, they call to it while holding it in the hand, "Jew, Jew, spit blood."

Kerchy. (Pro. *ker-tchee.*) A curtsy. A mode of salutation by females. Once very common, now nearly obsolete except in some remote country places where the women and children actually display good manners! In towns, the people don't often use such a form of salute in these school-board days.

Kerchy. A pocket handkerchief. "Where's my kerchy?"

Kivully. Loose, hollow, shelfy ground. *Pryce.*

Learys. A mining term for "old men's workings." Q.V.

Mabyers. Chicken, young fowls. Celtic Cornish *mab* a son, *yer*, hens.

Mock lead. Blende or black-jack. Sulphuret of Zinc. *Pryce.*

Mole. The fish, rock goby. *Gobius niger.* C.

Molly-caudle. A *she*-man who fidgets, and interferes with what is "women's work."

Nater. Provincial, and Celtic Cornish for, nature. "*Erbyn nater gans un cry.*" Against nature with a cry.

Near the day. Miner's term for, near the surface.

Penny-liggy. Hard up for cash.

Pilly ground. A fishing term for alternate stretches of sand, and rocks covered with sea-weed, under water. (Looe.) W.T.A.P. In Celtic Cornish *pil* means a hillock, as if to say, a hillocky bottom.

Poop, or Poopy. To go to stool. (Said by children.)

Quick sticks. "He made quick sticks of it," i.e., He soon did it, or soon settled the business in hand.

Rampant spar lode. A quartz lode. *Pryce.*

Rowler. A ruler, a governor. It is a Celtic Cornish word.

Rusk or Risk. The rind or bark. It is *risc* in Celtic Cornish.

Rux. Grains of gold were so called by tinners. *Pryce.* See **Hopps.**

St. Tibb's Eve. Neither before nor after Christmas, i.e., at no time. "I'll do et next St. Tibb's Eve." M.A.C. Like the "Greek calends."

Scaw-coo. The night shade. M.A.C. Celtic Cornish.

Scaw-dower. The water elder. M.A.C. It is Celtic Cornish from, *scawen*, elder, (*scaw* elders,) and *dour* water.

Scullions. (Onions. T.W.S.) Elsewhere called *scallions* or leeks. "The leek was worshipped at Ascalon, (whence the modern name of *scallions,)* as it was in Egypt. Leeks and onions were also deposited in the sacred chests of the mysteries both of Isis and Ceres, the *Ceudven* of the Druids. . . . . It may also induce one to think that the wearing of *leeks* on St. David's day, did not originate at the battle between the Welch and the Saxons in the sixth century, but that its origin lies in the remotest antiquity."

Hogg's Fabulous Histy. of Ancient Cornwall. p. 448.

Shortahs. "Masses of loose rubbish in slate quarries which have fallen in, and filled up cracks and rents." C.

Tarving. Struggling, storming, agitating. "Tarving about in a rage." In Celtic Cornish, *tervyns*, a tempest.

Teary, or **Tary ground.** Loose, fissured, or broken ground, or rock. In Celtic Cornish *tyrry*, to break, and *terry*, a breaking.

Turn-house, or **Turning-house.** "When (in mining) a *drift* is driven across the country N. and S. to cut a lode, they make a right angle from their *drift*, and work on the lode itself, which, as it is in a contrary direction to their past *drift* they call *Turning house*, in order to work on the course of the lode."

Pryce.

CURIOUS SPELLING OF THE NAMES OF DRUGS, &c.

(From actual Cornish manuscript of 40 years ago).

Alavadick pills.	Aromatic pills.
Aleboar.	Hellebore.
Allows.	Aloes.
Anne quintum.	Unguentum.
Apadildoldock.	Opodeldoc.
Brusoil.	Bruise oil.
Burgmott.	Bergamot.
Calamile.	Calomel.
Campure.	Camphor.
Campyer.	Camphor.
Carbinet olemonia.	Carbonate of Ammonia.
Cerbenated mansia.	Carbonate of Magnesia.
Couchenell.	Cochineal.
Coughanell.	Cochineal.
Dalby's communative.	Dalby's Carminative.
Davy's Lixture.	Daffy's Elixir.
Esens.	Essence.
Fernician red.	Venetian red.
Gum go acum.	Gum Guaiacum.
Hantaybilush piles.	Antibilious pills.
Hellyconpane.	Elecampane.
Hole peper.	Whole pepper.

Hoocologney.	Eau de Cologne.
Magnesha.	Magnesia.
Marcery.	Mercury.
Nighter.	Nitre.
Nightor.	Nitre.
Oil a bay.	Oil of bay.
Oil breik.	Oil of brick.
Oil deldock.	Opodeldoc.
Oil sowols.	Oil of swallows.
Oil of spiks.	Oil of spike.
Oil of swalos.	Oil of swallows.
Palm of city.	Spermaceti.
Pilacotia.	Compound Colocynth pill.
Pil rusus.	Pil. Rufi, or pill of aloes and myrrh.
Puder chilk.	Powdered chalk.
Puder ginger.	Powdered ginger.
Purl wight.	Pearl white.
Red arcepty.	Red precipitate.
Rowbarb.	Rhubarb.
Shugir.	Sugar.
Sprit win.	Spirits of wine.
Sprit of Nighter.	Spirit of Nitre.
Sperts terpine.	Spirits of Turpentine.
Sperm citta.	Spermaceti.
Turpine.	Turpentine.
Weait an quintum.	White unguentum, or the white lead ointment.
Whit precipit.	White precipitate.
White sipety powder.	White precipitate powder.

EXPLANATION OF THE REFERENCES, IN THE GLOSSARY.

H. Mr. Robt. Hunt, author of "The Romances of the West of England," &c.

E.N. The late Mr. Edwin Netherton, of Truro. He compiled the glossary in "Cornish Tales, in prose and verse," by J. T. Tregellas. Also, the glossary at the end of "The Exhibition and other Cornish Tales," by Forfar, and others.

U.J.T. William Sandys, F.S.A. The author of "Specimens of Cornish provincial dialect," by "Uncle Jan Treenoodle," *(sic)* the glossary by "An antiquarian friend." The portrait of Dolly Pentreath in this book, is taken from Mr. Sandys' work.

W.T.A.P. Dr. Pattison, junr., formerly of Duporth, near St. Austell. This gentleman has rendered valuable assistance to the writer in the compilation of this glossary, and in investigations about Dolly Pentreath.

T.W.S. Mr. Thomas Walter Sandrey, contributor to the "Cornishman" in 1880, of lists of "Old Cornish words."

M.A.C. Miss Margaret A. Courtney, of Alverton House, Penzance. This lady was so kind as to thank the writer for words which are included in the Glossary for West Cornwall, published by the London Dialect Society. Great thanks are in return due to her for the help which her compilation has afforded.

C. This letter refers to Mr. Thos. Quiller Couch, of Bodmin. It has been explained that the excellent glossary in the "History of Polperro," was in reality done by him and not by his father, as was generally supposed. The writer found much assistance from his glossary. See Appendix.

H.R.C. Mr. H. R. Cornish.

T.C. Mr. Thomas Cornish. } Both of these gentlemen have done good work for the glossary by Miss M. A. Courtney.

W.N. Mr. Wm. Noye. See the Appendix.

F.C. The Rev. Flavell Cook. He has collected many provincial words, which are included in the glossary by Miss Courtney.

B.V. Mr. Bernard Victor, Mousehole. Many old Cornish words, and even phrases, are known to him, and were published in the "Cornishman." See Appendix for his letters about old Dolly Pentreath, whose coffin was made by his grandfather.

W.F.P. Mr. Wm. Fred. Pentreath, of Mousehole, also contributed a long list of old Cornish words to the "Cornishman."

i.e. id est, that is.

Q.V. Quid vide, which see.

The writings of Carew, Lhuyd, Tonkin (as in Lord De Dunstanvilles Ed. of Carew), Pryce, Borlase, Polwhele, and others, have afforded the compiler a large number of words.

The *comparisons* with the Celtic Cornish language, so far as the writer has ventured to give them, are principally according to the "Lexicon Cornu-Britannicum" of Williams.

Great thanks are due to Mr. J. R. Netherton, of Truro, who, as an experienced publisher, has afforded much practical help in correcting and revising the list of writers on Cornish dialect.

The lists of words contributed by the writer to the "Cornishman," (a newspaper published in Penzance), in 1879, 1880, are, with numerous additions of his own since, added to the glossary.

In order to distinguish more clearly between provincial words, and those of the ancient language, the term *Celtic* Cornish instead of *old* Cornish is used.

APPENDIX.

DOLLY PENTREATH.

In Lake's Parochial History of Cornwall it is stated that the parish register of Paul, near Mousehole, contains the following entry. (The words in italics are put so by the writer of this.) "Dorothy Jeffery was *buried* Decr. 27. (1777)."

On the south face of her monument, erected, *not on her grave* but in the churchyard wall, in 1860, there is this inscription. "*Here* lieth interred Dorothy Pentreath, who *died in* 1778 * said to have been the last person who conversed in the ancient Cornish, the peculiar language of this county from the earliest records till it expired in the eighteenth century, in this parish of St. Paul. This stone is erected by the Prince Louis Lucien Bonaparte, in union with the Rev. John Garrett, vicar of St. Paul, June 1860. "Hononr thy father and thy mother, that thy days may be long in the land which the Lord thy God giveth thee. *Exod.*, xx, 12.

*If Dolly, as the Prince has stated *died* in 1778 and, as the parish register states, she was *buried* in 1777, (see above) it is clear according to this that she was buried alive !! which is absurd.

"Gwra perthi de taz ha de mam: mal de Dythiow bethewz hyr war an tyr neb an arleth de dew ryes dees. *Exod.* xx, 12."

"Old Dolly Pentreath" (see *Paroch. Hist. of Cornwall, Lake, vol. iv, p.* 26) "retained her maiden name until her death, which occurred in her 102nd year; her husband's name was Jeffery."

In the *Bibliotheca Cornubiensis* there is this notice of her—"Jeffery, Dorothy (generally known by her maiden name of Dolly Pentreath, dau. of Nicholas Pentreath), bapt. Paul, 17 May, 1714; d. Mousehole, Dec. 1777; bur. Paul, 27th Dec."—"All the accounts state that Dolly Pentreath was 102, but her real age at the time of death seems to have been only 63."*

The reader has seen what Drew says about Dolly Pentreath, and the positive statements contained in the letter by Daines Barrington. Drew was a careful and experienced writer, and the Cornish History done by him, and printed and published at *Helston* in 1824, was compiled by Hitchins, who lived at *St. Ives,* and died at

* There seems to be an extraordinary mistake in this. The question naturally arises, Why should she have been known by her *maiden* name all her life? If the reader will refer to Polwhele's *History of Cornwall,* under the heading "The Language, Literature, and Literary Characters of Cornwall" (page 19, in a note), he will find that Polwhele, writing about Dolly Pentreath, states positively and distinctly thus, "Her *maiden* name was Jeffery." From this then it must have been that she married a man called Pentreath, and was naturally so called afterwards throughout the rest of her very long life. The age 63 is certainly an error, and impossible, according to the testimony of Daines Barrington as given in his letter. (See back pp. 6, 11.) At p. 20, in a note, Polwhele says, "Old Dolly had no family." (Ed. of 1806.)

Marazion on April 1, 1814. Hitchins was, therefore, a near neighbour to Dolly Pentreath's place, viz., Mousehole. The collection of the materials for a Cornish History must have taken a long time, so that Hitchens, being so near Mousehole, and writing not so very many years after the time of Dolly's death, could hardly be other than well informed of the facts. It being hard to reconcile the above differences of dates, and the subject requiring further investigation, the writer went to Mousehole in the summer of 1881, and made inquiries. He convinced himself that, (notwithstanding the statement of so correct a writer as Drew, that Dolly died in "1788," or the inscription on her present monument erected by Prince L. L. Bonaparte that she "died in 1778,") the actual day of her *death* was Decr. 26th, A.D. 1777. She was probably *buried*, in the very beginning of the year 1778, a few days after her death.

This appears to be positively determined by the following valuable and interesting letters from Mr. Bernard Victor, of Wellington Place, Mousehole. He not only fixes the date of Dolly Pentreath's death, but also gives details of the true position of her grave, over which the monument, erected by Prince L. L. Bonaparte in 1860, should have been placed, instead of where it is at present, (1882.)

The writer of this was informed by Mr. Trewavas, of Mousehole, who in 1881 was in his 88th year, and pleasantly bright, clear, and intelligent, that "he does not remember anything on her (Dolly Pentreath's) tombstone or what was on it, himself, but he has heard that the first or old inscription on the supposed tombstone was—"Here lieth Old Dolly Pentreath, who lived one hundred years and two, was born and buried in Paul parish too. Not in the Church amongst people great and high, but in the Churchyard doth old Dolly lie."—(The tombstone here referred to, is the supposed one spoken of by Drew in his History of Cornwall, and not that erected by Prince L. L. Bonaparte in 1860.)

DOLLY PENTREATH AND THE OLD CORNISH LANGUAGE, &c.

SIR,

By the request of Mr. Trewavas, your correspondent, I avail myself of this favourable opportunity to furnish you with an incident, or two, relative to the above celebrated dame.

Though there were several of Dolly's neighbours who had an acquaintance with the old Cornish, she became more generally known as a living repository of the almost defunct language from her occupation as a fish-seller, or back-jouster, her particular vocation calling her to nearly all parts of the surrounding country, where the good, but perhaps parsimonious housewives, declining her terms, and refusing the fish. often drew from the ancient dame, in choicest Celtic, the outpourings of her wrath; for Dolly was a woman of spirit, and had a sharp tongue. It has even been said that Dolly used to swear in Cornish.

The house in which the ancient dame lived, at the time she followed the occupation of a fish-seller. is still to be seen at Mousehole,* and at present is occupied by two fishermen as a net loft, &c.

---

* See the frontis-piece—for house and portrait. The house is on the opposite side of the street, but a little lower down, than were stands the "Keigwin Arms," and sketched from near the porch of the old Inn.

It is believed the fire-place remains to this day.

Where she plied bellows,
Boiled her salted fish,
There she washed her trencher.
There she cleaned her dish.

She died Decr. 26, 1777, at the age of 102. At her funeral the undertaker was George Badcock. He being my grandfather, that is the reason I am so well informed; and there were eight chosen fishermen bearers to take her to her last resting place.

There was not anything erected on the old lady's grave as a tablet to her memory. I know quite well the grave where her remains are deposited.

The churchyard in which her remains are deposited is emphatically declared to be worthy of particular regard, and the monumental granite erected there by Prince Louis Lucien Bonaparte keeps her memory green.

Her old language, like the virtuous departed, being dead, yet speaketh.

"Ha'n Dew euhella, vedn ry
Peth yw gwella ol rag why."*

"And God supreme will do for you,
What He thinks best is good for you."

I should feel obliged if you would have the goodness to write me, and let me know if this information will be of any service to you.

My address (is) Bernard Victor, Wellington Place, Mousehole, Cornwall.

I remain, yours faithfully,

BERNARD VICTOR,

Mousehole, West Cornwall.

Decr., 1881.

To Dr. Jago, Plymouth.

* This, as written by Mr. Victor, is given in full by Pryce in his *Archæologia Cornu-Britannica* among his "Collection of Proverbs, Rhimes, &c.," as under—

ADVICE TO ALL MEN.

"Chee dên krêv, leb es war tyr,
Bithew gwrä, gen skïans fyr;
Ha'n Dew euhella, vedn ry,
Peth yw gwella ol rag why.

Thou strong man, who on earth dost dwell,
To-day, with prudence, act thou well;
And God supreme for thee will do,
What he thinks best is good for you."**

** *Literally*—'Will give what is best all for you.'

In May 1882, my friend Dr. W. T. A. Pattison, and also Mr. Bernard Victor of Mousehole, visited Dolly Pentreath's grave in order that the *exact* position of it might be recorded, and soon after the following letter was written.

Wellington Place, Mousehole,
May 16th, 1882.

Dear Sir,

I beg to inform you that I have visited the grave-yard of Doll Pentreath this day at noon, and I will give you the correct distance and compass bearing of the grave to the monument that was erected by Prince L. L. Bonaparte; also the distance from the grave to the Chancel door of the Church, and the compass bearing. I took a mariner's compass with me and a rule to measure with, so that it should be correct.

1st.—The head of the grave from the monument erected by Prince L. L. Bonaparte is south-east, a point easterly; distance, forty-seven feet.

2nd.—The head of the grave from the chancel door is south, a point westerly; distance, fifty-two feet.

I have sent you the plan of the Church; also of the grave and the present monument: so there can be no mistake.

The grave is quite close to the front wall of the church-yard, as you will see I have placed it in the plan of the grave-yard. I have also placed the trees as they are situated, close to the wall of the front of the grave-yard. The front of the Church (the south side is meant—F. W. P. J.) is as correct as possible, with the two doors and six windows; and the window at the west end.

The south front of the Church, and the church-yard wall that I have sent you a sketch of, face the Church road from Mousehole to Paul Church-town.

I shall feel glad if my information is satisfactory to you. Please send me a few lines and let me know how you like my plan. I saw Dr. Pattison yesterday; he gave me the note you sent to have plan.

I remain yours faithfully,

Bernard Victor.

To Dr. Jago, Plymouth.

The description as given above is quite clear for any one visiting Paul Church-yard, and the *plan* is not really required, although Mr. Victor so kindly took the trouble to make it.

On May 23, 1882, Mr. B. Victor was again written to. The following is an extract, the rest of the letter not being important :—

SIR,

"But how was it that Prince L. L. Bonaparte, in 1860, fixed Dolly's monument where it now stands? The inscription on it says '*Here* lieth interred Dolly Pentreath,' &c., when, by your account, Dolly's *actual* resting place is '47 feet south-east, a point easterly' from Prince L. L. Bonaparte's monument to her. Who told the Prince that Dolly lies where the present monument is? The public require proof; and how was such a mistake made about the exact place of Dolly's grave?"

I am yours truly,

FRED. W. P. JAGO.

Mr. Bernard Victor, Mousehole.

The following interesting letter is the reply :—

Wellington Place, Mousehole,

May 22nd, 1882.

DEAR SIR,

I will give you my opinion of where Prince L. L. Bonaparte got the information from to erect the monument where it is at present.

First, I will say as to myself I never saw Prince L. L. Bonaparte; if so, the monument, no doubt, would have been erected in its right place.

There was a William Bodener, a fisherman of this place, who wrote a letter in the Cornish language on the 3rd of July, 1776, so when Prince L. L. Bonaparte came to Mousehole, he came to the descendants of the before mentioned William Bodener; but I am not prepared to inform you whether they gave him any information as to the present erection of the monument, but the information that I have given you is from my grandfather, who was the undertaker at her funeral, which I gave you to understand before, and that she was carried to her grave by eight fishermen.

But I believe you have a doubt of my information being correct. If you were in Mousehole at this present time, you could see an old fisherman by the name of Stephen Blewett, who could give you the same information about the grave which I have given you; but, of course, he knew nothing of Dolly Pentreath. What he and others know about Dolly is handed down from sire to son.

I remember my grandfather quite well; he died with us, and I was fifteen years of age when he died.

Dear Sir, this I will inform you—that the descendant of William Bodener, who is alive at Mousehole at present, can give no information whatever on the ancient Cornish language, or about Dolly Pentreath, or her grave, or anything connected with her funeral procession.

I gave you the plan of the churchyard wall, and you see there are two gates in the long south churchyard wall, and the monument is placed in the position below the *upper* gate, but it should have been placed below the *lower* gate,* so *there* was the mistake by the person who gave the information (to the Prince).

This I can further say, that there was no person who could satisfy any visitors who came there to make inquiry about the grave before they came to me. There was always a doubt by the folks that the monument (of 1860) was not in its right place.

Now I have given you all the information in my power, and who is the person that can say that I am not correct? Who knew better about Dolly Pentreath's grave than my grandfather who made her coffin and superintended the funeral?

It is not to be said that the monument is in its right place because it was put there by the order of Prince L. L. Bonaparte, or by the Rev. John Garrett—the one a Frenchman and the other an Irishman!

I remain, yours faithfully,

BERNARD VICTOR.

To Dr. Jago, 21, Lockyer Street, Plymouth.

---

* The gate which opens into the path leading to the chancel door in the south side of Paul Church.—F. W. P. J.

To the preceding letter was the following reply :—

21, Lockyer Street, Plymouth,
May 26, 1882.

DEAR SIR,

Many thanks for the valuable information contained in your letter of the 22nd inst. respecting the *actual* position of Dolly Pentreath's grave in Paul churchyard.

I had no doubt of your statements, and only wrote you again to obtain the fullest information possible. Your letter explains very clearly that Prince L. L. Bonaparte, and the Rev. John Garrett the clergyman at Paul (the latter had only been instituted in Paul in 1857, that is, only three years before the present monument was erected), mistook the position, and instead of erecting the monument to Dolly below the *upper* gate, it should have been placed below the *lower* gate as you have described.

It is to be hoped that one day the present monument of 1860 will be placed in the true position so carefully described by you, and that the date 1778, now on it, will be altered to December 26, 1777.

Such information, coming from one so well acquainted with many words and even phrases of the ancient Cornish language, and this apart from books, renders it peculiarly interesting, and I am much indebted to you for your letters.

From my personal knowledge of you I am satisfied that you have written truthfully, and conscientiously.

I am, Dear Sir,
Yours very truly,
FRED. W. P. JAGO.

MR. BERNARD VICTOR,*
Wellington Place,
Mousehole.

The following question required an answer, viz. :—
How can it be explained that Mr. Bernard Victor's grandfather was old enough in 1777 to act as undertaker for Dolly Pentreath, 105 years ago?

---

* Mr. B. Victor has a son now (May 1882). residing at 12, Clowance street, Devonport. His father says that this son is also fully acquainted with the particulars concerning Dolly Pentreath. F. W. P. J.

The following is Mr. Bernard Victor's reply :—

Wellington Place,
Mousehole,
July 24, 1882.

DEAR SIR,

"In reply to your letter of the 21st inst., I beg to inform you that it is no trouble whatever to me to furnish you with the following particulars of the age of my grandfather (George Badcock), at his death, also his age at the time he buried Dolly Pentreath, and likewise my age.

My grandfather died in July 1832, at the age of 84 years, so that will make it 50 years since my grandfather's death.

Now from the time of his birth up to the present will make 134 years, and Dolly Pentreath who died in 1777 will make 105 years.

This will give my grandfather's age at the time he buried Dolly Pentreath to have been 29 years.

My grandfather was married at that time, *and his wife had one child, a girl, who was born in* 1777, *the year that Dolly died.*

My age.—I was born in this village, Mousehole, in the year 1817 on the 21st of August, so I shall be 65 on August 21st, which will be next month."

I am, yours &c.
BERNARD VICTOR.

DR. F. W. P. JAGO,
21, Lockyer Street,
Plymouth.

CONCLUDING REMARKS ABOUT DOLLY PENTREATH.

The foregoing letters contain full particulars, but to the casual visitor to Paul churchyard the following directions may be of use.

In going by the "Church road" from Mousehole to Paul, the south east angle of Paul churchyard is first reached on the right hand.

Close inside the churchyard wall there, next the "Church road," and lengthways between two trees, lies the grave with nothing to mark its place (1882).

Close to the west end of the grave is the gate opening into the path which leads dircetly from the "Church road" to the square headed chancel door in the south side of the Church.

Thirteen or fourteen paces more to the west of this (chancel) gate stands the misplaced memorial to Dolly by the Prince L. L. Bonaparte. The long inscription (already given) faces the road, and on the *north* side of the stone is a shorter inscription facing the churchyard, in these words —"Dorothy Pentreath who conversed in ancient Cornish, died 1778. This stone is erected by Prince Louis Lucien Bonaparte and the Rev. John Garrett, 1860."

There is good evidence notwithstanding the confusion of dates, that Dolly Pentreath was aged 102 when she died in 1777, (not 1778 as on the present monument).

There seems no reason to doubt that an epitaph in ancient Cornish, and a translation of the same into English was *written,* and which is referred to by Drew, Polwhele, and others, but there is no evidence to prove that such an epitaph was ever inscribed on stone, and placed upon Dolly's grave at or about the time of her burial.

If we are to believe writers who lived near the time of the events which they recorded, then Dolly Pentreath was the last who spoke Cornish as her *native* tongue, for in Drew's History of Cornwall, (vol. 1. p. 227), quoting Daines Barrington, it is said, "she does indeed talk Cornish as readily as others do English, *being bred up from a child to know no other language; nor could she (if we may believe her) talk a word of English before she was past twenty years of age.*"

Others who succeeded Dolly, although they could converse in Cornish more or less perfectly, yet they were born and *brought up as children to speak English.*

Thus, after all, Dolly Pentreath *was* the last known person *whose mother tongue was Cornish, and who knew no other language till she was a grown woman.**

* Dolly Pentreath's portrait on the frontis-piece, is a true copy of the one in "Uncle Jan Treenoodle," 1846. (by Wm. Sandys, F. S. A.,) and which is the same portrait as that in "Recreations in Rhyme," by John Trenhaile, published in 1854. See *Biblioth. Cornub.* Polwhele says that "in the Universal Magazine, (if I am rightly informed) there is no bad likeness of old Dolly as engraved by R. Scaddon."

NAMES OF WRITERS ON CORNISH DIALECT, &c.

The following notes have been made so that the reader may refer to such of the books and articles as have been written by those whose names are recorded below. The list may not be complete, but it may be useful.

It refers to those who have written on the Cornish language and dialect, and also to such as are authors of Cornish tales. The writer is indebted to the "Bibliotheca Cornubiensis" of Messrs. Boase and Courtney, but much fuller information can be had from their very valuable work. Several additions and alterations have been made by Mr. J. R. Netherton, of Truro, who has kindly revised the list.

B; H. F. B.—Under these letters are "Words used in Cornwall," in N. & Q., 1 S.; vi, 601 (1852).

BANNISTER, Rev. John.—The author of the Glossary of Cornish names of persons and places. "He began an English-Cornish Dictionary in an interleaved copy of Dr. Johnson's Dictionary—Also the Gerlever Cernouak, a vocabulary of the ancient Cornish language; and a Cornish vocabulary with copious additions to his printed work." There were also "Materials for a glossary of Cornish names, and newspaper cuttings on Cornish names."

The above valuable MSS. were bought for the Br. Museum. £15 was the sum paid for them!!

BELLOWS, JOHN.—"On the Cornish Language," in the Report of the Royal Cornwall Polytechnic Society for 1861, p. 28.

BLIGHT, ROBERT.—Among many others of his writings is an article in the West Briton, 1867, on "Old customs and provincial words in Cornwall."

BOASE, GEORGE CLEMENT.—A bibliographical list of the works published or in MS., illustrative of the various dialects of English—Edited by the Rev. Walter W. Skeat, M.A., Lond. English Dialect Society 1873, 8vo, pp. viii and 48.

The Bibliotheca Cornubiensis has this note—"The above work was in reality brought out in February 1875. It contains on pp. 19-28 a list of works relating to the English Dialect of Cornwall, originally made out by the Rev. W. W. Skeat, but re-written with additions and biographical notices by G. C. Boase and W. P. Courtney."

BONAPARTE, PRINCE LOUIS LUCIEN.—The Song of Solomon in the living Cornish Dialect, from the authorised English version, privately printed by Geo. Barclay, 28, Castle Street, Leicester Square, London, 1859, 16mo. The Prince had this "Song" translated into other dialects, Lancashire, &c. The translation into the Cornish dialect was very cleverly done by the late Mr. Edwin Netherton, of Truro, at the request of

Prince Lucien Bonaparte. Only 250 copies were printed. The Prince was much pleased with the translation, and expressed himself so to Mr. E. Netherton.

"On the expiration of the Cornish Language," a letter by the Hon. Daines Barrington, read at the Society of Antiquaries May 6, 1773. This letter was reprinted by the Prince in 1860. There were only twelve copies printed.

"The Literature and Dialect of Cornwall," Camb. Jour., 30 Nov., 1861.

BOTTRELL, WILLIAM.—Author of "Traditions and Hearthside stories of West Cornwall." This book contains a Glossary. He has written many things relating to Cornwall.

COUCH, THOMAS QUILLER, M.R.C.S., F.S.A.—Among his writings are "Obsolete words still in use in East Cornwall." *Journ. Roy. Inst. of Cornwall*, 1864, March, pp. 6-26; also April 1870, pp. 173-79, is an Appendix to a list of Obsolescent words and Local Phrases in use among the folk of East Cornwall" Also an article on "The Cornish language," 1864, pp. 76-77. In the Biblioth. Cornubiensis there is a further notice, thus (p. 1139).

"List of obsolete words still in use among the folk of East Cornwall." Truro, Netherton, printer, n.d. (1864), 8vo., pp. 22.

"Cornish words and Phrases," ib., 2 S. iii, 240, 1857, cf. also iii, 473.

"East Cornwall words," by Thomas Q. Couch. Pub. by the English Dialect Society, 1880.

DANIEL, HENRY JOHN.—"The Cornish Thalia; being original Cornish Poems illustrative of the Cornish Dialect"—"A Companion to the Cornish Thalia," &c., &c. He has written a great deal. See the Biblioth. Cornub.

DIALECT.—A western eclogue between Pengrouze and Bet Polglaze—signed "Cornwall"—Gent. Mag. xxxii., 287—(1762).

An old Cornish dialogue, Huthnance, letterpress and copperplate printer, Queen Square, Penzance, n.d. (circa. 1840) fol. s. sh.—124 lines,

Commences thus—

"Twas kendle teening when jung Mal Treloare
Trudg'd hom from bal a bucking copper ore."

List of local expressions, signed S., Gent. Mag. lxiii, 1083-84 (1793)—(Biblioth. Cornub., vol. 3).

EDWARDS, JOSEPH, of Wrington.—In "Poems" by Outis are included Rhymes by "Agrikler," *i.e.* Joseph Edwards, some of them in the Cornish dialect.—New ed. London, Houlston & Sons, n.d. (1870) 8vo.

ENGLISH DIALECT SOCIETY.—Published in 1880 a Glossary of Words for West Cornwall by Miss M. A. Courtney, and one for East Cornwall by Thos. Q. Couch.

ENGLISH, HENRY.—"Glossary of Mining Terms used in South America, *Cornwall*, and Derbyshire," 1830, 8vo. —Mr. W. J. Henwood, F.R.S., compiled the glossary of *Cornish* mining terms.

F.—The Cornish farmer and the squire (by F.), Netherton's Cornish Almanack 1869; reprinted in "Four Tales (Truro, Netherton), 1873," pp. 8-18.

Capt. Tom Teague's humorous and satirical remarks on Zebedee Jacka's real adventures at the exhibition in July, 1862 (by F.), Netherton's Cornish Almanack 1869. Reprinted in "Four Tales," pp. 23-42. (Biblioth. Cornub.)

FORFAR, WM. BENTINCK.—Has written many good tales in the Cornish dialect; see Biblioth. Cornub., pp. 158 and 1183. The *dialect* has been well done by this author.

FOX, CHARLES.—"A Cornish Dialogue between Gracy Penrose and Mally Trevisky" (1790?). Printed in Polwhele's "Cornwall," v, 25.

GARLAND, THOMAS.—"List of words in common use in West Cornwall," in the Journal of the Royal Institution of Cornwall, April 1865, pp. 45-54.

HIGHAM, T. R.—A Dialogue between Tom Thomas and Bill Bilkey, two Cornish miners—The Snake—by T. R. H(igham). Truro, J. R. Netherton; n.d. (1866). pp. 14.

The Cornish Farmer and the Squire, a Poem by T. R. Higham. Netherton's Cornish Almanack, 1868, pp. 11.

'Lisbeth Jane's Courtship, being another Dialogue between Tom Thomas and Bill Bilkey (by T. R. Higham). Netherton's Cornish Almanack (1869), pp. 2.

Note.—The above two are reprinted in "Four Cornish Tales" (Truro, J. R. Netherton, 1870, 8vo.) pp. 11 and 5 respectively.

Edwin Lukey's Trip to Town, *Anon.* Printed in Cornish Tales (Truro, J. R. Netherton, 1867, 8vo), pp. 66-70.

Betty White—Jimmy's Story, *Anon.*, *ib.* pp. 71-79.

A Dialogue between Betty Penstraze and Sally Trembath, *Anon.*, *ib*, pp. 132-47. (Biblioth. Cornub.)

JENNINGS, JAMES.—Compiled a Glossary of West of England words with a slight reference only to Cornwall; 1825, 8vo.

JIMMY TREBILCOCK, or the humorous adventures of a Cornish miner at the Great Exhibition. Camborne, printed by T. T. Whear, 1862; 12mo., pp. 16. Fifth thousand, 1863.

KINAHAN, GEORGE HENRY.—"Notes on the similarity of some of the Cornish rock-names and miners' terms to Irish words. Journal of Royal Institution of Cornwall, April 1873, pp. 133-39. (Biblioth. Cornub.)

LACH-SZYRMA, Rev. W. S.—Author of many valuable contributions to Cornish lore. Among them "A short history of Penzance, St. Michael's Mount, St. Ives, and the Land's End district." "The numerals in old Cornish," *The Academy*, 20 Mh. 1875, pp. 297-98. "The old Cornish language in questions and answers." "St. Just, the Plân-an-gwaré, and a Cornish drama;" *Journ. Brit. Archœol. Assoc.*, xxxv., 413-22 (1879). "Last relics of the Cornish tongue;" *The Antiquary* 1, 15-18, 63-66 (1880).

THE MONTHLY MAG., xxvi, 421, 544 (1808), xxix, 451 (1810), contains a vocabulary of Cornish Provincial words.

NETHERTON, EDWIN.—He was very well acquainted with the peculiarities of the Cornish Dialect. The glossary at the end of "Tregellas's Tales" was done by him. Also the glossary at the end of "The Exhibition and other Tales." Both published by Netherton and Worth, Truro.

NETHERTON'S, J. R., CORNISH ALMANACK FOR 1854.—Printed and sold by J. R. Netherton, Truro, and since continued annually. The following is a note in the Bibliotheca Cornubiensis :—

"This series contains the following pieces—

1861—Specimens of the ancient Cornish Language; Extracts from Cornish Tales, published by J. R. Netherton.

1863—Found drowned, and the Oysters, by W. B. Forfar.

1865—Rozzy Trenoodle and his leatheren bag, by W. B. Forfar.

1869—'Lisbeth Jane's courtship, by T. R. Higham; Luke Martin's cowld, by E. Netherton.

1870—The crock and the billies, or fuddled Jabez Hornblower; The flying angel, *alias* Beelzebub, from "Haunts and Homes."

1872—The billies and the magistrate; Tom Mitchell and the Redruth barber, from "Haunts and Homes."

1873—Nicholas Kneebone, *alias* Slippery Nick; Mousey Cock, from "Haunts and Homes."

1874—The perfect cure, by Charles Bennett; Wend, snaw, het, an' tha porpose plaaster, wether taabel, an' setra, by Herclus Polsu.

1875—Nick Dyer's pay day adventure; A sorrow bringing sovereign, by C. Bennett.

1876—Snaw, het, and wend, (continued), by Herclus Polsu; Amos Polsu's letter.

1877—The billy-goat and the pepper mine; A quack's recipe.

1878—The mistaken prescription, by A. Sumpman; A knight's adventure (Biblioth. Cornub.)

NOTE.—Most of the above, and those published since, have been reprinted with other Tales.

NOYE, William.—Contributed to the Academy, 1875, p. 402, on "Old Cornish," and to the "Cornishman" in 1879. Also on Cornish words in Symond's diary, 1878.

O'DONOGHUE, Rev. Francis Talbot, B.A.—St. Knighton's Kieve. A Cornish Tale, with a Postscript and Glossary 1864, 8vo.; Smith and Elder, pp. iv. and 304.

PARIS, John Ayrton, M.D., F.R.S.—In his book ("A gvide to Movnts Bay and Land's End," 1824, 2nd ed., by a Physician, *Anon.)* is a very good specimen of Western dialect. It is a "Cornish Dialogue between Grace Penvear and Mary Treviskey."

PASCOE, Charlotte Champion.—This lady is the writer of "Wan An' aell, a Cornish Drawel as Zung, Zold, and Spauken by Barzillai Baragweneth (pseud., *i.e.* C. C. Pascoe); pub. Penzance, F. T. Vibert, 1864, 8vo., pp. 24.

PENGELLY, William.—Among his very numerous writings is an article in N. & Q. "on Local Words" 6 S. i, 345 (1880).

SANDYS, William, F.S.A.—Author of "Specimens of Cornish provincial dialect, collected and arranged by Uncle Jan Trenoodle" (*i.e.* William Sandys). It contains a Glossary "by an antiquarian friend." Lond. J. R. Smith 1846, 8vo., pp. 108, 4s.

SMITH, John Russell.—Publisher, Soho Square, London. Printed a "List of works which have been published towards illustrating the provincial dialects of England," 1839, pp. 24. It contains a list of works on the Cornish dialect.

STACKHOUSE, REV. JONATHAN LETT.—He contributed to the Journal of the Royal Institution of Cornwall, May 1864, pp. 75, 76, an article on "Obsolete words still in use among the people of East Cornwall."

TALES.—Cornish tales in prose and verse. By various authors, including W. B. Forfar, T. R. Higham, with a glossary. Truro, James R. Netherton, 1867, 8vo, pp. 151.

Five tales in prose and verse in the Cornish dialect. Truro, J. R. Netherton, n.d. (1882), 12mo., pp. 61.

Cornish Comicalities, 9 tales in prose and verse, 12°. pp. 60, 1880.

A Cornish Love Story and 8 other tales, 12°. pp. 62, 2nd ed. 1882.

The Billy Goat and the Pepper Mine, and 6 other tales, 12°. pp. 64, 1882.

TREGELLAS, JOHN TABOIS.—He was born at St. Agnes on Novr. 1, 1792. Spent the greater part of his life in Cornwall, and died at Chester on April 17, 1867. Unequalled as a writer and lecturer on the Cornish Provincial Dialect. The whole of his works are now published in 2 vols., viz:—"Tales in prose and verse," and "Haunts and Homes of the Rural Population of Cornwall," (illustrated), published by Netherton and Worth, Truro.

WHITE, JOHN.—Writer of "The humorous adventures of Tom Trevail," 1872, 8vo., pp. 20.

WORTH, RICHARD NICHOLLS.—The well known author of the History of Plymouth, &c. In the Journal of the Royal Institution of Cornwall is "Some inquiry into the association of the Dialects of Devon and Cornwall, April 1870, pp. 180-83," written by him.

The pages of the "Cornishman," a newspaper published in Penzance, frequently contain characteristic specimens of the provincial dialect of Cornwall.

ERRATA.

Page 5, line 20, } for *nauidua*, read *navidna*.
,, 15, ,, 9, }
,, 12, ,, 6, for *plêa*. read *plêu*.
,, 19, ,, 2nd from bottom, for *Pnulus*, read *Pœnulus*.
,, 39, ,, 2nd from bottom, for *Eva*, read *Eve*.
,, 55, ,, 16. Omit one "in."
,, 73, ,, 2, for *writing*. read *writings*.
,, 103, ,, 20, for *scources*, read *sources*.
,, 108, ,, for **Agyfy**, read **Argyfy**.
,, 128, ,, 1, for *Flour spar*, read *Fluor spar*.
,, 141, ,, 21, for *fortuituously*, read *fortuitously*.
,, 152, } for *Bottrall*, read *Bottrell*.
,, 158, }
,, 166, ,, for **Fern-webb**, read **Fern-web**.
,, 167, ,, 13, for **Fichet**, read **Fitchet**.
,, 192, ,, 23, for *scrab*, read *scab*.
,, 203, ,, **Lace.** Omit, "*This is a Celtic Cornish word meaning.*"
,, 205, ,, 21, for *vegatable*, read *vegetable*.
,, 230, ,, 16, for *bill-hoook*, read *bill-hook*.
,, 240, ,, 19, for *tos*, to swear, read *toy*, to swear, *tos*, he swore.
,, 252, ,, 13, for *toothacke*, read *toothache*.
,, 255, ,, 12, for **Scabby-gulyun**, read **Scably-gulyun**.
,, 259, ,, 13, for **Sruff**, read **Scruff**.
,, 296, ,, 3, for *task*, read *cask*.
,, 316, ,, 2, for *crauny*, read *cranny*.